BLOOD
UNDER WATER

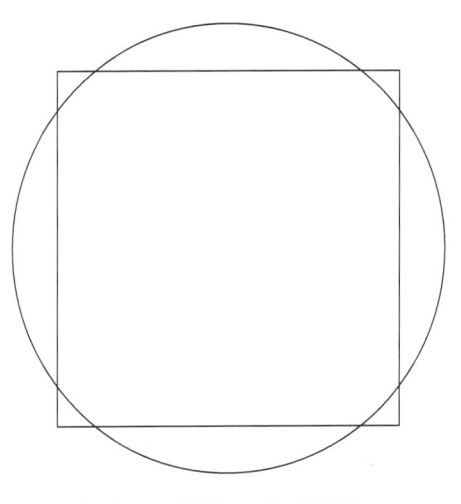

T.A. FROST

This is a work of fiction. Names, characters, places, and incidents either are the product of the author's imagination or are used fictitiously. Any resemblance to actual persons, living or dead, events, or locales is entirely coincidental.

Copyright © Toby Frost 2019

All rights reserved. No part of this book may be reproduced or used in any manner without written permission of the copyright owner except for the use of quotations in a book review.

First Edition
Cover Art by AutumnSky.co.uk
Typesetting by Ryan Ashcroft/BookBrand.co.uk
All rights reserved

It was hard to see the sun in the jungle, let alone to guess the time of day. Father Coraldo could have been walking for an hour, or all morning. He would not have been surprised if the weak light suddenly dimmed and they were obliged to make camp on the forest floor again. Frightened, but not surprised.

A root snagged his robe, and he slipped. His pack swung against him as if a child had leaped onto his back. Coraldo staggered, bit his lip and lurched upright again, fresh sweat itching on his brow.

"Can we stop for a while?"

The guide watched him nervously. "Holy Father, we need go fast. Zupai says you come today. If he says so, we must."

Coraldo shrugged his pack back into place. He looked at the guide, and saw that the native was afraid. *You're afraid, I'm afraid – that's what this godless place does to you.* He glanced back between the close-packed trees, at what the guide had called a path, and imagined evil festering between the leaves like plague.

"Let's go, then," he said.

They walked on. Coraldo had no-one to talk to but himself, nothing to think about but his own discomfort. A toad the size of a pie glared at him from the roots where it nestled. It looked like a turd given life. *This is the Devil's own land. These poor savages are all the humanity that he lets exist.*

Something thundered overhead. Coraldo ducked, his pack nearly overbalancing him, and saw a scaled body rush past as if he lay beneath an immense snake. He heard the thump, thump of wings against air, and then the monster was gone.

His fist was in front of his chest, holding out the holy

sign that hung around his neck. The guide looked at him. "*Couatl*," he said. "Is blessing us, Holy Father. Good."

Coraldo heard hissing up ahead and saw water between the trunks. Without warning the forest ended and they were out beside a stream. Sand like fine sawdust stretched to a little river. The water was impossibly blue. Pretty fish danced in the shallows. *Like a dream*, Coraldo thought, and he remembered the beauty of the place when he had first seen the New World from the ship that had brought him here: all green and shimmering, steaming like hot meat.

On the far side of the stream was a clearing and, in the clearing, a multitude of strange plants: black-red balls on leafless stems as high as Coraldo's waist. He stepped forward, and the sun hit his neck. In the jungle he had felt as if he were being boiled in a pot; suddenly he was exposed to the flame.

"Is safe," the guide said. "I go now. Is safe."

Coraldo walked towards the water.

"Safe to go cross, Holy Father. I go. Please."

Coraldo began to wade across. Halfway there, he cried out.

They were not plants, but hundreds of rotting heads, each one driven onto a stake.

"Savages!" He stumbled on, disbelieving, and was hit by the stink of it. He stood at the edge of the stream and retched.

When he looked up, there was a man among the heads. The man approached, and light glinted on his helmet and breastplate. He carried a mace. His free hand waved.

"Father Coraldo!"

The soldier stopped at the edge of the clearing. He

took his helmet off and tucked it under his arm. He had a hard jawline and light-brown hair, and in the sunshine he looked almost angelic. "Father."

"Thank God. It's so good to see an Alexian face," Coraldo said.

"I am Ignazio Arrighetti, commander here." The soldier grinned. "The natives call me Zupai. I'm glad you were able to visit us, Father."

Coraldo could taste bile. He tried not to look around. "God in Heaven, what a place," he said. "These heads, there must be a thousand.... What happened here?"

Arrighetti nodded grimly. "It's these whoreson savages," he said. "They're a spiteful, godless, ignorant bunch. You can reason with them all you want, but sometimes – well, you just have to show them who's in charge." He smiled. "But it will be easier with you here. They won't fight back so much, now we have a priest to bless our work." He gestured behind him. "Come: let me show you your quarters."

Arrighetti turned and walked into the clearing, into the smell of death.

Eight Days before the Hanging

ONE

Winter did not freeze Averrio so much as slow it down. Only the narrowest canals were frozen over, but the cold seemed to get into the city's veins. Men lingered for longer in taverns, boats crept from one landing-point to another, and on the network of bridges and walkways that stood in place of normal streets, people moved stiff-legged and slow.

The clerks of the Bank of Fiorenti were required to work with their sleeves rolled up, so they wore fingerless gloves that reached almost to their elbows. As he peered at Giulia's pay-book, the clerk at archway four rubbed his hands together, as if to polish the palms.

"I'm sorry, madam, but I can't do that. Only men can take out accounts. The Bank of Fiorenti does not lend to children, fey folk, women—"

"And dogs, I know. But I don't want to take out an account." Giulia leaned forward to address the cashier through the thin iron bars. "The money's already there. It's listed in the book."

"Yes, but it doesn't belong to you, madam. It belongs to the holder of the account, who is—"

"I *know* that. I can read." Giulia glanced around

the hall; apart from a worried-looking fellow two arches down, the place was deserted. "But the letter I've just given you, here, is from the man whose account it is. See? Sir Hugh of Kenton, there. That's his signature, to say I can discuss it with you."

"Is he your husband, madam?"

Do I look that bad? Hugh's old enough to be my father. Maybe my grandfather. "God, no. I work with him. In business. Look, if you really have to talk to someone with a— someone male, I can bring him in here…"

The clerk managed a caring look, as if informed of the death of someone he didn't know. "I'm terribly sorry, but I really can't help."

"Dammit, I only want to pay some money in! It can't be that hard, can it?"

"You want to pay money *in*? Oh, I see! Well, then." The clerk leaned forward. "How much money would madam like to add to the account?"

Giulia slid the little bags between the bars and watched as the clerk counted out the coins. He dipped his pen and scratched at her bank-book. Giulia heard boots just behind her; she turned and saw Hugh there, looking around the room with a kind of bemused optimism.

"Everything all right, Giulia?"

"Wonderful," she replied. "If there's one thing better than earning money, it's watching someone else get rich by sitting on it. Did you find the place?"

"Yes. It's called Horseman Square."

"Well, lead on. I'm finished here. I don't like being so close to money that I can't touch."

The street outside was narrow and cold. Giulia had taken to wearing her britches under her skirt: it was still freezing. They walked quickly. As they crossed the fifth short, high-backed bridge, a long boat slid beneath them as sleek and quiet as an eel. A man stood at the stern, punting it along with a pole.

"Damn, it's cold," Giulia said. She rubbed at the scars on her left cheek. They seemed unusually tender today. "I can feel my face going numb."

"It's often like this in Albion, especially in the north. When I was fighting the reaver-knights..." Hugh blinked. "Anyway, how much money have we got?"

Giulia pulled her hood up. "We've got one thousand two hundred put away, and about three hundred in loose coin. Not bad, for a couple of thief-takers."

"That's good. Once we know how much it'll take to hire a couple of fellows to help out..."

Giulia tugged her scarf tight around her neck. "More than a couple, Hugh. If we're serious about this wyvern business, I'd say four or five, at least."

"That sounds costly to me. We'd have to feed them, too. Perhaps we ought to try to get more wyvern scales. We'd make a much better profit that way."

Easier said than done. "Shall we steal them off the same bird, or two different ones?"

Hugh did not notice her sarcasm. "They're not birds, Giulia. They're more like lizards – like small dragons, to be honest. I don't know why you're so worried. The scales just fall off them. It's not as if we'll be doing battle with it."

"Small dragons. You're really encouraging me. We need to hire some good people for this." *A real-life wyvern. Shit. Well, you wanted adventure, and here it is. Where do they nest, anyhow? Probably at the top of a bloody mountain.* Giulia remembered something Hugh had said, just before they had left Pagalia: "*It's not an easy path, the Quest.*" *Well, no doubt about that.* She pulled her sleeves down over her fingers.

Horseman Square was small, and the tenement buildings that rose around it made Giulia feel like a mouse in the bottom of a box. A little crowd stood in front of a doorway at the far end of the square, where a herald on a platform was calling out names.

The horseman himself was a bronze statue on a plinth in the centre, in old-fashioned armour and a crusader's tabard. His shield bore the Sign of the Sword; his lance, cocked over his shoulder, acted as the pole for a limp flag. It showed the griffon rampant, the emblem of Averrio, rearing up over two crossed spears.

Hugh gazed up at the statue. Giulia nudged his arm. "Over there," she said, looking at the crowd. "That's our place."

They approached. The men wore breastplates and swords. Some carried bows and guns in wrapped parcels. Several had darker skin: she reckoned they would have come from Dalagar, Averrio's province to the far south. All of them wore feathered hats and sleeves slashed to show bright colours underneath.

Mercenary fashion.

"Six men needed to join a marine crew to Orromano," the herald called out. "Must be skilled with gun or crossbow, and willing to assist on the oars."

A couple of men had stepped forward; as the oars were mentioned, they grumbled and looked away.

"Lazy buggers," Hugh muttered, slightly too loudly. "Typical hirelings."

"Come on." Giulia slipped through the crowd and into the building behind.

Like many city tenements, the lower floor was open

as a shop. Unusually, there was only one business here: scribes worked at half a dozen desks, while customers chatted to company officials on armchairs in the back. Engravings on the walls showed soldiers brandishing pikes at one another.

A slim man in red velvet came forward to meet them. "The work's outside, sir," he said cheerily, blocking their way. "If you want to sign up, you can take the oath—"

"We want to hire some soldiers," Giulia said.

"Oh, I see. Well, I'm happy to discuss that. Your armour suggests that you're a captain-of-arms, sir—"

"I'm a knight," said Hugh.

I'm over here, you idiots. "We're hunters," Giulia put in. "We're getting a crew together to hunt beasts up in the mountains. We need to hire several men—"

"A couple," Hugh said.

"Quite a few men with experience of this sort of work. We'd pay on success."

"A few good fighters, eh?" The contractor gestured to the rear of the room. "Well, we don't get much call for hunting. Most of the mercenaries we use end up helping train the city levy, supporting the city guard and the like. May I ask what sort of beasts you'll be hunting, sir?"

"Wyverns," Hugh replied. "We're going to get some wyvern scales. To sell to apothecaries."

At the back of the room, a large, smartly-dressed man turned to look at them.

"They'll need to be good scouts," Giulia explained. "And good fighters, if it comes to it."

"I'm sure we can find just the men for the job." The contractor looked oddly pleased. Giulia wondered if he relished the challenge of finding suitable men – or if he was amused by the folly of stealing wyvern scales. "I need to have a word with a colleague of mine, but I'm pretty sure I know some people who might be able to help. May I take your name, sir knight?"

"Sir Hugh of Kenton."

"Excellent."

Giulia added, "And I'm Giulia Degarno."

"One moment," said the official, and he stepped away. Giulia had the feeling that he had gone to laugh about them with his friends.

She said, "He'd better not try to foist rubbish onto us."

Hugh frowned. "I don't rate most hired men, myself. What we need are knights errant, eager for glory, like in the books—"

"Wait," Giulia said. The big man was approaching from the back of the room, a little faster than seemed quite right. "Someone's coming over. Do you know that man?"

"Good lord," said Hugh.

The man walked straight up to them. "Hugh of Kenton? Is that you?"

"And none other," Hugh said. He was beginning to smile.

"Hugh!" The man thrust out a hand and Hugh shook it hard. "Good lord, fancy meeting you here!"

"Edwin! Good to see you, man!" Hugh stopped shaking Edwin's hand and they briefly embraced. Even for an Anglian, Hugh did not much like physical contact: this had to be a very great friend.

Giulia looked the man over. He was quite like Hugh – built for the same purpose, but from a slightly different mould. Edwin was big and bulky where Hugh tended towards wiriness: if Edwin stopped taking exercise, he would go to fat. He was slightly shorter than Hugh, and there was less grey in his moustache and hair. Edwin wore newer clothes and no armour: Giulia had almost never seen Hugh without some kind of breastplate.

"So," said Edwin, "who's this?"

"This is Giulia Degarno," said Hugh. "A friend of mine, a freelancer."

"Hello," Giulia said. She put out her hand and Edwin, looking slightly surprised, shook it. His grip was strong. He looked straight into her eyes, which meant that he was trying not to look at her scars. "I work with Hugh," Giulia explained. "I'm a thief-taker by trade."

"She's a good sort," Hugh said.

"Pleased to meet you, Giulia," Edwin said. "So, what brings you to Averrio, then?"

"We're looking to hire some fighters," Hugh explained. "We've got a job planned, but we need men."

Edwin nodded. "Likewise. I need some fellows to help guard my ship. It's not cheap staying safe, I can tell you!" He had a broad, honest-looking smile. "Here, that contractor fellow's staring at us. Let's go outside."

"So, a boat, eh?" Hugh declared as they stepped into the cold. "I never saw you as a seaman, you know."

They pushed through the crowd of mercenaries. The herald shouted out jobs over their heads as if he hoped that the statue on its plinth would answer him instead of the crowd. "Two dozen needed to join a company of pike! Lowlanders preferred!"

"Nor did I," Edwin called back. "It's hardly a big boat," he explained as they broke free from the crowd. "Twenty men, two masts – but she's quick. *Margaret of Cheswick*, she's called. I got together with a merchant called Gilbert Langton, who ships wool out here. Anyway, we're waiting to load a new cargo right now, so we've got a bit of time to kill before we can head back for home. Dammit," he added, stamping his feet, "I left Anglia to get *away* from this bloody cold! So, what about you? The last I heard you were guarding the ambassador up at – what's its name – Pagalia?"

Hugh smoothed down his moustache. "Yes, well, they got this new fellow in to help run the embassy. Marsby, his name was. Absolute idiot. One day he told me I wasn't friendly enough to his guests. Well, I'd had a few jars that morning, and I told him what I thought of that. And of him. So I left, and to cut a long story short—"

I found you drunk in a pub, and you helped me kill half a dozen men who'd been sent to murder me. Giulia looked left, between two of the high tenements. A serving-girl stood in the alley, beating dust out of a rug with a flat-headed brush. It made Giulia think of the slums of Pagalia.

"Elayne and I are staying at the Old Arms, up in the north," Edwin was saying. "It's pretty pleasant, as they go, and not too expensive. Popular with travellers and the like. Where are you?"

Giulia didn't like giving her location away. It was force of habit. "We've only just arrived—"

"Well, why don't you come and visit, eh? Come over. Bring your horses, too. It's just inside the city wall, on the land before you get to the lagoon. It's very pleasant there – good beer, too."

Hugh smiled.

"Ah, I knew that would make your mind up!"

Giulia said, "We'll think about it."

"Excellent. Elayne will be delighted. It's been ages, Hugh!" Edwin rubbed his hands together as though he had struck a good bargain, and looked towards the canal. "Well, I'd best get back to the stevedores. They'll do bugger-all unless someone's watching them. I think this hiring business is a dead loss today. Let's come back here tomorrow, and then we'll have a think about finding some men for you. Remember – there's nothing two knights can't accomplish, God willing! Am I not right?"

"Damn right," Hugh replied, and he smiled his deep, fierce smile.

"Then come up and join us, and we'll try to take the chill off a bit. You too, Giulia."

"Goodbye," she said. "See you soon."

She watched Edwin walk between the buildings: a strong, solid man in the winter sun. "He seems a decent fellow."

Hugh looked down at her. "Yes, he's an old friend of mine. We fought at the Bone Cliffs together, back in the war." The old knight ran a hand through his hair. "Do you think we should visit them?"

"Your friends? Of course. 'Course we should. Maybe Edwin could help us go after this wyvern of yours. Who's this Elayne, then? Another old friend?"

"Yes," said Hugh.

"So what's she like?"

"Skilled in the Art," the knight replied.

"A wizard, you mean?"

"Yes. She was always very talented. She's really quite remarkable."

***

The salls were closing in the Plaza of Wisdom. They were tiny and gaudy compared to the serene public buildings that hemmed them in: the Basilica of St Marietta with its five pale domes, the Palace of Justice and its massive clock tower, and the stern, white bulk of the Senate of the Hundred, where the City Council met.

Giovanni Benevesi watched the stallkeepers from the palace doorway. They were tough men, all older than he was, but the sight of them gave him an almost paternal pride. They were fellow pursuers of commerce, working their way up in life the way he had almost done, perhaps even borrowing money from his own bank.

The clock boomed the hour of five. Someone touched his arm, and Benevesi started: he hoped it didn't make him look guilty. Georgio Nones, an architect and fellow member of the Council of a Hundred, stood by his side.

"Not going home?" Nones asked. "The meeting's over, you know. You're a free man again – until tomorrow."

"Yes, thank Heaven." It had been a painfully boring session of the Council. Even the Decimus himself had looked as if he wanted to fall asleep, while his ministers had debated provisions for additional fire-watchers in the poor quarter. "I've got some business to do. A meeting of the bank elders."

"That sounds daunting," Nones replied. "But not as daunting as being late home to my wife!"

Benevesi made himself laugh, and watched as Nones scurried away. The smile dropped off his face.

A figure appeared in the entrance to the basilica. Tiny under the huge white archway, the man trotted down the steps and turned left.

Benevesi followed him.

The old man made no effort to cover his tracks, but Benevesi did not catch him up. They crossed two small bridges and turned towards the docks. On Four Saints Way, the old man entered an ale-house. Benevesi paused outside. He could see to the far end of the road, straight out of the city and into the bay. The Grand Griffon reared up out of the winter mist like a monster striding out to fight Averrio's enemies. For a moment, Benevesi felt that it was watching him. Then he ducked into the tavern, into the warmth.

The room was busy, full of merchants bracing themselves with drink for the cold walk home. Chatter filled the air like gas.

On the far side of the room, the proprietor put a cup of wine in front of the old man. Benevesi slipped through the clientele until he stood at the old man's side.

"Azul," Benevesi said. "I'd have gone for coffee, myself."

The old man looked around. Behind his spectacles, his eyes were shrewd and hard. His mouth naturally hung open a little, as if it were a small hole cut in a piece of leather. He looked at Benevesi as he always did, as if about to angrily rebut an accusation.

"A fad," Azul croaked. "It smells better than it tastes." He pointed at a space by the far wall. He was wearing gloves: Benevesi had never seen him without them. "Over there. It's too noisy here."

Benevesi bought a drink of his own. When they stood beside the wall, Azul said, "This wine could be better, too."

The banker sighed. "Perhaps we should have met elsewhere."

"This is good enough. You look natural here."

Too natural, Benevesi thought. *How many of the merchants know my name – and perhaps my face?* "Did you sort that problem out?" he asked.

"Soon," the old man replied.

"I hope so. I tell you, if this gets out, we'll both be in the shit."

Azul looked up from his wine. "I know that," he replied. "Do you think I'm stupid? I am well aware of what it is to live in danger, thank you. My man will deal with it by the end of today."

"Good. It needs taking care of."

Azul smiled. It looked false. "How are the Council of a Hundred these days? Ruling with wisdom?"

Benevesi took a sip of his wine. "Worse than useless," he said, lowering his cup. "They talk incessantly, but they do nothing. Except architecture, that is. Architecture and warships."

"That sounds like every council I've heard of," Azul said. "Always bickering. Merchants and politicians, eh?" He looked at the bar, across the smiling, well-fed faces. A group of tubby men burst out laughing. Azul scowled as if he had bitten into a lime. "Look at them, grubbing for coins. Not a soldier among them. You know, one day I think men like this will get a terrible surprise."

Benevesi wondered if Azul included him in that definition. He felt a slight twinge of fear. Did Azul joke about how soft he was to that weird tall woman who followed him everywhere? Benevesi glanced around the room, knowing that if Azul attacked him, none of these smooth, pampered men would raise a hand in his defence. But of course, Azul wouldn't do that. Not ever.

Azul sipped, and frowned as though the wine had offended him. "So, I assume there will be no change in the import laws."

"None. I tried, believe me, but the Hundred weren't

having any of it."

"As I thought. Well, thank you for trying. You can expect more payments at the end of the month."

"I will." They drank in silence, the hubbub of the ale-house surrounding them. Benevesi raised his cup. "Then I propose a toast. To success."

Azul took another sip. His throat twitched as if he'd swallowed a pebble. "Success," he croaked.

A man and woman walked in. They were tall and light-haired, healthier and younger than most of the clientele, and could have been brother and sister. The woman closed the door, and the man scanned the room; he saw Azul and grinned into his beard.

"Your friends are here," Benevesi said.

"They've come to collect me. It's dangerous for an old man to go walking alone," Azul said, and his mouth opened like a hatch in his face. A hard, wheezing laugh came out.

Benevesi made himself smile back. Azul's young friends unnerved him. There was something outdoorsy about them, a fierce heartiness that made him think that they'd roar with laughter one moment and slash your throat the next.

"Ah," the woman said, striding over, "you are drinking away the cold, eh?" Her accent was foreign, slightly lilting. Benevesi reckoned that she was some kind of Teut.

"I couldn't keep away, Alicia," Azul said, smiling. He glanced at the man. "Cortaag, is that little matter being dealt with tonight?"

Cortaag was a little more formal: more like a servant than a relation. "It's being handled right now, sir."

Azul looked at Benevesi. "Reliable people, these.

The best. Always surround yourself with good workers. It's the key to success, you know. And now," he declared, "I have to go. You can have the rest of my wine. I'll arrange a meeting soon."

As Benevesi took the cup, Azul pulled his cloak tight across his meagre shoulders. His bodyguards parted to let him through. "Until next time," he said, and he walked towards the doors.

***

Giulia waited for Hugh in the north of the city, where the canals met the land and where the merchants swapped their long, low boats for carts. It was just after dark, and the street was empty. Their horses were tied up in an alleyway across the road. In the canal behind the inn, the water lay as quiet and black as tar.

She leaned against the buttress of a church, deep in shadow, not truly hiding but reluctant to stand in full view. She had nothing to hide, but it was best not to give people an excuse to make a nuisance of themselves.

The Old Arms was unusual for Averrio: a long, low, sprawling building, whose stables stuck out from the sides like roots from a stump. The canal ran parallel with the rear of the inn; the front faced onto a road. It looked like something from the countryside. Rustic, perhaps, but not cheap: the road was lit by a succession of glowing alchemical lanterns, which meant that the locals had hired a lamplighter. It looked warm and safe.

Several streets away, a hoarse voice struggled to drum up trade. "Come and see the salacious dances of the forest folk! The dryad dance of fertility! It will entrance even the most—" The man broke into coughs and tailed off. It was too cold to be shouting in the street.

Orange light bloomed on the stones to her left. Two guards turned the corner, one carrying a lantern. The crest on their tunics showed a white griffon against a blue background. The man on the left carried a musket, the other a crossbow.

Watchmen, she thought: no-one else would go strolling around at this time of night, especially dressed like that.

Giulia stepped into view. The Watchmen would soon have seen her anyway, and it would be best not to surprise armed men.

"Everything well, friend?" one asked.

His tone of voice suggested that there was no good reason to be hanging about outdoors. "Just waiting," she replied.

"Oh yes?" The Watchman had a small, bony head on a long, wrinkled neck, like a vulture, and he pushed it out at her. "Waiting for what?"

For God's sake. She pulled her hood back. "For my uncle. He's sorting out lodgings in the inn." Giulia pointed across the street. "See those horses in the alley there? I'm watching them for him."

The Watchmen made a show of weighing up the situation. "Is that so?" the older man said, and she wondered if he was about to make trouble for her.

"Come on," said the other. "If it gets much colder my balls'll drop off."

Ah, you can't beat the Watch. Wherever you go, they're all the same.

Giulia watched them turn and go. It was only when they were out of sight that she realised she was still being observed.

There was a long dagger in her boot, under her skirt, but she slid her hand onto the little meat-knife on her belt. Quicker to draw, less suspicious to possess.

A man loomed out of the dark. He stood there, just separate from the shadows, carefully looking at nothing.

"Have the Watch gone yet?" He had an unusual accent, hard to pin down.

Giulia said, "They'd hear me if I called."

"Don't call them. Please."

His face should have been handsome, but the hard jaw and dark eyes were meant for a stronger, more arrogant man, a man Giulia would not have much liked. Instead he looked nervous, as if afraid that the tough customer whose face he'd stolen would come to take it back.

He looked enviously at the Old Arms. "Is that place safe?"

"I don't know. I'd think so."

"They get a lot of travellers in there?"

He wore black, she saw, a long robe down to his ankles. His boots were tough and battered; there were strips of cloth wrapped round his hands to warm them, like bandages.

"I get the feeling all sorts stay there. It's probably safe enough for a preacher," Giulia said.

"I'm not a preacher. I'm just a peddler, that's all. I just sell things."

So where's the stuff you're peddling, then? She tightened her grip on her knife, willing him to go away. She wondered if he was mad enough to think she was a prostitute, whether he'd start saying crazy sexual stuff. He'd be getting a fist in the mouth if he did. Maybe more than that.

"My name's Sebastian," he said.

"Amelia." *Go away.*

"You ever been in there?" Sebastian kept his eyes on the inn, as if worried that it would sneak away.

"No."

"I heard there were Anglians there." Suddenly he seemed agitated, as though the answer mattered a great deal. "Knights and suchlike. Pious men."

She wondered why he cared. Perhaps he wanted to convert to the New Church. If he somehow thought Hugh could help with that, he was in for a surprise. Hugh believed in what he called the Piety of Noble Deeds, which meant that he rarely bothered with going to church if he could charge about on horseback instead.

"I don't know," she said again. *Go away. Can't you tell that I want you to fuck off?*

Sebastian stared off down the street. He looked ready for something to happen – angry, almost. "I have to go. But thank you."

"It was nothing," she said, reflecting that it really had been nothing at all. She was glad to see him go; even if he meant no harm, fear stuck to him like a sickness.

A door opened across the road, and light and noise spilled into the street: voices singing and chattering, and the sudden smell of food. Hugh of Kenton strode out, smiling as he paced across the road.

"Ah, there you are! This is the place, all right."

"Good," she said. "Is there space?"

"Yes. Edwin had them keep a couple of rooms back. Elayne's in there with him now. That's the good thing about these city places – you can get a room to yourself. None of that sleeping on the floor nonsense."

"Great," she said. "I'm freezing to death out here." She looked down the street. Sebastian had disappeared.

"Everything all right, Giulia?"

She peered into the dark. Nobody. "There was a man just here. Dressed like a priest. He's gone now."

"I saw a fellow walk off." Hugh nodded to the north. "Went that way. You need something from him?"

"God, no. I wanted shot of him. He started talking rubbish at me. I can't stand it when men think they can just ramble at you."

"Really? That's no good. Ought to have given him a piece of my mind." Hugh looked around as if unsure how he'd got there. "Well, come in. Bloody freezing out here."

He held the door open for her. Giulia walked from the night to the orange firelight of the inn. A babble of voices hit her ears, and the heat made her skin prickle with sweat.

People huddled in groups around tables, hunched over beer and dice. Iron candelabra hung below the soot-blackened ceiling. A single, massive fire crackled at one end of the room. The air was full of noise and smoke and the smell of soot.

She walked deeper inside and Hugh followed, looming up behind her. At the far end of the inn a fat man in an apron dipped cups into an open barrel and handed them to a little cluster of people around him. Hugh found a couple of cups on the floor, knocked the rushes off them and held them out to be filled with small beer.

"Edwin and Elayne were here," he said. "Must've moved back..."

Giulia followed him, sipping, glancing from man to man. She did not consciously check the customers for weaponry, but her eyes moved there as if magnetised – to belts and sleeves and dagger handles protruding from the tops of boots, to the fresh scabs on a man's knuckles and the way another set his shoulders as he stood. Even in a decent inn like this, there was always a chance that violence lay waiting under the smiles.

In the rear of the room there was a walled circle, a tiny arena for dogs to fight packs of dockyard rats. Now, though, the pit was empty and half a dozen people leaned against the railing and talked.

A middle-aged woman was peering into the pit. She was tall and flimsy-looking. She wore a green, wide-sleeved dress, well-cut but a little out of fashion. Her features were fine, but her nose was steeply upturned, and had her eyes not been so friendly and so quick, she would have looked aloof. Giulia knew at once that it had to be her: Elayne Brown, the sorceress.

Hugh waved and Elayne smiled, revealing a lot of white teeth. For someone who had to be at least forty-five, Elayne had aged extremely well. *She knows magic*, Giulia thought. *Go carefully*.

"There you are," Hugh said.

"Here I am indeed," Elayne replied, grinning.

She looks mad when she smiles. Still, no scars on her face. She's doing better than some.

"This is my friend Giulia," Hugh said. He held his arm out towards Giulia as if welcoming a performer on stage.

"Hello," Giulia said.

"Hello there!" Elayne replied. "I'm most pleased to meet you. Elayne Brown. So, are you an adventurer like Hugh?"

It seemed an odd expression. The usual word was "thief-taker" and, occasionally, "mercenary". "I suppose so," Giulia said. "I mean, I've had what you might call adventures."

"Excellent!" Elayne said. "Have you seen any

unusual places on your travels? Any good monsters to tell me about?"

Giulia had seen monsters, some of them human, and on bad nights she dreamed of them. She made herself smile and said, "Well, none that I'd call *good*, but I'm not sure if Hugh would agree."

Elayne laughed. "How did you meet?"

"Well, it was back in Pagalia. There was a riot at the palace – a rebellion, I suppose – and we were on the same side when it all broke out. We kind of helped Princess Leonora take the throne. Anyhow, both of us couldn't stand the place, so as soon as the chance came we took the road out of there. And, well, for the moment the road's taken us here."

"A rebellion? You'll have to tell me all about it. Goodness, Hugh, I can hardly believe it's really you! Let's all sit down – you too, Giulia. We've got so much to talk about!"

Edwin suddenly appeared at her side, breaking free of the crowd as if he had been hiding among the customers to spring an attack. "Hello again! Who'd like another drink?"

They sat at a battered table on mismatched stools.

Edwin glanced at Hugh as he passed the jug around. "So, you've known each other for a few months, then? You're not, um...?" he said, nodding at Giulia.

"Oh no," the knight replied. "We're friends, that's all. Brothers in arms, you might say."

"Siblings, surely," Elayne corrected.

"So who came up with the wyvern hunting?" Edwin said.

Elayne smiled. "Was it Hugh, by any chance?"

Hugh smiled back. "Well, somewhat. We did some minor hired work on the way here," he said. "Bits and pieces, really—"

"Which doesn't matter," Giulia added. "We thought we'd have a change, and so we came to Averrio. So, er, what brings you here?"

Edwin took out a pipe and knocked the bowl into his palm. "We're picking up a shipment of glassware to take back home. People want lenses these days, for telescopes and things. Or at least that's what I'm here for; Elayne's come with me to visit some magician fellow. Porthoris, was he?" he asked her.

"Portharion," she replied. "He lives on an island off the coast, but apparently he's on good terms with the scholars' clubs here. They say he can call spirits out the air."

"You're a wizard too, aren't you?" Giulia said.

"I certainly am. A specialised one, I should say, but a wizard of sorts indeed."

Giulia had the feeling that talking to Elayne was always going to be like swimming against a current of words. "Can you do that? Call up spirits to work for you?"

"No, that's not really my field, I'm afraid. I know – when I meet Portharion, why don't you come along? We could all go, all four of us."

Edwin had started to talk to Hugh, but he stopped and looked back at Elayne. "Now, I'm not sure that's a good idea—" he began.

"Oh, it'll be fun! If Hugh's prepared to vouch for Giulia, I'm sure she's fine." She glanced at Giulia and gave her the big smile again.

Kind people, I'm sure, Guilia thought, *but not my sort.*

"So," Edwin continued, "buying and selling wool

and glass: that's what I do. There's good money in it, too."

Giulia finished her drink. She wanted to join the conversation, but could not think of anything to say.

"Still jousting?" Hugh asked.

"No," Edwin said, "not for a while. You know, about a year ago I was at a militia training ground, and I saw a levy-man put a hole in plate armour with one of those matchlock guns. It really shook me up. For the first time, a peasant like that could put a knight down before we could ever get close to him."

Hugh shrugged. "There's always been bowmen," he said. "And guns have been around for a while."

"Not like that. It used to be that you could rely on a gun either blowing up or not going off at all. Not anymore. So here I am – and in clothes that aren't falling apart, for once."

"Very dapper." Hugh looked unconvinced. "How're the others back home? Tarquin and Lionel and the other fellows?"

Elayne tugged at Giulia's sleeve; she looked mischievous. "Look at this." She took a little cloth parcel out of her bag and unwrapped it. Inside was a frame no bigger than four inches square and, in that, a piece of coloured glass.

Elayne passed the frame to Giulia. "Look in the middle," she said.

Giulia held it up. She could see the warm blur of the fireplace through the frame. As she peered at it, she made out a picture, stained – or maybe painted, somehow – into the glass itself. A translucent sky and, under it, waves. Land rose above the water at the horizon – an island with a single tower.

"There's a picture there," she said.

Elayne's smile was gentler now. "Keep looking."

Giulia stared into the glass, and saw that the sun really was shining in it, reflecting on the sea. No, surely not: it was the glow of the fireplace behind doing that. But the water – it was rippling. The room was a masculine hum of voices somewhere far away.

A trick of the light. She held the frame steady, and the water shifted.

"It's moving!" she said.

"Keep watching. It's just a picture."

A dark streak threaded through the water. It swayed, as if some tiny snake was crawling beneath the frame.

There's something under the water.

It broke the surface. Dark blue, shining, like a seal's back but much too long. Giulia's chest felt tight. *Just a picture.*

Something rose from the water, glinting in the glass, something she thought was a tail – but no, it was a neck like a swan's but far, far larger, and at the end was a head, shaped like a horse's and draped with seaweed. Slowly, languidly, it looked towards the island, and then swung as the body turned, back towards Giulia—

She thrust the glass back at Elayne. "There's something in there," she said.

"Did you see it?"

"I saw an animal in the water. It moved. What the hell is that?"

"It's a water-wyrm. Clever, isn't it?"

"That's one word for it. Did you make that?"

"Oh no." Elayne wrapped the frame up again. "It's an imprint," she said. "Like a painting. The glass is enchanted to show a moment that happened a long time ago. There's nothing in there really, nothing that could harm you. It just remembers the moment it was enchanted, that's all."

"Is it safe?"

"Totally. Only the greatest glassmakers can produce something like that, and only here. This piece is just an example, to show people what can be done. You can see why Edwin does business with Averrio."

"You trade wool for that? Hell of an exchange." Giulia got to her feet. "Would you excuse me for a moment? I need to get some air."

In a moment she was outside, standing under the porch at the back of the Old Arms, pulling up her hood against the winter chill. The sounds of the inn washed out behind her. Giulia sighed, watching her breath curl like smoke, and stepped out into the night.

The canal stirred gently by her feet.

Creepy damned thing, that glass.

Giulia walked to the stable, rubbing her hands together. She took her crossbow and her thieving gear from her saddlebag and hid it on a low rafter. She wasn't entirely sure if it was legal to own a crossbow in the city – usually, you could carry a bow so long as it was wrapped up – but the lockpicks wouldn't look good, and it was best not to take any chances.

Leaving the stable, she hesitated. Giulia didn't want to go back inside: for now, she needed to be on her own. Hugh's friends seemed kindly enough, but they lived in a different world. They had grown up on farms and estates, with swordplay and archery instead of fist-fights and the sudden shine of knives. Edwin and Hugh were soldiers, not thieves, and their lives had a kind of brave glamour that Giulia's would always lack.

She strolled along the pavement beside the canal. The water was still, and the light reflected off the occasional ripples was almost white. Across the canal, a solitary figure hurried along in a long cloak like her own, head lowered. Giulia caught a glimpse of a face – long and chiselled with enormous, beautiful, inhuman eyes. A dryad. No wonder it kept its head down: outside the district set aside for unbelievers and heretics, a dryad would draw attention, and as a pagan it could expect little protection from the law.

Giulia thought about another inhuman head, rising from the sea in Elayne's magic glass, and looked at the canal and shuddered. *No*, she thought, *things like that could never swim up here. Surely not.*

She missed being alone. Hugh's friends would be good company for a while, but soon enough Giulia and Hugh would have to earn some money of their own. Most of her reward from foiling the coup in Pagalia had gone on new thieving equipment, the rest on an expensive dress that she was beginning to regret. Besides, Giulia didn't like the way Hugh looked at Elayne. *He ought to be searching for companionship somewhere else*, she thought. *So should I.*

Somewhere, distantly, a bell was tolling, inviting paupers to a church where they could trade worship for warmth. In the corner where two houses met, a pile of blankets moved as the man underneath shifted in his sleep. She carried on.

Tenements rose up around her. Statues of saints clustered on a church roof, their faces angled down towards the canal as if about to jump in. A servant slept outside one wide-fronted house in an open boat, part-hidden by several cloaks. He opened one eye as Giulia approached, grunted, and went back to sleep.

The bell was still ringing as she turned and walked back towards the inn. She could see the light of the Old Arms, and by now she was cold enough to want to get indoors. Hopefully, the others would have finished swapping stories about people that she didn't know, and there would be a conversation in which she could take part.

There was a narrow wooden bridge almost opposite the inn, arcing across the canal. Nearly a dozen people stood on the bridge, looking at something in the water. A couple of men, probably from the City Watch, were prodding the object with a boat-hook.

Giulia stopped next to them, suddenly uneasy. "What's that?" she said. "What's going on?"

An old woman turned to look at her. "It's some poor bastard drowned himself," she said, and she looked up and made the Sign of the Sword across her chest. "Some children saw him floating. They thought he was an animal come up from the bay."

The Watchmen were arguing over the boat-hook. It caught on the body, and the man turned over lazily, his arm making a loose, drunken gesture that seemed to take in the sky and the crowd that had come to watch. It was a scene drawn in white, blue and black, as though the death had drained the colour from the air.

The man's empty face stared up at the moon, his mouth a shapeless hole. His throat had been torn out.

The Watchman yanked on the boat-hook and called, "Somebody bring the boat up, for God's sake. People drink out of there. Get the boat, Pietro!"

"Doesn't look like he drowned," Giulia said. People were leaving the Old Arms in a steady flow, eager to see the corpse: the inn was losing a lot of its trade to the dead man. As the hook tugged more of him into view, she saw the marks on his chest, rips in his clothing through which his white body shone as brightly as the moon. She saw his features properly. It was the man she'd spoken to outside the Old Arms, the man who had been afraid.

Giulia ran towards the inn.

She pushed past a thin stream of people going out and ducked inside. She saw Elayne's dress, ran over to the Anglians and said, "Hugh, we've got trouble."

Hugh tipped the contents of his cup down his throat. His Adam's apple twitched like something that had just been killed. "Fighting, eh?" he said, eyes gleaming.

"What's going on?" Edwin asked. Elayne reached out and took his hand.

"They've found a body in the canal that runs behind the inn. They're just fishing him out. Looks like he was stabbed."

"God," Elayne said, "how awful!"

Giulia spoke to Hugh. "Look, I think we ought to go. Maybe all of us should."

"Go?" Edwin said. "That's not going to look good, is it?"

"This doesn't look good anyhow," she replied. "They'll be looking for someone to bring in. You three are foreigners, and I'm – well, we don't look right."

"It's them who're the bloody foreigners," Hugh muttered. He rubbed his chin. "Right then, let's have a look outside."

Edwin said, "Perhaps we ought to get our things together, love."

She shook her head. "I don't know..."

Giulia thought, *This'll take all year*. "Elayne, Edwin, you get your stuff ready. Hugh and I'll fetch the horses."

"Right," said Hugh, standing up. "See you round the back."

The fresh night air sharpened Giulia's mind.

Watchmen had converged on the bridge as if drawn by a scent. There were half a dozen of them now, all trying to help bring the corpse to land. A boat had been found, and with the help of a couple of rowers they hauled the body out of the canal. Its arms dangled; it reminded Giulia of a hanged man.

"I'll check the horses," Hugh said.

"Do it quickly. We need to be going right now."

Men gathered around the body. Someone slipped and cursed. Voices babbled and overlapped. "It's not proper, just leaving him out here." "Put your cloak over him." "My cloak on a dead man? You think I want to catch plague?"

On the water's edge, a fat Watch captain dropped into a crouch and began to search the body as his colleagues shoved the onlookers away. Giulia saw him slip a square packet from the dead man's belt and drop it into a pocket in his cloak.

She clenched her fists; the urge to run was winding her taut inside. *Dammit, Hugh, hurry up!*

She looked at the body, at the crowd, hissed with irritation and ran back into the inn.

The Old Arms was three-quarters empty now. Giulia strode to the stairs and looked up.

"Edwin? Elayne! Are you there? Edwin? We have to go!"

The door banged open behind her and winter air rushed into the room. Giulia whirled around. Five Watchmen stood in the doorway. At their head was the tubby captain that she had seen outside.

"You!" he called. "You with the scars! You know a man called Hugh of Kenton – tall man, from Albion?"

"Yes," she said, "I know him."

"Then come out here."

For a moment she looked them over. There would be no point arguing. She nodded, drew her cloak close around her, and walked to the door. They stepped aside to let her through.

Outside, Hugh stood next to Edwin and Elayne. A young man with a pimpled face covered them with his crossbow. He looked ludicrous next to the three of them, a part-timer signed up for the extra coins and the chance to carry a bow. But the tip of the bolt was pointed at Elayne, and that was enough to secure obedience from the men.

Above them, far off, a hawk shrieked. Giulia glanced up and saw a black spot moving across the sky, silhouetted by the gibbous moon: a mixture of eagle and lion, four-limbed and winged.

The sight of it made her shiver, with awe as much as fear. It seemed miles away.

"Wild griffon," the fat captain said, looking at her. He gestured towards the heraldry on his tunic, and his mean, podgy face became dreamy and proud. "Symbol of the city." It hardened again. "All right, let's go."

She looked away from the moon, back to the Watch captain. "What d'you mean?" Giulia said. "Go where?"

The captain grinned. "Where do you think, girl? Your friends are going to jail until we've decided what to do with them. And guess what?"

"What?"

"You're going with them."

TWO

The cell smelt of earth and stagnant water. It contained two low benches and a trough on the floor. There was water in the trough, and algae at the bottom of it. Giulia was not sure of its purpose. After a careful search by the sole candle, she discovered that there was no way out except the barred, heavy door. Without weapons or lockpicks, they were trapped.

The four of them sat in a grim row on one bench. On the other bench was a thin girl with eyes like polished rocks. Giulia didn't like her; she looked wiry and fast.

Giulia thought about where she would have liked to be: a house in the countryside, perhaps a small manor, with neat, tame gardens outside. She imagined herself owning it, somehow. There would probably be a man involved, but she wasn't sure where exactly he'd fit in.

Two months ago I kissed Marcellus van Auer. And now Marcellus is building his machines and painting his pictures in a palace miles away. He's probably got a woman now, and a commission of his own. And I've got this.

"What you in for?" the girl opposite demanded, stretching out on the bench.

"I'm not sure yet," Edwin replied. "How about

you?"

"Whoring." She yawned. "They pull us in every so often: it happens."

Giulia leaned forward. "You've been here before, then?"

"Once in a while. Shithole that it is."

"What's the best way to get out of here?"

"The best way out?" The girl adjusted her dress. It was frilly and slowly falling apart, hitched up at the front to show off her legs. "Hard to say. But sucking off the guard tends to help."

"I'm sure we can get out soon," Edwin said. "I just need to talk to the right people, that's all. I'm sure it's a misunderstanding."

"Oh, we'll be fine once it's all explained," Elayne said. "Though I *will* be writing to the Anglian ambassador about this."

"I don't think there is one," Edwin said. "There's an embassy in Pagalia, though."

"Pagalia is fifty miles away," Giulia said. "And it's a different state."

"Bloody foreigners," said Hugh.

Elayne pulled her skirts up so they did not touch the floor. Her shoes were smart and delicate, but without the platforms that were in fashion on the Peninsula. The prostitute looked at Elayne as if considering robbing her.

Giulia took a deep breath and said, "So I suppose you can't just, er, magic us out of here, then?"

Elayne shook her head. "No, I'm afraid, though I wish I could. It doesn't quite work like that. To be honest, I wouldn't know how."

"Don't they teach you that at wizard school?"

"There isn't such a thing as wizard school.

Sometimes a great scholar takes on an apprentice, but that's it."

Giulia nodded. "So, er, what *can* you do?"

"I'm a summoner of winds. That's what I do on the ship. If we're becalmed, I can call up a wind to get us moving again."

"I thought most ports had their own storm-caller."

"They do, but it helps to have your own." Elayne smiled. "I can do a few other little things: help small wounds heal up quicker, get animals to obey, that sort of business."

"Animals? What about people?"

"It's harder. Sometimes I can get them to do things they wouldn't usually do, to change their minds. But it's difficult. People vary."

"Could you make the guards let us go?"

"I doubt it. It's exactly what they're not supposed to do. It's difficult to turn a person's mind around like that. I could push them a little way, though," she added. "Sorry not to be more use."

"That's all right," said Hugh.

Giulia tried not to grimace.

"Well, we'll just think of something else," Edwin said. "Don't feel bad about it, dear. We'll sort something out, you'll see."

Like what? Giulia thought. Her lockpicks were back in the inn, hidden in the stable with the rest of her thieving kit. *I knew this would be trouble, I bloody knew it. You idiot, Giulia. I could have fought off that fat Watch captain and run away. Why the hell didn't I?*

As soon as the thought entered her mind, she knew the answer. Hugh wouldn't leave Edwin and Elayne, and Giulia wouldn't leave Hugh.

"I say we break out," Hugh declared. "One of the ladies feigns illness, and then when the guard comes we jump him, get the keys and go."

"We've got no swords," Edwin said.

"Ah, that's nothing. The two of us against some part-time guard? We can take him. It'll be like the old days. Remember how we got out of the Chateau Dolour?"

Edwin said, "We got the keys then?"

"Yes indeed! Anwell made out he had gut-ache, then the two of us did the guards when they came to look. There were three of them then, and armed!" He crossed his arms and leaned back, smiling. "*That's* what we ought to do."

The thin-faced prostitute met Giulia's eyes for a moment. Giulia glanced away.

Edwin shook his head. "It wouldn't work, Hugh. It'd be too risky."

"Nonsense, old fellow: the ladies can go at the back. Besides, Giulia there knows a trick or two as it is. All we'd have to make sure is that you're safe, Elayne, and I can see to that."

Edwin shook his head. "It's too dangerous. I'm not putting you at risk, Elayne."

"Well, we'll all be at risk if we just sit here," Hugh said. "I tell you, I'm not having some bloody peasant thinking he can lock me up. I'm for getting out the proper way!"

Giulia looked at Elayne. "What do *you* think?" she said.

Elayne shrugged. "I'm not much of a fighter, to be honest. Can't we just try talking to the guard?"

"Definitely not," Edwin said.

"Nonsense, man!" said Hugh.

Giulia turned to the prostitute. "How do we talk to the guard? Without offering to suck him off, preferably."

The girl shrugged, stood up and walked to the door. She stood on tiptoe and put her face to the bars. "Hey, arsehole!"

A face appeared at the door, and the prostitute stepped back. "They want to talk to the boss."

The guard stood there, looking at each of them in turn with the same expression of bored disdain, as if forced to make a choice that would inevitably turn out to be disappointing.

"Just one of you. You, the woman. Not you, scarface; I meant the lady. You'll do."

The men were on their feet. "Now look here—" Hugh said.

"My wife goes nowhere without me," Edwin said.

Giulia turned to Elayne. "I'll do this," she said quietly. "I can take care of myself. Hey, you! I'll speak for them."

"No," said the guard. "Only one of you comes out, and it's the lady."

Elayne said, "You know, I think it would be helpful if we all came along."

"Maybe..." The guard shook his head. "No. I said one, lady. One woman, and not your friend with the cut-up face. A proper lady."

"It would be better if Giulia went. She knows the situation much better than me. You really should talk to her. It would look much better for you."

The guard looked around the cell, as if hoping one of the others would give him permission. "All right then. But her only."

He stepped close to the door and took a key from

his belt. Giulia met Hugh's eyes, and she gave a quick shake of her head. *Don't rush the door.*

"Come on, scarface," said the guard. "Let's get moving."

He led her upstairs, into a well-lit white chamber. There was a big desk in the corner of the room, its surface pitted with dents like a carpenter's bench. An elderly mastiff flopped beside the desk, all ears, chops and gangly legs. A man sat at the desk reading a letter, following the text with a fingertip. Every so often he would reach out blindly, and his hand would pat the air until it met the dog's head.

A few other Watchmen sat on the far side of the room, talking. The ceiling creaked over Giulia's head as someone moved about on the floor above.

The guard stopped Giulia in front of the desk. "This is the woman, Boss. Giulia something."

"Give me a moment. I just need to finish this." The man glanced up and saw Giulia, and his eyes widened slightly as he noticed her scars. "Who's this?"

The guard shrugged. "She's from the cells. They wanted to talk to the man in charge. I said one of the women could come up."

"Is that so? Looks like you brought up the wrong one."

"He brought the right one," Giulia said. "The other three are foreigners. They don't know what's going on. I do. I've dealt with this kind of thing before."

"Looks more like it dealt with you." He looked at her, expecting something that she couldn't work out, so she looked straight back. At the far end of the room, one of the Watchmen leaned out on his chair to get a better view, then leaned back again.

Something softened in the Watch lieutenant's eyes. "Sit down." He was tired-looking, weak-chinned, with eyes that made Giulia think of tunnels and mice. "You can go, Tommaso."

The guard grunted, turned and walked away. His boots scuffed and thumped on the stairs.

"So, then," said the lieutenant.

Giulia sat down and held out her hand, like a man. "I'm Giulia Degarno. Pleased to meet you."

He didn't shake it. "I'm Antonio Falsi, Lieutenant of the Watch. Which means that I pretty much run this place," he added, as if it had only just occurred to him.

Lucky you. Giulia said, "I'm glad to be talking to the right person. There's clearly been a mistake here."

"We don't make mistakes," Falsi said.

So you made this cock-up on purpose? I feel vastly reassured. "I'm pleased to hear it," she said. "I'm a thief-taker by trade—"

"That's horse-shit to begin with," said a voice from the back of the room. One of the men in the far corner stood up and strolled over to Falsi's side. He was tall and light-haired, with a lumpy jaw that looked as if the muscles were permanently clenched. "I was with Captain Orvo when he brought them in. A thief-taker would have rope, manacles, that sort of stuff. She had none of that." He looked down at Giulia. "The only thief-taking she's seen is thieves taking her up the arse."

Giulia kept her eyes on Falsi. "Look," she said, "I need to get my friends out of here. If you could tell me what you need—"

"You want to go? God, no." Falsi looked appalled. Behind him, the tall man emitted a short, snorting laugh, a laugh for a man who knew that he was tough. Falsi said,

"You and your friends are about the only thing I've got on that dead preacher they hauled out of the water last night. It looks like he was on his way to see you when someone did him over."

Was he, now? She remembered Sebastian's haunted face, his quick denial of being a clergyman. "A priest?"

"Damn right. He had all the robes and a sigil round his neck. It looks like a faith killing, if you ask me. The sort of thing Purists would do."

"Now wait a minute. I don't know anything about any faith killings."

Falsi's friend scratched his head. "That's funny, because as it happens we've got three Purists sitting in the cell downstairs. And here's another funny thing – they were very near the priest when he was killed. So funny it's hilarious, isn't it?"

"For God's sake," Giulia said. "They're not even Purists, they're – I don't know – New Church or something. Hugh's hardly a priest-hater. God, he doesn't care about any of that stuff."

"Irreligious, eh?" Falsi said, and he sighed. "Woman, your friends are in a lot of trouble—"

"A heap of shit, to be precise," said the big man.

"Shut up, Cafaro. Listen, girl: a priest is knifed and a dog set on him, then his body gets dumped in the canal. And who happens to be nearest to the killing? Three travelling Purists, or Objectors or whatever other New Church heresy they happen to follow, and not just them, but – well, you. It doesn't look good, does it?"

"God in Heaven," Giulia cried, "anyone could have done it! Your bloody dog could have done it!"

Falsi's mastiff glanced up, confused. It stared at Giulia for a moment, then settled back down. "Nah," said

Cafaro. "That thing's way too soft."

Falsi rocked back in his chair and looked at his thumb. "Two months ago a group of Purists tried to blow up the city arsenal," he said. "People don't much like the New Church at the moment. Like I said, if you want to walk away from this, I'd suggest you distance yourself from any heretics you might know."

Giulia looked him in the eye. "You can forget that," she replied. "I stand by my friends."

Cafaro smirked. "Probably hang by 'em, too."

Something landed heavily in the room above, and the timbers groaned. Giulia looked up: the roof bulged down slightly, like a belly against a tight shirt.

"The thing is that, as it is, you four are the closest we have to knowing who killed him. Chances are, you did it." Falsi opened his hands, as if to let her future fall out of them. *He doesn't believe that*, Giulia thought.

"I'd like to see the priest's body," she said.

"What for? Did you know him?"

"No. I'd just like to know that anything of what you've just told me is true. You said about a dog being set on him. We don't even *have* a dog. I'll bet the knife wounds are all wrong, too."

"You'd know, would you?" Cafaro said.

Falsi shook his head. "No, you can't see the body. If you were a relation, maybe, but... Sorry, no. He stays in the cellar. Besides, what do you need to know? He died of being stabbed and a dog mauling him. That's all there is to know."

"You don't want us," she said. "Really, you don't. My friends are important merchants. They do a lot of trade here. It wouldn't look good for the city."

Falsi rubbed the mastiff behind the ears. It opened

its mouth and began to pant. "Wouldn't it? Well, here's what's going to happen. You people will stay here until we know a bit more. Then, you go up before the magistrate."

"What for?"

"Murder, of course. Depends how the procurator sees it, though."

"Who?"

"The procurator. Head lawyer. Does the prosecuting. I thought you said you knew this city?"

"Look, what I do know is that Hugh didn't do it. Nor did any of them. Come on, man, this is a lie. And you know it."

"No." She was surprised how serious Falsi looked. It was as if she'd finally cracked through the armour of his disinterest. "I'm supposed to find some sort of answer. At the moment, you four are the best answer there is."

Cafaro put his hands on his hips. "Law and order, little lady, that's what the Watch is all about. If you can't have law, you settle for order."

Falsi looked around. "Cafaro, piss off."

"Just trying to help, sir." The big man threw a salute and strolled towards the door.

It burst open in his face. Hugh strode in. Edwin and Elayne stood in the doorway behind him. Giulia's stomach churned. They'd decided to do it Hugh's way - killing their way out of prison.

Falsi was on his feet. "What the hell's this?" Men got up at the back of the room. The mastiff leaped up and barked. Elayne made a quick gesture and it sat down again, suddenly calm.

But Hugh raised his empty hands. The guard, Tommaso, stepped out from the middle of the group. "I thought you'd like to see them," he said weakly.

"Why in God's name did you bring them up here?"

Tommaso's voice was very small. "Well, you've got her up here to begin with, and you said it wasn't the right woman, so I thought I'd get the right woman and then she said that you might as well see all of them..."

Cafaro laughed bitterly. "You fucking idiot."

Giulia noticed something that nobody else seemed to have done: Falsi was holding a pistol just below the table.

The lieutenant said, "Keep a bow on these people."

A Watchman came forward from the back of the room, a crossbow in his hands. "I've got 'em."

"We just want to talk to you," Elayne said. "That's all."

"Fine," Falsi replied. Slowly, he laid the pistol on the tabletop. It sounded very loud as he put it down. "You, sit down. The other two, keep very still."

Elayne took a chair and sat. The two men stood behind her and Giulia, as though they were all posing for a painting.

Giulia turned to the Anglians. "They're pinning it on us," she said. "The dead man was a priest, and since you're foreigners, they want to say you did it. As for me – well, I don't look too innocent, either." She glanced at Falsi. "Apparently, that's all the proof Lieutenant Falsi here needs."

"Shut up," Falsi said. "Listen, if you've got anything worth saying, say it. Otherwise, you can go back in your cell, and this time I'll put someone with half a fucking brain on the door. Anything you'd like to tell me?" He waited for a few moments. "Didn't think so. Men, put these good people back in the cell."

"Wait," Giulia said.

"You had your chance."

The crossbowman stepped forward. Cafaro reached up to a shelf. With a soft clank of metal, he pulled down a set of manacles.

Elayne said, "Listen to her. *Listen*."

Falsi raised his hand. "Wait."

"I can get you a name," Giulia said. "If you let us out of here, I'll come back to you in a week's time with the name of the person who killed the priest. You won't have to do anything except wait. Then, you can get the right man instead of us."

"That's a stupid idea," Falsi said. "How will I know you won't give me the wrong name?"

"It can't be more wrong than the ones you've got now," Giulia replied. She glanced at the others: Edwin was leaning forward, hands gripping the back of Elayne's chair as to drive his fingers through the wood. Elayne was sweating. She looked a little sick.

"Maybe," Falsi said. "But I still don't like it. What's to stop you just running off?"

"We have money," Edwin began. "Perhaps a donation might help?"

Falsi snorted. "A 'donation.' Do you seriously think I'd let you walk out of here just like that?"

"You could give us a chance," Giulia said. She glanced at Elayne.

"It's a good idea," Elayne said calmly. "Giulia's right: you know that. You can't keep us here."

"Maybe." Falsi patted the dog's head. "We might need the cells, I suppose."

"That's right," Elayne replied. "You could put us under house arrest instead."

Falsi looked at the man with the bow. "If I do that,"

he said, "you'll run for it. I reckon you'll just run straight out the city."

"That's simple," Giulia said. "Tell the men at the city gates to look out for us."

"No, you'd hold up a boatman or something, try to row your way out. You wouldn't get far, though."

Good, Giulia thought. *He's already thinking about how to control us, what to do once we're outside. He thinks he's being tough, but he's really making concessions. We're halfway to agreeing on this.*

"I won't go anywhere you don't want me to," Edwin said. "Provided you stick to your side of the bargain, you have my word of honour on that."

"Mine too," Hugh put in. "As a knight."

"None of us will be leaving," Elayne said. Her teeth were gritted, her face tense. "You know there won't be any problems. It's a good idea."

For a while Falsi was silent. He leaned over the edge of the desk to look at the dog, and did not sit back up for several seconds. Giulia wondered if he was unwell. Falsi screwed his eyes up tight, as though he was trying to remember something, or put it out of his mind. He shook his head as if to clear it, but he still looked confused.

"Well... I suppose it's only fair. Yes, that's... fair. And if you try to run, we'll know for sure that you're guilty. Right then: you, Giulia Degarno, you've got seven days. Come the end of the week and you'll be up in the courthouse – no second chances.

"The rest of you are under house arrest. You'll remain in the Old Arms no matter what. You can have your weapons back, but if I hear you've so much as drawn a sword in anger, you're dead. If you're seen on the street, my men will have the right to bring you in, however's necessary. And I *will* be checking," he added. "If you try to run, we'll take you, even if I have to call in the soldiers from the Arsenal to do it. But I don't think that will be necessary. You're not all fighters, after all." And he looked at Elayne.

That's smart, Giulia thought. *She's the way to control Edwin – and Hugh. And therefore me. Clever little fellow, aren't you?*

"Understand?"

"We understand," Edwin said.

"Yes," Hugh said darkly, "I see."

The Watchman turned to Giulia. "I'm giving you a lot here," he said.

"Don't worry," she replied. "I'll make sure you get something back."

THREE

Outside, the city was groggily coming to life. Along the streets and bridges people and goods passed back and forth; the first boats slid lazily down the canals. A statue of a saint stood in the back of a boat. Its arm was extended, as if it were waving Averrio goodbye.
Lucky bastard.

Five Watch guards with crossbows accompanied them to the inn, hanging back and talking while their captives walked ahead. One of the guards was Cafaro: he carried a sack containing their knives and swords. Giulia stopped to adjust her boot and found him staring at her when she glanced back. When he wasn't smirking, Cafaro looked as friendly as a robber's dog.

Hugh waited for Giulia to stand. "Damn it, Giulia. This is a bloody mess. You know," he said quietly, "we should have just stormed the place. I could have had that crooked Falsi fellow."

"With a bullet in you?" Giulia asked.

"Better me than you, or Elayne," Hugh said. "He'd have just given up, anyway. People like that are all mouth."

"I'm not sure," Edwin said. "He was pretty serious – for a Watchman. Damn," he added, "I wish we'd got taken by the Customs people instead. They've got a brain between them."

"Well, we're out for now," Elayne said, and she slipped her hand into Edwin's. "I've got a rotten headache. Pushing him was hard."

"Pushing?" Giulia said. "You mean you did magic on him?"

Behind them one of Falsi's men laughed, coarse and loud. *I could run*, she thought. *I could tear away down a sidestreet, creep out of this city and— no.*

"Absolutely." Elayne was sweating again, a fine line of water across her brow. Her breath was high and fast. "Sometimes you can help make someone's mind up for them. But it doesn't work on everyone. I tried to make him let us go at first, but he was too set against it. Goodness, I'm tired. I could do with a week asleep. Lieutenant Falsi might not have looked very proper, but his mind was strong. If he hadn't wanted to let us go, we'd still be there, I suppose."

"Wanted to?"

"A little bit."

"Guilt, I suppose," Edwin said.

"Watchmen don't do guilt," Giulia replied. "Not that I've ever seen."

They approached the rear of the Old Arms. The canal lay before them, innocuous in the light of day.

Giulia looked at the place where the body had lain, and a memory from last night arose as clearly as the remembered image in Elayne's magic glass: that fat Watch captain bending down and taking something from the body, some wrapped parcel that didn't look like a money bag. *What was that thing? Something Falsi wanted? He didn't mention it. Was it something the captain wanted for himself, to keep from his men?*

Edwin put his arm around Elayne's shoulders and she leaned in to him. As they walked he reached up and stroked her hair. Giulia glanced at Hugh. His face showed no emotion. "Not to worry," Edwin said. "We'll be back soon."

The guards tipped up their sack on a table, and Hugh's sword clattered onto the wood amidst a shower of knives. One of the men spoke to the landlord, and Cafaro sauntered over to bid the travellers farewell.

"I don't know what in God's name the boss is playing at," he said, "but make no bloody mistake, I'll be watching you. You may not see me, or my men, but we'll be looking out for you, don't you worry. We have our people, you know."

Giulia looked at the landlord, still quietly conferring with Cafaro's friend.

"Not just him. Men on the street, all over the place. So when I catch you, don't say you weren't warned. And you, you old whoreson," he added, "I'll be watching you especially."

Hugh did not so much ignore him as seem not to have noticed him from the start.

Cafaro gathered his men and they walked to the door. Giulia heard them muttering: "... that idiot must be half-crazy... lieutenant must be losing his wits..."

The door slammed behind them. Giulia followed the others upstairs.

She locked the door to her room and sat down on the bed.

Giulia looked down at her hands. There was a pressure building behind her forehead, like the beginning of a headache. Her body felt weak, deflated, leaving her a little less alive.

It shouldn't be like this.

It was the Melancholia, of course. Giulia had known she couldn't escape it, but she'd thought it was under control when she left Pagalia, that settling her scores there would somehow capture it for good. She grimaced and rubbed her temples.

It wasn't supposed to end up this way. I was supposed to get away from this – away from cheating Watchmen and dirty inns and false witnesses. I should be riding across the plains, having adventures, like people in stories do. And what do I get instead?

A knock on the door. "Giulia? Are you all right in there?"

She glanced up, relieved. "Yes – yes, I'm fine." She stood up and opened the door.

"You look sick," said Hugh.

"Just a headache, that's all. I've had better days." She looked past him, down the corridor. "I'm going to check on my things."

He nodded. "I'd offer to assist, but this house arrest and all... I'm not sure if I can go to the stables."

"Don't worry. I won't be a minute."

The landlord, a fat, strong-looking man, watched her resentfully as he swept up. He moved slowly, heavily, as if someone was riding on his shoulders.

"Just need some air," she said. "You know I'm allowed to go outside, right?"

"Uh," he replied.

She slipped up the side of the inn, to the little stable. Giulia didn't much like horses, and suspected that they knew it. Her own horse ignored her, as it tended to.

She jumped up, caught hold of a low beam and pulled herself up. A grey blanket was wedged between the ceiling and one of the lower beams. Giulia knocked it off, dropped down and caught the bundle as it fell. She opened it up.

Her crossbow took up most of the bundle. A set of lockpicks, a stiletto and a black-bladed fighting knife lay beside it, along with a pair of leather arm-bracers. She took the knives, the picks and the bracers, and pushed the bow back in place.

The door to Hugh's room was ajar. He sat on the edge of the bed, elbows resting on knees, hands clasped. He looked too big for the little room, as if trapped inside a nursery. The knight raised his head. "Giulia."

She stepped inside and closed the door. "What a shitty deal," she said.

"At least we're not still in that cell," he said. He sounded unconvinced. "When you said about finding a name to give the Watch back there, was that just a bluff to get us out?"

Giulia leaned against the wall. The room felt oppressively small. "No. At least, not entirely. I'll see what I can do, but no guarantees. Frankly, a lot of it *was* bluff." She sighed. "This is just what we bloody need."

"Don't worry," Hugh said, "I've been working on a plan. First, we knock out the innkeep. Then we get our gear on and head to the gate. And on the way, we teach a damned good lesson to any foreigner who thinks he can frame two Anglian knights." He was angry, she saw, winding himself up for righteous violence. "Then we break through the guardposts before they know what's happening and take off north." He sighed. "You know, being stuck here would be a damn sight easier if there weren't any women involved. No offence."

"That's all right. I can put up with it."

"Elayne can't. I don't mean to be rude, but she's not tough like you. She's... delicate. She always has been. Needs to be looked after."

"I expect Edwin will take care of her."

"I suppose."

Giulia said, "Look, why don't you go downstairs and have a drink, eh?"

"Look like I need it, do I?" He smiled.

"No more than any of us. I'm going out for a while," she said. "I'll find someone who can testify for us, then we can get the hell out of here." She forced a smile. "You know, I never thought wyvern hunting would seem such a good idea."

Hugh looked straight at her. "If you need any help, you know I'll muck in. Just say."

"Thanks. I'll let you know. But in the meantime, just keep calm, all right? Don't go doing anything wild. I won't be long, and we'll have some wine when I get back."

"I'll be fine. Where *are* you going, anyway?"

"To find out what really happened last night. I've got an idea of where to start. I don't think I was the only person to see that priest alive."

"Be careful, Giulia. Damned shame I can't come along. It could be dangerous out there."

"Don't worry – I'm prepared." She pulled up her skirt and he turned away, as if dazzled by the sun.

"Dammit, woman, I don't want to see that!" Hugh lowered his hand, saw that she had britches on under her dress, and looked at the knife handle protruding from the top of her boot.

"Got another one up my sleeve." Giulia grinned. "See you later, Hugh."

She headed downstairs. The innkeeper watched her leave, his eyes narrow and shrewd. He looked at her as if she were money he planned to steal. In a way, she was: no doubt the innkeep was being paid to keep a very close eye on them all. *Bastards*, she thought. *Nobody pins me down.*

The street looked different in daylight. Across the road, muffled sounds of a hammer came from a cobbler's shop. A boot dangled from a jig above the door, along with the stamp that indicated guild membership. The boot was shiny with frost.

Giulia walked carefully, her breath forming in a cloud before her face. She wondered why that happened when it was cold, and a face appeared in her mind – Marcellus van Auer, savant and engineer. *He'd have known why*. She put the image aside before she could start feeling bad. There wasn't time to think about that.

Last night, while she had left the Old Arms to get some fresh air, she'd glimpsed a dryad near the spot where the dead man had been found. The dryad might have seen something, might be able to help – provided that Giulia could track it down. The fey people had a knack of making themselves scarce, especially in the hostile territory of a human city.

Just before Giulia had encountered Father Sebastian, she'd heard the owner of an inn shouting about the salacious dancing of the fey. Giulia knew of such shows from back in Pagalia; they almost never included a real dryad, usually just some skinny dancer, hair down and face painted. But maybe this was real. Other than the Watch captain that she'd seen stealing something from the dead man, it was the only real lead she had. She quickened her pace, following the canal towards the place from which the sound had come.

Fifty yards down, she found an inn on the canalside. It had no name. The sign outside showed a barrel, and had not someone dropped a tankard and puked on the doorstep, it could have been a cooper's shop.

Giulia bashed on the door with her fist, stepped back and waited.

She struck again and tried to peer through the windows. They were a patchwork of tiny bits of glass. Half the window seemed to be lead, and the other half glass too filthy to allow her a decent view of the room beyond.

The shutters opened above her and a balding man poked his head out. He had a dented face that made Giulia think of boiled meat.

"Is the building on fire?" said the man.

"No, I—"

"Then piss off." He slammed the shutters closed.

Giulia picked up the tankard and threw it at the window. It clattered against the frame, and the shutters snapped open like the reflex kicking of a struck knee.

"What?" the man demanded.

"I'm looking for someone. Also, you've got a tankard under your window."

"Your man's not here. We throw 'em all out come sunrise."

"It's not a man I'm looking for. I want to talk to you."

"We're already talking, and I don't like it."

The cold pinched the end of Giulia's nose. "I'm looking for a dryad, a female one. I heard you calling in the street last night—"

"Yes – last night. Today I want to sleep. Come back later with the rest of 'em."

"I've got money," Giulia said.

The window closed. Sounds came from within. She folded her arms and slipped her hand into her left sleeve. The knife there felt like a friend.

A bolt scraped behind the front door, then another. The door opened a few inches and the man stood behind it, ready to slam it shut. He wore a loose white shirt which showed that his neck and upper chest were in the same condition as his face.

"So what do you want?" His left hand was on the door handle. She could not see his right.

"I'd like to see the dryad who dances for you," Giulia said. "Just to talk to her, of course."

A smile pulled the corner of his mouth upward, as though it had got caught on a hook. "Oh yes?" he said.

He stepped back, and she followed him into a wide, low-ceilinged room like the hold of an old ship. It reeked of beer and stale smoke.

The landlord held out his hand. "Five saviours," he said, "and don't try anything. I'll tell you when you're done."

She counted out five coins. He stepped over to a door at the rear of the room and rapped on it. "Visitor!" he called. "A young lady to talk to you. Here," he said. "You have a good time now, just talking."

Go fuck yourself, Giulia thought, and she opened the door.

It was a small, mediocre room, neither cramped nor squalid, but little better than that. There was a narrow bed, a small table and two chairs. A battered screen hid the back of the room. A plant was growing up the wall, a type of vine she didn't recognise.

The dryad sat on one of the chairs. The clothes indicated that it was female. The dryad's face was long and refined, with a small, delicate mouth above a pointed chin. The eyes were enormous and almond-shaped, twice the size of a human's. Her hair was straight and blonde, so lightly coloured that it seemed almost silver.

Giulia pulled the door shut behind her. She felt nervous in the presence of this thing. *Stay calm*, she told herself. *You're the one who's asking the questions. And don't call her a pixie to her face. They don't like that.*

"Hello," said Giulia.

"Hello," the dryad said. She spoke carefully, as though afraid it would hurt her to talk. "Would you like to sit down?"

"Please." Giulia sat. She had never been this close to a dryad before, and it stirred her emotions into an uneasy mix. Something twisted in her gut.

"What's your name?"

"Anasharallishomai," she said.

"Anna? Can I call you that?"

"Yes."

"I'm Giulia." She put out her hand. The dryad hesitated and reached out. Her fingers were long to the point of abnormality. Giulia felt them slip around her own hand, and she shuddered; the dryad glanced up. Giulia tightened her grip and they shook. She felt relieved to have her hand back, but guilty for shivering at Anna's touch.

"What do you do here?" Giulia asked.

"I dance, and sing. People come and watch me."

I'm sure they do, Giulia thought. "Are you happy here?" she said, and as soon as she had, she wondered why she'd asked.

"There are worse places."

"Better ones, too. How come you're not in the forest or something? They don't keep you here, locked up, do they?"

"I have debts to pay. It is difficult to explain, but I am not a prisoner in that way. I should not go back until they are paid."

"I see. So you dance here, and they pay you for it?"

"The man you met outside does."

"Does he pay you much?" she asked. She hadn't meant to ask that, either.

The dryad frowned. "Yes, I think so. We don't have money where I come from. Sometimes it is hard to tell."

Giulia pinched her brow. *God almighty, there's worse things than being a thief with a cut-up face.* "You know how to fight?"

"Of course. We all do, after the War of Faith."

"Why don't you become a mercenary, then? Hire out? Shit, you're good as selling yourself here."

Anna shook her head. "I would rather not take life."

Giulia shrugged. "Well, your choice. If you ask me, there's worse ways to make coins than fighting." She leaned forward. "Look, I didn't come here about that. I need to ask you something about last night."

Anna pulled her legs up onto the chair. She had a gymnast's body, boyish and slim. Her feet were bare and long, the big toes markedly separate from the others. "What would you like to know?"

"I think I saw you last night, outside. Near a place called the Old Arms."

The dryad tilted her head, a birdlike, twitchy movement. "Are you sure it was me and not another? You people find it hard to tell."

"I think so. You were heading in this direction."

"Oh." The dryad's expression hardly changed, but Giulia knew that she was afraid. "Are you from the Church?"

"No. I'm not from the City Watch either. I'm on my own." Giulia felt pity rise up again, and forced it aside. "A man died last night. They found him in the water. They think someone set a dog on him."

Anna stared back, her huge eyes empty.

"The Watch think it was a religious killing. They want to blame my friend for it. My friend is an Anglian, which means he's New Church."

The dryad looked blank.

"You know what that means?"

"Yes."

"So are his friend and his friend's wife. I need to prove that they didn't kill the man who died. The Watch have given me until the end of the week to find out what happened. If I can't, they'll hang my friend. And me, if they can."

Anna continued to stare. Giulia glanced around the little room, at the multi-coloured piece of string on the dryad's left wrist, and back up to her eyes.

"So I need you to tell me anything you might know. Anything you saw."

"Or else you will say that it was me who murdered him," Anna said.

That hadn't occurred to Giulia before. It would be very easy. She could simply shift the blame from an Anglian dissenter to something even lower down the scale: a pixie-woman, a pagan slut. And no doubt half the scum that came to leer at her over pints of ale would join the lynch mob that took her to the gallows.

"No," said Giulia, "that's not what I meant."

"His name was Sebastian Coraldo," Anna said. "He was one of your holy men."

"Holy men? A priest?"

"Yes."

"How do you know that?"

"He came here and spoke to me."

"Here?" The word jumped from Giulia's lips. "To look at you – to see you dance?"

The dryad raised her hand lazily and scratched the side of her head. Watching her made Giulia uncomfortable. Even now she gave out a kind of languid, casual sexuality. It was like some bewitching spell, some aphrodisiac she secreted instead of sweat.

"He watched, and when I went back here, he came after. He wanted to talk to me."

"What did he say?"

"I ignored him at first. But he asked questions. He was looking for someone to listen to him."

"What kind of questions?"

"He said he had to talk to someone, and that I would understand him because I was fey. He was wrong: I understood nothing. He said that he knew about the new order of the world. Those were his words."

"Did he say anything more? Anything about what that meant?"

The huge, soft eyes closed slowly and opened again, like a lizard's. "His voice was different. Like yours, but a little different. I thought that he was strange." She glanced away, looking for a phrase. "Touched by the moon."

Giulia frowned. The room seemed tiny, the dryad closer than she really was. Giulia crossed her legs. "Do you know where his accent was from?"

"I don't know."

"Did he say anyone was after him? If he was being followed?"

"No. But he looked scared."

"Anna, this might sound strange, but did you see any big dogs when you were out, any big animals?"

"No. Should I have done?"

"I don't know." Giulia frowned. Her thoughts were a jumble. *There's something – she must have seen something else – dammit.* "Thank you for your help," she said. She stood up and made herself smile. Reaching into her purse, she took out a few coins and laid them on the chair where she had been sitting. The purse felt light, and a pang of anger struck her as she remembered how much the innkeeper had made her pay. "Thanks. You've been a great help."

Anna rose up fluidly, and gracefully stepped past Giulia, her bare feet soft on the wooden floor. Her fingers wrapped around the door handle.

"Giulia," she said, "I would rather you did not talk about me to anyone."

"I won't, I promise."

"And come back and see me. I like you. You are" —she struggled for the word— "polite, and interesting. I would like to see you again."

Giulia felt a queasy mixture of discomfort and something close to lust, as if she'd been slipped a drug. She wanted to be out of here. "Well, thanks," she replied. "I'd better go."

The dryad opened the door, and Giulia stopped on a sudden whim and said, "You look out for yourself, yes? Don't let anyone push you around. I let them push me around, and—" She stopped. "Well, anyway, good luck."

Giulia stepped through and into the main room again. The door closed behind her.

The innkeeper smirked at her. "Have fun?"

"I got what I was looking for," she replied.

"I'll bet you did," he said.

"Come here a moment." Giulia waved him over. "I've got something to tell you." Giulia smiled. "A private thing."

He grinned and walked over. Giulia beckoned him close, so she could whisper in his ear. He stepped up close, his boots nearly touching hers.

"Don't smile so much," she whispered. "Your face wasn't made for looking happy."

She felt his eyes on her back as she left. She hated that sensation.

It was a relief to be back in the cold, away from the smell of smoke and spilt booze. The chilly air sharpened her mind, as if a spell had lifted. She no longer felt sad, or angry. The weird lust she'd felt in Anna's presence was gone.

Thank God for that.

Giulia pulled her hood up and walked back along the canal.

So, he was a priest, was he? A priest looking for a dryad and an Anglian. A priest looking for heretics.

Of course, she thought, the dryad might be lying. No, somehow it rang true. The problem was understanding what it meant. She felt a stab of pity for Anna, and tried to think about something else.

So, the corpse in the water was called Sebastian Coraldo. He had gone to see Anna, thinking that she would understand him, or perhaps that she'd be able to direct him to someone who would. Like most people who went to church and kept to the law, he probably thought that all pagans and heretics knew each other.

A gondola lay moored-up on the other side of the canal. Two men were helping the gondolier unload a cargo of rugs onto dry land. One of the men glanced up as she walked past, stared for a moment, and got back to work. She hurried by, wondering if these were the spies that Cafaro had mentioned.

Maybe Father Coraldo had been a member of some illegal sect who thought he could find safety at the Old Arms. Or maybe he had been a witch-hunter, hoping that Anna or the Anglians could lead him to rebel preachers. Being a member of the New Church was not illegal in most city-states, but trying to convert people to it was.

It didn't matter either way. For all Giulia might know about the dead man's past, she was no closer to knowing who had murdered him.

Edwin and Hugh were drinking in the main room of the Old Arms. They were the only people there. Hugh was explaining something with the help of hand gestures.

"Pulled out shield-side, came up behind the saddle and gave it to the bugger on the back of the escudgeon! So, they see he's unarmed, and a couple of them bear down on the off-flank to do him in. So what does he do? Whips off his shield and beats them with it and scores two more!" Hugh laughed, rocking on his stool.

Edwin smiled – a wide smile like Hugh's, but tinged with a little sadness. "Yes," he said, "I remember that. Those were good days."

"Some of the best," Hugh replied. "Ah, here's Giulia. What cheer, eh?"

"Not much," Giulia said. She dragged a chair over

to the table and sat down. "Last night I saw a dryad outside. I tracked her down and managed to talk to her. She wasn't much help, though. Where's Elayne, by the way?"

"Sleeping," Edwin said. "She exhausted herself working magic on that Watch officer. It's not her usual style."

Giulia nodded. "Fair enough. Just out of interest, if anyone tried that on me, I'd know, right?"

"Elayne wouldn't do that," Hugh said, and he gave her a brief, stern look.

"Of course. Just making sure."

"Did you find out anything else?" Edwin asked.

"The priest's name was Sebastian Coraldo. That's about it," Giulia said. "The dryad remembered things, but none of them added up to much. I don't suppose either of you know anyone with that name?"

Edwin shook his head. "Not anyone I remember. To be honest, I don't have much cause to speak to priests, not from the Old Church."

"Then I've only got one more lead to look into," Giulia said.

"And if that doesn't work," said Hugh, "we'll escape."

"It'd be hard," Giulia said. "And chances are, a hell of a lot of people would get hurt, even if we four got out alive."

"Maybe, but—"

"To be honest, I doubt any of us *would* get out. You heard what Falsi said about fetching soldiers from the Arsenal. I think he meant it. They'd just keep coming."

"Ah, yes," said the knight. "Perhaps you're right." He looked into his cup.

"All right," Edwin said, "we need another plan. One that doesn't get us killed."

"Yes."

Edwin sighed. "Well, what about buying our way out? I've got some money put away; after all, that's what I'm here to do, trade. And I'm sure you two have some you could put in. Maybe we could pay..."

"Pay these bastards not to slander and murder us?" Hugh stared. "You must be joking, man! I'm not paying that little rat in the Watch-house to let me go! I'll wring his damned neck and take the next boat from the docks!"

Giulia raised a hand. "Easy, Hugh. Even if *you* could make it out of the city, which I don't think you could, what about Elayne?"

"You need to stop thinking about yourself and consider the rest of us," Edwin added. He was sitting back in his chair, drink in hand, looking like a prosperous minister about to say grace.

Hugh glanced down and took another sip of beer. "The whole rotten peninsula's on the bloody take," he muttered.

Giulia stretched. "There's some good people around. It's just a shame we don't meet many of them. Look, if nothing comes of what I've got planned, we've got till the end of the week to come up with another idea. And remember that I can come and go as I like, so if we need anything, I reckon I could smuggle it in."

Edwin said, "So, what's this other lead of yours?"

Giulia glanced over her shoulder. Even though there was no-one else in the room, she leaned forward and lowered her voice. "I saw a captain of the Watch take something off the body last night, when they pulled him out the water. I don't know what it was, but I reckon someone in the Watch-house will. I'm going to go and find out."

Edwin shook his head. "It was probably just his money."

"Maybe, but I'm not sure. It looked square to me, like a book. I might be wrong, but I think there's more to it than just stealing."

"He was in the water," Edwin said. "A book wouldn't be readable after that. Besides, the Watch wouldn't let you see it."

Giulia looked at Hugh, and they both smiled.

"I wasn't thinking of asking," she said. She stood up and turned towards the stairs.

"Wait. Where're you going?" Edwin demanded.

"Upstairs, to sleep. What I've got planned, you don't do in daylight."

FOUR

Giulia woke in darkness. She got up, unlocked the door and lit a candle off the lantern in the passageway. Voices seeped up from the bar below.

A bell was tolling, the same one she'd heard last night. Six o'clock: late enough for the sun to set, early enough for people to still be out on the street.

Back in her bedroom she closed the door and took off her dress. Giulia put on her dark shirt and britches. She fastened a belt around her waist. She took out a small satchel, folded it flat and pushed it into her belt at the back.

Ah, yes. Almost ready to go.

Next, the knives. She strapped on two at her hips: a thin dagger that could double as a prying tool, and the fighting-knife she had been given back in Pagalia, stained black by the dwarrows so that the blade would never shine when it was drawn. She still wore a stiletto in the bracer on her left arm.

Giulia stretched and whirled her arms to wake the muscles. She closed her eyes and said a brief prayer to Senobina, patron of thieves. Then she threw her cloak over her shoulders and pulled the hood up. She would not need her crossbow tonight.

Downstairs, the Old Arms was getting busy. The inn was half-full, and several of the patrons were already drunk. It was rat-fight night, and stocky men held terriers with matted fur and ragged ears.

The landlord shoved past, a writhing bag held at arm's length in front of him. Rats for the fight, no doubt. He turned to look at her as he passed her by, and his eyes fastened on Giulia in a way no innocent person's had ever done.

She stepped outside and drew her cloak around her body, eager to get away.

The moon was almost full, and she counted off the landmarks she'd seen on the way in, this time in reverse: a square tower on the right, a narrow, hump-backed bridge and then a sign advertising a minor glassmaker, with the guild symbol in polished brass in the corner. The cold made her scars tingle. Giulia crossed a bridge over the black stripe of the canal, stopped and watched to see if she was being followed. There was nobody behind.

She walked down a narrow alleyway, the peeling tenement walls penning her in like cliffs. She passed an open window: inside, a couple were bickering. Giulia smiled as she passed, then remembered that she had no lover to argue with at all, and she hurried on.

The Watch-house was a square white fort, standing squat and alone in a tiny courtyard. The moon put a deep shadow on its pitted face, and where the plaster had chipped it looked as if someone had blasted the walls with boarding-shot. There were two windows on the ground floor: one normal-sized and closed with shutters, the other a dark, high hole crossed by bars.

That's the cell where they kept us.

Two liveried guards stood on either side of the front door. They chatted and passed a bottle back and forth, but they kept their eyes on the road. It would be impossible to creep past them.

The first floor looked more promising. It had several large windows, all shuttered but large enough to fit her body. The window in the room where she'd met Falsi hadn't been glazed. Hopefully the rest would be the same.

But how to get up there? She thought about the ways in and out of Falsi's room, the layout of the place. She slipped into the alley and worked her way to the back of the Watch-house. It wasn't promising: there was a window on the first floor, but its shutters were closed.

She looked at the tenement behind the Watch-house. Ten feet off the ground, a balcony jutted out. The balcony had a railing around the edge.

I could pull myself up on that. Maybe I could lean out and open the shutters.

She took a deep breath and rubbed her hands on her thighs. This wasn't going to be easy. Or quiet.

Giulia ran at the Watch-house wall. She jumped, hit the wall with both boots, pushed off and leaped at the balcony.

Her fingers brushed the railing, but it was too high. She dropped back down into the alleyway. She landed in a crouch and froze there, listening.

Did they hear that? No? No.

She stood up, took another deep breath.

"Thought it came from round the corner." A man's voice.

Oh, shit.

Giulia threw herself at the Watch-house. Her boots struck the wall and she kicked down, drove out with both legs across the alleyway. She caught the railing with both hands, gritted her teeth and arched her back.

Footsteps close below. Giulia pulled herself up, over the railing, and dropped onto the balcony. She tugged her hood up and lay there, flat on the dirty floor. Her arms ached.

Go away. Keep walking. There's nothing to see.

Light seeped between the railings: the men below had a lantern. "Sounded like it came from here."

Something touched her shoulder: a single delicate push, as if a rod was being gently pressed against her body. Then another, and another. An animal.

"Raaaow."

Fucking cat.

"Come on, there's nothing here."

A second man: "I don't know. I thought..."

It's nothing.

The cat jumped off her.

"Shit! There's something up there!"

She froze, tensed, held her breath.

The other man burst out laughing. "It's a cat! Saints, you're fucking jumpy!"

Giulia listened to them walk off, bickering. She rose to a crouch and peeked over the railing. The coast was clear.

She pulled the stiletto from her sleeve, climbed over the balcony railing and leaned out across the road.

The tip of the stiletto slipped between the shutters. She drew it up, felt a catch flick loose and used the point to ease the shutters apart. Behind them was the darkness of the room where she had spoken to Falsi.

Giulia replaced the knife and braced herself against the railings. Then she jumped.

Half a second in the air and she hit Falsi's window, grabbed stone and swung her legs up and through the window in the same movement. Giulia dropped into the Watch-house on all fours, held her breath and counted to thirty. Only then did she stand up.

She closed the shutters and locked the catch. The moon crept through the slats into the room.

There were two tables, including Falsi's own: big things that reminded her of tombs in the bad light. There was nothing to search: no drawers, no locked chests or cabinets. She found a chunky crossbow, a couple of bolts and a bag of lead bullets on a shelf – otherwise, it was bare.

Nothing to get stolen or broken. Like the front room in a bad tavern.

Strange to think that she'd been sitting here only this morning, holding back the urge to rage at Falsi as he patted his dog and threatened to have them all hanged. Time to get to work.

First, she needed to see the body of the priest. The door led straight onto the staircase. It seemed deserted. She sneaked downstairs, legs bent, pausing every few seconds to listen.

The guards must still be outside.

The stairs ended in a little hall, lit by a single lantern. A statue of Lady Justice stood in a niche, draped with a rosary. Giulia took a stub of candle from her bag and lit it from the lantern. The door to the cell stood opposite the stairs: dark old oak, reinforced with iron bands.

That's where they locked us up. She looked through the little hole in the door: the cell was empty. The prostitute must have made good on her promise to get the guard to let her go.

To the right was another door. It opened easily. A narrow flight of stairs led down.

Sickly, perfumed air rose up from below. She smelled lavender and, under it, the artificial tang of alchemy. This had to be the place. She closed the door behind her, unpleasantly aware that she was trapping herself, and descended.

There would be nothing alive down here, but she still felt as if she would be met at the bottom of the stairs. The urge to hurry grew in her, the need to get this done and get out.

A table stood in the middle of the room under a dead lantern, massive and battered like a butcher's block. Bundles of dried flowers lay on the table to keep the air clean. There were black marks on the wood, marks that became deep red as the candlelight fell across them.

Someone had pinned a sheet of paper to the wall. She held the candle up to it, saw the hand-inked script, and realised it was a charm against disease, the sort you could buy from a good apothecary. Giulia lit the lantern.

A body wrapped in white cloth lay against the back wall like a huge chrysalis. Giulia crouched down beside the parcel. She took hold of the cloth, pulled it back and looked into the empty face of Father Coraldo.

"Hello again," she said.

It was strange to think that this lump had once been a living man. The priest looked like a doll now: a pallid mannequin. She made the Sign of the Sword across her chest. *Blessed Lord, rest this man.* Then she pulled back the sheet.

His chest was a ploughed field. To the right, just below the navel, there was a small puncture wound, the sort of thing a blade would do. That would have hurt, would have crippled him, but the killing blows had not been made by a man. Perhaps he'd been hit by the knife to keep him still while the dog did its work. *If it was a dog at all.*

A single blow had finished him: a massive downward swipe from shoulder to gut, done by something with four claws. She felt a little sick.

Giulia held her hand over his chest and spread her fingers out. A man could have done it, if he wore a metal hook at the end of each digit. Was there a weapon Easterners used, like that? Hugh would know; he'd frequently bored her with stories of his exploits on the Silk Road. Whatever it was, it was not a dog. Dogs and wolves killed with their teeth. And no dog was big enough for this.

She crouched in the dim light, trying to think. Some kind of huge cat? She'd once seen a mountain lion in a show at the Pagalian arena. That must have been ten years ago. Perhaps a beast that big could carve a man up like this. But what kind of madman kept a lion as a pet?

Something jarred in her mind, something she'd seen that night – the griffon she'd glimpsed a long way off, silhouetted against the moon. Hadn't someone said something about there being wild griffons on the edge of Averrio? For that matter, even if it was a big cat and not a griffon, who would have the money to keep an animal like that?

City elders? Hell. If they were the people pulling Lieutenant Falsi's strings, she'd be better off fleeing from Averrio while she still had a chance.

She shuddered. A dead priest, some kind of huge animal, and money behind it all. It felt like a conspiracy, like the signs of black magic. Giulia made the Sign across her chest again. It was time to go, thank God.

As she pulled the sheets back over the body, she thought, *They shouldn't do this. They shouldn't be allowed to kill a priest.*

The thought surprised her. She was not especially religious, and had liked few of the clerics she'd ever met. She hadn't even liked Sebastian Coraldo: he had seemed half-mad, a man made shifty and dangerous by fear. Yet she felt angry as she covered his face.

There was a lot still left to do. The fat Watch captain had taken something from Father Coraldo's body, and she needed to find out what it was.

Giulia blew out the candle as she returned to the entrance hall. She was in the doorway when the floor above her creaked.

Someone was upstairs. Well, there was no getting out of this. She walked to the stairs, flattened her back to the wall and began to climb.

She reached the first floor and kept going. As the second floor came into view, she heard the steady thud of something soft being hit over and over again. A nasty sound.

The stairs opened onto a corridor. There was a door on either side of the passage, and the one on the left was open. At the far end, a ladder led to a trapdoor in the ceiling. She walked down the hall, placing each boot down carefully, feeling the give in the planks underfoot. At the edge of the open door, she crouched down and peered around the corner.

A short, broad man stood with his back to the door. His arm rose and swung a truncheon into a practice dummy made out of sacks. Behind him there were weapon racks and a couple of archery targets. There was a big ring of keys on his belt. His blue tunic looked as broad as the sail on a galleon.

As she watched, the man put down his truncheon and took a deep swig from a bottle of wine. A second bottle lay on the floor behind him, uncorked and on its side.

Drunk and violent. Only the finest need apply.

She crept silently past the doorway. The sound of the guard battering the dummy was a muffled drumbeat behind her.

The door across the hall was smarter than the others, with a polished handle and new iron bands across the wood. This looked promising. Less promising was the large brass lock set into the door.

Damn it. She thought about creeping back and stealing the keys off the man's belt. *Too risky.* She crouched down and took out her picks.

After five minutes, her legs started to ache. Her left knee seemed to be rusting shut. She counted the tumblers as she worked: the first one was easy, then came the gradual, reluctant yielding of the second, and finally the third, rolling back with a sharp click. Giulia slid the picks out of the defeated lock. Her legs felt weak as she stood up again. She turned the handle and opened the door.

Moonlight streamed in through a broad window, over clean walls and a patterned rug. There was a painting of Saint Josua Lexicatus on the far wall and a woodcut of the Archangel Alexis in his armour behind the wide, empty desk. On a shelf behind the desk was a copy of the Holy Codex and a thin accounts-book.

Giulia closed the door behind her and took the books down. She checked the Codex first – she'd seen criminals cut a hole in the pages to hide keys. Nothing except holy writ. She opened the thin book and saw names and offences: it was a roster of crimes discovered and pursued.

Giulia flicked through to the last page of writing. She stood near the window, holding the roster up as if to offer it to the moon.

"Priest in Cannal. Dead, stabbed. Anglans in cell, look like Mersenries. Told Proc will hang them soon."

And that was it: her life and achievements summed up in "will hang them soon." It amused her, in a bitter way. She put the roster back and rifled the desk. It had two drawers, both unlocked. The first one contained paper, ink, a couple of quills and a letter-stamp with the emblem of the Watch carved into it.

From down the corridor, there came a sudden pounding of boots and a clumsy thud. A drunken voice called out, "Ah, shit!"

She waited. No movement. Maybe he'd knocked himself out.

There was a red candlestick beside the desk. She pulled out a piece of thieves' tinder from her bag, spat on the end and watched it sizzle into life. She touched the candle to the flame.

Giulia sat at the desk and waited until the candle-wax was soft and hot. She tore a piece of paper from the roster-book and dripped wax on it until there was a thick coating on the paper the size of a coin. Then she took the stamp and pushed it into the wax.

The impression was good. Giulia removed the stamp and returned it to the desk.

The man in the practice room had fallen silent. Perhaps he'd passed out. Somewhere outside, a dog began to howl. Giulia stashed the wax imprint in her satchel. Then she turned her attention to the second drawer in the desk.

She pulled out a wad of old letters. None of them looked important. She reached in to the back of the drawer and her fingers touched something cold and hard, wrapped in a rag. She slid it out and laid it on the desk, then lifted the cloth away.

Yes. It was a tile of some sort, a red clay square about four inches wide. There was an image sculpted onto the tile. Giulia tilted it at the window, so that the moonlight caught on the ridges in the clay.

The picture looked as if it had been drawn either by a child or someone long ago. It showed a man in a loincloth lying on the ground. Strings were coming out of his head: hair, presumably, or maybe blood. Standing over him was a man in a cuirass and a plumed helmet. The standing man waved a sword in the air. His free hand pointed to the ground. Objects lay scattered beside the dead man: bowls, plates, what might have been a statue or a small animal.

It made her feel uneasy, as if it was enchanted. She watched the shadows catch on the tile as she turned it in her hands, wondering whether, if she looked at it for long enough, the clay blood might run back into the victim's head, or the little killer might dance with glee. She remembered the water-wyrm in Elayne's glass, rising up from the depths.

Suddenly Giulia knew that this business was more than a mistake, more than the casual corruption of Watchmen too lazy to do their job: somewhere out there was evil, real and alive, closing in on the four of them like poisonous smoke.

Is this what he was murdered for?

She would steal the tile. It might be vital for tracing the killer. When the captain noticed that it was gone, what would he do? He could hardly send his men out to find the thing, seeing how he'd stolen it off the body of a priest. Giulia wrapped it up in the cloth and slipped it into her satchel.

She felt something in her back. She was being watched.

Giulia turned around. There was nobody there. Strange: for a second she had been certain that someone was in the room with her, some cloaked stranger creeping up on her. She waited, staring at the door, but it did not open.

She put the paper and pens back in the desk and closed it up. Giulia blew out the candle, shut the office door behind her and locked it with her picks. As she pulled her hood up, she heard a voice.

"We're doing what we can, Procurator." It came from below. The stairs creaked under two pairs of boots.

Shit!

"Oh, I don't doubt it for a moment. I'm sure you're doing everything you're capable of. But this has to be resolved *quickly*."

They were close – five, six seconds away. The office door would take too long to unlock. The practice room was silent, but wide open. Giulia looked back and saw the ladder leading up to the trapdoor at the end of the hall. She cursed, ran down the hall and scrambled up the rungs. In one quick movement she yanked the bolt back – it sounded deafening – pushed the trapdoor open, slipped through and climbed onto the roof.

Cold air hit her. She wanted to slam the door down; she forced herself to lower it quietly. Light rain pattered against her bare hands. Giulia took a deep breath and imagined her heart slowing, becoming calm. She got on all fours on the cold stone roof and put her ear to the trapdoor.

"...precisely why the whole business is such a worry," the cultured voice was saying. "It's completely unacceptable that a priest should be found dead. It makes us look absurd."

"I know."

"It needs cleaning up, and soon. I don't like loose ends."

"I've got some suspects. They're foreigners just arrived in the city. Three of them are New Churchers. Falsi has them under house arrest."

"House arrest? Why aren't they in the cell?"

The deep voice paused. "I think he wants them to confess. He can be like that, sir. A reliable man, but he likes to do things formally, you know—"

"I see. Well, make sure it's dealt with properly. I don't want anybody to be able to say that we weren't fair. Now then, this stone you found on him—"

"Right up here, Procurator."

Giulia lifted the trapdoor an inch and squinted through the gap. Two men stood in the corridor, facing one another as they talked. One was a Watchman in a polished breastplate, tall and wide enough to almost completely eclipse his colleague. He was the fat captain she'd seen stealing from the dead priest. The other was slight and dapper, his hair thick and fluffy above a high forehead. He wore no armour, just expensive-looking clothes and a smart, short cloak.

The Watch captain had a ring of keys on his belt. "I put it in here," he said apologetically, "for safe keeping. No-one else knows." The captain opened the door for his visitor.

"Let's see what we've got," said the other man. They stepped into the office, and the door closed.

As soon as they were out of view, Giulia opened the trapdoor and climbed back down the ladder. She crept past the office door, almost on all fours.

She glanced into the practice room. The Watchman lay flat out on the floor. The training dummy stood over him, as though it had bested him in combat.

As she reached the head of the staircase, the voices jumped up a notch. Giulia hurried down the steps. The office door clattered open. "It *must* be here!" the captain said, and she ran downstairs.

In the hallway above her, they were arguing.

"—no need for that. I'll tell my men," the Watch captain said.

"Whatever it takes. Just get the bloody thing back!"

Giulia slipped through the doorway and was back in the room where she'd met Falsi. She walked to the window and opened the shutters.

She climbed onto the windowsill, turned and lowered herself down until she dangled from her hands. Giulia dropped the last few feet and landed neatly in the street below. She ran down the alleyway, and the shadows swallowed her up.

***

The inn was busy when she returned. People crowded round the rat pit, calling out and laying bets. A trader swept a heap of coins into a bag. Giulia slipped past a thuggish man carrying a wounded dog as gently as a baby. "Damn thing turned cur on him," someone said to her left, and a woman laughed, her voice full of drink. Giulia picked her way through the bar and went upstairs.

Hugh sat in his room, dozing. As she stepped into the doorway his eyes flicked open, as if she had snagged a tripwire to jolt him awake. "Hello there. How did it go?"

"Not bad, thanks. Let's get the others," she added. She felt flushed with success, almost gleeful, the way she often did when a job went well. "I've got something to show you all. It's been a busy night."

Hugh knocked on Edwin's door. "Come in," Edwin said. He and Elayne sat at a table in their room, playing a hand of one-and-thirty. Elayne smiled and gathered the cards up as Giulia entered, making her look both dreamy and conspiratorial.

Giulia said, "Evening, everyone. I need to talk to you all."

Edwin gave Giulia his seat, and Hugh leaned against the door, in the shadow. With four people in it, the room seemed minute.

She felt weary. *I must have had about five hours' sleep since I got to Averrio. If that.*

"So, how'd it go?" Edwin asked.

Elayne nodded several times. "All well in the city tonight? Did you find anything interesting?"

"Oh, yes," Giulia said. "But listen, we need to be careful. If we have to talk openly, we only should do it up here."

"I second that," Elayne replied.

"Giulia's right," Hugh said. "Can't trust these buggers."

"Then it's agreed," Edwin said. "What did you find out, then?"

"I went back to the Watch-house," Giulia said, setting her bag down on the table. "I broke in and had a look around."

Edwin stared at her. "You mean the place where we were locked up?"

"That's the one."

Edwin leaned across the table. "Is that a good idea? If they knew you'd done that—"

"They don't."

"But if they did—"

"Giulia here knows her stuff," Hugh said. "If she says she got away clean, I'm sure she did."

"I don't think it's the sort of thing we should be doing," Edwin said. He took out his pipe and examined it, as if the discussion had ended now.

"As opposed to doing magic on a Watch lieutenant," Giulia said. Edwin shot her a hard look. "I hate to say it," she added, "but someone's got to get us out of this shit, and I'm the only person who can get much done right now. The Watch played dirty with us, so we've got a right to play dirty with them. When the rules no longer favour the weak, the weak have a right to make new rules."

"That's very profound," Elayne said.

"It's not mine. I heard it in a play."

The sorceress leaned forward, eyes gleaming. "So then, tell us about what happened when you broke in. What did you find?"

"First, I went downstairs, to the room next to where they kept us, and I got a look at the dead man, Father Coraldo. Somebody stabbed him, but it wasn't being stabbed that killed him. Something ripped him up a treat." She shook her head, remembering the torn, waxy flesh. "It wasn't a dog, I'm sure of that. I don't think it was a wolf, either."

Edwin frowned. "A bear, perhaps?"

What the hell would a bear be doing here? Giulia checked herself. "It's possible, I suppose. It could have been some sort of big cat, too. Maybe even a griffon. I don't know. But it was claws, not a knife. Someone set something on him, or else they made it look as if they did."

"But why?" Elayne said. "I mean, I don't know anything about this sort of thing, but if you wanted to kill someone, you'd just – I don't know – stab him or something, wouldn't you? Almost everyone carries a knife of some sort. If you did that, it could be anyone, couldn't it?"

She looked from face to face as if appealing to them to prove her wrong.

Giulia nodded. "That's what I'd have thought. But someone must have really wanted him dead to mess him up that way." She shook her head, remembering the furrows in the corpse's chest. "Something."

"I wouldn't worry about *that*," Hugh said. He rubbed his hands together. "Edwin and I are rather knowledgeable when it comes to slaying beasts. It couldn't have been a wyvern, could it?" He sounded hopeful.

"Look at this." Giulia opened her bag and took out the clay tile. She removed the cloth and pushed the tile across to Edwin and Elayne. Hugh leaned over to get a better view. Giulia said, "Anyone know what this is?"

"Hmm," said Hugh. "What is it, a roof tile?"

"I don't know."

The old knight smoothed down his moustache. "Where did you find it?"

"It was in the Watch-house. Last night I saw one of their captains, a big fat man, taking it off the priest's body. I thought it might be worth looking at."

"You *stole* from the Watch?" Edwin said.

Hugh was grinning. "That's Giulia for you."

Edwin flopped back in his chair. "I don't believe this. How the hell do you expect to get them on our side if you steal from them?"

Giulia said, "I don't. They're not on our side, and they don't want to be: in five days' time they'll come back here to string us up. All of us. The only reason we've not already got dropped is because of Elayne's magic. Right now, we need anything we can get. If that means stealing, so be it. Or were you thinking of fighting the whole Watch when they come back, and all the soldiers they'll have with them?"

Edwin sucked angrily on his pipe. "Of course not."

"All right, then. Besides, how are they to know it was me who took it?" She smiled at Edwin. He continued to scowl. Elayne put her hand on his arm. Giulia said, "So, can anyone tell me what this thing is?" She leaned back and let them look at the tile.

"It's a picture of some sort," Edwin said, to no-one in particular. "There's a man, and he's on the ground, and another man, and... it looks like they've had a fight..."

"It's certainly not from Alexendom," Elayne said, peering at the stone. "Not dwarrow or dryad either." She pressed her fingertips to it. "It doesn't feel magical, either. Could it come from the Indies or the New World, perhaps?"

Something seemed to move in the back of Giulia's mind. *Someone told me something like that, about a new world...*

"Definitely looks foreign," Hugh said.

Edwin sighed. "We're abroad, Hugh. Everything within a thousand miles is foreign."

"The New World," Giulia said. *Of course – the dryad dancing girl, in that pub.* When she'd met Father Coraldo, he'd asked her about the "new order of the world." She must have misheard him.

Elayne pushed the tile aside with her long, clean fingers. "The southern island, that is. Maidenland takes up the north island; we have a peace treaty with their king. Their pictures don't look like this. As to the south, though... I don't know."

Giulia leaned back in her chair. "Do you think that's what they killed him for?"

"Who knows?" said Hugh. "I suppose it's possible."

"Whatever it is, you'd best keep it hidden," Edwin said. "If it's worth stealing, it must have some value."

Giulia nodded. "I will, don't worry. It means something, but until we know what, it's staying out of view." She yawned.

"We should all get to bed," Elayne said. "It's late."

"Good idea." Hugh moved towards the door.

"Wait," Giulia said. "I overheard two people talking while I was in the Watch station. One was the Watch captain – the same man I saw taking this thing off the priest when they pulled him out the canal. The other one I didn't recognise. I'd know him if I saw him again, though."

"Did you get a name?" Edwin asked.

Giulia shook her head. "Only a title. The other one called him 'Procurator'. Falsi mentioned him, I think."

Edwin and Elayne glanced at one another. "I know what that is," Edwin said. "That's to do with the Council."

"Council?"

He nodded. "The Council of a Hundred. They rule Averrio. It's them that advise the Closed Council, and the Closed Council advises the Decimus. I think the procurator's some sort of lawyer. They find things out, tell the Council what the law is, stuff like that. He's a serious man around these parts."

"Could I talk to him? He sounded like he could get us out of here."

"I've no idea. I doubt you could just walk in there. You'd need a recommendation, I suppose."

"I see." Giulia glanced at her bag. "How about a letter from the Watch?"

Edwin laughed. "I'm sure that would work perfectly. The question is whether they'd write it for you."

"They might not have to," Giulia said. She sighed. "I'm still not sure what's going on, but maybe I'm closer than I was. I've learned a few things this evening – but what any of it means, I don't know."

"It's very good of you to do it, anyway," Elayne said. "You took a big risk. We're grateful."

"Thanks." Giulia felt oddly flattered. She stood up. "Well, I need to get some sleep – a lot of it. If nobody minds, I'll take this with me."

She gathered up the tile and crossed to the door. "Goodnight, everyone."

"Yes, goodnight," said Hugh. "Think I'll turn in too." He nodded to Edwin and leaned in to kiss Elayne on the cheek. "Night, all."

Outside, in the corridor, Giulia said, "Are you all right, Hugh?"

"Yes, I'm fine. Why?"

"You're sure? It can't be much fun, being kept

locked up in here."

Noise floated up from downstairs, the sound of drunkenness in the bar.

"No," he said thoughtfully, "it's not ideal. Still, it's good to see Edwin and Elayne again. Just a shame about all this."

She lifted the lantern down from its hook on the wall. "Why don't you go down and get us something to drink, Hugh? I've never seen you go to bed sober before."

He smiled. "Excellent idea. I'll be back shortly."

Giulia walked to her room and closed the door behind her. *Poor bastard*, she thought as she lit up the candles. *So much for the big reunion.*

She sat down on the edge of the bed. She felt weak, her limbs heavy and loose, her head aching slightly from lack of sleep. *Will I end up like Hugh*, she thought, *stuck looking for mercenary work while the people around me get on with their lives and leave me behind?*

The Melancholia stirred within her, gathering its strength. She exhaled and rubbed her eyes, tried to point her thoughts elsewhere. She tried not to think about the Watch, about the free world outside, about the chances of a pauper with a faceful of scars getting some money, a home, a man. She tried not to think about Marcellus, who had liked her in a way, and who she'd told that it would never work out. He was still in Pagalia, recognised as the genius he was, building machines for the new prince and probably now the most eligible man in the principality.

I'm sure it did work out, for you.

That was the thing with the Melancholia: the same images kept rolling through your mind like teeth on the same cog. Hugh and Elayne – missing her chance with Marcellus – her future shrinking down into this shabby prison of an inn—

Someone knocked on the door.

It was Hugh. The knight had a bottle of wine and two cups.

As he poured the wine, Giulia opened her satchel. She took out the piece of paper on which she'd made the imprint of the Watch captain's seal and examined the quality of the stamp.

"Here we go," Hugh said, holding out a cup.

"Thanks." Giulia took a sip. "Your good health." She drank. "They seem like decent people, your friends."

"They are. Good sorts."

"She's a friendly girl – woman – that Elayne."

"Yes, very pleasant."

"Distinctive-looking." She took another drink. The wine tasted bitter and cheap, but she was glad to have it all the same. "It must be strange seeing her again. Hugh, were you and her ever, you know..."

"Yes, for a little while. I used to court her, back in the day. Like in the books."

"And you were friends with Edwin back then?"

"Yes, good friends. We had some adventures together." Hugh leaned back, a little distant. He was no longer wholly in the room: part of him thundered across a plain under a vast and open sky, calling to his comrades above the wind. "Yes, we did some pretty wild things, although I say so myself. I remember there was this madman keeping a woman locked in a tower, and we had to fight some kind of drake to get past, Edwin and me." He refilled his cup. "Hell of a scrap it was, too."

"Was that Elayne, in the tower?"

"Oh, no. I met Elayne much later, when I was recovering after a raid we did. I was with a marine party in the war, attacking an Inquisition port. I took a hit to the head, and when I came round... well, there she was, looking down at me. She'd come to help heal the wounded, you see. We got on well, and we just sort of went from there. Excellent company, she was. Pretty, and a good laugh, too." He looked into his glass. "Didn't make a very good job of it, though. Can't even remember ever telling her she looked good, for God's sake, and you have to do that with women, don't you?"

"It helps," Giulia said.

Hugh frowned like a master-craftsman inspecting shoddy work. "I've never been good with women. Just not in my nature, you know? I'm only really good at killing things. My own fault, really."

"I'm sorry it turned out that way."

He shrugged. "Not to worry. Probably for the best in the long run. She's better off with old Edwin. He looks after her."

"But it's not better for you, is it?"

"Could be worse, I suppose. She's happy, at least."

"Look, Hugh, don't you think that perhaps you ought to, you know, find someone else? There's a lot of ladies out there, you know."

"Hmm. Think I'll turn in now," Hugh said, getting up. "Thanks for the wine, Giulia."

"It was you that bought it, Hugh."

"Yes. Right. Well... thanks for listening to me spouting off, anyway."

"Any time. Goodnight."

FIVE

Lieutenant Falsi strolled into the Watch-house just after dawn, half an apple in his hand. As he entered the hall, two men struggled out of the side door, carrying a long bundle between them. It looked a little like a rolled-up rug, but Falsi knew what, and who, it really was. *No mistaking a corpse*, he thought, and he took another bite of his apple.

"Morning, Rupe; morning, Seb. Taking our wandering preacher out for his final service?"

"That's right, Boss." The nearer man grunted. "They're rowing him out to the Isle of Graves this morning. Talk about hearts of iron – this bugger weighs about a ton. Hey, you'll like this – they found Louis this morning in the armoury. That stupid whoreson was training drunk last night – so drunk he fell over and passed out!"

"Bloody Louis. That man's a halfwit. I'll give you a hand getting the preacher underground."

"No."

Falsi turned.

Captain Orvo stood in the doorway of the Watch-house. "You're walking the shops round Printers' Way today. Cafaro's taking care of the body." The captain looked down at the corpse. "From pulpit to poor-pit, all in two days." He shook his head. "I need a word with you."

"Of course." Falsi followed him into the Watchhouse. Behind him, Rupe wished Falsi good luck. Falsi pretended that he hadn't heard.

They trudged up the stairs, past the mess-room, up to the second floor. Orvo opened his office door and they stepped inside.

"Problem, sir?" Falsi said as he closed the door. *Out with it*, he thought.

"Maybe," Orvo said. He sat down. "'Tonio, do you know if anyone has keys for this room besides me?"

"No-one, I think. *I* don't. Why?"

"I've lost something. I was sure I'd put it down here, shut it away, in fact. It's a square made out of clay, like a tile. It's got a picture of two fellows fighting on it, carved into it."

"I'll keep an eye open."

"It's not valuable – not money-wise, anyhow. It's got sentimental value to me. Just tell me if you find it, will you?"

"I will, sir." Falsi moved towards the door.

"One more thing."

Falsi stopped. *Here it comes.* "Yes?"

"Those four you brought in about the dead priest: am I right in thinking you put them under house arrest?"

Falsi braced himself. "That's right. They're at the Old Arms, down by—"

"I know where it is. I just wondered why you let them stay there." Orvo raised his eyebrows. It was meant to look chummy, to take the edge off the question. It didn't.

"Well, sir, it seemed like the best thing to do. We couldn't just keep them here. They're down there under strict orders not to leave. If they try anything, they're dead men. And women. I mean, they're not going anywhere, and if they do, we'll know it. The innkeep's one of ours."

"Hmm. That's not what Cafaro said. He said you gave one of the women the run of the city to clear her name."

Falsi said, "Yes, I did do that." *I just wish I knew why.* "She's got to come back, though. She's close to the others. She won't abandon them."

"What did she offer in return, might I ask?"

"Nothing, sir."

"Nothing at all? Are you sure? I mean, it happens sometimes, right? You do the trawl, bring in some whore or other, she's got no money to pay a fine, so one makes an, er, an arrangement—"

"No. I just thought they deserved a fair chance." He stopped, aware how stupid he sounded. "I doubt it'll make much difference in the end."

Orvo said nothing. He cupped his chins in his hand, as if testing their weight. "Can you move this along a bit? Get them back in here, perhaps?"

"Why? I mean, they'll swing at the end of the week as it is - it just makes us look better to give them a chance. Besides," he added, "I gave them my word, and they gave me theirs. I don't think they'll try to run. They've got a ship in the harbour, for one thing."

"Fair enough. But I want this finished. Come the end of the week, they need to be in the courthouse in the morning and on the scaffold by midday."

Why? Why do you care so much? "I'll make sure of it."

"Good. You do that." Orvo picked at a scab on his

thumb. "Tell me about this woman, then. The one who's meant to be saving their hides."

"She's called Giulia Degarno. Youngish, but not *really* young. She looks like a cat tore her up. Seriously, she's got two scars running down her left cheek, like this." He made a V with his fingers and laid them against his face, secretly enjoying giving the captain the Bowman's Salute. "You'd know her if you saw her, believe me. Apparently she's a thief-taker up from Pagalia - personally, I think she's one of those bodyguards some noblewomen get - you know, dressed up as ladies' maids and the like."

"Really? I'd like to meet these people." Orvo stood up. His eyes moved to Falsi's pistol. "You're still wearing that cannon, I see. Let's go and make sure they haven't overslept."

He stepped out of the office, Falsi following. Orvo carefully locked the door behind him. As he started towards the stairs, Falsi considered bending down to see whether the lock was scratched, but the captain turned to face him before he had the chance. "Coming?"

"Right away," Falsi said, and he followed Orvo downstairs.

***

Giulia dreamed. She was standing on a bed, looking out of an open window at a storm. There were trees outside and a thin man was dancing in them, a lurching puppet's dance that made her afraid even though it looked absurd.

Thunder pounded on wooden walls. The capering man was gone: outside, she could see the moon. Giulia shifted and the dream was gone. She was lying in bed, the hem of a blanket tickling her ear. Thunder again - no, not thunder, a fist beating at her door.

A woman's voice. "Giulia! Wake up!"

She sat up, grabbed her stiletto from beside the bed and slipped it under the sheet. "What's going on?"

"Giulia, it's Elayne. The Watch are here!"

"I'm coming."

She dressed quickly: long dress, white undershirt and boots. There was only time to strap her knife inside her sleeve and shove the things she'd stolen last night under the pillow before she heard feet clattering on wood. She opened the door to her room, not quite alert enough to be properly afraid.

Hugh stood on the landing. He held a scabbarded sword before him, barring the way up the stairs. Edwin loomed behind him, hands open. Elayne stood beside them, in a long gown.

"Aha!" Hugh cried as a man stepped into view, the griffon of the Watch painted onto his cuirass. "*Now* we start!"

Giulia said, "Put the sword down, Hugh," but he ignored her. "Hugh – put it down!"

Elayne was at Hugh's side in a moment. Fear had made her eyes wide: she looked like a startled horse. "Hugh, please. Let's not hurt anyone."

"Yet," he growled, but he stepped back and lowered the sword. "Very well. But if they try anything—"

"Stay here. I'll find out what's going on." Giulia slipped past them all and down the stairs. Half a dozen Watchmen milled about in the main hall. They wore swords and maces on their belts. Three carried muskets, one a crossbow.

Falsi stood at the bottom of the stairs. His face was tired and seemed to hang off the bones, as if little weights had been sewn into the skin to drag it down.

Giulia walked straight up to him. "What the hell's this? You said we had till the end of the week."

"We've come to search the place," Falsi said.

"*Search* here? You want to *search here*, do you?" She made her voice loud, so the others would hear. *Get the stuff I stole last night*, she willed them. *Hide it now!* "What for?"

The Watchmen were looking under tables, overturning chairs. In their midst was the fat captain from the night before. Three men shoved past Giulia, their boots pounding on the floorboards. "Hey, wait!" the landlord cried.

She turned to move, and Falsi grabbed her arm. She looked into his face, and she saw something that she could not decipher there. "A word of advice," he said. "Just leave it."

Edwin shouted, "Get your hands off my wife!"

Giulia turned. A Watchman went stumbling back down the stairs, nearly losing his footing. Edwin blocked the staircase like a statue, feet wide apart.

"Out of my way!" the Watchman shouted, and as he ran back up the stairs to meet Edwin, both Hugh and Elayne stepped into his path.

The Watchman jabbed his mace at Edwin; the knight slipped aside and grabbed the shaft, and the two were face to face, grappling for it. Edwin slid his arm into the Watchman's, locking it, and the man began to fold, bending back so as not to fall. "I need help!" he shouted, and his friends ran up to rescue him, cudgels in their hands, cursing.

"Shit!" Falsi said, reaching to his belt.

Giulia darted forward. "Wait!"

Falsi's pistol went off like a cannonet. Chips and splinters whirled past Giulia's face and she ducked back, hands up to shield her eyes. She lowered her arm, and saw Falsi standing at the bottom of the staircase in a column of swirling dust, his gun still pointed at the roof.

"Listen," he shouted, "let's have some fucking order here! You lot – stand back!"

"But, Boss—" one of the Watchmen said.

"I said *stand back*." Although it was empty now, he still waved the pistol about like a badge of office. The Watchmen waited around him, threatening but unsure. "And you, Anglian – give that man his stick back."

Edwin released the mace and held up his hands, palms-out, towards the Watchmen. He took a step away. Hugh and Elayne shuffled back out of view.

"Listen," Falsi said, "no-one's going to get hurt, not if everyone keeps calm. Just let us do our job, and we'll leave you in peace. All right?"

"Until the end of the week," Hugh growled.

Giulia stepped close to Falsi's side. "What're you doing here?"

He carefully pushed his pistol back into his belt.

"Do you actually know why you're here?"

"Shut up," he replied, and the fat Watch captain swaggered up to join him, thumbs hitched over his belt.

"This is a search for stolen goods!" Captain Orvo yelled up the stairs. "We are looking for stolen goods!"

Giulia hissed, "Here? We haven't been out the bloody building!"

Falsi shrugged.

She looked upstairs. Edwin was shielding Elayne from view, as if he feared that the Watchmen would rush the staircase. Hugh waited at the top of the stairs, expressionless. Nobody seemed to have remembered the tile in Giulia's room. Or the lockpicks and the knives.

She felt her body quicken. A sudden urge hit her – to run upstairs, to tear past these people, grab her bag and leap with it out the window, and immediately she knew she didn't have a hope. She'd have to get through half a dozen armed men – and leave Hugh behind her.

Giulia leaned close to Falsi's ear. "This is ridiculous. You don't even know what you're looking for."

She looked up to see Elayne welcoming the Watchmen onto the landing like the lady of the house greeting late guests.

No, Elayne.

Falsi grunted. "Not my idea," he said. "I've got a job to do."

Giulia ignored him and started up the stairs. Perhaps she could warn Elayne, catch hold of her dress through the banisters or something—

Smiling and benign, Elayne was giving the Watch a tour. Two miserable-looking toughs followed her out of Hugh's room.

"Now, this way is where Giulia sleeps. Let me just..."

Giulia's skin crawled as Elayne opened the door, like something withering in the heat. *Don't do it. For God's sake, don't let them see. Elayne, if you can hear me—* Giulia held her ground. The urge to flee tore at her like an itch under a plaster cast.

"Look closely," Elayne said. "Take a *good* look around. You see the bed? And that chair? Nothing special, is there, now? Nothing on the walls, or the floor. Nothing worth looking at."

They turned and walked out of the room. Elayne closed the door behind them.

"That does the upstairs," one of the men shouted down the stairs. "You want us to go through the rest of it?"

"Ah, don't bother," Falsi called back. "We're done here."

The Watchmen stomped down the stairs. Halfway down, the last man paused and rubbed his jaw, as if trying to remember something. He turned.

Elayne stood sweating at the top of the stairs. Edwin had his arm around her waist, virtually holding her up. Hugh waited beside them, his gloved fists clenched.

The Watchman met her eyes, shrugged, and walked back down.

Giulia turned away from the others, closed her eyes and took ten slow breaths. Elayne was leaning against the wall now, and the two knights were tending to her: Edwin close up, Hugh hovering a step behind. Giulia felt the sweat start to cool on her skin. She walked downstairs, light-headed.

"Come on, lads, back to the Watch-house," Falsi said.

"Damned right," one of his men replied. "I hate this early-morning stuff."

"Sorry to get you gentlemen up," Giulia said.

The Watchman turned to her. He had heavy brows and bad skin that looked as if it had been scrubbed with grit. "Did you just say something?" he demanded, two feet from her face, "Because if you've got something fucking clever to say—"

Falsi took him by the arm. "Leave it. She's being stupid. She does that."

"Maybe someone needs to shut her up."

"I *said* to leave it."

The Watchmen loitered near the door like drunks being ejected midway through a party. Giulia heard the fat captain call them all together from outside, and they wandered out. Falsi did not bid her goodbye.

The innkeeper slammed the door behind them and looked back at Giulia with hard, suspicious eyes. He began to put the tables back in order. A few cups stood about; from the look of it, Falsi's men had taken the opportunity to have a quick drink. As Giulia approached, the innkeeper glanced away, as though they shared a past of which they were both ashamed.

Slowly, he put up the last chair. He reached to his back and pulled out a folded piece of paper, looked at Giulia and tossed it onto the table.

"The Watch left that for you," he said, as though it disgusted him.

Giulia looked at him. He stared through her. She reached out and picked the piece of paper up.

For the truth, it said, *seek Ricardo Varro, boatmaker.*

Giulia re-read it, trying to dredge up a memory that might make sense of the words. She looked at the innkeeper.

"You said the Watch left this here?"

"That's right."

"Lieutenant Falsi gave it to you?"

"Just a Watchman, that's all. I don't know what it says," he added. "I don't read."

"Thanks," she said.

The innkeeper took a step towards her. He smelled stale. "I see you people," he said. "You, her upstairs, those two old men: you're unnatural, all of you. Heretics and wizards and God knows what else. The sooner you're gone, the better." He took a step back from her. "Just saying."

"Thanks for letting me know. Now shut up and fuck off," Giulia replied, folding the paper in her hands. "Just saying."

She walked upstairs. Elayne stood uneasily, propped between the two men. Hugh was watching her keenly. Giulia was surprised by how alert he looked. Normally the vague look only left Hugh's face when he was fighting someone.

"How are you?" Giulia asked.

"I'm fine," Elayne managed. "That last one was rather difficult, that's all. He really wanted to have a nose around."

Giulia glanced into her room. The door was open, and the pillow was clearly visible through the gap, too high on the bed not to be hiding something underneath. "Good work," she said.

Elayne smiled weakly. "Well, one tries."

The men guided Elayne to her room. Giulia followed them, wanting to hurry them along. *Five days more. If we're lucky.*

Giulia waited by the door.

"Really," Elayne said, "I *am* fine, you know."

Giulia said, "Look, everybody: we need to talk. Someone left this downstairs." She passed the note to Edwin and watched as they all read it.

"The innkeeper said one of the Watch left it behind," Giulia said. She turned to Elayne. "I don't suppose you could tell...?"

"That's not my area, I'm afraid," Elayne replied, and she gave Giulia a big, queasy smile.

"Maybe it's worthless, or maybe it's a lead," Giulia said. "Whatever it is, I ought to have a look. I'm going to set off to find this Varro pretty soon. While I'm away, I want you to think about how to get out of here. Anyone who owes you, anyone you could bribe, or hire, any tricks you could pull – anything. We need a proper plan. We can talk about it when I get back."

Hugh followed her out, and the door closed behind him. "Watch yourself," he said. "Take your kit with you. Damn it, I wish I could come along too."

"Well, you can't. You're under house arrest."

"To hell with house arrest. Giulia, you can't understand, but this is no life for a fighting man. It shames me, being stuck here while those bloody peasants barge in and root around, threatening—" He checked himself. "All of us."

There was a tightness in his voice that she didn't like, a hint of craziness. "Look, Hugh..."

"Yes?"

"As soon as I'm done, we'll be out of here. A day, two days, and we'll be free, I promise. You know I'm doing whatever I can. You've got my word on that."

His face was grim. "We don't have long, Giulia. Not with those bastards creeping about, looking for excuses to string us up."

"I know."

"I could cut us a way out of here tonight."

"It wouldn't be safe. Not for Elayne. For you or I, fine, probably for Edwin too – but she couldn't. You know that."

"I suppose not. Dammit!" he said. "I should never have let them bring us here. But if we'd not come – there wouldn't have been anyone to defend her – no-one still a knight, that is..." He tailed off, barely addressing her.

"Well, it's happened now." *If they hadn't brought us*

here... "Just stay here a while. I won't be long, I promise."

She turned and walked along the corridor. *I used his code against him*, she realised. *I used his loyalty to Elayne to keep him here.*

In her room, she tidied up her dress and tied her hair back neatly. *Not too bad, leaving aside the scars. Damn, I wish I knew where a good alchemist was.* She thought about it, and realised that finding the right shop could take all day. *Perhaps I could just stand in profile*, she thought. *Show Varro my better side.* She gave her pocket-mirror a small, bitter smile.

If they hadn't brought us here...

Giulia stepped into the corridor. She paused, feeling curiously nervous, and knocked on Elayne's door.

The sorceress was reading from a little book, scratching notes into the margin with a goose-feather quill. She glanced up as Giulia came in, and stifled a yawn.

"Sorry to interrupt," Giulia began. "I just wanted to get your opinion on something."

Edwin was sitting at the table with a cup of wine. "Could you do this later?" he said. "Elayne's still very tired."

The wizard waved a hand. "No, no, it's fine now. Go ahead."

"I'll be with Hugh," Edwin said grumpily.

Giulia looked at Elayne and wondered what to say. She felt more at home with either of the men, tough creatures used to war and travelling, than this clever, gentle woman. It was not because Elayne knew magic: it was because she seemed never to have known hardship, or suffering, or what it was to hate someone.

"Goodness me! Going somewhere grand?"

"Thanks. I, er, thought I'd get your opinion, if you don't mind. How do I look?"

Elayne laid down her pen and stood up. "Well, very good indeed! Yes, most well turned-out, I'd say." Her voice was quick and twittering. Giulia wondered if she was nervous, or whether Elayne thought much faster than normal people, like a bird must do.

"I look all right?"

"You look fine," the wizard said. "It's a good dress; it suits your hair. It's cut very well, don't you think?"

"The barber did it for a few coppers."

"I meant the dress."

"Oh, right. It's just the usual one." Giulia looked down. She felt a stab of pleasure. Far away from the pragmatic part of her that knew about thievery and survival, a small bit of her mind grinned with delight at the thought of being pretty. It was nonsense, of course, but difficult to resist.

"Going somewhere good?" Elayne asked.

"I don't think so. I've got to ask someone a few questions. It can't hurt to look right."

"True. Do sit down, by the way."

Giulia took a seat. "Thanks."

"So, what's it like, being with Hugh? Does he make you go on quests?"

Giulia smiled. "Not exactly. But he doesn't stop, that's for sure. He's fitter than a man half his age. He once told me that if a knight stayed true to his vows, he wouldn't age like a normal man. Is that really what happens?"

Elayne looked serious. "Maybe. What vows do you mean?"

"Well, being honourable, helping people, that sort of thing."

"I see. Yes, perhaps there's something in that.... If you don't mind me asking – and don't reply if you do, if you see what I mean – how come you and Hugh are – well, friends at all?" Elayne flashed her wide, open smile. "I don't mean to be rude: it's just that he and you seem, well, rather at the opposite end of things, so to speak. Not that you're not a very decent person, as far as I can tell—"

"Well, they say opposites attract," Giulia said blithely, and immediately wished she hadn't. "I mean, not like that."

"Of course," Elayne said, and Giulia suddenly realised that she knew everything, that the situation was obvious to her. "You know he still cares for me, don't you?"

"Yes."

"I wish he didn't. It makes things rather awkward."

"He can't help it, you know," Giulia said. "It's not as if he does it to annoy you." Her voice was harder than she'd meant it to be.

"I used to be close to him, but that was a long time ago." Elayne's eyes flicked to the book again. "I wish he'd just forget. It's not good for him."

"I don't think he's very good at forgetting things." *Although it depends how much he's had to drink.*

"Well, I wish he would!" Elayne wasn't built for arguing. The angrier she got, Giulia thought, the more feeble she would sound. "It's not fair, not on me or Edwin, for him to keep on thinking like that. And he ought to find someone else, Giulia, for his own sake. It can't be good for him to keep on wishing – when really he must know that there's no chance—"

"I don't reckon he works like that."

"Can't you say something to him?" she said. "Can't

you try to tell him yourself, make him understand?"

"I'll do what I can." Giulia stood up, eager to go. She felt guilty for mentioning it. "So I look all right, then?"

"You look very good."

Apart from the face, she thought, suddenly hard and cold. She wondered if Elayne had simply been lying all the way, thinking Giulia was sufficiently desperate to swallow whatever compliment she threw at her. "Thanks," she said. "I'll see you later."

"Wait," Elayne said. Giulia paused. "I've been thinking. You know I mentioned Lord Portharion, the mage, when you asked me about magic? He might be able to help us. I don't know how to get in touch with him directly, but there's an organisation here that he was connected to – a club for artists, I think..."

"Go on."

"I only heard in passing, ages ago. The Cornello Scola, I think it was called. My tutor Doctor Dorne gave a lecture there, years ago. He was cross because they put Portharion on before him. He said they had no right to put another wizard's name at the top of the bill..." She stopped, half-smiling. "Well, anyway, you could try there."

"You think this Portharion would be willing to help us?"

Elayne opened her slim, soft hands. "I don't know. But I know he's respected. If nothing else, the Watch would have to listen to him. There's not much solidarity between wizards, to be honest, but – well, it's worth a try, isn't it?"

"Right now," Giulia replied, "I think pretty much anything is."

As Giulia left the Old Arms, she pulled her cloak tight against the morning air. She paced down the road, heading south. She passed the little bridge from which they'd hauled Father Coraldo in to land, then followed the thin canal deeper into Averrio. Houses rose up on either side like cliffs flanking a river: it seemed to Giulia that she was walking into a tunnel, or the main gate of a castle.

The shutters were open in the tenements on either side. A man burst into song above her. *Third floor, second window*, she thought. The song followed her down the canal.

There was a little staging-post further up. The path dipped almost to the level of the water, and a thin boat had moored up there. The boatman sat in the stern, eating a chunk of bread.

He saw Giulia, put his food down and waved. The boat hardly rocked. "Good morning, milady! Need a ride to somewhere?"

"Yes, please."

"Anything to get away from that God-damned singing, eh? He makes that racket as regular as tides. Where to?"

"Do you know somewhere called the Cornello Scola?"

"Scola san Cornelio? Big place off the Great Canal. Where the painters go. I'll take you there for six saviours."

"Four."

"Done. Climb in; careful, now."

I should have held out for three, she thought, and she settled into the cushion-covered chair at the bows.

The boatman pushed them away from the canalside. Unusually for Averrio, he used a pair of oars instead of a punt. There was something strange about his rowing style:

she realised that he was strapped to the back of his seat by a wide belt.

"How come you use oars?" she asked.

"I've got bad legs." He pulled back the blanket that covered his legs, and she saw that they were thin, as if starved, held in place by leather straps. A pair of crutches was stashed beside them. She also saw a wheellock pistol by his hip. She reckoned that he wanted her to see it, too.

"What happened to them?"

He hauled on the oars and shrugged. "I don't know. I was born like that."

"That's bad luck."

"It's not easy, that's for sure, but I've seen worse things happen to others. I may be slow on land, but on water, I'm like a swan. I'm no alms-case, not me. I always tell people that I've got no problem with my *alms* – it's my legs that bother me!"

He laughed at the pun, and she made herself chuckle along with him.

They slipped through the canyon of houses and weaved left into a wider canal. The oars dipped into the water as regular as a machine. Giulia watched the buildings go past. The water-marks on the old stone made her feel both tranquil and sad, although she didn't know why. Voices called and laughed in a distant, echoing square. Everywhere smelt wet and slightly stale.

Another boat slid past, and the boatmen greeted each other as they passed. "What cheer, Mattia?" "All's good; what cheer with you?" Giulia glimpsed the passenger in the other boat – a curly-haired, moustached man – and they were gone. "Saints watch your back, pauper!"

The boatmen talked like street-gangers back in Pagalia. She remembered how she'd been rowed into

Pagalia, ready to take her revenge on the men who had scarred her and left her to drown. She'd been the hunter then. Now she looked at the damp sprawl of Averrio and wondered who, and where, her enemy was.

The canal widened and twisted. More boats appeared; cranes loomed over the water like huge wooden storks. "You'll like this," Mattia the boatman said, nodding at the bows. He gestured grandly. "This, madam, is the Great Canal."

It was as wide as a pasture, a bottle-green expanse of rippling, slapping water. Vast bridges spanned the canal, big enough to support entire streets.

Boats swarmed the canal. She saw thin passenger craft, like her own; wide barges piled with sacks, chests and heaps of food; floating houses covered in a rash of balconies and jury-rigged improvements; Customs skiffs with cannonets and grappling ballistas; even an ocean-going merchantman being guided towards the Arsenal by clockwork paddle-boats like a fat trader protected by his sons.

Along the far bank, a row of great houses stopped at the waterfront itself. To the left, a stone dome loomed over the skyline. Beside it stood a bundle of towers, each topped with a hemisphere like that of the main building. It made her think of pictures she'd seen of the Holy Land, of temples and minarets.

She pointed. "What's that?"

"Palace of the Hundred," the boatman replied. "Where the Council meets. The Decimus lives in there too."

"It looks like something from Jallar."

"That's not surprising. They get the stones from Dalagar, out east. We own it."

Dalagar. Another place I'm not going to. Morning light twinkled on the domes. Giulia sighed. *How many people must live here? How many of them could have killed the priest?*

A ship picked its sluggish way towards them, a high-sized floating castle, incense billowing from the bows. Its figurehead was Saint Allamar the Fisher, trident raised, and the sail was painted with an archangel. Boats swerved to let it through; sailors stood up and made the Sign of the Sword as it passed. The air twinkled: people were throwing pennies onto its deck.

It's a church!

"Can we pull up here?" Giulia asked.

"'Course," the boatman replied, and they drew up beside the floating chapel. The boatman called out, and a monk threw a rope down. "Stay here," Giulia said. A sailor helped the monk pull her on board, and she climbed onto the painted deck.

"Good day, sister," said the monk.

Giulia dipped her head to him. "Holy brother. Can I pray for help here?"

"Certainly. There's a chapel in the forecastle, just there."

He opened the door for her and she ducked inside. It was low-ceilinged and dim. The walls were riddled with niches for statues and collection-plates. Giulia felt uncomfortably close to God, as if trapped in here with him. The planks moved gently under her feet.

A small altar stood at the far end, and above it was a painting of the heavenly court. Candles the length of femurs burned on either side.

She found Saint Senobina at the edge of the picture, depicted with a smile on her lips, as though the celestial host struck her as slightly absurd. Giulia knelt and touched the saint with her fingertips.

Blessed Senobina, patron of thieves. I'm sorry I've not come earlier, but, well, I've been busy. I need your help again. I need you to guide me to the truth. Show me who killed Father Coraldo. And keep me hidden from my enemies. Bless me and watch over me. Amen.

She took a few coins from her purse and laid them on a collection plate. *It's not much, but I stole them, like the tradition says.*

Giulia left the chapel, bowing to the monk as she left. Her boat lay waiting for her. She felt ready now.

The Scola san Cornelio was four storeys of off-white stone, surrounded by a high wall that ended right at the waterside. The building's facade was covered in scrollwork, ornaments and little reliefs, as though challenging Giulia to climb it. There were poles outside for tying up boats, and a jetty about three feet long.

Giulia got out, told the boatman to wait, and knocked on the door in the wall. A man opened a slit in the door. Suspicious eyes watched as she explained why she had come.

"Lord Portharion?" The eyes in the door narrowed. "He's not here. He's gone away."

"I've got a message to give him."

"Put it through the hole and he'll get it when he comes back."

"It's not written down."

"Wait there." The slit clacked shut. Giulia looked at the canal and thought, *What else can I do? Swim away?* Just looking at the water made her feel cold.

The door opened. "Come on," said the man, and Giulia walked in.

She followed him through a garden, towards the house. The grounds were curiously unkempt, as if forgotten. They passed a small glade of stubby trees, which would have been pretty had someone trimmed it back. Perhaps the artists of the Scola thought it looked dramatic. She'd seen almost no other trees in Averrio.

They reached the back door, and the servant ushered her into a hall. Giulia listened to him trudging away. The walls were white, and the pale statues that stood against them looked as if they had grown out of their alcoves. She waited.

A man entered the room at the far end. He was slight and tanned, his eyes shining and hair fluffed up, as though by the wind. He wore a smart jacket and a shoulder-length cape, and his bootheels clicked as he approached.

"Battista Iacono, madam." He stopped and bowed with a quick, birdlike dipping of the head. "I live here."

"Giulia Degarno. Pleased to meet you, sir."

"Likewise." Iacono smiled and rubbed his hands together to warm them. It made him look conspiratorial. "I understand you wanted to pass a message to Magister Portharion, am I right?" Without pause he added, "I'm afraid he's not here right now. He's in Montalius for a wedding: we don't expect to see him until next month."

"I know; your servant said. I need to get a message to him. It's from Elayne Brown. It's very urgent."

Iacono looked blank.

"She's a wizard. She's a student of Doctor Dorne, from Anglia. He's also a wizard."

"I know of Doctor Dorne. He advises Queen Gloria. Technically, he's a mathematician, but I've heard of his interest in matters spiritual." Iacono sounded mildly annoyed. "Look, I can take a message and pass it on if you'd like. I'm sure Portharion would be interested in anyone skilled in the Art; goodness knows they're rare enough..." Iacono grimaced. He seemed to be undergoing some sort of internal struggle. "You'd better come through. Could you follow me, please?"

"Thank you," Giulia said, and he squinted at her as if he could spot sarcasm in her eyes. She realised that he hadn't looked at her scars yet. Perhaps he was too polite to stare, or perhaps she wasn't important enough to merit the attention.

Iacono turned and Giulia followed him across the hall. "So," she said, "is this your house, then?"

"Oh, no. I have a bursary to work here. It's one of the privileges of being the secretary of the Scola. Portharion is one of our patrons, you see."

"Does he live here too?"

"No. He has his own island."

"Oh."

The corridor opened into a well-furnished, warmer room. A maid knelt before the fire, feeding it coal.

The pictures on the walls depicted a range of scholars. They brandished sextants, scrolls, books, holy signs and more; behind them, there were boats, armies, great buildings.

"Those are people who've addressed the Scola," Iacono said. "We have a portrait painted when they lecture: it's something of a tradition, you see. Do sit down."

She took a seat. The chairs were very soft. "Who's that?" Giulia asked, pointing. A tall, messy-haired woman smiled out of a picture, gesturing awkwardly at an easel.

"That's Amelia Brunelli," Iacono replied. "A painter. She's known for her portraits and religious scenes."

Giulia turned to look at him. "Do you paint?"

"I'm a cartographer. I make maps. As a matter of fact, I was the first person to map out the entire city. Look, can we—"

"That's very interesting. I'm a thief-taker by trade. I use a lot of maps."

"Is that so?"

Ah, that's got your attention. "I doubt I'd have used yours, though. They'd be too expensive for someone like me. I would see them more as things of pure art."

"Well," Iacono said, "they are known to be of quality, you see. Who knows, maybe one day you'll be able to afford one. I always think that a map can look just as pleasing as a painting, provided it's framed properly."

"Definitely. Sir, I really need to send a message to Lord Portharion. I have to tell him that Elayne Brown is in great danger and needs his help."

"What sort of danger?"

Giulia paused a moment. *Why not? Now's hardly the time to hold back.* "She's accused of murder. At the end of the week, the Watch will take her to the court-house, and she'll hang that afternoon."

"And she hired you to send this message?"

"No. I'm accused as well."

"I see." He leaned forward, as if only just starting to listen.

"Elayne, her husband, my friend Hugh and I were all accused. It's because they're from outside the city. The Watch think they're an easy mark."

"Go on."

"A priest was killed outside the inn where we're staying. Someone stabbed him and set a dog on him – or at least that's what the Watch said. I think it's bullsh— I think it isn't true. They've pinned it on us because we're an easy catch."

"I'm shocked." He wasn't.

"Look," she said, "will you tell Portharion that? We don't have much time. We have to act soon."

Iacono said, "I can't promise anything."

"Could you try? It's very important."

His eyes hardened, and for a moment he seemed never to have spoken to her before, as though she was something he'd only just been forced to see. He glanced away and sighed. "I'll try my best. You have my word on that."

Giulia swallowed. His complacency annoyed her; she had been close to raising her voice. It wouldn't help to get angry. "We're staying up at the Old Arms, in the north quarter. If you need anyone to vouch for me, once this is all sorted out they can talk to Marcellus van Auer or Grodrin of the Forge back in Pagalia. Either of them can testify to my good name."

"Van Auer, eh?" Iacono nodded. "I've heard of him. Is he a printer?"

"That's his father," she said. "Marcellus is a natural philosopher. He works for Princess Leonora." She made herself smile. "Perhaps one day he'll have his portrait on your wall."

"Perhaps so. Well," the cartographer added, leaning forward, "rest assured that I'll try to get Magister Portharion—"

"Please. It's very urgent." Giulia stood up, and Iacono did the same. "Thank you for seeing me." *Even though you're going to do shit-all about it.*

"A pleasure." Iacono gestured gracefully towards

the exit. Giulia took the hint.

The door closed behind her, and the old servant led her back to the canal. She stood on the tiny jetty and scowled at the far side of the Great Canal.

So much for the wizard. Now we really are alone.

Boats of varying sizes crawled past: on the back of one, a fat woman reclined under an awning, propped up on one elbow like a Quaestor's wife. A man, perhaps her husband, was showing her a bottle of wine. Giulia tried not to pull a face.

The boatman looked up at her. "Where to now, milady?"

She reached to her purse. "Take me to Ricardo Varro, the boatbuilder. And go quickly."

***

Iacono stood by the door for a few seconds, enjoying the quiet of the hall. He was glad to have got rid of Giulia Degarno. She had been too quick, too clever – especially for a woman, and especially one from the lower orders.

He saw a slim figure in the doorway to the right. The newcomer's huge, almond-shaped eyes were calm, but Iacono still felt as if he were being judged. "Sethis."

The dryad stepped forward and stood before the fire. "That was interesting," he said. He turned around, warming the backs of his legs. Sethis raised a hand and rubbed his smooth, pointed chin with fingers longer than a man's. "What an unusual woman."

"You should have seen her face," Iacono replied. "She had two huge scars on her cheek."

"She sounded honest, though." The dryad crossed his arms. He was a little taller than Iacono.

"I thought she sounded like a lunatic. Were you listening in?"

"Not deliberately. I just happened to overhear a little."

"Hmm. You've been to Anglia," the mapmaker said. "Do you know this Elayne Brown she was talking about?"

"No, but I know of James Dorne. He's a very powerful wizard, if a bit – well, odd. But Grodrin of Pagalia is a good person. If he can vouch for her, this Giulia Degarno can't be all bad."

"That's as may be, but I didn't trust her." Iacono scowled. "I mean, is this the sort of person we want to be dealing with at all?"

"I can't see why not," Sethis replied. "The fact she merely looks unusual shouldn't preclude us from talking to her. After all, I hardly look like the most normal of folk, do I?" He waited a moment before he smiled.

"You think there's some truth in what she said? All of that about Portharion's friends being in danger?"

The dryad shook his head. "Probably not. But what I think isn't really the question, is it? The question is whether, on the off-chance that it isn't nonsense, we should tell Portharion. And, I suppose, what we'd do if it turned out that she was right."

"So where is Portharion right now?"

Sethis shrugged. "Probably on his island, I suppose."

"Can you find out? You know people..."

"I can ask. It's been a while, though. Some of them don't trust me very much these days." Sethis nodded several times. He seemed to have come to a decision. "I'll see what I can do. It's rather more my side of things than yours. After all, where Portharion lives, maps don't work."

***

Ricardo Varro's boatyard faced straight onto the wide Sarreri Canal, close to the opening of the lagoon. To the east, the vast military dockyard known as the Arsenal loomed over the civilian yards like a monstrous castle.

Giulia shielded her eyes and looked south, across the cold, calm waters of the lagoon to the great harbour walls, where batteries of cannon turned slowly on clockwork pedestals. The Golden Griffon stood out in the bay on top of its column, its huge claws raised over the ships as they came in to dock.

As Giulia stepped onto land, half a dozen barefooted, sweating men were hauling a skiff up the slipway and into a cavernous shed. From within the outhouses came the continual tinkle of muffled hammering.

Giulia approached the boatsheds. A dripping brown figure lumbered from behind the skiff: leather-skinned, goggle-eyed, trailing a tendril from its head. Giulia tensed. Her right hand slid into her left sleeve, fingers closing around the handle of the knife stashed there.

The water-man reached up and pulled a leather helmet from his head. A pale, soggy human face appeared. *It's some sort of armour*, she realised, and she felt foolish for having reached for her blade.

"Nothing underneath that I could see," the man announced. "Damn, it's cold in there," he added, and he trudged up the slipway and out of view. Giulia realised that he'd somehow been walking about under the water. She was a long way from home.

A sign hung above the boatyard: a painting of a galleon. A pennant on the ship's mast bore the word *Varro*. Giulia paused, smoothed her dress down, and walked in.

In the yard, half-built boats lay on trestles like the skeletons of sea-beasts. Smooth, curved lengths of oak were propped up against a long shed. A man stood shaping a keel with a two-handed plane. Curls of pale wood lay around his shoes, as though he had been shearing sheep. As Giulia walked over, her boots deliberately loud on the cobbles, he raised his head and stared at her. She wondered if he was eyeing her scars or trying to recognise her face.

"Help you?"

Giulia wasn't going to sound like a local. She made her voice a little tighter, a little more exotic. "I'm looking for Master Varro," she replied. "It's about a commission."

He looked past her. "Just you?"

She nodded. "Just me."

The man nodded and laid down the plane. "I'll take you to him. This way."

They walked up to a long shed together. Giulia followed him inside, hand close to her knife again.

The shed was dark and stank of pitch and stagnant water. The walls seemed infused with the smell of the canal, even more so than the waterway itself. Even the windows were clogged up with green stuff, as if they had been salvaged from the deep.

The smell unnerved Giulia. It reminded her of the place in Pagalia where her enemies had left her to drown, her face ripped open, her lungs desperately straining for air. *Stop it. That was a long time ago. Those men are dead.*

A man was stirring a pot of pitch with a spoon at the rear of the room, gazing into it as if hoping for a revelation. He wore a leather apron. As he moved, Giulia realised that he was the same person who had emerged from the canal. The workman coughed, and he looked up.

He was big, with a broad frame and heavy muscles and a beer gut. His damp hair was light for Averrio, the colour of sand. The face under it was tough, friendly and round, and as it saw Giulia it smiled.

"Woman to see you, Boss."

"So I see. Good afternoon, madam."

For the first time, Giulia realised just how high the ceiling was: needle-shaped skiffs hung in it as if roosting. Water rippled in the frosted window behind Varro's head. In the yard outside, the light, steady hammering pattered away like rain.

"You too," she said. She made her accent a little more refined. "Are you Ricardo Varro?"

"That's me," the big man said cheerily. He pulled off his heavy gloves and approached, sticking out a hand. They shook, his fist enveloping Giulia's. His hand was as pink and meaty as a ham. "Ricardo Varro, at your service."

"Giulia Corvani. Pleased to meet you."

Varro glanced at his man. "Back to work, Luca." He watched Luca go, waiting until the door closed before he said, "So, madam. Is that House Corvani of Pagalia?"

"Only a distant relation, I'm afraid. I was schooled in Vorland. Which is where I got these," she added, waving a hand at the long scars on her face.

"From duels? I heard men fought them, but women...?"

"A hunting accident. Boar, you see."

"I thought boars struck at the legs, rather than the face?"

Oh fuck. "That, sir," she replied, "depends rather on the boar." She made what she hoped looked like an aristocratic shrug.

Varro raised his eyebrows, but she couldn't tell

whether he was impressed or amused. "I'm sure. Well, you're not the first Corvani to come here. We did some repairs on Lady Tabitha's barge when she visited Averrio a few years ago."

"Really? I never actually met her. I've heard she was a truly remarkable woman." Giulia remembered her own encounter with Lady Tabitha and thought, *Remarkable indeed. Crafty, power-hungry and very slightly mad.* "I'm new in town, as a matter of fact. I've come down from Montalius. Averrio is very beautiful."

"It's a lovely city to look at," Varro said. "Just try to ignore the smell." He laughed. "Actually, you picked the right time to visit. Come summer, the canals stink. They say when God looks down at Averrio he holds his nose. Now, how can I help?"

"Well," said Giulia, "it's a long story."

"Then come and sit down. Take a seat, please."

He pointed to a table and two battered chairs. Giulia sat down while Varro took a bottle of wine down from a shelf and hunted for something to drink from. Giulia got a clay cup, Varro a dented tankard. The boatbuilder poured the drinks out carefully, trying to make them equal, then he sat down opposite her. "Ah, that's a bit better. Sorry if the wine's not up to much."

She sipped. "It's fine." She looked at the rowing boats that ran along the roof, the oars and parts resting against the walls. Her eyes stopped on the underwater helmet, now drying on a workbench. It looked like a hangman's hood, with big glass lenses where the eye-holes should be. A leather pipe ran out of the hood, ending in a wooden object the size of a bell.

"Oh, that," Varro said, seeing where she was looking. "It's a water-suit. It lets you work underwater.

We use a couple: that one's not sprung any leaks yet, but I think the enchanting's wearing thin." He looked back to her. "So, then, are you thinking of commissioning some work?"

"Not exactly. But there is money involved."

He rubbed his hands together and grinned. "Always good. I'm like a dwarrow miner when it comes to gold."

"It's a delicate matter. You see, I've been told you can help me – but I don't know who told me, and I don't know how."

Varro frowned. "I don't follow you."

"A friend of mine has been falsely accused of a crime. She's under house arrest. As you can imagine, I'm reluctant to tell anyone her name. I got a message today from one of the Watch, telling me to go and talk to you. It was left for me to see it."

The boatbuilder took a slow, thoughtful sip. "They told you to come to me? What's your friend accused of?"

"The murder of a priest."

"That's serious business."

"I know. They found him in the canal, cut up. His name was Sebastian Coraldo. He was floating outside the inn where we're staying. That was enough for the Watch to pin it on us."

"How did he die?"

"He was stabbed. And a big dog was set on him. He might have drowned after that. Overall, someone didn't like him very much."

Varro shook his head and took a gulp of wine from his tankard. "And that to a priest. Terrible. What was he, an apostate?"

"I don't know. I wondered if you might be able to help me there."

The big, round head shook from side to side. "Sorry. I don't know anything about it. Do they think he was pushed into the canal from a boat?"

Giulia tried to imagine Falsi, or any of his colleagues, coming to such an elaborate conclusion. "I don't think they know. I've not heard it said."

Varro stood up, walked to the fire and stirred the bucket of pitch. He walked back, looking thoughtful. "I don't see how I can help you, then. Unless it was some madman who bought a boat from us. But I don't see how. I don't sell to the fey folk, or to dissenters, God help them, and if it was a madman who bought the boat from me – then I'd know, wouldn't I?"

Giulia felt the conversation sliding from her grip. Varro knew nothing: the only connection with the murder was that someone had dropped his name. *What if they gave me his name just to waste my time? God-damned Watch bastards.* "I suppose you would." She glanced around, trying to fit this together, feeling the frustration that would soon swell into outright anger. "Can you think of any reason why they would have told me to see you?"

"Who's they?"

"Someone in the Watch, I suppose."

Varro stood up. "Would you excuse me for a minute? I just need to tell my foreman something."

He stepped to the door. She heard it open and saw it swing closed.

Giulia glanced around the room: at the paddles propped like brooms against the walls, the greened-up windows, the boats roosting in the roof. She looked at her hand, at the broken knuckle on her little finger. *He's gone to get the Watch. No, he hasn't. Why should he?*

The door opened again, and a sudden thunder of

hammering followed Varro back into the room. He closed the door. The noise continued, slightly muffled.

"Sorry, we've got an important job on. I have to keep checking, or else the lads slack off." He smiled and sat down. "Now, then: is there anything else you know? Anything that might help at all? Did this Father Coraldo have any friends? Perhaps I might have known them."

"Well, he spoke to someone before he died."

"Who was that?"

Giulia remembered Anna in her little room. "Nobody much. Just a prostitute."

"What was this whore like? Can you describe her to me?"

"She wasn't much. Just a girl. Dark hair, held up with combs. Nothing special."

"What did he say to her?"

"She said he just talked about anything. The new order of the world, she said, stuff like that."

"The new world order, did she say that?"

Giulia frowned. "Why?"

"Is that what she said?"

"Yes, I think."

"The New World Order." Varro paused. "No, I'm sorry. Doesn't mean anything, I'm afraid."

He took a deep draught from his tankard, lowered it from his lips, and drove it into the side of Giulia's head.

She twisted away, but not fast enough. The tankard hit her temple, her chair tipped over, and the ground rushed up and struck her palms. She scrabbled aside, rolled and came up, and as Varro lumbered in, she plucked the knife from her sleeve and threw it at him.

He dodged and her knife clattered against the wall. Varro dropped into a fighting stance, arms up and hands open, fingers tensed. Giulia's stinging hands folded into fists.

Varro filled the room: he was the room. His hard breath and the hammering, the stink of pitch that crawled into her mouth and lungs, all came from the same place, the same net that surrounded her.

The hammering became loud and desperate, loud enough to drown out screams. She yanked her dress up to reach the knife in her boot, and Varro came scuttling in, quick on his big flat feet, and his fist swung out at her eye. She skipped aside, his hand shot past, and she drove her thumbs one-two into his ribs.

He did not even flinch; his arm dropped around her shoulder and suddenly she was wrapped in his embrace. Varro snarled, and his arms closed bear-like around her waist and hauled her, thrashing, off the ground.

He waded across the shed with Giulia squirming round trying to get at his face, and she saw what he was going towards – the fireplace. Varro threw her down hard, and before she could get her footing he had knocked her onto her knees, one arm across her shoulders to keep her in place, his hand on the back of her head.

Varro pushed her down towards the bucket of pitch that bubbled on the hearth. Giulia saw it open up before her like a hole into Hell, saw the crusted black filth around the rim, the spoon sticking up from it, her desperate face reflected in the bubbles on its surface. The reek of pitch flooded her mind.

She couldn't quite reach her boot.

Her neck was nothing compared to his arm. The hammering rang through the room like drums. The simmering pitch was six inches from her face. Her knife felt like a mile away.

Giulia reached out, seized the spoon and flicked it at his face.

He screamed and staggered back, hands clamped around his eye. Giulia grabbed her skirt, pulled it up and snatched the knife from her boot. Varro tripped and stumbled away, babbling something behind his hands, and she lunged in and punched the blade into his neck. He fell against the wall like a drunk, slid down and flopped onto the floor.

Varro lay on the floor, legs stuck out in front of him, blood spreading over his front. The right side of his face was raw. He was still breathing; soon he would be gone. Giulia stepped back, knife in hand. She was breathing hard, not quite panting. Her body ached. She crossed the room and picked up her stiletto, slid it into her sleeve, and bent down to put the other knife back into her boot.

Varro laughed. It was a low, dirty chuckle, hardly audible over the pounding racket from outside. She looked up. He shouldn't be able to make a sound like that.

The burn on his face was shrinking. It looked as if the red marks were evaporating, like droplets of water on a hot stove. His skin was sealing up, coming back together again, pushing the tar out of the wound like black sweat.

"Clever, isn't it?" He got up as awkward as a toddler, rolling onto his hands and hauling himself to his feet. The light caught his face. He looked a little sunburnt.

How? How could that happen?

Varro brushed his hands together. "You've got to try harder than that, girl!" He looked drunk with glee. Delighted with her shock, he yelled something that she couldn't make out, then: "Surprise, little lady!"

He lunged. Giulia sprang back and, as his punch swung past, she snapped her left hand around his wrist.

Giulia kicked him in the shin and yanked his arm. He lost his balance and stumbled forward, and she shoved his arm against a gondola, turned her body and punched her knife straight through the back of his hand.

The knife sank into the wood up to the hilt, pinning him to the boat. Varro howled, a long, mad, castrate whoop.

She stepped back, eyes racing over the room. Varro gawped at his hand, horrified, but it couldn't be long before he tore free.

Giulia glanced around and saw what she needed. She bent into the shadows and came up with a paddle.

Varro's eyes were wet with pain, but they fixed on her. There was something wrong with his mouth, she saw, as though he'd packed out his gums with wool. "You do that," he snarled through a mess of teeth, "and I swear you'll fucking pay."

She smashed the paddle into his skull. Varro's legs gave way and she hit him with it again, knocking him to his knees. She raised the oar a third time, judged her aim and broke the blade over Varro's head.

Outside, the hammering continued. She tossed the paddle on top of him.

Varro lay on his front, arm still pinned to the boat. More than his corpse, or the blood all over his head, the raised arm made her feel sick. She stepped in and pulled the knife out. Varro's arm dropped.

They set me up, she thought. *They sent me here so he could kill me.* He looked dead, but she kept the knife ready, held down by her side.

Giulia stood by the far window, listening. The hammering was coming from the other side of the boatyard. She crossed the room and bolted the door, and then she returned to the window.

She used the knife to cut out some of the lead in the window-pane, until she could hook the blade round and bend the window down to her. Giulia tore the window open and looked out. The prows of finished boats jutted out like arrowheads.

Varro didn't move.

There wasn't enough room to sit on the sill, but she could squeeze her shoulders through the gap. Halfway out, she heard cloth snag and rip. *Fucking dress*. She crawled out the window, onto her scratched palms. Grimacing, she slid her legs out and stood up.

Giulia brushed herself down and checked the skirt: the tear was only small. She took a deep breath and walked between the prows, away from the waterfront.

Quickly and neatly, Giulia crossed the yard and slipped out the gates. The hammering went on behind her. Somewhere far away, a dog barked its response.

SIX

The streets were full of the sound of work. Men called to one another across the canal. Two robed scholars argued as they walked by. A barber chatted with his neighbour outside his shop, proudly displaying the blood on his apron to show how busy he was. Any of them could have been a friend of Ricardo Varro.

Giulia took the long way back to the inn, keeping to backstreets, doubling back on herself, ducking into shops and doorways to watch the road behind. She had to walk: a boat could have taken her across the bay in half the time, but Varro was a boatbuilder. Who knew how many of the local boatmen were his customers? Suddenly the whole city seemed to turn its eyes to her, and it no longer felt as if a murderer hid in Averrio, but that all its inhabitants were part of the same conspiracy. She hurried on, with her head down and the chill of winter closing around her cheeks and hands, wishing for nightfall to hide her face.

She reached the Old Arms in the mid-afternoon. Hugh sat in an alcove in the main bar, his head nodding. She thought that he was asleep, but he glanced up as she approached. He looked tired and sad, like an old hound.

"We've got a problem," Giulia said. "A big one."

"What happened?"

"I followed that note up. It was a trap. The man whose name was on that bit of paper tried to murder me."

Hugh was fully alert now. His eyes were hard. "What did you do?"

"I'm not sure. I thought I'd killed him, but he just – I don't know – healed back up again. I think he was some sort of wizard."

"A wizard?"

"Enchanted, maybe. Shit, Hugh, I don't know the fucking word for it. We got talking, and he was asking me about all of this. He must have been listening for me to say something, because all of a sudden he came at me. He was tough, very tough, but I put a knife in his neck. Then he got back up again."

"What did you do?"

"I hit him with an oar. Right here," she added, tapping the back of her head. "I think I killed him. Then I got the hell out of there." Even describing the fight had made her a little short of breath. "Shit. I was lucky to get away."

"You'd have been luckier if I'd have been there." Hugh smoothed down his moustache. "Do his men know he's dead?"

The innkeeper wandered into view, holding a broom in hand. He started to sweep up, the bristles scraping the floor. Hugh looked at him. "Fetch us more wine, would you, please?"

The innkeeper grunted and moved away.

Giulia said, "They must do. I didn't hide him – I wish I had, now. I didn't tell him who we are, or where. But I reckon he must have known."

"It sounds like it," the knight replied. There was a bottle beside him; he reached out and took a deep swig from the neck. The bottle caught the light as he put it down, and Giulia saw that it was almost empty. She thought: *This place is rotting you.* Hugh said, "Do you think this Varro killed the priest?"

Giulia was surprised to realise she hadn't considered it. She shook her head. "I don't know. Maybe. Look, Hugh, this changes things. I thought the Watch just pinned this shit on us because it was convenient, because they were too stupid and lazy to find the real killer. But one of them – maybe all of them – sent me to Varro to get me killed. This is a conspiracy, Hugh."

"I think you're right. Seems strange, though. Why not wait to the end of the week and just have you arrested?"

"Maybe I've been getting close to something. Is there anyone who has a grudge against you? Anyone ever cross you, try to rob you, ask you for bribes that you wouldn't pay, anything like that?"

He shook his head slowly. "No-one I can think of. Maybe a few people back in Pagalia, perhaps. But I've not got a feud – what do you call it? – a vendetta against anyone."

"Me neither. Can you ask Edwin and Elayne if they do? I think it would be better coming from you."

"I doubt they would have, Giulia."

"Just check for me. You never know."

"All right." He took another swig from the bottle. "By God, I'll be glad to see the back of this place. Sitting here like a bloody target, waiting for the Watch to try to get us..."

"I agree," Giulia said. "I'm not for staying here either. Did anyone come looking around while I was gone?"

He shook his head. "Only the innkeeper."

"Good. Listen: I need you to get Edwin and Elayne ready to ride out of here the very moment I say, all right? Get them packed up and ready to go."

"Right. What about you?"

"I'm going to get ready. I'm going back out."

***

Antonio Falsi was wasting his day. Up at some stupid hour to look for God-knew-what in that inn where the Anglians were being kept, and now a pointless patrol of Printers' Row with two of the most slack-jawed halfwits that the Watch had ever managed to recruit.

They were a pair of idle youths with the scrawny quickness of pickpockets, eager to flaunt their status and unwilling to do any genuine work. All the time he had to chivvy them – wait here, go there, stand up straight – like a couple of beggar apprentices. Rubbish, real rubbish.

Falsi strolled through the street ahead of his men, hoping to lead by example and wondering whether they might just slip away while he wasn't looking. He didn't much care if they did. People liked to see the Watch out in force, as it made them feel safe, but to get anything done, to catch any real criminals, you needed trained men, not these sewer-rats.

To the right was Jansson's Folios, the largest print shop in Averrio. The steady thump of a printing press pulsed out of the doorway like the beating of a metal heart. On the left was Frannie's, and he nodded to her as she shook out a blanket outside the door. It was the only brothel in this district, discreet enough not to offend the printers, and the Watch protected it in return for payment. Falsi had heard stories about the state of the beds and some of the girls, and he always took his cut in money, not sex. Besides, his wife would murder him if he got up to tricks like that.

"All well, Frannie?"

She was a wide-hipped woman with big fists and straw-coloured hair. She grinned at him, showing off a large gap between her front teeth. "Fine, thank you, sir. All well with you?"

"Oh, fine." Her eyes moved from him, and he looked around and saw one of his men in conversation with a page-seller, ten yards behind. "Hey! Come on!"

"Orange, Boss?" the other of the new men said, appearing at his side.

"No. Hey, where'd you get that?"

"Fruit cart," the youth replied. "Owes me a favour, he does."

"You're here to work, not call in favours," Falsi said. *Cocky little bastard*, he thought. The youth shrugged.

A stocky man ran into the road from an alleyway, apron flapping in front of him like a crusader's tabard. "Thief! Thief!"

The man spun to a halt in front of them and jabbed his finger down the street. "Thief! That way!"

"What's he like?" Falsi said.

"He stole a leg of mutton from my stall!"

"What does he look like?"

"Young, white shirt, dirty face! He went that way!"

Falsi turned to his men. "Right, you two, time to earn your pay. Go down there and get the hue-and-cry up. See if anyone's seen him. I'll head round the back." They blinked. "Go on, get to it! Run!"

Let them do it. Lazy buggers.

"We'll get him," he told the stallkeeper, managing to sound confident. "Don't worry. You follow my men and see if you can pick him out." *While I have a quick drink*, he added to himself, trying not to smile at the thought of it. After a morning like this, he felt that he deserved it.

He watched the two Watchmen run around the corner, the stallkeeper keeping pace with them. Young men were better runners than he was, after all. One of the youths glanced back as he turned the corner, as if to check that Falsi wasn't going to leave him on his own.

Actually, son, I am.

Falsi knew Printers' Row well, and he walked three houses down and slipped into a door on the left. It was someone's front room and it smelt of animals, or children. Two men with inky hands sat at a little table. A short woman in a leather apron appeared at Falsi's side. "Cup of whatever you've got," Falsi told the proprietor, and she leaned into a hatch and came up with a pitcher. Falsi sniffed the black, hoppy-smelling beer and passed the woman a coin.

The beer was strong and sour. Just the taste of it made him feel more manly, somehow, more professional. He lowered the cup and sighed louder than was necessary. "Ah, that's good."

Let the others do the hard work. They'd sent him on this shitty errand, like a part-timer – why shouldn't he enjoy himself a bit? By all rights he ought to be rowing back from the Isle of Graves by now with Sep and Rupe after putting that priest in the ground. Typical Cafaro, stealing the easy jobs. He wondered why he'd not been involved, and took another sip.

"Falsi." He felt breath on his ear. "Don't look

round. Come into the alley outside. I've got news for you." Something was wrong with the voice: he took a second to realise that it was a woman's.

He turned and saw a figure slip out the door. Falsi took a deep swig of his beer and pulled his cloak away from the pistol on his belt. He could draw it faster than his sword, and it was easier to wield: a wide-bore wheellock with a low-strength enchantment on the mechanism to stop it misfiring. It had cost a lot, but it had kept him alive more than once.

He walked outside with the cup in his left hand. The cold air robbed him of the confidence that he'd felt indoors. His beer looked as tasty as pondwater. Falsi peered around the corner and looked into the gap between the houses. It was hardly a yard across. Quietly, he set his cup down and drew his gun. If this was some bastard trying to rob him, or a felon looking to settle an old score, they were in for a surprise. The sweat in his hair made his scalp prickle.

He had taken eight steps before something scuffed behind him. He started to turn, but she said, "Don't move. I've got a crossbow. Put your gun down, good and slow."

Suddenly everything was very difficult. Swallowing, keeping control of his bladder, even breathing took great concentration. Falsi held his fingers away from the trigger. He crouched down slowly and put the pistol on the ground. It occurred to him that if he'd dropped it right, it would have gone off, startling her. Perhaps that would have given him the chance to fight back. No time now, no time.

"Turn around."

She was in black stuff: he didn't make out the details. His eyes only saw her white, scarred face and the glint of metal on the crossbow she was pointing at his chest. It occurred to him then that she looked very professional. He took half a second to recall her full name: Giulia Degarno.

"Let's talk," she said.

His mouth was dry. There was a pebble in his throat. He nodded, then said, "If you want."

"Someone tried to have me killed today. They sent me to talk to a man who tried to murder me. I want to know whose idea it was to send me there."

He found words. "I don't understand."

"All right, let's try again – and if you're stalling me, you're good as dead, so listen well. After your people searched the inn this morning, the innkeeper gave me a note. He said a Watchman had left it for me. It had a man's name on it. I went to see the man whose name it was, and he tried to stick my face in a bucket of boiling tar. I didn't let him. The way I see it, my face is messed up enough as it is."

"Oh, fucking hell," he said.

"So tell me who put that note there."

"It wasn't me. I don't know anything about a note." Falsi shook his head. "It must have been someone else."

"Not you, eh?" She lifted the crossbow to head height, closed one eye and lined it up. His stomach churned; he clenched his bowels. If he was to die now, he'd face the end without actually shitting himself. Not much of a victory, but something. "I don't want to know who it *wasn't*. Who put it there? What about that fat man?"

"Orvo? He's the boss. He might have put it there. God, he's the only one other than me who knows how to write." Falsi laughed once, then stopped.

"The man I saw this morning, ordering you around?"

Falsi grimaced. "Yes, that's him. He's captain round

here. Look, my men will be here soon—" He half expected her to tell him they were already dead.

"Then you'll send them away. This morning, when you searched us, what were you looking for?"

"Stolen goods."

She said nothing.

"Look, they don't tell me much, all right?"

"Don't give me that. You're the fucking lieutenant, for God's sake. Didn't any of your men know what you were looking for?"

"I don't—" His voice caught in his dry throat and he could not speak, and for a terrifying second he thought she'd shoot him for holding out. He swallowed and said, "I don't think so. All I knew was to turn the place over and look for anything unusual. Orvo had lost some thing of his - a picture or something."

"That's all?"

"Yes - yes, I promise it's all I know."

"So your boss, this Orvo - *he* left the note."

"I suppose... You've got to understand: I didn't see anyone, but I don't see who else it could be - unless one of the men did it."

"But your men are illiterate. You just said so."

"My men are shit," he said bitterly.

"This goes higher than you, doesn't it?"

"Yes."

"How much higher?"

"I don't know." Anger pushed through his fear. "Look, woman, I took you people in because I was doing my job, understand? They told me you killed him. Why shouldn't I believe it?"

"Because we said we were innocent?"

"Oh, come on! That's for the magistrate. They

told me to arrest you and get you through quickly—" He stopped. Something dropped into place.

She'd seen it in his face. "Quicker than normal, right?"

He said nothing. He felt terribly naked all of a sudden, as if the clouds had split and a great eye was looking down at him from above.

"So whoever really did it would get away. Is that what Orvo said?"

"I don't know," he said.

"I thought so." Something changed in her voice. It was still tight with anger, but the rage was no longer directed at him. Hope sprang into his mind: he might get away unscathed. She licked her lips. "You don't have to do this, Falsi. You know it's horseshit. And if you do go through with it, I promise that you'll be answering to me and then to God really fucking soon."

Fearing the answer, he said, "What do you want me to do?"

"I want to talk to whoever's higher than your boss. Can you get me to the procurator?"

Falsi put up his hands. "Now just wait a moment. I can't do that. I can't just valse in and ask him to—"

"The procurator knows about this, doesn't he?"

"I don't know. But I *do* know that I can't just fetch him for you. He's an advisor to the Council, and the Council is way, way above where I am."

"The Council of a Hundred? Is this about them, then? Is that why the priest was killed?"

Falsi glanced around. He wanted to turn his head to check the alley behind him, but he did not dare. "Maybe," he said. "But I don't know for sure."

She paused, frowning, and something seemed to

relax a little inside her. "Right, then. I'll tell you what's going to happen. You've seen me get the jump on you. You know that if I want to, I can get the jump on you again."

"Yes."

"Good. You are going to tell *nobody* about this conversation. You're going to tell Orvo you think we're innocent. You will do everything in your power to slow this horseshit down. And if anyone asks you, you think the case against us is weak – because you know it is."

He nodded. "Right."

"I'll find you if I need anything, but until then, we stay well apart. Understand?"

"But what if they make me go after you? If they put pressure on me to bring you in early?"

"Then you might want to think about what pressure I could put on *you*." She took a step backwards, towards the street. She glanced at the ground beside her boot. "I left you a present. Something to take home for dinner."

She stepped out of view. Falsi flopped against the wall. The smoky air suddenly tasted sweet. He looked at the place she'd been, as if she had left a trace of herself there.

After a minute Falsi stood up and walked over to his beer. He picked it up and drank the whole lot quickly, his parched throat pumping as he drained the cup. There was a parcel on the ground, a bit of white cloth. He bent down and looked inside, then tucked it under his arm.

He felt elated as he walked out of the alley, but it was a silly elation, the giddiness that came with relief. Under it, he was weary and depressed.

The two young Watchmen stood outside Frannie's, beside the stallkeeper who had raised the hue-and-cry. Between them was a scrawny beggar in torn hose and a white shirt. "We found the thief, sir!" one of the Watchmen said as Falsi drew near. "We caught this fellow creeping round the backstreets. Of course, he's hidden the meat he took, but he'll talk soon enough."

Falsi opened the bundle he held under his arm. "Here," he said, and he passed the leg of mutton to the stallkeeper.

The beggar shook himself free of his guards. "God-damned Watch," he said, and he dipped his head and spat on the ground. He stomped off, head still down, muttering as he walked away. "Always looking for a poor man to beat... God-damned..."

Falsi looked down at the white shirt he still held. It was speckled pink where it had been wrapped around the meat. "Back to work," he said.

***

"He just healed up, as if the cut I gave him hadn't happened." Giulia poured herself another cup of wine and put the bottle back in the centre of the table. "He didn't wave his hands around, say magic words, or any of that stuff. Have any of you ever seen anything like that before?"

They sat around the table in the room that Edwin and Elayne shared. Giulia had been back less than an hour, and she had already drunk half a bottle of cheap red wine. It tasted like sucking on a copper penny, but she knew it would seem better in another cup's time. She looked across the table at Elayne. "Is that a thing *you* can do, just heal up like that?"

"Not that quickly," the wizard replied. "And not that easily either. If you stuck a knife in my neck, I wouldn't be getting up at all. Of course, there might be other mages who'd know how to do that, but they'd have to be very powerful, and they probably wouldn't spend their time making boats."

Giulia nodded and sucked at her thumb. There was a long, shallow cut across the pad, gained when she'd climbed out of sight to get the drop on Falsi. A nail must have been sticking out of the tiles. Whatever it was, the damned thing wouldn't stop bleeding.

"Hugh, Edwin? You've seen some strange things. Ever heard of a man's wounds just closing up like that?"

Edwin rubbed his brow. "No, I've never heard of anything like that before. This whole business is insane." He grimaced and rubbed his eyes. "Could he have been a mort, or some sort of ghost?"

Giulia frowned and said, "I don't think so. He looked normal, that's the thing. But he shouldn't have got up after a wound like that. And tar would have burned his face off. It just seemed to boil away." She rubbed her temples, feeling sleepy and worn out.

"You've hurt your hand," Elayne said.

"It's just a cut."

"It won't heal up easily: it's in an awkward place. Here, give me your hand."

"It's all right," Edwin said helpfully.

Uncertainly, Giulia held out her arm. She had never trusted magic. Back in the old days, when she'd been more pious, she had thought of magic as one of the things that sped your way to Hell. More recently, she'd come to see it as a tool of the wealthy and insane.

Elayne took Giulia's hand in her own: Giulia felt the woman's nails lightly scrape her skin. Elayne's hands were paler and cleaner than her own. "Don't worry," Elayne said, and she closed her eyes. "It'll be fine," she said softly, and her voice became first a whisper, then nothing.

Giulia's thumb tingled. She looked down: the wound was closed and scabbed over, the blood dried around it. The digit was numb, as if she had rested something heavy on it, cutting off the flow of blood.

Elayne mouthed something, finished and looked up. She opened her eyes and smiled. "Good as new. Look."

Giulia lifted her hand and looked at it. The scab was now a stripe of old blood, like rust. She bent her thumb, feeling the joint prickle. "It feels strange," she said.

"It will for a little while," said Elayne. "That tends to happen. Don't worry: it won't drop off." She wiggled her fingers and grinned.

Giulia made herself smile back. "Thank you."

Hugh leaned forward. "I've been thinking," he said. "The way Giulia puts it, there's no guarantee that this Varro man is actually dead. I think we need to finish him off."

Giulia shook her head. "I'm not going back there. Not in the daylight."

"Actually, I thought I could. I reckon I could sneak out, with a bit of help from Giulia."

"I don't think that's a very good idea," Elayne began.

"That's a bloody terrible idea," Edwin said casually, without anger.

Giulia glanced at Hugh. He did not look offended. "Why's that?" he asked.

Edwin said, "Well, let's see. We're wanted criminals, for a start, we're under house arrest, and the City Watch is looking for an excuse to wring our necks. How's that?"

"I suppose so," said Hugh. "But what if this Varro

man is still out there, looking for Giulia? We should take him on properly, get this conspiracy out where we can see it. We could do some proper fighting for a change."

Edwin said, "The only problem with that is that we'd be doing this 'proper fighting' in the middle of a city where everyone wants us dead. Come on, Hugh, talk sense. You really are up in the clouds sometimes."

The knight sat up as if jabbed with a fork. He stared feverishly across the table. "Then what *shall* we do, eh? Just sit on our arses, waiting to be hanged, like we've been doing ever since Giulia and I got here?"

"Now look, everyone—" Elayne began.

"I'm sick of sitting here like I've gone soft! It's not right that someone should try to do us for killing a vicar – Old Church or New – when we weren't even bloody there. I say we move fast, because if we don't do something, it won't just be you and me on the line – it'll be these two women as well." Hugh shifted in his chair, shrugged impatiently. "I won't have ladies suffer on account of us just sitting here, Edwin. I won't."

Edwin leaned forward. He seemed bigger, suddenly. "Look, man. We can't just run away. It's too bloody dangerous."

"I've got a plan," Giulia said. "Tomorrow I'm going to go—"

Hugh snorted. "Dangerous? It's dangerous enough as it is! They'll come for us all at the end of the week! You're getting slack, Edwin."

"Slack? I don't know if you've noticed, but I have some responsibility these days! It's all very well for you, prancing around like some errant knight in a song—"

Giulia raised her voice. "Will you two listen to me, for God's sake?"

"Prancing? You can talk! We used to fight evil, not hide from it!"

"I have responsibilities! I have someone to look after!"

"Shut up!" Elayne screamed.

They were silent. Hugh opened his mouth, moved his jaw up and down like a fish, and closed it. The men glared at each other across the table, furious but mute.

Elayne said, "I gather you've got something to say, Giulia."

She nodded. "Thanks. I know what I'm going to do. Tomorrow morning I'm going to see this procurator, whoever he is. I heard him talking to the captain of the Watch last night, the fat man who was here this morning – Falsi called him Orvo. I overheard him telling this Orvo that he wanted this sorted out. I reckon the procurator must be able to help."

Elayne said, "What if the Watch won't let you see him?"

"I've got that taken care of. I should be able to go in over the Watch's head. With a bit of luck, he'll hear me out and help get us out of here."

"What if he doesn't?" Elayne asked.

Giulia sighed. "Then we'll just have to do it ourselves. Listen, when I spoke to Falsi he sounded uncertain about this. I don't think it was just fear. He knows this stinks, as much as we do. If you got a second chance to talk to him, Elayne, he might just agree to help. I doubt it'd be much more than promising to look the other way while we sneak out, but still, it's something."

"Sounds good to me." Elayne looked around the table. "Right, then. Does anyone have a problem with that? Edwin?"

"No," he said.

"Hugh?"

"No. But we're running out of time."

"I know," Giulia said. "If this doesn't work, I say we take our chances fighting our way out of here. Now, I need to write a letter, so I'm going to need some ink and a pen, and some paper to practice on. This is going to have to look just right."

She closed the door to her room and wedged it shut.

Edwin had brought in the small table from his bedroom, and Giulia had pushed her cloak under the legs to keep it steady. It was now covered in a stubby forest of burning candles. A glow hung over the tabletop, like a shrine.

Giulia approached the table like a surgeon approaching a difficult operation. She opened her bag and took out a piece of folded paper, torn from the Watch's record book. The wax seal of the Watch lay on the paper like clotted blood.

Elayne had given her a few sheets of fresh paper and a stoppered bottle of ink. Giulia took a fresh quill, cut a sharp nib with her knife and dipped it in the ink. She tested it on the spare paper and paused, the pen hovering above the page. Then she readied her neatest sheet of paper and wrote:

To whom it may concern, let him who reads this know that I grant authority for—

No, she decided, *no false names*. It had to come from her: she needed this procurator as an ally, and it would not do to be caught out deceiving him.

Giulia Degarno to discuss the matter of the Death of the Priest outside the Old Arms inn, which occurred three days ago. I request that she be allowed to make Inquiries and receive Information as though she were of the City Watch, and that she be granted admission to Matters of Importance as would a Watch-man. Sirs, I thank you in advance for your co-operation in this matter. Yours in Faith,

She scribbled 'Orvo, Captain' at the bottom, so badly that nobody could have guessed what his name actually said. She intended to take the letter back as soon as she had shown it to the relevant authorities. It could prove useful more than once.

Giulia re-read the letter. It seemed sufficiently pompous. For a final touch of realism, she drew lines under the signature down to the bottom of the page. Rich people did this to stop rogues like Giulia adding extra sentences to their letters. Rich people clearly didn't suspect that the entire text might be written by a rogue.

Once the ink was dry, she folded the letter in on itself. Giulia pulled one of the candles close, took the paper with the Watch seal on it and very carefully held it over the flame.

It took only a few seconds to warm the rear of the seal. Giulia tapped it, felt the wax become the consistency of mortar, and took it away from the candle. She sliced the wax away from the tattered page of the Watch record book. Then she pressed it onto the letter.

The letter was now sealed with the Watch stamp. She blew out the candles and went to bed. For once, she didn't dream.

SEVEN

Giulia woke late. The midday sun poured into her eyes as she sat up. She felt something against her side. There was a scabbarded knife under the covers with her, and she shook her head sadly as she took it out, as though some prankster had left it there for her to find.

Out of bed and standing in the middle of the little room, Giulia swung her arms and stretched her back. Slowly, working from the main joints to the smaller ones, she warmed up until she was ready to move quickly and quietly. It made her feel alert and strong.

She put on a low-necked undershirt, then pulled the better of her two dresses over the top. After the cold of the day before, she kept her britches and boots on. She fastened the leather bracers under her sleeves, pulled on her cloak and went downstairs. The dress made her feel cumbersome and slow.

She filled a small bottle with wine and slipped it into her bag. Hugh sat near the door, as if awaiting permission to leave. He nodded to her as she left the inn. "Good luck."

The streets were full of people too cold to stand still.

Giulia walked down to the edge of the canal, crossed the bridge and headed towards the place where she had found a boat the day before. She passed a man selling hot wine from a tiny stove, and she gave him two coins and quickly drained a cup. The seller stared at her face, but the warm alcohol made her feel much better.

Mattia the boatman waited at the same dock, sitting in his boat. "Good morning, milady!"

She climbed into the boat, gathering her skirts so they would not touch the water.

"You're looking very fine today, milady. Where would you like to go?"

"I need an alchemist," she replied. "I need to get something to hide these scars."

The boatman nodded, as if this sort of thing happened every day. Giulia wondered if you saw things differently if your legs didn't work right.

"I'll take you to the brother of a friend of mine. He has a good shop: quiet, very cheap. What's the word? Discreet."

They kept to narrow waterways, where the canals were almost deserted. The boat slid between high tenements. Giulia pulled her hood up. A window clattered above and a cheerful-looking woman looked out and studied the sky as if expecting it to rain money.

It took half an hour to find the alchemist's. It faced onto a narrow back-canal that the boat could barely enter, opposite a butcher's that looked as if it would stock not just horsemeat but anything the locals pulled out of the water. "Tell him I sent you," Mattia said.

The inside of the shop was poky and dark. The proprietor wore a leather hat that looked like an overcooked pie. Giulia knew what she needed, and she watched him grind up a powder from four types of crushed leaf and a grey dust that smelt of lavender, then made a mental note of the place in case she had to return.

"Where to now?" the boatman asked, as she dropped back among the damp cushions in the bows.

"Where can I find the procurator?"

"The procurator? The lawyer fellow? That'd be the Palace of Justice. No way you're getting in there, though. That's for the nobles."

"Has he got an estate?"

"Got a mansion to the south-west. It's a fair way: eight saviours to take you there."

"Fine."

"I don't know if they'll let you in. With respect, you don't look like his sort of people."

"We'll see when we get there."

She took the bottle from her bag and opened the packet that the alchemist had given her. She tipped the powder into her mouth and took a deep swig of wine, then sat back and waited for the magic to get to work.

The boat swung onto the Great Canal. It was late afternoon, and there was less traffic than the day before. Only a few barges crawled down the waterway. Narrow ferryboats like her own moved around them, flies around cattle. A boat passed by, and as the boatmen greeted each other, the other passenger looked straight at Giulia: a small, prim nobleman, looking both haughty and stricken with guilt. She wondered where he was going.

In the far distance she could see the masts of seagoing ships, ready to head to the Glass Islands and beyond. Something twinkled: one of the big houses on the far bank was plated in silver, too bright to be just polished metal. It looked like something from a story, a magical place knights might encounter on a quest. Giulia looked at the splendid row of mansions on the waterfront and thought, *This place could be beautiful – no, it is beautiful.*

"Slow down," she said. "Stop the boat."

He feathered the oars and brought them to a halt. She leaned over the edge and checked her reflection in the canal. The potion had done its work: the scars were invisible. Her cheeks looked entirely smooth. Giulia sat back up. The boatman stared at her face for a moment, then rowed on.

So, it works. She ran a finger down her face, feeling the scars. So long as he did not touch her, the procurator would be fooled. And he wouldn't be touching her.

Seeing her face without the scars was like meeting some long-lost sister. What would she be, this other, uncut Giulia: the wife of a wealthy artisan, used to luxury? Just as likely she'd be a petty thief still, or a washerwoman with half a dozen brats. Life might be hard, but she took nobody's orders now. She could fight for herself.

Which was precisely what she might have to do. There was a killer out there, hiding among thousands. She stared across the water at the magnificent sprawl of Averrio, and thought, *Where the hell are you?*

The grounds of the procurator's mansion backed onto the waterfront. Two guards stood on a broad jetty, and behind them steps rose up to a wall and an iron gate. The guards wore red-and-yellow striped uniforms and smart new armour.

The boat swung in towards the jetty, and one of the guards walked down to take the rope while his colleague stayed back, crossbow in hand.

"Afternoon," said the guard. He held the rope, not

tying it off. "What's this, then?"

"I'm here to see the procurator. I've got a letter." Giulia opened her bag and fished out the paper. She passed it to the guard. Under the jetty, the water lapped softly at the poles.

The guard looped the rope around a post. "Stay here," he told Giulia.

The two guards closed the door and left her on the jetty. She waited. The boatman folded his arms and dozed.

Behind the wall, in the grounds of the procurator's house, came the steady *ting* of a hammer on steel. It made her think of Varro's boatsheds. Where the hell was the guard? *Come on, come on, what's keeping you...*

The door opened, and the guard looked out. "Here you go," he said, and he gave her the letter back. "You can come up now."

"One moment, please." Giulia crouched down and counted out a pile of coins. "Here's ten saviours. You've been a real help, Mattia."

The boatman took the coins and stashed them out of view. "It's a pleasure," he replied. "Always good to have an interesting passenger. Would you fine fellows cast off the rope for me?"

One guard opened the gate while the other ushered Giulia through.

She was in a long, walled garden, beautiful and orderly like a tidy paradise. The grass was greener, the urns whiter than she'd ever seen in a city before, especially in winter. *Alchemy. They must put something in the soil.*

"This way," said the guard, and she heard his colleague step in close behind. She began to walk.

A paved path ran from the gate to the rear door of the house. Milk-white statues flanked the path, gazing over her head. One bearded figure stood over a fountain, a huge seashell in his hand. Another wore nothing but a crown of leaves, toasting the air with a massive cup. A huge statue threatened the clouds with an upraised club.

Giulia carried on, trying not to stare. The grounds had that smooth perfection that came from extreme wealth. Nothing showy, just everything in the right place. *Imagine robbing a place like this.*

Stone soldiers stood at the end of the path, as if to remind the procurator's men of their duty. Two more guards waited at an arched doorway. A bird twittered in a branch overhead. The guards stepped aside and one held the door open for her.

She walked into a cool, high-ceilinged room floored with a chequerboard of marble tiles. Religious paintings hung over fireplaces: on her left, Saint Jehann the Annunciator helped cherubs place a crown on the infant Alexis; on her right, Alexis himself hovered above a wondering crowd, wings outstretched. The gentle, reproaching eyes of the saints gazed out at her. They knew her guilt, she suddenly felt, knew how much forgiveness she would need to get into their Heaven. *You're just nervous*, she told herself. *Keep calm.*

She heard footsteps. A young man trotted down a staircase to her left. "Are you the young lady?"

Giulia resisted the impulse to look around for other young ladies. "Yes, that's me."

"If you would follow me, please?"

She followed him up two long flights of stairs, onto an airy landing. The wooden panels glowed in the afternoon sunshine as though they were about to catch light. Another pair of guards stood outside a wide, heavy-looking door. They carried halberds and wore armour and polished helmets. They looked like people used to violence.

The young man opened the door and slipped inside. He returned a moment later. "The procurator will see you now," he said, and ushered her in.

It was a plush, neat, slightly prissy room, dominated by a long desk of dark reddish wood. A thin man stood at the big window, arms crossed, watching the dusk creep across the garden. The light turned him into a near-silhouette. "One moment," he said crisply, not turning round. "Do sit, please."

Giulia pulled a chair back and sat down. The chair had curved, delicate legs, lacquered to a smooth shine. Everything in the room seemed sleek and perfect. She looked for somewhere to hang her cloak, saw nothing and shoved it under her seat.

"Francesco," said the procurator to the garden, "I need you to go to the Arsenal and tell them that they've had all the bronze they're getting off me. I'm not having those people melting my pieces down to make more stupid cannons. Have them lean on Moraldi: he collects the most awful tat. Got that? Can you do that for me?"

"Yes, sir," the young man said, and he left the room, pulling the door behind him. Giulia heard the latch click shut.

"Now, then." The procurator turned around. He wore a smart jerkin in the Berganian style, with a thin knife in his belt. He approached with his right hand raised slightly, like an actor about to declaim. He reminded her of Iacono, the mapmaker from the Scola.

Nobles. All alike.

She stood up and curtseyed. "It's an honour to meet you, noble sir."

For a second he studied her face, and something changed in his eyes. She wondered if he had seen through her disguise to the scars below – but the procurator merely smiled. "Likewise," he said. His voice was too clipped to sound friendly. "I apologise for not greeting you properly as you came in, but something of a crisis seems to have arisen. Do you know anything of art?"

"A little," Giulia said. "I've come across some bits in the past."

"Then I'm sure you know how *grim* it is to have someone try to strip one bare," the procurator said. He motioned to the objects on the walls: pictures of ancient scenes, and busts on little plinths. "And they want to make cannons out of my collection. For the good of the city, they say." The procurator huffed as he sat down. "For the good of a bunch of idiots! Would you like some wine?"

"Please."

He reached across to the wall. A length of red cord hung down beside the curtain. He tugged it, hard. Outside, a bell rang. The door opened and a guard looked in. "Bottle of wine, two glasses, thank you. And make it the good stuff." The door closed.

He turned back to Giulia and rubbed his chin. "Now, I understand you have a letter of authority from the Watch to come and see me about something. Could I see that, please?"

"Yes, sir. I thought they'd given it to you."

"No. My servant Francesco will have looked it over." He held out his hand; Giulia gave him the letter.

The procurator sat up as he studied the letter, as if expecting to have his portrait painted reading it. She waited, the fear of exposure winding a little tighter in her chest.

"Who wrote this, please?"

"I'm not sure, sir. A Watchman wrote it for me. He said he was quite high up."

"A large man, quite coarse?"

"I think so."

"Ah yes. It looks like 'Orvo' down here... Yes, this seems in order. Here."

"Thank you," she said, trying not to grin with relief. She took the letter back and folded it up.

"It is rather irregular of him, writing to me. I'd have thought he would simply raise the matter in the normal way." There was a hint of suspicion in the procurator's voice. "Do you know why that might be?"

"I'm afraid not, milord."

"I see. It's just that – well, no matter."

Giulia had been thinking he was going somewhere with this. *No*, she decided. He had simply wanted to point out how used he was to having things done his way.

"You're not from here, are you?"

"No, milord. I'm from Pagalia, originally."

"I don't recognise your name. I know most of the noted Pagalian families."

Do you, now? I've run into a few of them as well. Been inside their houses, too. "Well, there was a feud on the other side of the family, and some of us had to leave for fear of reprisals."

"Ah. A terrible business, vendetta. A cousin of mine had to flee Montalius in similar circumstances – poor, dear, sweet girl. Not as bad a situation as yours, from the sound of it, but she is from an exceptional family, and perhaps more delicate... It's a beautiful place, Montalius, but *fiercely* so. Now, then, to business. How can I help you?"

"It's about a friend of mine. He's been wrongly charged with a crime."

The procurator crossed his thin legs. "Go on."

Carefully, as if laying out the parts of some delicate machine, she told her story, starting with her arrival in Averrio. She explained about Hugh – a bold knight who had offered to ride with her as bodyguard – and Edwin, whom she described as a merchant of considerable standing with the Anglian parliament. Elayne was simply his wife: the Averrian authorities were not noted for their love of wizardry. She did not mention the Scola or the dryad dancer – there was no need to bring them into this. Nor did she describe her return visit to the Watch-house.

Her friends were victims of a plot, she explained, and for reasons unknown had been framed for a murder. Was it laziness among the Watch, or just mistaken identity? She couldn't possibly say. Although they could petition the Anglian government, it would be far quicker to go straight to the procurator. And of course, he could get the matter sorted out quietly, without all the embarrassment that the government of Anglia would cause.

He nodded sagely. "You say you looked into the matter somewhat. Do *you* have any idea who might be behind all this?"

Giulia paused. She had wanted to leave Varro out, to play the innocent newcomer. But whatever the conspiracy was, whoever was behind it, Varro was involved. And if she could direct suspicion towards Varro – who, if he had not murdered Coraldo, had certainly tried to kill Giulia – the four of them would be safe.

"Yes," she said, "I do."

Someone knocked on the door. A servant entered with wine. She sat there, watching the procurator test the bottle before allowing it to be poured. Rich people liked to make you wait for things. It was a way of showing that they had power over you.

"Carry on," he said, as the servant withdrew.

As she spoke, he got up and wandered to the window, staring out into the evening. It was getting dark now. He stood there, glass half-raised to his lips, listening.

"... and I was luckily able to grab a knife and cut him with it, before he had a chance to murder me," Giulia said. "I don't believe I killed Master Varro, merely wounded him, but I ran away as fast as I could, and I didn't see him after that."

"You didn't kill him," the procurator said. "I have it on good authority that he was in his yard today."

"He – he was?"

"Yes, of course. Go on."

She hesitated. What did that mean? Fear settled on her like the growing darkness outside, as if she'd just been told that Varro was in the building, healed and looking for revenge. "So, ah, I went back to the inn, and came out to talk to you. I thought you might be able to help."

The procurator turned from the window. "Yes, well, I'm not sure my powers extend quite that far. Do you know exactly what I do?"

"Not exactly, milord."

"I'm not a minister as such. I'm more a lawyer than anything else. I give advice to the Council of a Hundred where necessary. They tend to take it. But I think I may be able to help you out a little, yes." He sat down again. "So, what is it that you want me to do?"

"I'd like you to let us go," she said. "Milord."

"Which is presumably rather difficult at the moment. It would be far easier if we knew who killed this

Father Coraldo, wouldn't it, yes?"

"Yes."

"So once we have a man for that, there'd be no need to keep your friends here, would there?"

"No."

He frowned. "You're in some rather deep water, young lady. Rather deeper than you know, I think. I'm not sure you're telling me *quite* everything, but it doesn't matter. It can still be sorted out."

"Really?" She was surprised. Perhaps this man was useful after all. Perhaps the way out of this mess was clear from the lofty position he occupied. Maybe he could cut through the lies and hand her the solution on a plate.

"Oh, yes. We can sort it right now, in fact."

"Right now?" Something felt wrong. "You know who did it, then?"

"Of course. You did."

Gears seemed to lurch inside her. The whole room looked somehow different. "What?"

"You did it. Or at least that's what you're going to say." He leaned back in his chair and put his fingertips together.

She hadn't heard him wrong. "Me?" she managed to say, still astonished. Like a chill, the news was soaking through her.

"Of course. The answer to all of this seems simple to me. You're suffering from a derangement of the mind, brought on by illness. You killed Father Coraldo in your sleep, owing to an imbalance of the humours. Then, so deluded was your mind, you cooked up a story that a respected artisan like Ricardo Varro murdered him in some sort of black magic ritual. We can have a man in to write it up right now."

"You're mad," she said.

"Not at all. I'm the one trying to sort this mess out. I think my version of events is rather more credible than yours, don't you? There's a hospital on the Isle of Quarantine, where deluded people are allowed to stay. You'll be taken there, and looked after by the authorities—"

"Are you saying you're sending me to a fucking madhouse?"

"That's not a very tactful way of putting it. The treatment is very good. People do come back, you know. Anyway, in return for your agreement, your friends will be put on the first boat to Anglia. They'll go free."

"But I didn't do it."

"I think that's a matter of opinion."

He was too casual. There was no concern there, no fear that a murderer might be on the loose. "You do know who really did it," she said. "Don't you?"

"No, and if you think that I'd—"

Her voice was tight. "You know."

A smile crept out onto his face. "Do you really want to know?"

His smile pushed her over the edge. There was no reason to be servile now, no reason to show anything but fury and contempt. "Are you out of your fucking mind? You want to set me up as a murderer – a priest-killer – and you sit there and ask if I fucking *want to know*? Of course I want to know!"

Someone knocked on the door behind her. "Problem, sir?" the guard called through the door.

"No, no," the procurator called back. "All's well, thank you."

Giulia thought about the knife in her boot and the knife in her sleeve. "If I confess, my friends won't believe it. They'll come back for you. These are serious people I'm talking about. Connected people."

"That's a chance I'm willing to take." He opened his hands. "In this job, you take difficult decisions. I can live with that."

Rage made it hard to speak, to do anything much except stare and will him to die. The world seemed to narrow down to his face, as if she was looking at him down the barrel of a musket. *You bastard, you fucking bastard.* "And I'm just a decision," Giulia said.

"Quite. Not one I particularly like to take, though." He sat upright, as if he had been in danger of drifting off to sleep. "So then: the confession. Shall I attempt a first draft?"

"Yes, let's," she replied. "How about we start with 'Fuck you'?"

There was a moment's silence. The procurator seemed to be considering her suggestion. Suddenly he jabbed his head forward, and all the grace and poise was gone. "Now listen to me, my little friend," he hissed, "listen closely, because I'm about to give you a few home truths. You're nothing. You don't mean a thing here, not – one – thing. You're not worth a tenth of any one of the paintings in this room. The world's full of people like you, ugly little people all trying to crawl their way up to where they don't belong. You came here to fleece me with your shitty letter, this second-rate forgery, in my own home and now I've got you, and you don't even have the decency – *the basic decency!* – to admit that you're caught." He prodded himself in his narrow chest, his eyes wild. "*I'm* the one putting my neck out here. You don't know how much *I'm* looking out for you and your pissy, worthless friends – God knows why. I could have you all killed just like that." He snapped his fingers. "But I won't if – *if* – you agree. You can take what I've offered you, you can behave decently and leave this city with a degree of honour that I'll bet my life you've never had before."

She looked at him and thought, *If he screams, the guards will be in here in a second. This evil bastard knows that. But he reckons I'm unarmed. No-one's as clever as you think you are, Procurator.*

The procurator leaned back, sighed, and he was composed again.

"Or, you can choose not to take my advice. In which case, I'll pass you to my guards, who will do as they see fit with you, and then to the Watch, who will no doubt do likewise. And after that, you can make your confession to my friends in the proper authorities, who may well decide that you're not just a lunatic but a criminal and probably a heretic – and then, believe me, it won't be quick or clean at all."

Giulia looked at the dead man opposite, the trumped-up fool who thought that he had her pinned down. She wondered if he could ring the bell before she drew her knife, whether he could scream before she cut his throat.

"You really think you're something special, don't you?" she said.

"I'll count to ten, shall I? That might help you make up your mind, and I really don't have all day."

She looked over the desk. It was about three feet high. Nothing on the surface. If he wanted a confession, he'd need to fetch some ink. She looked around the room. There was ink and paper laid out on a table by the wall, artfully spread into a fan. In an alcove to her right, a small bronze maiden was riding a dolphin.

"One," he said, putting his fingertips together, "two—"

"I'll sign."

"I thought you might."

"Paper," she said, shifting in her chair.

He twisted around to look, and she leaned forward, tensing her legs. He saw the paper on the table at the wall. "Ah, yes."

The procurator turned again, and Giulia stood up and grabbed at the alcove. Her hand closed around cold bronze. He heard her and turned, and she swung the statue. It met his head just above the ear with a thick, heavy sound, sending a jolt up her arm. He staggered back, eyes wide, and stumbled into his chair like a drunk. His mouth opened and closed as if underwater. Then he slid onto the floor.

"Son of a bitch," Giulia said. She was panting.

She glanced at the door. Nothing. She looked back. Behind the desk, the procurator was moving. He moved very slowly, without any clear purpose, like a crawling beetle.

Giulia wondered if she should cut his throat. She hesitated.

The procurator threw himself against the wall. His shoulder bumped loudly against the plaster.

Giulia lunged and grabbed the bell-rope, lifted it out of reach. The procurator's hand rose and clutched the air spasmodically – and then he fell back down.

Very slowly, Giulia lowered the bell-rope. It didn't ring. She sighed.

There was a knock at the door. A voice called, "Sir?"

She spun to face the door. Giulia glanced about

for weapons, ways out – anything. There were none. The procurator kept paintings on his walls, not swords.

"Sir?"

"Um, we're fine in here," she said, her voice as deep as she could make it. She put the statue on the desk.

"Sir, I thought I heard—"

"No, we're fine," she called out, looking for something – anything at all – that would help. "Thanks all the same."

"Sir, I think I—"

She stepped to the door and slid the bolt. She slid the other bolts, top and bottom. A fist hammered on the door. "Sir!"

Giulia looked at the window. She was four storeys up, with guards and paving stones below.

Oh God no.

She reached to her back and loosened her dress, then yanked it over her head. It dropped onto the floor in a puddle of cloth.

Giulia stood in her undershirt, britches, and boots. She put her cloak on and pulled up the hood. The air felt cold on her face and hands.

The hammering became pounding. "Open up! Open up right now!"

She threw the window open and looked out. It was nearly dark.

It must be fifty feet to the ground.

No chance of getting down, then. The only way out was up. Something heavy hit the door.

Cold night air wrapped itself round her, and she shivered. This was going to be hard.

Another blow struck the door. Only moments to go. She climbed onto the windowsill.

Dear God, dear Archangels, Saint Senobina, patron of thieves, protect me.

The wind whipped across the building, threw her cloak against her. Giulia looked up. The front of the building was covered in statues and ornamental pillars. There were stone columns on either side of the window, and a plaster pediment across the top of them. *Handholds.*

She turned and stood up on the outside of the windowsill. The sense of being outside, being able to fall, almost overwhelmed her.

Come on. Do it.

Giulia grabbed the top of the pediment, braced herself and pushed up with her legs. Her shirt came untucked: the stonework grazed the skin of her stomach. She hauled with all her strength and got her elbows onto the top of the pediment, legs thrashing below.

Another crash against the door. Wood crunched. Giulia gritted her teeth. Her boot knocked against something, bumped off, found the column again, and she dug her toes into the fretwork and pushed herself up onto the roof.

The door broke open. Boots pounded into the room beneath her, a voice yelled "Oh my God!" and a second cried "The window! The window!" Feet rushed across the room.

Up, now. The roof was gently sloped, with a white railing around the edge. She grabbed the railing and pulled herself up.

"The roof! There's someone on the roof!"

She glanced back: in the gardens, tiny people pointed up at her. "Fetch a musket! Somebody get up there!"

Her arms ached: her upper body was sweat and ice.

Someone had climbed onto the window-ledge, and his friends were passing him a gun.

She braced herself and thought, *Go!* Giulia pushed with her legs and heaved herself over the railing.

A musket fired. Giulia rolled onto the roof, cloak ripping as a bullet tore straight through. She flopped onto on her back, exhausted, panting at the sky.

"Can't get him!" the man cried below. "Dammit, give me that!"

She lay there, her muscles screaming at her, desperate to rest and knowing that her enemies were closing in. Her arms felt as if they had been torn on the rack. *Get up*, she told her body. *Get up, damn you!* Giulia moaned and rolled over and struggled to her feet. Something streaked past her face, and she flinched back into the dark. A crossbow bolt clattered on the roof.

Her belly was scratched, her shoulder raw. The cloak hung off her back like a dead tail.

Got to go. Find Hugh. Get off the roof.

How? The night was full of voices: there was no chance of getting down the front of the building. Giulia ran to the other side of the house and saw her chance: a tiled roof like the back of a church, built beside the mansion but a storey lower.

I can do this. I just need a run-up. I can do this.

She jogged back, and a bolt sailed over her head. People shouted under her, a jumble of voices all saying the same thing: Get her, shoot her, get the woman on the roof.

Giulia ran, legs pounding under her, heard a gun crack to her left, sprang onto the railing and jumped. Her legs drove out, her body flicked forward like the arm of a catapult. Then she was falling – the wind rushing in her ears, cloak flapping behind her – and there was nothing underneath. She seemed suspended, looking down at her flailing legs and the long, fatal drop, with only the wind and cold and the sickness in her gut to tell her that she was moving at all.

She hit the tiled roof, rolled, came up staggering. Tiles slithered under her boots, dropped off the edge and tinkled as they smashed below. An old man's voice cried "Hey, look!" and she made herself run again, along the building's spine.

Keep moving. Jump down in stages, house-to-house.

Someone shouted behind her. That meant they had people on the procurator's roof. A gun cracked and tiles burst a yard from her feet.

Giulia saw a chance and went left. She scrambled down the tiles, onto the ridge of a dormer window, sped up to keep her balance and jumped again, only six feet this time, hit the next roof in a crouch and paused to take a breath.

And there was Averrio in front of her, a mass of rooftops, each a scale on a dragon's back, threaded with canals like veins. She saw the Palace of a Hundred squatting on the waterfront, the silver mansion she'd glimpsed this afternoon still twinkling in the dark, the five milk-white domes of the cathedral rising up on the far side of Palace Square as if to challenge the palace of the Decimus. She drew in a deep breath, awed despite herself, and then heard her pursuers closing in.

Torches were gathering in the streets, weaving their way towards her. A dog barked, a low, throaty sound.

They'll try to cut me off.

Giulia jogged across the roof. She recognised a square tower to the west: that was the way to the Old

Arms. Keeping low, she turned that way and saw what she'd wanted: a tenement with an outside staircase.

This time it was hardly a jump at all. She went down backwards, easing her grazed body over the edge, dangling from fingertips until the last moment. Giulia dropped onto the stairs in a shower of loose tiles.

She wanted to rest. *Not yet*. She hurried down the steps on aching legs. Halfway down the stairs she saw a wall below, and behind it, an ornamental garden.

It was easy to slip under the handrail, to jump onto the wall and drop down into the shadows of the garden. In the dark, surrounded by the smell of grass, Giulia leaned against the rough bricks and tried to recover.

I killed him, she thought. *Self-defence, but that doesn't matter. It's all ruined now. Everything's done. Have to get the others, get far away from here.*

From somewhere to the left she could hear men calling to each other. Their voices were loud but indistinct. She waited. They didn't come any closer.

There was a little wooden door on the far side of the garden. It ought to lead back into the city. Once there, she could slip through the streets and be away. She started towards the door, keeping close to the wall.

Falsi had been right: this went deep. The procurator knew who had murdered Coraldo. And he ran the Watch. *God, the whole fucking city's in on it.*

Now that she was going slower, the cold closed in on her, tightening like a fist. She felt something, and she pulled her hood up and stopped.

An animal stood on the far side of the lawn. It was too broad to be a dog, but too long and skinny for a bear. Fear swelled up inside her like fever.

Steam pumped from its muzzle. Patches of bare

skin shone where there was no fur. The creature wore no collar, but someone had tied a belt around its upper arm. It took a step into the moonlight, snorted, and stood upright.

Ghoul.

Its mouth opened and she saw teeth glint like polished marble. It yawned.

You can't see me, she thought. *Don't look at me.*

The beast's head swung left, then right. It sniffed the air, raised its hands and thoughtfully cracked the knuckles.

The truth dropped onto her like a weight. She was looking at the murderer. It loped away from her, deeper into the garden.

Giulia took a step to the left. She kept in close to the wall, deep in shadow. She took another step. The sweat felt freezing as it dried on her stomach and back. She slid the knife from her sleeve.

Keeping close to the wall, Giulia started to walk towards the door on the far side of the garden. Ten steps in and she looked behind her. The thing had gone. She opened the door and slipped into the city. Fifty yards on, she gave in to her instincts and ran.

EIGHT

She stepped into the Old Arms and stopped dead. The front room had been torn apart. Chairs and tables were smashed, a window broken. A long smear of blood ran down one wall.

Movement on the left. Giulia turned, reaching for her knife. Elayne rushed over to her, sleeves flapping. Alarm caricatured her face, accentuating her wide eyes.

"Giulia, thank goodness! She's here, everyone!" Then, "My God, what happened to you?"

"I'll explain later," Giulia said. "We're leaving."

"Damn right we are," Edwin said. He stepped out of the rear of the inn, his face set and hard. "We're getting out, right now."

"Where's Hugh?"

"Getting the horses ready."

Giulia looked about, trying to find some reason for the mayhem around her. "What happened? Where is everyone?"

"They ran," Elayne said. "An animal broke in. I don't know what it was - magical, I think. It came in through the window there. It was like a mastiff, or a wolf, but much bigger. We managed to kill it—"

Giulia said, "Did it walk upright? On two legs?"

"How did you know?"

"I saw it. Or I saw something like it, I'm not sure. Listen, things turned really bad out there. The procurator tried to pin the murder on me. He was in league with whoever did it. I knocked him out... I think."

"What happened to your dress?"

"I had to do some running. It's back there with the procurator." Giulia pinched the bridge of her nose. "Falsi said this went high up. Shit... What did you do with the animal?"

"We dragged it over there, round the corner." Edwin grimaced. Giulia took a step towards the back of the room. "You won't like it."

A body lay in the shadows. It looked like a starved, shaven bear.

You could know what was coming, but still be repulsed all the same. The lower body was an animal's: the legs were jointed wrongly and half-furred, as though the man's pubic hair had spread over his thighs and back like mould. The feet were particularly horrible, she thought: the contorted delicacy of the toes made her nauseous. It looked like something she'd seen in a picture, a cavorting thing from the deep woods. A satyr, that was the word. She felt oddly relieved to give this abomination a name, however ill-fitting.

"We all fought it," Elayne said. "Hugh and I distracted it, then Edwin hit it in the back of the neck—"

"Through the spine," Edwin said. "It wasn't like any animal I've ever seen. Dog, bear, God knows: it looked like a whole load of things."

"I thought it was a ghoul," Giulia said. "I saw them at an abbey, back in Pagalia. Wait—"

She crouched down, half-knowing what she would see. Giulia made herself examine the creature's face. The lips bulged with teeth, and the nose was smaller than before, but she recognised its features all the same. She made the Sign of the Sword across her chest.

"It's Varro, the man from the boatyard. The one who tried to kill me." Giulia looked round at them. "God almighty. No wonder his wounds sealed back up. He was a monster."

Hugh called from the doorway. "Giulia? Are you all right?"

She straightened up and nodded. "We've got to go. They'll be looking for us."

"I know," he replied. "The horses are ready. I put all your things in your saddlebag. You need another shirt," the knight added. "You'll catch a cold like that."

"In a minute. Let's get moving."

"The north gate'll be sewn up tight," Edwin said. "I suggest we keep to the back alleys and work back towards the harbour. We can get out on my ship. The crew should all still be on board."

Hugh said, "What's the wind like?"

Elayne said, "I can summon a breeze to get us out of port. After that, it'll be fine."

"Your ship'll be watched," Giulia said.

"I don't see that we've got much choice," Edwin replied. "Besides, we beat this monster. We can deal with whatever else we find."

Hugh smiled. "Well said."

"What about the horses?"

"We'll try and get them onto the deck," Edwin said. "My crew can help." He looked from face to face. "Anyone got a better plan? No? Then let's go."

As she stepped outside, she saw faces: good citizens of Averrio, watching. Giulia saw a woman in a cloth cap shrink back like a revenant confronted with a holy sign. People stared at them from the edge of the road, from upstairs windows – horrified and appalled, but not so much that they didn't want to see.

"Let's move," Giulia said.

They hurried to the stable at the side of the inn. The horses were nervous, shy in their stands. "Must've smelt that thing," Hugh said. "Whatever it was."

Giulia fished her black shirt from her saddlebag. As she pulled it on, she saw that her arms and stomach were dirty and grazed. She fastened her knives to her belt as Edwin untied the reins.

Hugh took hold of the stirrup. "No," Giulia said. "We'll walk to begin with. Easier that way."

Giulia's horse drew back, head raised. Its teeth flashed in the moonlight.

"Damn thing's lost its nerve," said Hugh.

Elayne slipped inside the stable and whispered something to the nearest horse. It lowered its head, placated. Giulia looked over at Hugh. He had gone quiet as well, watching Elayne. The blank smile on his face made Giulia feel uneasy.

Edwin was last to be ready. "All set?" he asked, fastening a cloak across his shoulders.

Elayne stepped back. "Yes, I'm fine."

"Let's go," Edwin said, and they led the horses into the street.

Giulia's crossbow jutted out of the saddlebag, lurching with the horse's every step. She glanced back. Figures moved towards the inn at the edge of her vision, like little animals creeping out under the cover of night.

Maybe they wanted to see the damage, or maybe they just wanted to steal the wine.

"Quickly, now," Edwin said.

They left the Old Arms behind them, empty and wrecked. *Good fucking riddance*, Giulia thought.

***

Azul's knee was giving him trouble again. It was a steady, constant ache, behind the kneecap. It was weak to give in to pain, but he still scowled as he climbed the last few stairs.

The procurator's guards waited on the landing. They were well-equipped but slack, Azul thought. Soldiers were, these days. Horror had knocked the discipline out of them and turned them into startled, frightened men.

The one on the right said, "Halt and state your name and business."

"My name is Ramon Azul. My business is with the procurator."

The guard hesitated, then said, "They told me you were coming, milord. You can go through."

"Did my man Cortaag get here?"

"He's inside, milord." The guard opened the office door for him. "Milord, is the procurator going to live?"

"Go downstairs with the rest of the guards," Azul replied. "Watch the doors. If a woman called Alicia shows up, send her to me."

Cortaag waited inside. He stood up in the centre of the room, his broad shadow falling across the body at his feet. The procurator was sprawled across the carpet as though he had fallen out of the rafters. A dress lay under the window.

Azul turned and closed the doors. "Is he dead?"

Cortaag shook his head. He looked as if he'd been running. His hair was ruffled, sticky with sweat. His jacket lay discarded on the chair. "He's breathing. But only just." He picked up his jacket. Standing over the procurator as he pulled it on, it looked as if Cortaag was leaving after an illicit liaison.

Azul took off his spectacles and scowled at the lenses. "I take it you couldn't catch her."

The big man glanced away, as if he expected to have to soak up a blow. "She was too quick."

"That's unfortunate."

"She hit him with this," Cortaag said. He held up the bronze sculpture. The corner of the base was dark red.

"And then what?"

Cortaag nodded at the window. "She took her dress off and climbed out there."

"What?"

Cortaag glanced at the floor. "She had men's clothes on under the dress. She must have been expecting trouble."

"I'm sure she was." Azul stepped over to the window, opened it and looked down into the gardens. "It's a long way down."

"She went up," Cortaag said.

Azul looked up. He leaned out of the window and took in the complex façade, the columns and handholds. *Yes,* he thought, *someone could do that, if you had the skill. It would take a hell of a lot of determination.* It was interesting how the prospect of imminent death weakened some people and strengthened others. Some wilted and just froze, or wept, in the face of danger. Others became filled with rage and cunning. You never knew which you'd get until they were tested.

"She climbed over the rooftops," Cortaag said. "The guards tried to catch her, but..." He ran a hand through his thick hair. "She lost me in a garden to the north. She got away."

"So I see," Azul replied.

Two bronze horses reared up on either side of the fireplace. Busts of Quaestan emperors stared blindly over the body in the centre of the room. Azul stood there for a moment, breathing it all in.

A light breeze blew through the window, and the curtains stirred like seaweed in the tide.

"Felsten, this has not been a good week for you."

Cortaag looked at the floor. "I know. I'm sorry, sir."

"First the priest, then this. It won't do."

"I apologise."

Azul stepped in close to him. "Lift your head, Felsten. Present yourself like a soldier, not a schoolboy."

Cortaag's back stiffened; his heels struck together. He stood bolt upright, tensed. Azul looked into Cortaag's eyes and knew that his servant was trying not to flinch. Azul had seen that look many times before. He'd be wondering where the blow would fall.

"Much better," Azul said.

"Varro should have dealt with the others by now," Cortaag said. Azul knew he disliked silences. "I sent Alicia to check on him."

"Good." Azul crouched down and pressed his finger to the procurator's neck. The pulse was faint. He looked over the body, saw the blood on the side of the man's head. Very gently, Azul touched the wound. It felt spongy. Fractured.

He removed the glove from his left hand. His left

thumb had no nail. Below the knuckle, the skin became dry and smooth. The end of his thumb was covered in scales.

A slit opened at the tip of his thumb, widened, became a wet, pink mouth. Two long fangs folded down, slick with venom.

Azul pressed his thumb to the procurator's neck. The snake's jaws pinched the procurator's flesh, and the fangs slipped through his skin. Azul willed the poison to flow, and felt a little rush down his arm as the venom glands emptied into the lawyer's bloodstream. He lifted his hand away. The mouth closed.

"She murdered him. It's tidier this way," he said, standing up again. He pulled his glove back on. "I never liked him. He was like a scallop: hard on the outside, but soft deep down."

Cortaag smiled.

Someone knocked on the door. Azul called out, "Enter."

It was Alicia. She closed the door behind her. "Varro is dead," she said.

"What? Where?"

"The Old Arms, where they were staying. They are gone. We found his body there."

"Shit!" Azul's mouth drew down into a scowl; his cheeks drew in. "They'll try to leave the city. Cortaag?"

"Sir?"

"Get down there now. Remove Varro's body. Destroy it – I don't want another corpse floating in the canal. Get your men together and find these people. Take them alive if you can, but if they give you any trouble – kill them."

"Yes, sir!" Cortaag bowed and left the room.

Alicia stood near the door. She looked dreamy,

almost wistful. "Warn Benevesi about this," Azul said. "Tell him to make sure nothing leads back to the bank."

Alicia nodded. "I will."

"Five days until our guests arrive," Azul said. "I trust you have your party dress ready?"

Alicia beamed. "Oh, yes. I'm all set for it. The servants are ready, the food's been brought in."

"Good. Because this fucking mess had better be cleared up by then." Azul looked down at the procurator. "Fetch the guards. Tell them that their master is dead."

***

The city was dark and cold, and a light, chill rain sliced the sky. Giulia could see her own breath. *I want to be out of here*, she thought, and with the thought came a tremor of fear. Her horse paused as if it sympathised. *Easy*, she told herself. *Stay calm.*

It had been a bad idea to bring the horses at all. She had seen a few bored mules in the streets of Averrio, but nothing larger. *We stand out like this, even more than usual. I'd try to ride out, if I didn't think I'd end up in the canal.*

As they walked, she tried to think about the last few days as if she wasn't involved. It made her feel a little better. The scraps of information seemed to turn and slide together in her mind, starting to form a blurred, incomplete picture.

The procurator had known the identity of Father Coraldo's murderer, but she'd not had the chance to get a name out of him. Chances were, it had been Varro, but that wasn't important now. Varro was dead and the Watch wouldn't believe her anyway.

She glanced left and right, looking for enemies,

feeling like a sitting duck. *We should have left the stuff at the inn and just run*, she thought. *What the hell is in Elayne's saddlebags that's worth dying for?*

She felt sure that the procurator was not at the top of the conspiracy. He had been ruthless, yes, but he seemed to lack something, some degree of originality, or the sheer balls to come up with such a bold, callous plan. That meant that somebody very important was pulling the strings. But why had Coraldo been killed at all?

It didn't matter very much now. In an hour, with luck, they would be on Edwin's ship, slipping out of the city and away from danger. By dawn they could be twenty miles down the coast.

She felt a pang of regret that she would never be able to settle up with the bastard who had tried to frame her. It would have been good to know that he'd got what he deserved. Still, at least she was alive. After this evening's events, that was good enough.

"Here we are," Edwin said. "Stop here."

They were on the eastern edge of the Great Canal. They stood beside a wide, empty square. The canal ran along the right side of the square. On the far side, a forest of pillars stood in front of a huge white building.

"That's the ship," Edwin said, and he pointed. Giulia peered towards the canal: she saw the low bulk of the *Margaret of Cheswick*, the masts sticking up like spines. *Fifty yards away, at least.*

"Can we call your crew?" Hugh asked.

Edwin shook his head. "Best not risk it."

Giulia said, "You think it's a trap?"

"I don't know. Do you think it is?"

"It's very quiet," she replied. "But that could mean

anything."

Almost nothing moved on the canal. A few lanterns bobbed on small boats like lazy fireflies. Moonlight brushed the water: without it, the Great Canal could have been a dark canyon through the city's heart.

Edwin pointed to the pillars. "The House of Exchange," he said.

"What do you think?" Elayne said.

Giulia found her mouth was dry, even though the air felt damp. "I'll look ahead. It seems clear, but..." She slid her crossbow from the horse's saddlebag. She loaded up a bolt. "I'll check there's no-one there. If you see me wave, come across."

"Right," said Elayne.

Hugh had been gazing across the square. "Will you be safe?"

"I should be." Giulia checked the bow.

"We'll wait here," Edwin said.

Elayne reached in and embraced Giulia. "Good luck," she said.

It's only fifty yards, Giulia thought.

She ducked low and ran along the side of the square. Above her, two pale statues gazed overhead: wide-hipped women, tridents in their hands.

Giulia reached the pillars and slipped between them, into a forest of dead white trees. She stepped into the shadow of a pillar and pressed her back against the stone.

The shadows were like great bars along the ground. The world seemed to be drained of colour, pitch-black and marble-white.

Giulia looked behind her. She could just make out the others at the edge of the square. They were discussing something. It looked like a minor argument. Giulia jogged into a shaft of moonlight, then the next shadow dropped over her. She looked back again, and Elayne waved.

Giulia wanted to wave back, but the way was not yet clear. Then she realised that Elayne was not waving, but pointing: not at Giulia, but at something to her left.

Giulia looked left. She raised her crossbow and looked down the line of columns. Nobody moved.

Hugh stepped into the square. Giulia showed him the palm of her hand. He paused and moved back into the dark.

Slowly, silently, Giulia crept between the columns. She stopped and pressed her back against the reassuring stone.

She saw movement on the side of a high building, and the bow flicked up in her hands. Something slid across the roof. It looked like a falling leaf. It was a tile.

Someone's up there.

Footsteps behind her and she whipped round. Her finger relaxed. Hugh stopped beside her, out of the moonlight.

"Dammit, Hugh, didn't I tell you to stay back?"

He spoke in a low, hoarse whisper. "Elayne saw somebody. Over there."

"On the roof?"

Hugh nodded. "Let's get him."

"What about the others? Are they safe?"

"She's fine."

"Good. Follow me."

Hugh pulled his cloak around his scabbard, muffling the sound as he drew his sword. Giulia scurried forward between the pillars. She heard him behind her, light on his feet, breathing carefully as he ran.

Elayne screamed. Giulia turned and saw people on the building behind them, half a dozen of them, a row of men and half-men scrambling over the peak of the roof. Hugh yelled, "Elayne!"

The men on the roof let out a ragged cheer. Giulia aimed and fired. One of the beast-men stumbled and rolled towards them. Hugh tore across the square, sword raised. Edwin was drawing his own sword. Elayne shouted something and threw out her hand. A man paused on the roof, framed against the sky, then staggered back and dropped out of view.

There was no time to reload. Giulia drew her long knife and ran after Hugh.

Lights shone on the water, swinging in to the bank. What was that? Giulia saw a long, low boat, plated with armour at the bows, great wheels spinning behind it. As the men poured into the square, a crewman on the boat tore a sheet back, and Giulia saw a bundle of tubes threaded onto a clockwork spindle. The man swung the tubes on their mounting, lined them up with Hugh—

She screamed "Hugh!" and the organ gun roared. Hugh vanished. She looked right, saw him crumpled on the ground, and she ran towards him, shouting his name. Something howled in agony; Edwin was bellowing like an ox. A great weight slammed into her head – the world went white – and she lurched upright, spitting and cursing, swiped at a shadow and her legs gave way again. She fell onto all fours, and then the world was swirling away from her like so much steam, spinning away until all she saw was blackness, and then not even that.

NINE

The world was one long tunnel, and Giulia was at the end of it. No, not a tunnel, a well: and she was at the bottom, looking up.

She could feel her back, then her legs. Suddenly she was alive again, and knew that she was somewhere with a low roof that smelt of earth. *Earth*, she thought. *I must be underground*, and with that the pain in the back of her head seemed to flood her skull and swallow her, and it all went dark again.

***

Hugh came around slowly, piece by piece, but he did not move. Lying on the ground, one eye open, he looked at the sky and tried to work out how badly injured he was. There was a vague, steady pain down his upper left arm, and his chest ached as he drew breath. The breastplate didn't seem to fit very well. For a moment that worried him, and then he realised that it had taken the force of the blast. They must have used grapeshot.

He heard boots crunching on stone, to his left. The men were eight or nine yards away, two of them.

Hugh remembered the dryad instructor from years ago, teaching him how to get the jump on dishonourable enemies. He imagined his soul drawing back into his heart, hiding there like a badger lurking in a sett, bracing itself to spring.

Very carefully, Hugh moved his hand to his side.

A voice said, "This the old man, then?"

"What's it look like? Better check him. He might be shamming."

"Will do. Don't want the boss coming down on me. Right, you old whoreson: end of the road."

Hugh listened to their foreign sing-song accents, imagined the men waving their hands as they spoke, the way they did abroad. He closed his fingers around the knife on his belt.

A boot came down close to his head. He shut his eye, which was the most painful thing he'd done so far. The man gave a little grunt as he swung something up into the air.

Hugh rolled over, drawing the knife as he moved, and punched it into the side of the man's knee. The thug howled fit to split the sky. Hugh hauled himself up as the would-be killer fell. Hugh shoved him aside, picked up the hammer the man had dropped, and stood up straight. He swung the hammer to test its weight.

The second man stood a little way back, a knife in hand, watching his comrade rolling on the cobbles.

Hugh put a foot on the fallen man's neck and whipped the hammer down into his skull. He wrenched the hammer-head free. The knife-man gasped and turned to flee. In two strides Hugh caught up with him. The first swing of the hammer took his legs out, and the second shut him up for good.

Hugh nodded, satisfied. He hurt, but it wasn't too bad. It took more than a couple of louts to stop a knight. Getting up had been the hard part. The rest would come easily.

***

Giulia felt cold against her lips, smooth, cold glass. The bottle tipped and water ran into her mouth and trickled down over her chin. She swallowed. It tasted sour and sharp, like bad wine. She coughed and spat.

A hand touched her brow. "It's fine. It's a healing drink." An old man's voice, soothing and gentle. The bottle tipped again, and she took another sip. "There."

She opened her eyes and saw a small man in an empty, dark-walled room. The candlelight glinted on his scalp. He wore dark gloves and a leather apron. His sleeves were rolled to the elbows.

Her body ached. It was very warm in here. A strand of hair had fallen in front of her eyes. She wanted to brush it away, but her arm wouldn't move. Why was that?

She was tied to the chair.

Wide awake, horrified, she thrashed in the seat, yanked her wrists back and forth. The chair shook but nothing broke. She tried again, one big, long pull against the ropes, heard herself grunt. It did nothing. She stopped, panting. The old man took a step back.

Fear churned in her stomach like a live eel.

"It's all right," the man said again, and she knew that he was lying. "I gave you a potion to help wake you up," he said. His voice was a slow, educated croak, the accent hard to place. He had that permanent scowl that came to some old people, as if he disapproved of everything he saw.

"It also causes alertness and loquacity," he explained. "It loosens the tongue." His tortoise face managed a smile. "Which will help both of us."

Someone was standing behind her. She thrashed again, and the old man waited for her to stop. Her face was wet, and she realised it was sweat. She needed to piss.

"You won't be violated, don't worry. I have no interest in you, in that respect. As a matter of fact, I find you very unattractive." The little man folded his arms. A huge scar ran from his elbow to his wrist, curling around his arm and disappearing into his glove. It had been tattooed to look like a serpent: not blue ink, but some kind of shiny stuff to resemble snakeskin. It glistened. "All I need you to do is answer a few questions for me. Truthfully, of course."

The person behind her stepped out. For a moment there was a blur at the edge of Giulia's vision, and then she saw her: a tall, long-necked, sandy-haired woman, handsome but hard along the jawline.

"So you better talk, eh?" the woman said, and as Giulia noticed that she had a strong accent, the woman hit her in the face.

She heard the slap of the woman's hand. The world flashed white for a moment, and then there was pain across her cheek and ear, and the little man barked, "Alicia! Never strike a prisoner unless I say!"

The woman stepped back quickly. There was a stupid grin on her face. *Crazy*, Giulia realised.

"I will see you later, then," she said, and she strode out of the room.

"My apologies," said the old man. He sounded as if he meant it. "I am many things, but a barbarian is not one of them. Now, then." He approached, shrugging his shoulders. Giulia drew back as far as the chair would allow. He stepped off to her right, out of view. She saw that there was another man at the back of the room, a broad-chested fellow with a beard. He had no expression at all.

The old man was doing something behind her. She needed to know what it was, but she desperately didn't want to know. She realised she could hear a crackling sound, a sound that she would hardly register, normally. A fireplace. He was tending the fire.

"Look," she said, "I don't know who you are, or what you want, but— I don't know anything. I'll tell you what I know but, listen to me, you've got the wrong person."

"You are a very resilient young lady," the old man said. "The last few days are testament to that. I admire your fortitude."

Metal scraped on brick. She wanted him to stay there forever, because when he came back, something terrible would happen.

"But the work of my little group cannot be jeopardised, not now. I need to know who sent you here, what your mission was, and how much you know about us."

She heard him stand up. Light came with him, and as he stepped into view she saw the poker in his hand. The whole world shrank down to the glowing tip of the poker.

Her breath came out in shuddery little gasps. "Now wait, listen to me—"

"Oh, I will. Have no doubt about that. My friend and I here, we're very good listeners. We may as well start at the beginning," said the little man. "I think we've got time, haven't we?"

The big man said, "We've got time."

Giulia drew back from the poker, up against the back of the chair. She struggled again, tensed her legs and arms.

"Tell me what you know about the New World Order."

"Please," she said, "I don't know anything."

"Are you quite sure about that?" he replied, and he pressed the poker against her arm.

She talked. There was no question of holding out.

The important thing, the only thing, was to talk as much as possible, to keep the poker away from her. She had to keep speaking, had to keep him interested.

So she started with the easy things, things that didn't matter. She told him about herself. He liked that. He nodded as she explained about Pagalia, about Astrago, about thief-taking. She told him that she could read and write, and that sometimes people had paid her to write letters for them. That didn't interest him much, and he stood up and wandered towards the fire.

"I want to know about the knight," he said.

God in Heaven, her arm hurt. He'd touched the poker to her upper arm for a few seconds, but the pain had felt as if she was going to die. It had burst out of her arm like a parasite, flooded down to her fingers, soaked through her shoulder and neck. She thought she could smell herself burning, roasting like pork.

Every breath hurt. Sometimes, for a whole few seconds, she'd have it under control, but then it would rush back, pounding through her flesh like a drum that couldn't be silenced, as though she'd started to rot.

He stepped out of view and she heard the poker on

the hearth. He was heating it up again. Terror flooded her, made her crazy with fear. "Listen to me, listen to me!" she yelled.

So she told them about Hugh. The man listened for what felt like an age. She told him what Hugh was like, how they'd met – the old man raised his eyebrows and she swore it was true – anything she could think of to avoid getting to the other stuff. Talking about Edwin and Elayne terrified her, because she didn't know much about them and he wouldn't believe her.

He stepped back into view, without the poker. Maybe that was a good thing. Maybe he would be friends.

"Your colleagues don't interest me, Giulia," he said. He spoke very carefully. "I want to know all about the New World Order."

"I – I don't know what that is."

He hesitated. "Hmm." Stepped out of view. Then back and – *Oh, God, please no* – the poker was back in his hand.

"Your arm will scar," he said. "It won't be pretty, but it won't be painful, either." He turned to his chair and carefully touched the poker to the middle of the seat. He watched it scorch the wood. "The New World Order, Giulia. Does that sound familiar to you?"

"Please, I don't know. Please."

"You're not trying. Remember what I can do to you."

She screamed it at him: "I *am* trying! I don't know! I don't fucking know! Listen to me, I don't fucking know what it is! Why won't you listen to me? Open your fucking ears, you deaf little prick! I – don't – know! I – don't – know!"

"I didn't ask if you knew what it *was*. I asked if

you'd heard of it before. *Think*, please. I know you're very frightened, but if you don't think, I will push this deep into your flesh and give you wounds that will never heal." He lifted the poker and examined the glowing tip. "It is possible to die of pain, you know. They killed one of the kings of Albion that way, many years ago."

"The priest said about the New World Order," she said. "Father Coraldo."

"Good!" He glanced at the bearded man, who nodded approvingly. "See? You do know. You can do it when you put your mind to it. Good girl."

He reached forward with his empty hand, towards her face, her eyes. The snake tattoo writhed as if there was a live serpent beneath his skin. Giulia cringed back, found there was nowhere left to go. And to her absolute revulsion, he smiled and ruffled her hair.

***

Azul tapped Cortaag on the shoulder and they left the room. In the corridor, he pulled off his gloves and said, "She's told us all she knows."

"Then can we clear up and go?" The big man took up the whole passage, like a portrait too large for its frame. "I'm sick of listening to her. Besides, who is this Publius Severra, anyway? Did she really kill him, like she said?"

Azul licked his lips. "He was a minor nobleman from Pagalia. A thorn in our side, as a matter of fact: he was trying to strike a deal with the Anglian embassy when someone cut his throat. If she did murder him, which I very much doubt, she did us something of a favour." Azul looked at the door, suddenly very aware of the woman on the other side of it. "But if she did half of what she says,

I'd be surprised."

Cortaag scowled. He leaned forward slightly, ready for violence. "She's lying, even now?"

Azul shook his head. "Not knowingly. By this stage she'll just be telling us anything she thinks we'd like to hear. It happens." He looked at his left hand. "I'm out of venom for now. Get Alicia and walk our guest out to the yard."

Cortaag nodded and moved towards the door.

Azul raised a hand. "Oh, and not the canal this time. Put the body on the cart out back and take it to the warehouse. We'll get rid of the remains once we're there. And don't allow yourself to change. Have some self-control this time. It's that which got us into all this trouble to begin with."

It took a few minutes for Cortaag to fetch Alicia from upstairs. She came down, scowling.

"You took too long," Azul said, looking the pair of them over. "What were you doing?"

"Nothing," she said.

"You were sulking. You need to sharpen up, both of you. Varro got slack, and look what happened to him. We've got hard work to do before the others get here. Understand?"

"Yes, sir," Cortaag said.

"I understand," Alicia replied.

"Good." Azul turned to the door. "Now, let's deal with our guest."

Giulia Degarno sat slumped in the chair, head drooping. Her dark hair had fallen forward, and it hung over her face as if wet.

Azul clapped his hands. Giulia's head rose slowly, as though lifted by a winch. She looked at him, dull-eyed.

"Good news!" Azul said. "We need detain you no longer. You can go. Cortaag here will escort you outside, and from there on you're your own woman again. I'd suggest you seek attention for that burn," he added. "It looks nasty. Cortaag, would you?"

Cortaag stepped over to the chair. He bent and unlaced the cords holding her right arm in place. Meekly, she lifted her arm onto her lap and flexed the fingers as if she was not quite sure what they did. Cortaag moved on to her left arm, his big hands making heavy work of the knots. Alicia looked at Azul and smiled. "He has fat fingers," she said, and she knelt down and undid the ropes around Giulia's feet.

Giulia's hand flicked out and knocked against Cortaag's side: hardly a blow at all. He glanced down – and Giulia lurched up and left. Azul saw a blade in her hand and shouted, but only a ragged croak came out. Giulia's hand caught Alicia's head, yanked her off balance, pulled her chin up to reveal her throat. Alicia knelt on the floor before her, head drawn back like a sheep being sheared.

Giulia yelled, "Back! Keep back!"

Cortaag turned to Azul with his hands raised. The dinner-knife was gone from his belt.

Giulia jabbed the tip of the blade into the tendons of Alicia's neck. Alicia howled. "Don't move!" Giulia shouted. "Touch me and I'll kill her! I'll cut your whore's throat, I fucking swear I will!"

Alicia's eyes swept the room. They were big and scared. "She will, she will!"

"Damn right I will." Giulia grinned at the men. "Well? Get the door open! Touch me and she fucking dies!"

"Step away, Cortaag," Azul said.

Cortaag stood back, heavy and awkward in the little room.

A bit of hair fell in front of Giulia's eyes and she flicked her head. She bared her teeth and spat.

"You're not well," Azul said. "Not well at all. You should put the knife down before you hurt yourself."

Giulia's shoulders twitched. Azul stared, unable to tell whether she was laughing or crying.

"You've had a bad experience," he said. He took a single step towards her. "A very bad experience. You must be feeling very unwell right now."

"Get away from me."

Alicia stared at Azul, terrified.

"I said you could go, and you have my word on that. There's no need for you or anyone else to get hurt. Just calm down." Azul took a second step.

Giulia looked down. "Get up," she said. Alicia drew up her legs. Azul glanced at Cortaag, took another step. Alicia started to rise.

"It doesn't have to be like this," Azul said. "You need to rest." Close now. Two yards from her. He could lunge and grab her arm where he'd burned her. The pain would make it easy to overpower her. He opened his hands. "Come on. Be reasonable now. Just pass me the knife and we can all be friends."

Giulia gasped again. It sounded like a sob. Her will was flagging. They did that sometimes: all the fight went out of them and they just folded up and cried. Azul held out his hand. "Just give me the knife, Giulia."

Her arm flicked out. Searing pain raced across his palm and he snatched his hand away. The mouth in his thumb opened and hissed.

Giulia's knife darted back to Alicia's throat, drove

half an inch into the meat of her neck. Alicia squealed.

Azul looked down at his hand. Blood leaked across the palm. He bit his lip and clenched his fist. He felt water in his eyes. "Bitch!"

Alicia blubbered.

"Touch me again and I'll slit her throat," Giulia said. "Door. Now. Open the fucking door!"

Azul turned, scowling, to Cortaag. "Open the door," he croaked.

***

Cortaag opened the door. He stepped aside like a sullen footman.

"Good, good." Giulia's left hand pulled Alicia's chin up, revealing her pale throat. Her right hand held the knife. Sweat ran over the handle. "That's it. Everyone keep back." Giulia and Alicia edged towards the door together, a creature of four legs, two heads, one blade. They began to back through the door.

Alicia drove her elbow into Giulia's ribs.

The knife tore free, Alicia weeping and snarling at once, and Giulia shoved her away. Alicia stumbled back into the room. Giulia grabbed the door, slammed it shut and tore off down the corridor. The door burst open behind her: grunts and bellows filled the passage as she bounded up the steps, heart ripping at her chest. Azul shouted, "Get the guns, get the guns!" and a crazy whoop drowned him out, Alicia no doubt, and Giulia reached the top of the stairs and ran into a kitchen. A man sitting at the table saw her and started to rise, so she drove Cortaag's knife into his neck and he went down choking on blood.

Sudden pressure on her upper arm, and agony turned the world white. Her back arched and she screamed. Cortaag leaned in over her shoulder, grinning as she shrivelled like an ember from the searing pain in her arm. "Now I've—"

The door burst open in front of her and a figure ran in, shoulder down, and charged straight into Cortaag's side. He released Giulia's arm, his eyes wide, and she saw that there was a sword buried to the hilt in his gut. Cortaag stood impaled at the top of the stairs, gasping.

Hugh drew his leg up and stamped into Cortaag's chest as if kicking down a door. The sword slid free and Cortaag fell back, clutching the air. He bounced down the stairs, end over end.

"Hello, Giulia," Hugh said.

"Hugh?" He seemed incredibly precious in this evil place. "We've got to get out. We've got to go. Oh God – I'm going to puke."

She retched. Nothing much came out.

"Come on," she said, and she stepped towards the door, her right arm holding the left straight by her side.

"You're hurt," Hugh said. His eyes widened and his lips drew back from his teeth. "By the lord God," he bellowed, "they've *tortured* you!"

"Got to go," Giulia said. Getting out was all that mattered now: getting far away and hiding somewhere, armed.

She struggled into the hall. It was a big house, deserted, probably abandoned long ago. Giulia glanced up the stairs and saw darkness. No sound came from behind them. Pain soaked through her arm like gangrene.

A man lay sprawled across the hall. His death had been fast and messy, without the chance for much sound.

Giulia headed towards the door. Hugh picked up a bag lying by the stairs. "Got your things here," he said.

Giulia put her back against the front door. Waves of pain soaked up from her arm, setting her head spinning. Her saliva was sour and hot.

"Give me the crossbow," she said.

Hugh lifted it out. "I'll load it for you."

"Good. Quick." She watched him work the ratchet. The dark of the house was creeping in on them. She wanted to snatch the bow from his old, slow hands. They could be anywhere: in the cellar, in the streets, upstairs, summoning reinforcements to drag her back downstairs—

"Here," Hugh said.

She took the bow in her right hand, kept the injured arm flat by her side. Her breath came out in shudders. "Let's go," Giulia said.

The night air was nauseatingly cold. *Keep your eyes on the street*, she thought. *Keep watching.*

There was a dead man in the shadows. He looked as if he'd charged head-first into the wall. The bulk of a mastiff lay beside him. Giulia spat and tried not to think.

"Boat's this way," Hugh said.

The walk blurred into pain. She felt herself wobble with each step, as if she stumbled down the deck of a ship in a gale. *Got to go, got to go*, she thought. *They'll come back.*

"Where're we going?" she asked. She looked down, wanting to peel the singed cloth away. It was stuck to the wound with dried blood. "God almighty, my arm fucking hurts."

"We're nearly there," Hugh said. "This way."

A boat lay beside the canal, a sliver of a boat with an axe-head prow. A man stood up in the boat. He climbed onto the bank and very gently helped her in, hardly touching her. Giulia dropped onto a pile of cushions in the bows, still holding her crossbow. Hugh climbed in and nodded to the boatman. "Get moving."

"Don't worry, I'm going," he said. "Is she all right?"

"I'm fine," Giulia said. "Just fucking go."

The man pushed off and the boat swung awkwardly into the middle of the canal. *Watch him, Hugh*, Giulia thought. *We don't know if we can trust him.*

The boat slipped down the canal like a snake down a rabbit-hole. Giulia tasted hot spit and gritted her teeth. Under her, the cushions smelt of damp. "Wait," she said. "Where're we going?"

Hugh looked over his shoulder at her. "It's all right. We're going somewhere safe."

"*Where*, Hugh?"

"The Scola san Cornelio."

"No," she said. "Go north. Up near the Old Arms there's a tavern with a barrel over the door. There's a fey woman in there, a dryad. Tell her to get out."

Hugh's frown echoed the droop of his moustache. "Are you sure?"

"Of course I'm sure. Her name's Anna. Go and get her. I mean it. They'll be after her."

"Yes, but why would they want—"

"Because I told them about her."

"Oh," said Hugh, and he turned away to talk to the boatman.

The Kingdom of the Dogs

TEN

Giulia heard the voices long before her brain made sense of them. One was a low, droning grumble, the other slightly higher: a young man's voice, perhaps. *I know you*, she thought, as the deeper voice began again. *I know you...*

She woke again. Her shoulder and upper arm were numb; her mouth felt strange. *What? What's happening?*

She opened her eyes and there were faces looming over her, inhuman faces with enormous eyes, their little mouths making sounds. A memory rushed into her mind of being trapped, tied down, people leaning in to ask questions and hurt her. She yelled and lunged. The faces whipped back, their big eyes full of dismay.

A hand grabbed her wrist. "Please, I'm trying to help you," one of the faces said – a man, she thought. There was a sharp pain in her shoulder, a sense of something colder than water being painted onto her skin, and she screamed and thrashed, shouted every curse she knew, but the world was already fading.

Where am I?

The room was white and strangely-angled, as if

she was in an attic. There was a woodcut on the wall. It showed a bearded man in baggy trousers, carrying a pike over one shoulder. He looked like a mercenary.

Giulia was sitting up in bed. Time had passed, she knew that, but she did not know how long. Light streamed in through a small window.

It must be morning. She couldn't think straight, but it didn't frighten her. Nothing did. Her mind was clear but everything felt distant, as though she was thinking about people far away, who had nothing to do with her.

There were two chairs near the door, and Hugh was sitting on one. "Good morning," he said.

Suddenly, she knew that she had to get out. "Hugh? What's going on?" Panic broke loose in her mind like a startled bird, and she stood up quickly, leaving the sheets behind. "We've got to go!"

Giulia stopped and looked down. She wore a white dress, without sleeves. It ended a few inches below her knees. She felt awkward to be wearing so little. "What is this place?"

"We're in the Scola," Hugh said. "You're safe."

"The Scola? Where're my things?"

"Over here," Hugh said. He pointed to a dark pile beside his chair. "It's quite safe here. I'm keeping watch, don't worry." He glanced at the window. "You've been asleep for a while, you know. There's a dryad fellow who's been looking after you. He seems decent enough."

Giulia nodded. There was something she hadn't remembered yet: it was as though her mind was waking up piece by piece. "Yes," she said. "I saw him, I think." Memories waited to come back to her, but she couldn't quite reach them. She imagined them hiding out of sight, like fish under the water. Where had she seen that image before? In an inn, when someone – Elayne – had showed her a piece of glass that moved. Elayne... she'd been shouting something – something about a square, full of pillars.

Giulia pulled her left arm across her body. It was numb. A bandage had been wound around her arm from elbow to shoulder. She could feel the tightness of the bandage on her skin. It smelt of cut grass.

Elayne screaming – moonlight between the pillars – men on rooftops, in boats – waking up on some kind of chair – an old man with a sour face –

The truth dropped on her like a rock.

"Oh, God," she said. "Oh my God."

"It was a bad business," Hugh said. "You're safe now."

Giulia sat down on the bed. She put her face in her hands. When her head stopped aching, she looked back up. "Yes," she replied. "Thanks for coming to help."

"Not a problem," Hugh replied. "Rescuing maidens is what I do." He smiled, without any irony.

"What about Edwin and Elayne? Did they get away?"

"Yes, their ship's gone. We did the job." Then he was quiet.

"Good... good. I'm glad," Giulia said. Her voice sounded strange to her. It seemed to come from someone else. "I need to get dressed," she added.

Hugh stood. "Of course. I'll wait in the corridor. Let me know when—"

"No – just turn around. It's all right. I'd rather you didn't go."

"Right, then." Hugh stood up and turned to the wall. "I'm not looking," he said. "Tell me when I can turn round again." He put his hands behind his back as she picked up her things and carried them to the bed.

She dressed. She was careful in putting her shirt on, and the bandage did not hurt. Someone had patched her sleeve, where the poker had burned through it. "I'm all ready now," she said as she strapped on her knives.

Hugh turned and looked her over. "Excellent," he said. "All set, eh?"

Giulia walked to the window. There was an ornamental garden outside, with a little grove of trees in the centre. The garden was very large by Averrian standards. She'd been led through it when the boatman had brought her here, when she'd spoken to Iacono the mapmaker.

Pretty.

She knew what she had to say: the words were like a stone in her mouth, waiting to be spat out. "I told them everything," she said. "All of it: you, me, Edwin, Elayne – shit, I even told them about Severra."

Hugh didn't say anything.

"I mean, I tried not to, you know? They didn't get it out of me easily, Hugh."

"Yes," he said. "I know that."

Outside, boats were moving across the window, up and down the canal. None of them seemed very important. "I held out as long as I could, I—" Another stone in her mouth. Deep breath. "They made threats. Bad ones."

Hugh stood up. He looked around the room impatiently, as if waiting for someone who had failed to arrive. His knobbly fists were straight down at his sides.

His silence made her angry. He was taking it too well: she wanted to argue with someone, to justify herself. "I mean, what was I supposed to do, Hugh? They'd have killed me otherwise. I didn't have another choice. I did what I could – I – *fuck*!" She drove the flat of her hand against the windowframe, hammered it with her palm. "Fuck, fuck, fuck!"

Hugh took a step towards her. "Hey, now."

Giulia's chest lurched and she drew in a huge, wheezing breath and suddenly she was head down, shoulders bucking with hard, raucous sobs. It felt like being sick, as if she could purge the misery from her body, as if she could puke it out if she cried hard enough. She heard a noise like a broken bellows coming out of her. She reached up and put her hand over her eyes and at once it was wet. Her head swam. "I tried – I bloody tried, I swear it—"

"Come along, old girl. Let's sit down, eh? You'll feel better sitting down."

She wrenched the breath back into her lungs, took one long, shuddering breath, then another calmer one. "Right. Right."

Giulia quietened and turned away from the window, rubbing the water off her eyes. She saw him gesturing to the chairs like an idiot footman, and she remembered what a good friend he was, and she was crying again. Her chest hurt, her eyes hurt; she seemed to be nothing except this puckered-faced, weeping wreck, a person she'd despise, and it made her sick with fury.

"Come on, Giulia, let's sit down."

His hand was on her back, almost round her shoulders, guiding her towards the chairs. Three steps in and she wanted him to take it away – for a moment she hated him for it – then she was desperately glad that he was here. She let him show her to the chairs.

She sat down. Quietly she said, "It wasn't supposed

to be like this."

"I know. Nothing you could do."

"I was supposed to have a new life. I was supposed to get *away* from this. I thought killing Severra would—" She stopped and shook her head. Hugh patted her back. Grief wrenched more croaky words out of her. "Ah, fuck it."

Hugh sat down beside her. For a moment, he didn't move. Then he leaned in and dropped his arm across her shoulders. He hugged her quickly, hard, as if welcoming a drinking companion. Giulia felt desperately grateful.

"They made me betray you, Hugh."

"Nonsense. You had some bad luck, that's all." He looked around the room, as though worried that he was missing something interesting elsewhere. "Look, ah, Giulia... they didn't, ah, you know, mess with you, did they?"

"No."

"Because if they did, I'll butcher them."

"No, they didn't. Too professional for that."

"Well, that's something, isn't it? Eh?" He patted her on the back. "Come on. We'll sort it out. Your arm'll heal up – it'll scar a bit, but not much—"

"Just another scar, eh?"

"Absolutely!"

"Another fucking scar." She took a deep breath and opened her hands, knowing there was no point trying to explain. "I don't want any more scars. I spent six years hunting down the man who put these on my face. I want – I don't know, I'd like to live like a fucking proper person for once." She was surprised how quiet her voice was. It sounded like someone else's, so measured it was almost threatening. "Sometimes I think I went off the path a long time ago, and no matter what I do I can't get back. The more I try, the further away I get."

Hugh said nothing. She looked at far side of the room, feeling the wetness around her eyes, seeing the bed distorted through the water in them.

"I just can't get back on the path," she said. "I'm not sure I ever will."

"Listen," said the knight, "that fey apothecary, the fellow who patched up your arm, he says he can get you back to Pagalia. There's a way they've got that they don't usually use for our sort, a magic way. He says you'd be back home in a day or so."

"Pagalia isn't home," Giulia said. Her voice was harder than she'd expected.

"Well, wherever, then. I'll ask him, if you like."

Yes, I could. Go back to Astrago, where the criminals live, or Pagalia, where I got my scars. Live off acquaintances for a while, and then from crime. Make enough to rent a room in a tenement block and spend the rest on drink and tinctures against Melancholia. Just find enough drink, and work, to stop thinking about my glorious adventure and how it all went wrong – how it ended in a cellar with that little bastard holding a poker to my arm.

"You mean retreat."

"You could go wherever you want," he said.

"Fuck that," she replied. "I'm not going anywhere.." She swallowed twice, and her voice was normal again. "I need something to do. I can't just sit here, getting miserable again. Can we trust the people here, in the Scola?"

She expected him to say, "Oh, of course," to naively accept that they were friends just because they'd treated her wounds. But Hugh thought about it. "I think so," he said. "But I'd tread carefully."

"Do you know when they want us to leave?"

"Not for a while. But they do want to talk to us."

"We must be wanted by the Watch, you know. We're pretty trapped up here."

Slowly, thoughtfully, he said, "The dryad fellow, Sethis, said that he wouldn't tell anyone that we were here. I got the feeling that whatever he wanted to talk about, it wasn't quite, um, legal."

"Oh yes? How d'you mean, exactly?" It felt good to talk business again.

"Well, I've been doing a bit of thinking, over the last day or two. I reckon you were on to something – we all were – about the priest, about that man Varro, the whole thing. It's all connected. I've talked to the people who run this place, and we're getting a crew together. They're not fighters here, but they know people. They could help us. They've asked to talk to me, in the garden. You can come along if you'd like."

"I want this bastard dead," Giulia said.

"That's the plan."

"No trials, no magistrates, no lying bastard procurators. Just a knife in the back. Actually, make that the front. I want him to see who he's crossed."

"Right."

"These people you've spoken to have to understand that. I'll help them find him, but then he's mine. I'm going to pull down whatever he's got going here, every bit of it. Are you all right with that?"

"Sounds fine to me. The justice of cold steel, eh?" Hugh stood up. "Let me know when you'd like to talk to them."

Giulia looked at her hands. She could feel the bandage on her arm when she thought about it: not the wound itself, but the tightness of the cloth around it. She needed to make a plan, to work out how to wreak her vengeance. If she evened the scales up enough, it might blot out the terror and humiliation of being in her enemy's hands. She got to her feet. "May as well get started," she said.

The room opened onto a narrow staircase. Cautiously, Giulia began to walk down the stairs. "I've got a room up here too," Hugh explained. "I put our stuff in there."

"They gave both of us rooms? They must really need us for something."

"Yes. I got the feeling—"

A figure stepped onto the stairs: a dryad man in normal clothing, smartly-dressed but not showy. He had the same huge eyes as Anna, at once gentle and unsettling. He wore spectacles perched on his small nose. Giulia remembered the faces leaning over her when she had woken, and wondered if one of them had been his.

He smiled and held out a hand. "Hello. You're awake, I see."

Giulia stopped on the stairs. "Hello." She reached out and shook his hand. The long fingers were warm and strong. The dryad was a few inches taller than her.

"I'm Sethis."

"Giulia."

"I'm pleased to meet you, Giulia."

"He's the doctor," said Hugh.

"Well, in a way," the dryad replied. "I'm not a trained apothecary, of course. But I've had a few lessons in anatomy." He raised a hand and scratched the side of his neck. His hair was short and dark brown. "I'm glad to see you're up and about. How are you feeling?"

"Not bad, considering."

"Good. You've woken up earlier than I expected: I thought you'd sleep for another day or two."

"A day?" Giulia said. "How long have I been asleep, then?"

"Two days," Hugh said. "I did mean to say."

"Two *days*?"

"We gave you a potion for the pain," the dryad said. "Your wound needed treating, and it was the easiest way to do it. Besides, it looked like you needed to rest."

"I did."

Nobody said anything for a moment.

"Well," Sethis said, "we'd best get off the stairs, I suppose. There's food downstairs, if you want it," he added, and he turned and began to walk down. Seen from behind, he looked like a slim, slightly athletic human: he could have been a tumbler or an acrobat.

Giulia followed. "Thanks."

"I've been speaking to Sir Hugh here," Sethis said, "and I think that you and I have got quite a lot to talk about. You see, I'm fairly sure we're both working towards the same end."

"Is that so?" Giulia said, as they reached the bottom of the stairs. They stood in a wide corridor, lined with paintings. It looked like a rich man's house.

"You must be hungry," Sethis said. "There's plenty of food in the dining hall. I've got to do some work, but if there's anything you need, call me."

As with Anna, Giulia could not tell how old he was. He reminded her of a young man, somehow: perhaps it was the sense of awkwardness, the eagerness to get things right.

"There is something you could do," she said. "You

said you know anatomy." She spoke quietly. "Just between you and I, do you know how to make a tincture against Melancholia? It doesn't need to be particularly strong." She felt ashamed for asking, for admitting that she might need it.

"Not a problem. I can't make it myself, but I know just the man. I'll get him to sort out a tincture for you. Just between you and I." Sethis smiled cautiously, like someone trying it out for the first time. She smiled back. "I'll see you later, I believe," he added. The dryad stepped back, raised his hand to wave goodbye, turned and hurried off down the corridor.

Giulia watched him go. "When I came here before, they nearly threw me out the front door," she said. "Looks like we're worth keeping now."

"And worth feeding, it seems," Hugh replied. "They serve decent meals here. The beer's not bad, either."

They started along the corridor. Giulia said, "Just be careful. We don't know these people."

"He's a fey," Hugh replied. "They were on our side in the war. He'll be fine."

"Right," Giulia said. It seemed best to change the subject. "You did find Anna, didn't you?"

Hugh nodded. "The dryad girl? Yes, I went there. You gave me directions, remember?"

"Did I? I don't remember much at all," she added, and a face appeared in the foreground of her mind: an elderly, intelligent face, cold and inquisitive, lit by the glow of a poker. There was no malice to the face, no spite – just the calm disdain of a man who did an unpleasant job. It was the face of a man pouring a pan of hot water over an anthill, watching the ants wriggle as they boiled alive. *Yes*, she thought, *I remember you. And by the time I'm done, you'll remember me.*

"Well," said Hugh, "let's get something to eat. I'm bloody starving – and you should be too!"

"Good idea." Giulia envied the simplicity of Hugh's needs. It must be wonderful, not having to fight your own Melancholia, worrying only about the source of the next helping of beer and stew. Then she remembered Elayne, and was not quite so sure.

The stairs curled down into an entrance-hall – not the hall Giulia had seen when she had visited the Scola, but a grander one. A statue stood in the centre, of some ancient sea-captain posing with one foot upon the globe, like a hunter beside his prey. The banister curved as gracefully as the hull of a ship.

Well, Giulia thought, *they wanted me here. May as well make the most of it.*

At the rear of the hall was a pair of high wooden doors. Giulia took hold of the handle – cast in the form of a curling dragon, in the dwarrow style – and opened the door.

She stood in the doorway, looking into a great single chamber that must have taken up most of this floor. Long windows let in light: there was a fire burning in an ornate grate as tall as she was, and the sight of the poker lying beside it made her hesitate.

Giulia forced that down and stepped inside, feeling that she was walking into a palace.

The floor was neatly tiled. The windows were huge and flanked by columns; she could have driven a cart through them. Life-sized statues of robed men stood against the walls, holding tools: telescopes, quills, chisels. Huge paintings hung between them, showing a variety of scenes: a picture of Holy Alexis rising from the pyre stood beside a depiction of the dwarrow king Sarus founding the Temple of Temples in some valley far away. Giulia imagined the members of the Scola dining here, discussing their various branches of savantry under the statues.

Above the fireplace, a life-size portrait hung. It showed a black man in ornate armour standing on the docks of Averrio, making a speech to a group of soldiers. The man had a long, intelligent face and a strong jawline. The soldiers gazed up at him, rapt.

"Good lord," said Hugh. "Look up there."

She looked up. Some genius had painted castles and mythic scenes onto the ceiling. A woman nursed a baby in front of a decrepit temple, while a soldier in modern dress looked on. Satyrs and plump, pink women frolicked beside a stream.

"This is something, isn't it?" Hugh said.

She nodded. *The last time I was in a place like this, I sneaked out with the candlesticks.* "Come on. Let's get fed."

They ate stew in a small dining room behind the great hall. The room was bare by comparison, but the stew was spiced and expensive-tasting. Hugh watched Giulia carefully as she ate.

"Is something wrong?" Giulia asked as she spooned stew into her mouth. She was surprised how hungry she'd been.

"No, not at all," Hugh said, peering into his beer.

"Are you sure? You're not eating much."

"Giulia, are you certain you want to carry on with this? I don't mind if you want me to do this alone. I realise you've had to sort things out yourself in the past – and you've done more than most men ever could – but I'm happy to avenge you on my own, you know." He took a sip of beer.

She looked up at him. *What do you mean?* she thought. *That I can't do this, that I'm not good enough? Don't be stupid. He's trying to help. He's just bad at saying it.*

"Thanks," she said, "but I'm in for this. I can't not be."

She tore off a chunk of bread and began wiping up the last of the stew. Giulia remembered a line from *The King of Caladon*, the play she'd watched while she'd prepared to take revenge on Publius Severra for cutting her face. She thought of Lord Macgraw, given the chance to flee from the kingdom he had usurped: *I have swum so far in blood that it would drown me to turn back now.* She leaned forward. "Look, Hugh, you know I've done some pretty bad stuff. Vendetta and all that."

"Yes..."

"You know how I killed Publius Severra, right? When he cut my face?"

"Yes. It's a shame you had to do it on your own, but, yes, I suppose honour was satisfied, in a way."

"If I leave now, everything I did there will have been a waste of time. It's hard to explain, but after all the effort it took to get even with Severra, to walk out now would be – it'd be like saying I was wrong all along."

"It's a matter of honour, you mean?"

"No – more than that. I trained for years to get Severra, and to leave now... I just couldn't. It would be like saying I've wasted my life."

Hugh smoothed down his moustache. He sat silently, frowning, thinking it over. He looked severe, like the elderly father of a grand family. Then he smiled. "Yes, I know that feeling. Used to happen in my questing days. You ride out, and you see how big the task is before you, but you can't back down from what you're meant to do –

you're too far in to turn back. Yes, that's the questing life, all right." He leaned back, contented and very slightly pompous, like an old actor Giulia had once seen talking about the stage.

Something like that. Except with less chivalry and more slit throats. "Yes, I think that's right."

Hugh smiled. "You and I see it the same. Of course, it's a bit strange, you being a woman and all, but I understand."

"So we're both in?" she said. She pressed her upper arm, testing the bandage. It was still numb.

"Absolutely."

"Good. Let's find out what Sethis and his people have to offer. If they can help us, fine – if not, well, we'll just have to do it alone."

ELEVEN

Sethis was waiting for them in the great hall. His head was cocked back so he could admire the ceiling, and he seemed completely lost, as though gazing at the face of God. Except, of course, that wasn't his god up there at all. He looked down, and Giulia was struck again by the neat strangeness of his face: the small mouth, high forehead and kindly, inhuman eyes, glittering behind his spectacles.

"Hello again," he said. "How are you feeling?"

"Much the same as an hour ago," Giulia replied and, realising she sounded ungrateful, she added, "Not too bad, thanks." He seemed much more human than Anna had done. Giulia did not feel the same strange attraction around him, nor quite the same unease.

"Good. I remember when they first painted that," he added, glancing upwards. "Quite an event. Scaffolding everywhere."

Hugh gestured to the portrait of the black knight addressing the troops. "Who's the heathen fellow?"

"That's General Attelani," Sethis said. "He's not a heathen, actually: he's in your Church. Anyway, the painting shows him about to take on the pirates of Sarpesi.

He won, if you're wondering."

"I thought he might have done," Giulia said.

"He's actually a patron of the Scola. Seems sort of right, somehow. We've both got our detractors in the city. Now, then," he said, "we're ready to discuss this business when you are."

"Who's 'we'?" Giulia replied.

"Sorry, I should have explained. We are myself, of course, and my friend Arashina. We'll also be joined by Vurael, who serves Lord Portharion."

Giulia said, "Portharion the wizard?"

"The very same."

"Who does Portharion work for?"

"Nobody. He works for himself."

"So who do *you* work for?"

"Me personally?"

She gestured at the hall. "All of you."

"The Scola works for the good of the city, and of scholarship in general. But I don't suppose that answers your question, does it?"

"Not really."

Sethis thought for a second. "Well, the Scola is an organisation for the promotion of learning and the arts, mainly painting. Members pay a fee for the upkeep of the building and grounds, and get to exhibit their work here in return. The Scola provides a place where we can meet and talk freely."

"Are you a painter?"

The dryad smiled. "Sadly, no. I've tried, but it's not for me. I just help out. So then: are you happy to talk to us now?"

Giulia nodded. *I hope I'm ready for this.*

"Great. We're meeting in the little garden outside.

Don't worry," Sethis added, with a conspiratorial smile. "It's quite warm."

He led them down a staircase, towards the front of the building. Giulia recognised the room on her left, with its pictures of worthies who had addressed the Scola. It was the place where she had met Iacono. They turned right, into the servants' wing.

Sethis opened a small door and held it for her. She stepped into the chilly garden. It was not cold enough for snow, but there was a sterile crispness to the air. The scars on her face felt tender and exposed.

"Where're we going?" she asked.

The dryad pointed towards the little clump of trees at the end of the garden. "That way."

Giulia glanced over her shoulder at the pale bulk of the Scola, and saw an attic window that could have led into her room.

"I do various bits and pieces for the Scola," Sethis said. "Among other things, I'm a kind of messenger." He strode across the wet grass. "The members sometimes need the help of the fey folk. I act as a link between the two. This way," he added, gesturing at the trees. "There's a canopy inside."

Giulia looked at the cold trees, their bare branches crossing like bars. If there was a canopy hidden away between them, it would be small and damp. She glanced at Hugh, who seemed entirely uninterested, and watched Sethis stroll into the little wood. Giulia took one long look behind her, back at the house, and followed him.

"I suppose you might call me a sort of ambassador for my people," Sethis said, "although that's a bit grand for it. I've spent quite a lot of time among you humans, so it's easier for me to make friends."

Which explains the normal clothes, Giulia thought.

Perhaps the trees on the edge of the copse kept the wind away: at any rate there seemed to be more greenery past the first row of bare trunks. Autumn appeared not to have really ended here: yellow leaves still clung on to branches, and the grass seemed more verdant, more alive. The pines looked fatter, and the deciduous trees were fleshed out with foliage as if winter had never come. Perhaps these savants had poured something into the soil.

"Why do you have these trees?" Giulia asked. She no longer saw her breath when she exhaled.

"To be a meeting-place," Sethis said.

"Hmm," said Hugh.

The path weaved a little, and it was hard to tell how far they had gone. Ten, twenty yards, perhaps? They'd be coming out the other side soon. Sethis was humming something under his breath; above them, birds twittered.

That was wrong. There shouldn't be so many birds at this time of year. Light filtered through the trees, warming her face: not the hard sunlight of a clear winter's day, but warm, life-giving light. She was walking out of winter, into spring. Giulia followed the dryad into the forest, as his humming mingled with the birdsong.

Giulia fell back a little, level with Hugh. She leaned in close. "Look at the leaves!" she whispered. "Where *are* we?"

Through the trees to her left she glimpsed something moving. She peered after it, thinking it was a horse. A stag weaved between the trees thirty yards away, its antlers seeming to merge with the branches. It stretched its thick-furred neck upwards and let out a hoarse bellow, turned, and was lost to view.

She looked back: no sign of winter, or the way

out. To her left, she saw a wide length of light-blue cloth stretched between the trunks, weaving away like the wall of a tent. Suddenly, Giulia noticed movement: a sleek figure stood watching them a little way off. It was a dryad, unarmed, its sex impossible to determine at this range. She felt the first tinges of sweat on her body, from heat and apprehension.

"This is fey business," Hugh said. "Keep going."

"Nearly there," Sethis announced.

There were sheets between the trees. Swaths of cloth in soft orange and blue had been threaded through the trunks, guiding them into a corridor. There was no doubt that this was magic, Giulia thought: no way that she could still be in the little wood at the bottom of the Scola gardens. Where was she, then? *Faery*, she realised. She felt uneasy, not quite scared. *It must be Faery: where the fey people live, where humans can't go without a guide.*

"Here," Sethis said. He reached over to the blue cloth and unhitched a section from the branches, holding it back like a door. Giulia stepped through the last trees and stopped, astonished.

They were on a hillside. The bottle-green meadow rolled away from them like an ocean. There was woodland in the distance, so thick and bright that colour seemed almost to pulse out of it. A river ran glinting through the valley like the back of a snake. The sky was almost cloudless. In some of the far pastures horses grazed, and little man-shaped specks walked and sat and talked. Some of the specks were pink all over – *Naked? Surely not.* The fields were dotted with tents and pavilions, elegant and brightly-coloured, painted with symbols that she did not understand.

"Hugh?"

"I'm here," he said by her side.

"Are you seeing all this?"

"Yes," Hugh replied. "Pleasant view, isn't it?"

"You ever see anything like this before?"

"Not for a long time."

A group of tiny fighters were sparring in a paddock half a mile off, kicking and leaping. Behind them, in the very distance, a long-necked creature lumbered across the horizon. Its back was studded with delicate minarets like a little city. *It must be the size of a siege tower*, she realised with a rush of alarm and a strange, crazy delight.

Giulia looked away, afraid for her mind if she saw much more. Very carefully, she hooked her thumbs into her belt and made her hands stay still. *These are friends. Easy now.*

"My God," she said.

"Mine, actually," Sethis said. "This way, please."

Just outside the forest, someone had laid a stone patio half a dozen yards across, like the dais of an altar. Birch trees rose around the edge of the patio. Cloth had been wound between the trees to form walls. Thirty feet up, the cloth stopped and the branches stretched across to one another as if to shake hands, cut and shaped to form a living wicker roof.

A table stood in the middle of the patio, and behind it sat a dryad woman. She was still: pale and doll-like, as though she wore a mask. Her hands rested on the table in front of her. A thin cigarillo smouldered between her long fingers. The air smelt of burning herbs.

Quietly, the woman stood up and stepped out of the shade. She was almost beautiful, and slightly like some insect that had shaped itself into nearly-human form.

Her hair was long, black and extremely thick. *Like a*

wig, Giulia thought. The woman held out a hand. Giulia's skin tensed.

"My name is Arashina. Please, come and sit down."

Giulia glanced towards Hugh. He shrugged. Sethis caught her eye and smiled. *Easy for you*, she thought. *You belong here.*

The seats were polished and carved, the sort of thing you would find in the home of a nobleman. Giulia pulled one out and sat down. There were clay cups and a big jug of wine on the table. Hugh took the seat opposite.

Birds chirruped. Judging by the shadows and the sun, it was early afternoon – here, anyway.

"This is Giulia Degarno, and this is Sir Hugh of Kenton," Sethis said.

"A pleasure, madam," Hugh said.

"Pleased to meet you," Giulia added.

"Thank you." Arashina raised her hand and sucked on the cigarillo. "Welcome." Her mouth was wider than Sethis', but thinner at the edges, like a scar. *She's even less human than he is. Maybe the longer they spend in our world, the more they look like us.*

"I represent the hunting party of the Lord and Lady of the Woods," Arashina said. "Sethis here is our voice in the Scola san Cornelio. Vurael attends on behalf of Lord Portharion."

She gestured vaguely at the trees. Giulia looked around, and started. A small figure stood there, robed in dark red like a tiny monk. The hood was big, almost absurdly so, completely obscuring the face. The arms were folded: she could see no hands. It could have been a child, or a piece of cloth propped up on sticks.

Giulia wanted to make the Sign of the Sword across her chest. She thought, *Saint Senobina, if you can hear me here, watch over me.*

Sethis poured the wine and passed the cups out.

"So," said Arashina. "You are mercenaries, I assume?"

"Not so," Hugh replied. "We are adventurers. I myself am a knight of Anglia, veteran of the Battle of the Bone Cliffs. Giulia here is – well, do you know the stories about Robehood, or John Greenwood? Like that, but in the city."

Arashina nodded. "You steal from the rich, and give to the poor?"

"To an extent," Giulia replied. "We came to Averrio from Pagalia. We've been doing some thief-taking work: supporting the guilds and things like that. I'm a friend of Grodrin the dwarrow," she added, hoping it might win her some respect.

"We know him," Arashina replied. "If you are a friend of his, I'm sure you can be trusted."

"Thank you," Giulia said. She sipped her wine. "So, um, you wanted to talk to us."

"Yes I did. We have enemies in common. You have seen them. You can tell us where to find them. You could lead us to them."

"Wait a minute." Sethis raised a hand. "I think we ought to explain the situation here."

Giulia said, "It would help."

Arashina shrugged and drew slowly on her cigarillo. "As you wish. We are looking for a group of your people," she said. "Old enemies of ours. They have acquired – no, *stolen* – certain abilities that originally derive from the Lady, our goddess. This cannot be permitted."

"What kind of abilities?"

Sethis looked her in the eye. "Changing shape."

Arashina nodded. "The difficulty is, none of us have seen these people for decades – at least, none have seen them and survived. We gather you have."

"I saw them, all right," Giulia replied. "They're the bastards who burned my arm."

"Well, yes." Sethis sounded uncomfortable. He chose his words carefully. "I understand that you and Hugh killed one of them—"

"That's right." Hugh sat up in his chair. "Fellow name of Varro. He made boats, I believe. He was a tough bugger, too. Their wounds seal up, you see."

Giulia gave him a wary glance. There was only a certain amount she wanted him to say.

"The moon allows it," Arashina added. "They draw strength from it."

Giulia looked at Sethis this time. Arashina was strange, otherworldly. If she was to get any straight answers, they would come from him. "Look, what are these people? Are they even people at all?"

Hugh said, "Werewolves, surely. In Teutland—"

"Not exactly." Sethis said. "They can change shape, that's right, but it's not really wolves they turn into – not just wolves, anyway." He frowned. "They become beasts. Wolves, bears, ghouls and other things, all mixed together."

"A perversion," Arashina said. She blew scented smoke towards the roof.

Sethis nodded. "Yes, a perversion. That's the word for it." He took his glasses off and polished the lenses on his sleeve.

"Which we intend to destroy." Arashina exhaled slowly, watching the smoke curling up into the branches over her head.

"That's what I want, too," Giulia said. "I've seen their leader. I want to hunt him down."

"Their leader?" Sethis put his glasses back on. "Who's that?"

"Don't you know?"

"We have no idea," Arashina said. "An alchemist, I assume, someone skilled in black magic. Beyond that—" She shrugged, and her dark hair shook.

"I don't know his name," Giulia said. "But I could describe him." She licked her lips, suddenly unwilling to talk. These new friends might not be trustworthy: they might want to keep that evil piece of shit alive, or worse, they might want to steal the privilege of killing him for themselves. *What if they just don't believe me?*

But then she remembered the old man's prim, sour face, and fury flared up inside her like white flame. "He's a little man, a bit shorter than me. Old, too, as old as Hugh. No offence, Hugh."

"None taken."

"He looks... angry. Like he's in pain."

"Is he?" Arashina said.

"Not yet. He had his sleeves rolled up. There's a long scar, from his elbow down to his wrist, maybe further. It's got to be a bad one: it's raised up from the skin, the way a bad burn is. You know what I mean?"

They did.

"It was tattooed to look like a snake. It was really convincing, too. Must've hurt like hell, tattooing a scar like that."

Arashina looked at Sethis. She said something in the dryad language.

Giulia said. "I'm sorry? I didn't hear that."

Sethis hesitated.

Giulia said, "Look, I mean no offence, but I need to know what I'm fighting here. If there's anything you know, it would help."

"She's right," Hugh said.

"That's fair enough," Sethis replied. "I'll start from the beginning. This might take a while."

She reached out for the jug. "I've got time."

"All right. Well, I'm sure you've seen that out in the villages, people aren't so, er, precise about the difference between the old and new faiths. They worship your god in church, but honour ours in the fields. There's a place on the road to Pagalia called Gellani—"

"Where they hang ribbons from the trees?" Giulia remembered it from the journey to Averrio. She hadn't stayed very long. Something about it had struck her as wrong, unsuited to her.

"That's the one. Well, the world is full of places like that. Where this world and Faery overlap."

"That's right." Hugh stretched out and yawned. "There's a place in Cerno where, if a man sleeps on midwinter night, King Alba's ghost appears and challenges him."

Giulia thought of Hugh praying in a field, and realised, *You know about this pagan stuff, don't you?*

"Exactly," Sethis said. "Places of overlap. To the east of here is a district called Cerandi."

"I know the name," Giulia said.

"It's near where I grew up. When I was young, Cerandi had a reputation for - well, not heresy as such, but leniency in religious matters. There was a tradition in one village, for example, that at midsummer one of their young women would—"

Arashina said something in her own language: one

long, lisping word.

"Right," Sethis said, "anyway, in Cerandi, there used to be a sect called the Berendanti. There weren't many of them – a few hundred, perhaps a thousand. They worshipped your god, they had a church and a priest, but they were close to us as well. We would come and visit them, and celebrate with them when they drew the harvest in." He frowned. "They had the blessing of our Lord and Lady as well as your god, and it granted them certain abilities. They could change shape."

Giulia sat up. "Go on."

"The Berendanti could pass into our land without a guide, into Faery. It wasn't easy for them, but their elders could do it in summer and winter. People called them 'wise walkers'. But because the border was weak where they lived, creatures from our land sometimes ventured into theirs. Harmful creatures; spirits. The Berendanti learned to change shape to fight them off."

"Into wolves?" Giulia said.

"Wolves, bears, horses, even into birds, some of them. Even we cannot do that. The favours of the gods are strange." The dryad smiled sadly. "Then the war came, and the purges. The Inquisition burned their villages to the ground. Some escaped, some we took with us when we destroyed our gate."

"Your gate?"

"The pathway to the forest. Like the wood in the Scola gardens. Those we took with us are dead now, but they died peacefully, at least."

"So what happened to the others, the ones that didn't get away?"

"Most were taken alive. We didn't see them again." Sethis stopped and glanced up at the trees, as if he had only just noticed how tall they were. "Sometimes," he said, "you make friends with strangers, even though they are very different to you. Perhaps because of it. At any rate, I had a friend among the Berendanti. The soldiers took her away."

"I'm sorry to hear that," Giulia said.

"It was near the end of the war, when the Inquisition turned on the Berendanti. By then, the smarter inquisitors knew that they were going to lose. They needed anything they could get, I suppose, any advantage, no matter how heretical it might have seemed when they started out. So they took the Berendanti to their alchemists, and tried to become like them." Sethis had stopped talking to them now. He looked out into the trees. "I would like to think my friend told them nothing," he said. "But it's hard to tell. I wouldn't know which pile of ashes to ask," he added, and Giulia could hear the rage wound up tight behind his voice.

"The Berendanti tried to strike a deal with the Inquisition," Arashina observed. "But in all things, your god is cruel. And the Inquis never leave a man alive when they could murder him instead."

"So that's what the things we saw are, then?" Giulia said. "Inquisition men?"

Sethis said, "The older ones would be. They'll probably have younger men working for them, though - too young to have been soldiers. I expect that they would just be criminals."

Arashina leaned forward. "The one we are looking for is called Leth. He is an alchemist, a sort of apothecary. He learned how to turn the soldiers into what you saw. He was unusual, in that he had no desire to make himself rich. But Leth was one of the worst. He was very old, and evil long before he found the Inquisitors. He kept himself alive with alchemy, you see."

"Leth," Giulia said. "So he's their leader."

Sethis shook his head. "I very much doubt it. Leth is in hiding. He has been for a long time. He was ancient when the Inquis recruited him: by now, he would look nothing like a human being."

"But he's the one you're looking for," Giulia said.

Arashina nodded. "Among others."

"So who was the man I saw?"

"We don't know."

It occurred to Giulia that she was the youngest person at the table, perhaps by several decades. *This is an old man's fight*, she thought. All of them seemed like relics suddenly: Hugh with his aging friends, Sethis with his burning villages, Arashina with her undying alchemist. They all bore old wounds, scars from a war that had finished almost before she had been born.

Sethis poured himself a fresh cup of wine. "I never was one for vendettas, you know. I couldn't see the point in something like that. After all, when there's a war, most people just get on with their lives once it's over. You have to carry on. There's no point brooding over things, just poisoning yourself." He paused. "But sometimes—"

"Sometimes you can't help it," Giulia said.

The dryad nodded slowly. "Right. You just can't."

For the first time she realised that she could understand him. Old scores or not, perhaps they could get along.

"Fair enough," she said. "You've levelled with me. My turn."

***

Falsi put his head around Orvo's door. "Afternoon, Boss."

The captain was cleaning a pistol at his desk, poking at the barrel with a tiny mop. A map of the city hung beside the window in a smart frame. Falsi hadn't seen it before. He wondered if it had formerly occupied a space on the late procurator's office wall.

"Falsi," Orvo said, almost looking up. "I've been looking for you."

Horse-shit you have, Falsi thought. For the past two days the captain had been away from his desk, leaving the running of the Watch-house to his men. "Well," Falsi said, "here I am now." He noticed that his own pistol was a good deal bigger than Orvo's. The knowledge gave him an odd sense of satisfaction. "It's pretty bad about the procurator," he said. He'd never much liked the man.

"Stone dead," Orvo replied. He put down the pistol. "It's terrible, of course, but at least it's ended now."

"So the Anglians killed him? That's what the lads are saying."

"Damn right. Crept in his office and beat the poor bastard to death. Word is, the assassin climbed out the window and ran over the bloody rooftops. Foreigners: lunatics, all of them."

"You said 'the assassin'. So only one of them killed the procurator?"

Orvo frowned. "No, that's not what I meant. Only one of them did the killing, for sure, but they were all in on it. A conspiracy, you see."

Falsi nodded. "I see."

"Then they ran for it. They got pretty far, too. The river boys got them, down at the docks."

"Did we get the bodies?"

Orvo frowned. "No, of course not. The Customs people took them away. They'll be in the Isle of Graves by now. All of them." He picked up his gun and got to work with the mop again.

"So that's that, is it?"

"Done and dusted." Orvo paused, tools in hand. "You know, it would've been better if you hadn't put them in that inn. You were too soft on them. All they did was plot to escape. You can see now why they had to be killed."

"It's not our finest moment," Falsi said. "You're right about that."

"I'll tell you what it *is*, though." Orvo looked the most alert he'd been for weeks. "Tidy, that's what. And everyone likes a tidy town."

"Too bad we won't get paid for the work," Falsi said sourly. "What with our boss being dead and all."

"They'll find another procurator." Orvo grinned. "Maybe I'll put myself forward."

"I doubt it. No offence, Boss, but that's noble's work."

"Now you," Orvo replied, wagging a hairy finger in Falsi's face, "are a nay-sayer. You hear the good news and you throw it back at me, just like Saint Jonas the Questioner."

Falsi chuckled. "You're quoting scripture at me. I think I've seen it all now." He glanced down the corridor, towards the stairs. "I've got things to do. I'll, er, leave you to the prophets." He turned and walked away.

"Ye of little faith!" Orvo called after him, laughing as he did.

Falsi stopped smiling. He thought about Giulia Degarno, telling him she was being set up as she pointed her crossbow at his head. *So then, Giulia, you tried to run for it. But why kill the procurator? How was that supposed to help your cause?*

He walked downstairs, turning it over in his mind and knowing that he didn't have the answers. *Even if I knew everything, I doubt I could work out what really happened.*

It didn't matter any more. *Tidy way for it all to work out*, he thought as he walked across the narrow hall, into the sunlight. He paused, suddenly convinced he was being watched: not by his colleagues, but by something else, something high above him. Falsi glanced back at the tower, and a sentry on the rooftop waved at him. There was nothing to worry about.

Very tidy indeed.

***

"And then you both escaped?" Sethis said.

"That's right," Giulia said. "Hugh broke the door in and we both got out. I – well, I don't know after that." She looked at her hands. "I was in a lot of pain."

"And then you woke up here. In the Scola."

"Yes."

Arashina picked the cigarillo out of her mouth, leaned to one side and ground it out on the underside of her chair. "And you want to go back up against them, then?"

Giulia took a deep breath. "Yes, I do."

She looked over her shoulder. The thing they'd called Vurael was still there, standing at the edge of the trees in its hood and robe. She suspected it was a model, like the crude figures villagers made for saints' day processions. She turned back to the others.

"Look, I'll be honest with you," Giulia said. "I'm

going to kill that old bastard no matter what. If you want to help me, feel free. If you want to stand back and let me get on with it myself, I don't mind that either. But if you don't want to help, I'd be grateful if you didn't get in the way."

Arashina sighed. Hugh watched her. His eyes were half-closed, as if he was about to fall asleep.

"I don't mean to be rude," Giulia said. "That's just how it is."

"Have you ever killed anyone before, in cold blood?" Arashina said. She stretched in her chair, but she didn't yawn. "It is one thing to steal, quite another to take a life."

"Plenty," Giulia replied, and disliked herself for putting it so crudely. "I've killed a few people. Most of those were ones I needed to pay back for my face. Others were self-defence. I can't say I'm proud of that, or that I enjoyed it – but knowing the kind of men they were, I can't say I regret it too much, either."

"True," said Hugh. There was a moment's silence.

"So where do I find them?" Giulia asked. "The only lead I've got left is Varro, the boatbuilder, but he's dead. There may still be something at his boathouse, but if they've got any sense, they'll have cleared it out by now." She shrugged. "They killed the priest for a reason, and the only one I can think of is that he knew something about them. But as to *what* he knew... well, I've no idea." A thought surfaced in her memory. "Have you ever heard of something called the New World Order?"

"The New World is known to us," Arashina said. "King Paratan of Maidenland is a good friend to our people. But an order – no. Is the New World Order a group of monks, perhaps?"

"I've got something that might help," Sethis said.

Giulia looked at him. "Oh yes?"

"A while back I did a little looking around," the dryad said. "Most of the inquisitors kept the money they stole. They hid it underground, stashed it in wine barrels, that sort of thing. But a few of them were more, er, forward thinking. A while ago I heard a rumour that the money the Inquis made from looting Cerandi had gone into the Fiorenti Bank, right here in Averrio. So I asked on behalf of the Scola to see the bank's records. To be honest," he added, "I was pretty surprised when they said yes."

"Did you find anything?" Giulia asked.

"Doubt it," Hugh muttered.

"Nothing that I could understand. They have a new system – double entering, whatever that means – and of course the man who showed me was one of the bank's own people. He had an interest in me remaining ignorant. Though it didn't seem right, somehow. I might be wrong, of course, but I think they were hiding something. So I contacted Arashina here – and well, now this has come along."

Giulia said, "So no proof at all, then."

"None that would satisfy the Council of a Hundred." Arashina looked round slowly, as if she was just coming to. "But we are not wrong," she added. "They are here in the city, the last of them, still using the magic they stole off the Berendanti. We've suspected that for a long time. And now you have confirmed it."

***

Azul tore off a crust of bread and transferred it to his mouth. He squinted as he chewed, as though it hurt him to eat. "They aren't dead," he said, wiping his lips. "Not one of them is dead."

He sat in the port offices of the Fiorenti Bank, in the private rooms of the Master-Banker, picking at pilchards in sweet sauce and drinking a bottle of cheap wine. Cortaag lurked by the wall. His stomach had been bandaged, and he could not sit. Outside, the air was full of gulls and the creak of ropes. Men called out in different languages; raucous laughter rose up from below.

Benevesi stood by the window, watching the ships. For him, Azul reflected, commerce was a virtue in itself, a representation of the will of great men to succeed. Azul felt nothing for this place. The sailors disgusted him. *Mongrel louts, all of them.*

"Several of our hired men were killed," Azul continued, poking his bread with a thin finger as if to get its attention. "That I can live with. But the woman and the knight got away. That is *not* acceptable."

"So?" Benevesi turned from the window. "If they've got any sense, we'll never see them again."

Azul frowned and sucked on his cheeks. "I don't think they *do* have any sense. You know, I'm beginning to wonder what we're dealing with. The woman said all kinds of rubbish when I questioned her, about assassination, vendetta and the like – at least, I thought it was rubbish at the time. On second thoughts, I think there might have been some truth in it all."

"Maybe," Cortaag said. "They know how to fight, that's for sure. Or at least the old man does."

Azul stared across the room. "Believe me, Benevesi, they'll still be here. They'll be hiding out somewhere, making a plan. If what that woman said is true, she's probably sharpening her knife right now."

"No doubt," Cortaag grumbled.

"So then," Benevesi said. "What should we do?"

"Hunt them both down." Azul tore off a scrap of bread and dipped it into the sauce. "Finish the job off."

"Couldn't've happened at a worse time, too," Cortaag growled. "I bet that priest timed it to happen now. The last thing we need is for this shit to come to light with the old brothers in town."

"Calm down, would you?" Benevesi said. "Maybe it's just chance."

"Don't tell me what to do!" Cortaag took a step forward, hands at his sides curling into fists. "What the hell do you know about it? I got a blade through the gut for you to tell me to calm down? For these people to shit all over us?"

Azul glanced up and smiled thinly. "Sit down, Felsten – if you can. You're scaring our friend. He's not used to violence."

Cortaag leaned back against the wall. Benevesi sighed. "Look," said the banker, "can't you just pay some people to take care of this? I mean to say, the Watch aren't the best, but there've got to be some Customs men we could hire, or mercenaries. Heaven knows we've got enough money coming in—"

"We'll do it ourselves," Azul replied. "This is a private matter. And besides, I doubt a few hired men could do the job."

Benevesi sighed. "You're getting worried about a madwoman and a broken-down old soldier. What is this man – pushing sixty, and still throwing his weight around? And this woman follows him about like a squire? It's like something from *Don Alonzo Rides Out*. If you ask me, these people sound like relics."

Azul scowled. "Do you consider me to be a relic,

too?" *Soon*, he thought, *you will realise how foolish an attitude that is. All of this – the city, the world around it, will be changed. The proper order will be restored, and the nonsense of the last two decades swept aside. Then, then you'll realise what a relic I really am. You judge the strength of a ruler by force of will, not money or age.*

Benevesi was smiling at him. "Here," he said, "I've got something else for you. You'll like this." He stepped to the door. "It's this way. Come on."

Benevesi led them down through the building. They passed through a hall of shipping clerks who sat scribbling at their desks like oversized schoolboys, surrounded by the scratchy whisper of pens.

Azul tapped Cortaag on the shoulder. "Did you find that dryad girl, the one the woman mentioned?"

Cortaag scowled. "Gone. The fat pig of a landlord didn't know where, and trust me, we pushed him hard."

"They took her with them," Azul replied. "That's the only explanation."

Benevesi took a narrow staircase to the ground. He opened a small door and they emerged into the afternoon sun.

"You can't see it from upstairs," the banker explained, leading Azul around the corner, "but there – look."

Azul squinted into the light. Benevesi pointed to a ship, a two-masted carrack big enough for ocean trade. An Averrian ship would have flown the griffon flag, by law; this didn't look as if it had come from the Astalian Peninsula at all. Men swarmed over the rigging, tucking in the rolled square sails. It had obviously been brought in for repairs: clockwork cranes held the ship at either end, anchoring it to the dock. Things like great sausages lay alongside the hull like piglets against a sow: buoyancy floats, made from the skin of young water-wyrms and inflated with brass pumps.

Two people moved about on the deck of the ship, the newness of their clothes marking them out from the stevedores and crew. The man wore a wide-brimmed hat with a roc feather. The woman's dress was green: it reminded Azul of plumage as it caught the light.

Azul had never seen the two of them before, but he knew them all the same.

"Their ship took in water two days ago," Benevesi said. "A Customs boat escorted them here. It appears there was damage beneath the waterline."

"Varro's last gift," Azul replied. He smiled. "A water-suit and an auger-drill."

"He was a good man," Cortaag muttered. "A brother."

"Bring that tar up, quickly!" a foreman yelled on the quay. "Keep stirring it!"

Benevesi pointed to the man in the hat, watching from the rail of the ship.

"That's the owner," he said, "and that's his wife. My men are repairing their ship – very slowly. They're under my personal protection as a member of the Council. I told them that the Watch investigation was over. That is right, isn't it?"

"Absolutely. We'll be taking this from here. It's much easier that way." Azul rubbed his hands together, suddenly sprightly. "Well, then, shall we say hello?"

***

It was mid-afternoon in the forest. The cloth walls threw

cool shadow over the pavilion. Giulia looked back at the trees and saw that the creature called Vurael was gone.

"It's been a pleasure to meet you," Arashina said.

"You too," Giulia said. "It's been interesting."

Hugh blinked a couple of times. He looked like an old man kept away from his supper – which, Giulia realised, he pretty much was. "Oh? Yes, definitely. A pleasure."

Arashina stood up and walked around the table. She wore leather sandals and loose, dark trousers. She looked relaxed and capable. Sethis leaned in and said something to her quietly, and she nodded and put out her hand. "Goodbye," she said. "And good luck. I will keep watching."

She had a strong handshake. "This way," Sethis said, gesturing.

They entered the trees again. Sethis walked beside Giulia, Hugh wandering along behind. "Thank you for hearing us out," the dryad said. "It sounds like we're pretty much on the same side."

"I think so."

"Arashina must seem rather strange to you," Sethis said. "She's been around your people much less than me. Some of the older dryads regard any contact with humanity as something of a betrayal."

Giulia nodded. "Reminds me of what the dwarrows said, back in Pagalia. When the Inquisition showed up, they weren't surprised. They said they always knew mankind would try to finish the job off."

"I don't feel like that. Some of your people are good, some are bad. The rest are just easily persuaded."

"That sounds about right," Giulia replied. The cold was gathering, the foliage becoming thinner on the branches. "We need a plan. The way I see it, there's two ways to go from here: Varro's workshop and the Fiorenti Bank. Right now, the workshop sounds more likely. If the bank wouldn't open up for you and the Scola, I doubt it'll do so for me."

"They may do," Sethis said. "You are human, after all."

"I'm poor and I'm a woman. They barely allow me to take my own money out; I doubt they'll let me anywhere near their secrets." She wondered about breaking into the bank. No, that could wait. She'd try the workshop first. Of course, there was a fair chance that the conspirators would have cleaned the place up after Varro's death, but she wouldn't know until she'd looked.

"I need to go back into the city," Giulia said. "Hugh, can you find something to do for the rest of today?"

"Easily."

"At the Scola, I mean. We ought to keep out of sight for now."

"We have a library," Sethis said. "You're welcome to look round there."

The knight frowned. "Well, I suppose I can. But we've been pinned down for too long, Giulia. It was being stuck in that damned inn that got us into trouble in the first place." He paused. "Could I stay here for a while, in Faery? It's good to get a bit of sun."

Sethis said, "I'll escort you back, once Giulia's returned to the Scola."

The afternoon light streaming through the trees looked crisp and cold. Giulia was almost back in winter again. "Do you know anyone who could lend me a dress?" she asked. "A commoner's dress, that is: nothing too showy, nothing memorable."

"I'll see what I can do," Sethis replied. "I'm sure someone can lend you something."

Branches crunched under their boots. Giulia felt the cold on her hands. She could see her breath. "I could really do with a drink," Hugh said wistfully.

She thought of the pavilion, the lurid green pastures and the strange creatures on them. And the prospect that they had allies now, that she and Hugh weren't alone. "Right now," she replied, "that feels like a pretty good idea."

***

Dusk crept over the water, and Falsi decided he was going home. He looked out across the wide canal, at the red roofs of the skyline, and felt sick of everything. He swung his stick onto his shoulder, dismissed the two men he had been leading through the streets on a pointless search for crime, and turned back the way he had come.

A fire-watcher strolled past. He gave Falsi a nod, and the Watchman scowled back.

Go home, friend, stop wasting your time on a thankless job. Who cares if the city burns down? I wouldn't. Nobody gives a shit.

It wasn't just weariness. It was the sense of being cheated, passed over, either watched suspiciously or ignored. Something was going on, that was obvious – almost as obvious as the fact that he wasn't invited to it.

I should get myself moved to the Southern Quarter. Maybe I could leave the watch and join the Customs. I'd put in a request, if the two men above me weren't a crook and a corpse.

"Fat bastard," he said out loud, and he spat into the

canal as he strolled by.

He reached the Pagalian Bridge, a long, wide expanse of white stone and brick. Prince Leonine of Pagalia had paid for it, years ago: Falsi had lined up with a dozen other Watchmen and cheered as the prince was carried across. Now the bridge was almost empty, and the only people on it were workers hurrying home.

Out on the canal, two young ladies stood at the bow of a pleasure-craft. They drank wine as three men worked the oars behind them. Falsi watched them with a vague sense of envy, tinged with lust. There wasn't any point in feeling much: they were so far out of his reach that he hardly knew what to think about them.

Everything's out of my reach. Slowly, bit by bit, my job is dripping away from me.

He rested against the rails and stared across the water. He thought about Orvo, the procurator, and the four main suspects suddenly and invisibly dead. Then he thought about the sense that had followed him since he'd left the Watch-house, that he was being watched.

A shadow stopped beside him, the dark blur of a body in a cloak.

"Don't move," a woman said. "There's a knife at your back."

"Ah, fuck," he said. It was an effort not to say *Fuck off and leave me alone*. He spat into the canal. "You again."

"Me," Giulia said.

Falsi didn't turn around. "Well, at least it's not a crossbow this time. Does that make us friends yet?"

She snorted. "Not yet. I just didn't think the crossbow went with this dress."

Falsi looked at the water and the houses. "They told me you were dead," he said.

"On balance, I think they were mistaken."

"They said all of you were." Anger crept into his voice. "What the hell is this all about, anyway? They said you killed the procurator, and you were shot trying to get out the city. According to my boss, you're in a winding-sheet on the Isle of Graves." He waited for a reply. "Well?"

"I didn't kill that priest, you know."

"I wish you had. It'd be a lot easier that way."

"You know I didn't, don't you?"

He sighed. He felt as if he were shrinking, like a camp-ball with a puncture. "Yes," he said. "I don't think you did."

"It sounds like they told you a few lies," Giulia replied.

"That's what I thought. Shit." Falsi stared down at the water. He could see her reflection, the white of her face under her black hood. She wore a cloak over a dark, simple dress. It made her look like a ghost. "Well," he said, "there's nothing I can do now. It's not a Watch matter anymore."

"Not since I died, eh?"

Now I know just what I am, he thought, *just what value they put on me. I do what they say: when they tell me to work, I work, and when they tell me to stop and forget, I do just that.*

"It fucking *stinks*," he said, and the fury in his own voice surprised him. A bell began to ring to the east: perhaps on a church, more likely on a boat, warning travellers or calling them to board.

"I need your help," she said.

"Oh yes? And why should I help you?"

"Because it stinks," she said. "You hate that as much as I do. You remember that man Varro? The one they sent me to see?"

"The one who tried to kill you?"

She nodded. "I need you to find out some things about him."

Falsi looked around slowly, as if waking from a dream. "What do you want to know?"

"Anything that looks wrong—"

"This whole business looks wrong," Falsi said, but he was interested now. He straightened up and said, "Go on."

Giulia glanced left and right. "Listen, Varro was a member of a gang. I don't mean a street-gang, though: these people are all older. A conspiracy, that's the word. Varro worked for an old man, a little man. If he's who I think he is, he's the one who killed the priest."

"This old man's the gang leader, then?"

"Yes. He must be at least sixty. He's rich, bald, quite short but not weak. There's a tattoo on his arm, like snakeskin. It might have some kind of magical effect. He's well-spoken, although he sort of croaks, like he's got a bad throat. I need you to find out who he is."

"How?"

"Varro will have had records of his business. All I need you to do is look at them and tell me if there's anything unusual."

Falsi rubbed his chin. "What sort of thing?"

"Unusual payments, requests, anything like that. Anything that stands out."

A slow, devious smile crept over the Watchman's face. "And what makes me so suited to doing this, instead of you?"

"They know my face down there. It'll be much easier for you."

"I can't promise anything, but I can take a look.

Where do I find these records?"

"They might be in the big shed at Varro's yard. But my guess is you'd be best off starting to look in your boss' office. Have you got a key?"

"No, but there's ways. But I guess you know that better than me." Falsi thought for a moment. "Meet me at eight tomorrow, in the ale-house on Printers' Row. Where you found me last time."

"I'll see you there. Thanks for doing this."

He shrugged. "If it stops you creeping up on me, I'm glad to help."

She nodded. "Good luck. And be careful. These are serious people. Don't take any risks you don't need to."

Falsi felt happy to be of use again, almost drunk on his sense of purpose. "Don't worry. I'm fiercer than I look."

"No, really. These people are experts. If anyone comes for you, run. I mean it."

He stopped smiling. "I'll look out," he said, and he patted the big pistol on his belt. "Just one thing. How did you find me?"

"I asked one of your men near the Watch-house, and he said you were walking the waterfront. Then I waited."

"Were you following me this morning?"

"No. Only just now."

"Hmm." Falsi glanced over her shoulder, ready to leave. "By the way, how did you find out about this old man? What did he do to get you on his tail?"

Giulia turned to go. "He tortured me," she said. "So I'm going to cut him to pieces. Any problems with that?"

***

As Giulia returned to the Scola, she felt her aggression start to fade. Falsi's fear seemed to be catching: by the time Giulia reached the side entrance, she was checking windows for watching eyes. She felt the energy drain from her and the Melancholia start to creep through her body like poison. She wondered whether she could do this, whether the whole venture was a terrible mistake. Of course it wasn't. She'd beaten Publius Severra, and this would be no different. Her arm had begun to ache. She wondered what it must look like under the bandages, and tried to think about something else.

One of the Scola's servants ushered her into the hall. A young man was holding forth to two bearded fellows in the rear hall. "But the limited palette," he explained, making a grabbing gesture into the air, "only makes the chiaroscuro more powerful. It's not drab – it's stark!"

Giulia didn't know what he was talking about, but it sounded like art. He wasn't bad-looking, and his enthusiasm was appealing. *Yes, you'd suit me fine. But what could I give you in return? Not a lot.* She trudged up the grand staircase, leaving the artists to their argument.

At the top of the stairs, a dwarrow was sitting on a bench, moulding something between his big hands. It looked like badly-mixed putty: it could be marble, she realised, for the dwarrows knew how to shape hard stone. He reminded her of her old friend Grodrin, back in Pagalia.

"Giulia?" Sethis stood in a doorway behind her. He looked inquisitive and optimistic, as if he thought she would give him good news. "How are you?" he asked. "Is the dress suitable?"

"The dress is fine. Say thank you to your friend from me."

"Amelia Brunelli. She left it here: it's one of her painting dresses. It's not many people who get to wear the clothes of a great artist." The dryad lowered his voice. "Here, I've got something for you. It's a tincture against Melancholia, a good one. I got it from one of the best apothecaries in Averrio." He held out a folded packet.

"Thanks." Giulia had expected him to give her a wad of picked herbs, or something he'd made himself: it seemed wrong for a dryad to go to an apothecary.

"Everything else all right?"

"My arm aches a little."

"I'll sort you something out. Hugh's in the library, over there." Sethis pointed. "Let me know if you need anything else."

"Thanks," she said again. "You're very kind."

The library was warm and well-lit. Six shelves of printed books stretched out in rows for the artists of the Scola to peruse. Hugh sat in the corner of the room, a wine bottle and an open book before him, staring out the window. There was a bland smile on his face. He nodded as she came in, then looked back to the window.

Giulia knew a fair amount about books: originally, from stealing them to order. The pictures had always intrigued her: wanting to know what they meant had inspired her to learn to read, years ago. She felt almost hungry as she looked over the spines, thinking about the stories that the books contained.

She picked out half a dozen titles and piled up them up on a table by the wall. "What're you reading, Hugh?" she asked.

He handed her the book. She was not surprised to see it was *The Death of Alba*, his favourite.

He had dog-eared a late page. There was a woodcut

of a rider lancing a dragon, while a maiden looked on. The woodcut was a copy of a painting Giulia half-recognised; the dragon looked like a huge plucked chicken.

She looked up and realised that Hugh was falling asleep. Giulia took the bottle from the table and sat down. She unfolded the packet Sethis had given her and tapped a little pile of grey dust into her palm.

It looked like the tinctures against Melancholia she'd taken before. *It could be anything.* There were stories about the fey folk, about them drugging people – women – and taking them away. *It could be poison, an enslaving drug, a love potion – to Hell with it. Why shouldn't I trust him?*

She tipped her hand against her lips, tasted the dust like fine sand coating the inside of her mouth, and licked her palm. Giulia lifted the bottle and took a swig. A quick swallow and there was only a little residue in her mouth. A second swig and it was all gone.

Good. That should stave it off for a while. Now, the books.

Her first book was an old work: John Mornville's *Travels in Africy*. She wetted her fingertip and ran through the pages, through the descriptions of the strange creatures that dwelled in the plains south of Jallar. Her eyes flicked over floating cities, dog-men in chainmail, weeping river-dragons and grey unicorns with skin like armour plate. She stopped at a picture of two men in loose britches, turbans on their heads. They were climbing up a cliff towards an enormous nest, on which sat a monster bigger than a horse, the result of the interbreeding of a lion and a bird of prey.

The symbol of the city.

She'd seen a griffon on the night Father Coraldo had died. Maybe it belonged to the killer, maybe it had just been flying overhead. But it was worth remembering.

The second book was *A Grammar Spiritual*, by John Dorne, Elayne's former tutor. Dorne was a great sorcerer and a very wise man, apparently, but the book was simply baffling. It looked more like a guide to mathematics than magic. Giulia closed it, vaguely relieved that she didn't understand the symbols and formulae inside.

The next was more promising. This was *The Magical History of the North* by Olaf Magus. Magus glowered from the front page, a stern, churchlike man. *Yes*, Giulia thought, *he'd know*. She picked through the pages, using the pictures at the head of each chapter as a guide. She stopped at a woodcut of a thing like an upright bear, and her eyes followed her finger down the page.

...taking on a Bear's aspect, as did Norskers in ancient days when they ate the berserking herb, or indeed wolves, as Publius Nasus relates in his Book of Changes. For it is well known that the stories of the Quaestan Empire contain transformations said to be wreaked by pagan gods upon those very Imperators...

Was it all like this? She turned the page and ran her eyes over the words, trying to find something that might help. She stopped halfway down.

... That wretched man did declare that he, Piter Stumpff, had been given a belt by Devils of the Forest and drunk of the blood of a man-wolf mixed with his Beer, whereupon he did tie that belt upon his arm and could at once change into a Beast and sate his hungers upon the goodfolk of the town until he chose to become a Man and walk among them ... To the Judges he said that he could alter as he pleased, but was strongest at the fullness of the Moon, and that no Disease would take him, nor any wound be struck that would not close within the Hour, lest

that blow was to his head or heart, or the Blade forged of lunar metal, so great was the devilry in him...

She carried on to the bottom of the page. "Hugh?"

The knight looked up and grunted.

"Wake up, would you?"

"I am awake. What's happening?"

"Have a read of this. That man you killed back in the inn – Varro, the wolf – this is all about it. Here."

She pushed the book over to him and tapped her finger on the middle of the page. Hugh leaned in close, squinting. He followed the text with a finger as pale and knobbly as a birch twig.

"We're going to need better weapons," she said. "It says they just heal up unless you kill them straight off."

"Edwin hit Varro in the neck," Hugh said. "That seemed to stop the bugger."

Giulia nodded. "It makes sense: that's where all the pipes are on a man. Maybe that'll stop them no matter what." She scratched her head. "The lunar metal's silver, isn't it?"

"Yes, that's right. I never was much good at books," he said gloomily. Giulia reached out for the next volume on her list.

They were setting the tables for dinner in the Scola. Women laid out plates, giving each a quick final polish before setting it down. The younger servants slacked where they could, but whenever the head maid turned to them, they hurried as if it hurt to be caught in her gaze.

Sometimes Giulia had thought that, had things gone differently, she would have ended up as a servant in a big house. It occurred to her that, even in a comparatively pleasant environment like the Scola, she could never have got used to being told what to do. She wandered over to the head maid, a brooding, thick-armed woman who had the bored, hard glare of a toad.

"Hello," Giulia said. "I'm due to stay here tonight, as a guest."

"Yep," said the woman.

"I'll be dining in my room. Could I, ah, borrow one of the spoons?"

The woman stared at her.

"I'm eating soup."

"Take what you like," the woman grunted. "I'll remember you took it. I remember everything."

"Thanks," Giulia said, and she picked up a shiny spoon and fled. She fetched her cloak, armed herself and slipped into the city.

Nightfall in the Western Quarter, where pagans and heretics lived. In torchlight, unbelievers and apostates hurried home from their work. The sky was darkening, swelling with rain.

A Purist couple passed by, the wife lagging a few steps behind her man. Under the hat-brim, his eyes were sharp and hard, shining with joyless enthusiasm. He looked like an Inquisition soldier – not just in his dark clothes, but also in his keen, bitter face. Giulia watched them go.

"It's not right," a cracked voice said from the side. Giulia looked around: an old woman stood beside her. The woman's face was small and wrinkled, her back and hands bent. She looked as though she were shrinking, folding into herself until she disappeared. "It's not right," the woman said again.

"Sorry?"

"They beat their wives, you know. They all do. With their praying all hours of the day, carrying their heathen books about... it's not right."

Giulia looked at the Purists, the grim man and his meek, broken-looking wife, and reflected that even if Purists didn't beat their wives, they certainly weren't doing themselves any favours. And yet she resented being told so.

"I'm looking for a smith," Giulia said.

"There's one," the crone replied. "He's one of 'em as well."

"A Purist?"

"An angel-killer. Black as midnight, he is. This used to be a good place," the woman said. "Third street on the left, if you want. I wouldn't use him," she added, and she made the Sign of the Sword across her chest. "Was it the Purists that cut your face?"

Giulia walked off.

"I'm closing," said the smith. He was tall, strong-looking, with a round, dark face that looked as if it ought to be smiling. His hair was neatly plaited down his back. He was an Idacian, a Jallari sect who denied the existence of angels. Or at least Giulia was fairly sure that was what they denied. Whatever it was, it was enough for them to burn when the authorities were in the mood.

"I need some work done," Giulia said. "It's urgent. I can pay."

"I'm sure you can," the man said. His voice was deep and pleasant. He turned and started gathering his tools. "I'm finished for today, though. Come back tomorrow and I'll do it first thing."

Can I wait a day? No. Best strike while the iron is hot.

She thought of the tip of the poker, felt water gathering in her eyes and nearly hissed with anger.

"It won't take long," she said, making her voice stay level. "It's just a piece of silver—"

Patiently: "Then get a silversmith."

Giulia took a deep breath. The room smelt of fireplaces and greased steel. "I need it done quietly. There's a man out there – a sorcerer – and I need silver on my knife to wound him."

The smith paused, head tilted to one side. "Is that so?"

"This sorcerer is enchanted. He used to be in the Inquisition. He killed a load of magical people and stole their powers during the war. Last week he murdered a priest and tried to have my friends hanged for it, then he came after me. I need a silver edge to protect me from him."

The blacksmith said, "And this is true?"

"Yes. I don't expect you to believe me—"

"I don't. Show me the knife."

She drew it and passed it over.

"It's a dwarrow weapon," he said. "That's an unusual thing for anyone to carry, let alone a woman on her own."

"Well, I am unusual."

"So I see." Wryly, he said, "It's fun to stand out, isn't it?"

"Oh, it's just wonderful."

The smith looked at her knife as if there was a message written down the blade. "I'll put a strip on the side, near the cutting edge. It won't be the finest work I've ever done, but if you need him to feel the silver, he will. Will that do?"

"That'll do fine." She took out the spoon she had taken from the Scola. "Here. Melt it down. You can keep what's left over."

"Tomorrow morning, then. If you don't come back, I keep your blade. And your silver. Fair?" He smiled and held out his hand to shake.

The Scola was empty, the dinner finished, and there was something cold and bleak about the statues in the hall. They seemed to judge Giulia as she passed by.

The cleaning crews were busy now, as they would be in any big house. A couple of women passed her in soft shoes, pulling a little cart laden with buckets and mops. They nodded to Giulia and she smiled back, wondering whether she was supposed to give them a coin.

Her arm had stopped aching now. She strolled through the corridors, wondering how badly the wound would scar. She could imagine it now, a band of pale skin, crinkled and unusually soft. It wouldn't be too visible, but she would know it was there. She didn't mind thinking about the wound itself. It kept her mind off the circumstances in which she'd received it.

They didn't break me. If I was broken, why would I still be here?

As Giulia climbed the stairs, she realised that she didn't want to go to bed. In the dark, the events of the week would run back through her mind. She would see all of it again, ending in the cellar and the agony in her arm. She would remember what she had been pushing to the back of her mind: the shame of talking, of betraying herself and her friends.

I am not broken, she thought.

On the landing, Giulia waited to get accustomed to

the dark. She climbed another, thinner set of stairs, past the servants' quarters and up into the attic. She looked at the door behind which Hugh slept, and for a moment thought of waking him.

What good would that do? Sooner or later, you're going to have to sleep.

She opened her door and slipped inside. Moonlight streamed through the high window. Giulia took off her boots and borrowed dress in the dim light, then pulled her kit out from beneath the bed. She put on her trousers and her black shirt.

There was a little parcel on top of her bag: the tile, wrapped in its scrap of cloth. She lifted it out and looked at the dead body lying at the soldier's feet. The soldier was one of Azul's men, she was sure of it. It felt heavy in her hands. She wished that she'd shown it to Sethis – and then felt that it was her business only, as if Father Coraldo had entrusted it to her like a quest, a wrong that she had to avenge.

Hugh had left her crossbow beneath the bed. Giulia sat on the bed and held it, pleased at the feel of the wood in her hands. *No, I'm not broken*, she thought. *I'm the one who breaks things.* She worked the ratchet until the string was fully drawn. Giulia laid a bolt in the groove and got up. She looked out the window and lifted the bow, peering down the bolt as if to shoot the moon.

TWELVE

"You've got a strip of silver down the blade, just behind the cutting edge," the blacksmith said, turning Grodrin's knife over in his hands. "It's the best I can do for now – not perfect, but if the stuff is poison to them, they'll taste it well enough. Here."

He held out the knife and watched Giulia as she examined it. Giulia took the weapon and tested its weight. It looked as if a single bead of molten silver had trickled from the handgrip to the tip of the blade. The morning light filtered into the forge and, as the sunshine caught the blade, the stripe of silver looked almost white against the matt black steel.

She made a little jabbing motion, not wanting to wield it properly in front of this man. "That's good. I like it."

The blacksmith watched her sadly. "A woman shouldn't fight," he said. "Her husband should take up arms for her – if she doesn't have one yet, her father. It's a shame to see a woman armed."

"I don't have either," Giulia said. She felt pleased with the knife. "And besides, this I'm doing myself. I'm the only person I'd trust to get it done."

The blacksmith shrugged. "Then we're finished. Good luck to you."

He put out his grimy hand, and they shook.

"When you find this Inquisition man, put a notch on him for me," the smith said, and he turned back to his work.

Giulia stood in the chilly sunshine and breathed in the fresh air, listening to the sound of the hammer on the anvil in the forge behind her. The street was busy, even now. A spicy, greasy smell came from a food stand beneath an awning; a Purist carpenter sawed away across the road, his face running with sweat. Two Marmurin priests walked past in their smocks, muttering in unison.

Busy people, these heretics.

It was time to meet up with Falsi. She caught a boat in the next street down and headed for Printers' Row.

The boat slid past peeling white buildings and open windows that the shadows turned into black squares. They slipped into a narrow canal with tenements on either side. High walls blocked out the sun, and it was chilly in the shade. Giulia pulled her hood up.

Looking down the canal, she felt that she was passing through a gate. After two days' rest she was back in Averrio: not as a suspect or a fugitive, but as a hunter.

She'd once read that there was a sort of fish which died if it stopped swimming. *That's me*, she thought. *I can't stop now: all I can do is outrun the Melancholia and keep fighting until all my enemies are dead. The moment I stop, I'll be admitting failure – and then I'll sink.*

Twenty minutes later, the boat drew up to the bank. The printers' shops were small and smelled of alchemy. From behind the open doors she heard the steady, slamming thump of print-blocks striking paper. Someone had thrown a bucket of runny ink into the road, and it was dripping into the canal. A boy sat outside one shop, slotting metal squares into a frame. He didn't look up as she went past.

The pub was the one where she'd ambushed Falsi a few days ago. Even in the morning sun it managed to look poky and dark. There were no other customers.

"Help you?" the publican's wife inquired.

"I'll take a cup of small beer, please," she said. As the woman passed her a beaker, she put a couple of coppers on the table and said, "I'm supposed to be meeting a friend. I don't know if you've seen him."

"What's he like?"

"He's older than me; he's clean-shaven and tired-looking. A Watchman."

The woman nodded. "What's your name?"

"Giulia."

"Wait here." She shuffled into the rear of the room and came back from the shadows with a flat package in her hand. "Here. He left this for you. Said you'd know what it's about. He said he had urgent business to deal with."

"Thanks." Giulia took the package and her cup and sat down by the wall. She picked the string open. Inside was a slim book without a cover, the outer pages dark with grease. A loose sheet had been pushed into the front of the book. She opened the sheet up and read the big, careful writing inside.

Your man is called Ramon Azul. Sorry about before. Remember me when you get rich.

Giulia began to read.

She was looking at a record-book. She had seen things like this before, but only from a distance: it didn't make for easy reading. She ran her eyes down the various columns, just about able to work out what they meant. Varro had built dinghies, repaired hulls, commissioned figureheads. He'd bought in timber and pitch and sent out bills to noblemen, guilds and merchant freelancers. He had been busy, but innocent.

Someone, presumably Falsi, had ringed a set of purchases. Giulia followed the circles, tracing Varro's work across the pages. She had no instinct for figures, but Falsi seemed to have an understanding that she lacked. Giulia turned another page, squinting in the bad light, and saw a pair of crosses in the margin, like a warning. Her finger slid down the page.

Two hulls sold to a man named Azul, she thought. *Hulls?*

She flicked through, looking for something else. No, this seemed to be on its own: Varro had provided two identical hulls – "modified", whatever that meant – along with a set of enchanted machinery bought in from the Clockworkers' Guild. Someone called Azul had ordered them for the guild of glassblowers.

Interesting, but hardly proof of anything illegal. Most large guilds in Averrio had their own boats. Payment for the hulls had been received some months after the delivery of the goods. Falsi had ringed that too. Giulia re-read the dates. Nothing strange there.

So who was Azul? *A high-ranking member of the Averrian guild of glassblowers, from the looks of it.* So a serious man, a powerful merchant. Giulia sat back and tried to visualise it all, to lock the people into their roles. She thought of Varro and his jolly, lying face, and then the old man, with his sour mouth and calm, ruthless eyes. *A glassmaker. God.*

So this Azul – whoever he may be – is a merchant. He needs two boats. Is he the link to the New World? Did he sail them there? Thoughts shifted at the edge of her mind like smoke, too vague to quite grasp: Sethis' talk about the bank, Varro wearing his underwater suit, the strange tile that the dead priest had been carrying.

It all comes down to the port. Edwin and Elayne, the priest, the Glassmakers, Varro himself. It's all about ships. Is he some kind of smuggler?

As soon as the thought was in her head, she wondered why she hadn't realised it before. Averrio was the perfect place to bring in goods, a sprawling port with links from Dalagar to Albion, whose trade routes reached deep into Bergania and the Teutic League, all the way to Maidenland and Santa Carilla across the World's End Sea. It was a nexus of trade, a gateway to other worlds. Anything could come in and go out, provided that it could slip through the Decimus' Customs patrols.

So is Azul bringing in illegal goods? How would he get them past the Customs? Disguise them as glass? Is it glass itself that he's smuggling?

Elayne had thought that the tile on Father Coraldo's body had come from the New World. Perhaps the priest had been there too. She wondered what he had done: discovered a criminal conspiracy, or decided to do a little illegal business of his own, and been crossed in the attempt? She thought about Arashina, and her talk about the Inquisitors twenty years ago. Churchmen of a sort, all of them.

The New World Order.

She returned to the entries about the two hulls.

There was a delivery address. Varro had sent the parts – or whatever he had made with them – to a warehouse near his boatyard. That was sloppy, but then nobody had been expected to check.

Not until now. It was time to talk to Hugh.

***

"So what's the job?" Falsi called to Orvo over the thwack of oars against the lagoon. Behind him, he could see the two galleons that marked the edge of the city proper. They were ancient things, decommissioned from naval service and permanently moored in place. Huge waterwheels jutted from their sides instead of cannon, turning in the tide to wind up the clockwork that powered the rotating gun-turrets and watchtowers of the city armoury.

There was a choppy wind out in the bay, and the two paid rowers had to work hard. One of them locked his oar, and the boat lurched. Swearing, the man freed his blade and they started up again. It wasn't dangerous weather, not yet.

"Morts," Orvo said. "The gravediggers brought up some stiffs a couple of days ago. They say they were putting them in the hole when they started thrashing about." He shrugged. "I don't know if it's true, but you've got to check, you know..."

"It's not those three Anglians and that woman, is it? The ones who tried to escape? You said they'd been buried out there."

"No, it's not them." Orvo looked uncomfortable, Falsi thought. Perhaps it was just the rocking of the boat. "They're good and buried. Why d'you ask?"

"Just wondered. Aren't we going to need masks, in

case it's the Grey Ague bringing them back?"

"There'll be masks when we get there," Orvo said.

The Isle of Graves lay low and dark before them like a giant crown sitting on the water. Its perimeter wall backed directly onto the lagoon. Behind the wall, trees stood on small hills. Falsi thought that the trees seemed trapped by the brick wall, like animals in a pen.

The main dock reminded him of the facade of a grand house. Nobody came down the steps to greet them. Orvo took the looped rope and tossed it over the mooring-post. He was strong as well as fat and, sweating, he drew the boat in close.

As he stepped onto the land, Falsi wished that he had brought a friend. He looked up at the stern white gatehouse, at the neat peak of its roof and the squat buttresses, and thought that it would not have surprised him to see a rotting face pressed against the round, porthole-like windows, the mouth gaping with the endless hunger of the undead. He wished his mastiff was here, or a priest. *They buried that priest out here as well – or at least that's what Orvo said.*

The rowers handed up boat-hooks. They had wide heads to shove the revenants back, ending in narrow spikes to drive home a finishing blow. You had to puncture their skulls, or else smash them apart. That would turn them back into corpses.

Orvo nodded to the boatmen. "Stay here." He walked up the steps, to the great gates.

"We need more gear," Falsi said as Orvo pushed his key into the padlock. Orvo opened the gate and beckoned him through. *He's going to lock me in there*, Falsi thought. *He's going to shut me in and row away. Oh God*, he thought, and he stepped through.

Orvo followed him and pulled the gate closed behind them. He slid the bolts. "Morts can't work bolts," he said. "They're too stupid."

They looked across the gardens. The lawns were pleasant in the morning sun. The walls blocked the wind, and only the tops of the trees swayed. The tombstones looked as if they'd grown here. Dotted among them, the robed figures of angels seemed genuinely at peace.

"It's not bad here," Falsi said. "All things considered."

Orvo pointed. "We need to go over there."

They started up the path, carrying their boat-hooks over their shoulders like labourers. Their boots crunched on the stones.

"Been a hell of a week," Orvo said. Falsi thought, *Yes, so hellish you couldn't even show up for the last few days.*

"How so?" he replied, looking between the trees. He'd never seen a mort before. There were special squads for this sort of thing, elite units of the Customs and the army that dealt with natural disaster and the Grey Ague. After fire, the Council of a Hundred feared nothing as much as plague.

Killing morts isn't proper Watch business, Falsi thought. *Assuming we actually manage to find them.* And then, with a creeping unease, *Assuming there are any to find.*

"Oh, just things," Orvo said. "These Anglians, for one thing."

Falsi nodded, feeling his heart start to accelerate. "But that's finished now, isn't it? I mean, they're all dead, so who cares, right?"

A little chapel stood on the hill about forty yards away. It was a pretty little place, shining in the sun. The front door opened, and two men walked out.

"Look over there," Falsi said. The men wore long coats and masks, like plague doctors. The masks covered their heads, ending in cones over their faces, packed with enchanted herbs.

"They're helping us," Orvo said.

The masks made them look like crows. Each beaked man held a staff. Falsi knew at once that they were not his friends.

"They're still alive, you know," Orvo said. "Those Anglians and the woman with the scars. They got away."

"I thought so," Falsi said.

"You didn't think anything," Orvo replied, not raising his voice. "You knew."

"What is this?" Falsi demanded. His heart had risen in his chest, pressed against his ribs like a bird trying to break out of its cage.

The plague doctors were still coming, unhurried.

"We need to talk, you and me," Orvo said. He looked nervous too.

Falsi stopped walking. "Talk? You can talk to this," he said. His hand was smooth and swift, and suddenly there was a gun in it. He glanced at the two doctors. "Stop there!"

"That thing's not loaded," Orvo said. "And if it is, the powder can't still be dry."

"We can find out easily enough," Falsi said. "That's enough!" he shouted up the path. "Stop there!"

"You heard him," Orvo cried. "Wait!"

The men stopped, and their beaked heads exchanged a glance. They stood in the path, waiting.

Falsi didn't feel scared any more. Wild strength ran through him, and suddenly he felt sharp, keen, as if he might go berserk at any moment. He wanted to vent this craziness, to whoop or laugh. He thought, *If I start laughing now, I'll never stop.* Fighting his voice down, he said: "Who put you up to this?"

"Nobody 'put me up'."

"Was it Azul?"

"I don't know who that is." Orvo's voice shook as if it was about to break. The wind picked up, making the treetops hiss.

"Yes you do. Did he kill the priest? Did he get you to do that?"

One of the doctors leaned in towards the other. They were making a plan.

"I didn't kill him," Orvo said.

"Who did?"

Orvo said nothing.

"Come on, man, it's a fucking priest! They killed a priest and tried to have us hang four people who'd done nothing wrong. It's one thing to take a bit of money on the side, but God almighty, you can't go along with that. Right?"

"It was Azul," Orvo said. "One of his men did it. I thought—"

He lunged. Orvo's hand grabbed the barrel, tugged, and the gun banged and kicked in Falsi's hand. Orvo took a step back, half-bent at the waist, his face screwed up like a baby about to howl. He sat down with a soft thump. Falsi smelled cordite.

Blood ran from Orvo's hand. It was pressed against his chest. The tip of his middle finger was missing, but most of the blood leaked through from the hole in his chest. Slowly, he pitched onto his side.

Something touched Falsi's hand. He glanced down and saw a droplet of rain on his wrist.

Falsi looked back up the path, as though he had been caught stealing. The masked men paused for a moment and began to move towards him. They broke into a slow, lumbering jog. Falsi glanced at the boat-hooks, then over his shoulder towards the gates. He looked between the men and the gates, trying to make a decision. Then he ran.

***

Two dogs were gearing up to fight in the road. Giulia watched them as she walked, a memory teasing the back of her mind. Varro's records had proved more interesting than she had expected, and a full perusal had taken up most of the afternoon. It was almost four, almost starting to get dark.

Azul, she thought. *So that's what you're called.* She would need more information, but it felt good to have a name to hang on him, a target for her fury.

One of the dogs had lowered its shoulders as if trying to bow, dipping low before the other. Giulia remembered Giordano, her lover years ago, joking about the Kingdom of the Dogs. He'd been an expert talker of nonsense, which had made him seem both funny and rebellious. He could take an idea and follow it to absurdity, and she'd join in, inspired, each adding to the other's silliness until they were both laughing drunk.

When Giulia had fled from Pagalia, her scars still raw and new, she'd lost touch with him. A year later Gio had been kind enough to write to her to say that he had found someone else, and the Kingdom of the Dogs was no more.

Giulia kept on walking, tired and wistful. Water

slopped softly on stone. The road was wide, for Averrio. On the far side, a lamplighter prodded a taper into a brazier. The Scola was only a street away.

As she reached the Scola she realised something she had always known, but never quite put into words: that Giordano had been one of the greatest opportunities of her life, and that that opportunity would never be coming back.

She turned the corner, into San Cornelio Square. There were men outside the Scola. She glimpsed blue surcoats and something dropped inside her like a rock. Giulia pushed her back against the wall, breathed in. She thought of Sethis, Hugh, Iacono the mapmaker, the trees at the bottom of the garden and the creatures who had sat in there with her.

Not good.

Five men loitered around the closed doors. Four wore dark clothes, but the light still caught on sword-belts and knives. The fifth was something else: taller and thinner than the others, dressed in a blue tunic; he swung a stick almost cheerfully as he watched the road, tapping it against his boot.

Giulia shielded her eyes and peered at him from thirty yards away. It was Cafaro, Falsi's rival from the Watch-house.

Shit.

She'd have to get in via the rear. She remembered the little dock at the back, facing onto the Great Canal. The gate there would lead into the garden, with its walls and thick foliage. *Lots of cover*. Yes, that would do.

She walked back up the road and crossed to the shadows on the other side. The guards were clustered in front of the door, talking. Giulia slipped into the passageway between the Scola and the smart tenements that neighboured it.

The wall was ten feet tall and too smooth to climb. No doubt the scholars wanted to keep their work quiet, and thieves away from their art. She kept close to the wall, in its shadow, following it down to the corner at the rear of the garden. The air was cold on her face and hands.

Hugh, Sethis, Arashina – where were they? Inside the Scola, in prison, something worse? She smelled smoke from behind the wall, but she couldn't hear the crackle of flames. She kept going to the corner.

Giulia stopped, crouched down, and put one eye around the edge. She flinched back – a man stood on the jetty. A rowing boat lay low in the water behind him. Water slopped gently against the pier.

The setting sun turned the man into a silhouette. The canal stretched away from his boots, full of the colours of sunset. It looked like oil. The man had a beard, long hair and a military crossbow. He wore a dented cuirass but no helmet.

Mercenary.

Giulia reached to her belt and drew her long knife. It felt reassuringly solid, as if its weight anchored her to her task. She flexed her fingers. *If you've hurt Hugh*, she thought, *if you've so much as touched him—*

Giulia stepped out behind him, onto the jetty. She lifted her hand level with the side of her head. A good blow would put him out cold.

No boats were coming on the canal.

His thumbs were hitched into his belt, crossbow wedged under his arm, and he sighed contentedly as he stared out across the water.

Giulia covered the distance in long, bent-legged

steps, her boots quick on the slimy wood of the pier. His back rose in her vision like a cliff as she approached, and she raised the knife higher, tensed the muscles in her arm and willed him: *Don't look round. Don't look round, you can't see me—*

She swung the knife down. He started to turn and the pommel smashed into the side of his skull, sending a judder of force up Giulia's arm. The mercenary stumbled, his knees buckled, and he went down with a puzzled little groan, a tiny sound for a man of his bulk.

Yes! Giulia hooked her arm around his chest and tried to lower him gradually, to minimise the noise. Her foot slid on the slick timber and she dropped painfully onto one knee, the man flopping across her lap. She lowered his head onto the jetty. When she was satisfied that he was out cold, she stood up.

The mercenary lay sprawled at her feet. Why not cut his throat, or put a stiletto into his spine? No. It wasn't needed. She drew his sword and tossed it and his crossbow into the canal. *Now to get this bastard out of sight.*

He was almost impossible to drag. She managed to roll him to the bottom of the wall, where perhaps he would be mistaken for rubbish, or a sleeping drunk. It would be wrong to push him into the water. Years ago, Publius Severra's men had tried to drown her, and the thought of the cold water enveloping her made Giulia shudder. She would not have wished that on anyone.

Well, almost anyone.

The gates were closed. Giulia crouched down and checked the lock. There was a tiny gap where the door met the frame, and through it she saw that there were bolts on the inside. *Shit*, she thought, *I won't be opening that.*

Giulia pulled her leg up and put the toe of her boot

onto the door handle. She took a long, slow breath.

She drove up from the ground with her right leg, pushed down on the handle with her left, and grabbed at the top of the gate. Her fingers hooked over the top and she hauled herself up. She dropped down on the other side and froze.

The garden was in disarray. The little wood was a damp ruin, dripping sadly where the conifers had once been fat with needles. The branches had been hacked down, the trunks scorched as if to cauterize the stumps.

Damn, they didn't mess about.

She crept up the garden, keeping close to the wall. The ground was wet and tangled. Thorns snagged her cloak; trailing branches lay in wait to trip her. Suddenly the whole place was her enemy.

That was why they'd wrecked the forest, she realised. It was an escape route. Burn the trees and you'd close the way out. She wondered if the others had been able to get into the forest before the Watch had destroyed it. Perhaps Hugh and the others were in Faery, trapped there. Or perhaps their bodies were piled up inside.

Eight yards from the gate, she saw her first corpse. It was a man lying on his side in the bushes, his back a mess of red and brown. He'd been slashed from behind, a single long blow from shoulder to hip, probably inflicted as he tried to run away. She didn't recognise his pale, empty face. Giulia crept on, faster now.

The second dead man lay beside the Scola's back door, slumped like a drunkard. He was tubby, and his stomach stuck out in front of him. Blood had run from his neck, covering his chest in a black stain.

Light moved on the right. Giulia pulled back and crouched down behind the ruined trees. A tall man emerged from the back door, a lantern on his belt. He carried a little bag, swinging it as though it was a cosh.

Giulia slid the stiletto out of her left sleeve.

The tall man crouched down beside the corpse. His sword stuck out behind him like a tail. He whistled softly and began patting the body down.

Giulia stepped out of cover. The man had opened the corpse's shirt, and was searching his neck for jewellery. Giulia crossed the ground in five long strides.

He did not notice her until her shadow blotted out the lantern-light. He started to turn, but he was too slow. She hit the back of his head with her left hand, shoving his chin down, and punched her stiletto into the back of his neck. He spasmed, hand twitching towards his neck, and flopped across his victim with a sound like a saddle being tossed onto the ground. He lay there, his hands fluttering, then he was still.

Giulia's arm ached a little. It all felt very simple, as if she had been pulling a splinter. She raised her hood to hide her face, and went inside.

There was just enough light to see. She crept down the passage with her weight on her back foot, keeping close to the wall to minimise the creaking of the floor.

Giulia reached the bottom of a staircase and dropped into the deep shadow below it, wishing she hadn't left her crossbow in her room. She waited, listening, head cocked to one side.

No sound came from within the Scola. It had begun to rain outside, and the patter of water on the windows was like a brush on a drum. She felt alone and very small, but ready and unafraid.

Giulia climbed the wide stairs two at a time. At the

top she paused, listening. Still nothing. She approached the great hall, bracing herself for what might be beyond.

The hall was empty, lit only by the moon. A little mechanical trolley lay in the doorway. Its clockwork innards spilled across the floor.

A long table stood in the centre of the room, laid for a banquet that would never begin. One of the dining chairs had fallen over backwards, as though someone had leaped up and fled. She thought about the ghostly thane in *The King of Caladon*, denouncing the king at his coronation feast.

At the end of the table was a corpse in a chair. It wore a blue Watch tunic, with a bib of blood. The head lolled back. It looked familiar.

She took a step forward, her silver-edged knife in front of her. As she passed the deserted table, the head swung down and Falsi's one open eye fixed on her. She sucked in her breath and froze.

"Help," he said.

She glanced around, saw no-one, and hurried to his side. Falsi lay in the chair as if he had fallen from above. He looked tiny and lost, a prince without courtiers. His blood was black in the moonlight.

"What happened?" she said. Her voice sounded high and desperate.

"We got in," he said, as if that answered everything. It nearly did.

"Where is everyone?"

Falsi licked his lips. They were puffy and split. The right side of his face was badly swollen, the right eye entirely shut. *Broken cheekbone*, Giulia thought. "They ran off," he said. "Pixies took them into the garden. They all ran off."

"All of them?"

"Most."

"What about Hugh?"

Falsi nodded slowly. "Him too, I think. He was holding us back with some of the others, till they all got out."

"What happened to you?"

"They got me this morning," he said. He winced, a convulsive twitch that made Giulia start. "Got me on the Isle – Isle of Graves. Orvo's dead. Brought me back here to see their man. God knows why, I've told them all I know... Cafaro, he did this. Must've been waiting for an excuse..." His mouth moved very slightly, as if it wanted to smile. "Looks like it was my turn."

Falsi's face turned away from her, and he raised his head carefully and looked at the roof. Above them, the horned man and the chubby women romped at the waterside, swigging from jugs of wine.

"Wish I was up there," he said.

"Come on," Giulia replied, suddenly furious with everything – with him, herself, her enemies, this whole stinking business. "We're getting out. Can you walk?"

"I don't know."

"Let's find out. Where're you hurt?"

"Leg and side."

She peered at him. "Right. Let's get you ready." Giulia crossed the room, drew her knife and slashed at the curtains. They were thicker than she'd expected: she had to hack at them before a length of cloth came away. Quickly, she bandaged Falsi as best she could: he had lost a good deal of blood, she realised, and his shirt and britches were stiff with it. She crouched beside him and tied the bandage tight.

"Left me here," Falsi said as she tied off the tourniquet on his leg. "Said they'd come back. They went to fetch someone."

"I know who," she replied. "That's the bastard I'm looking for."

"He's not here. He's at a warehouse. The one in the books."

"A warehouse?"

"Where they bring the glass. Fuck."

"Listen," she said, "I'm going to help you out here, but I need to get something. I'll be two minutes, then I'll come back. All right?"

He came to life: his eye was wide and desperate. "Don't leave me here."

"I won't, I promise."

"Be fucking quick. I mean it. Please."

Giulia touched his hand, felt embarrassed, turned and ran out. She knew the way well enough; she ran down a corridor, turned, then climbed the staircase that led up towards the roof.

Hugh's door gaped open. Hers was shut. She touched the handle and a long hair came away on her finger. She'd put it there this morning.

Three steps took her to the bed, the boards creaking softly underfoot. She crouched down and reached underneath. Her fingers found the crossbow and she pulled it out.

Giulia slung the crossbow over her shoulder and hurried back downstairs. She was twenty yards away from the hall when she heard a man's voice.

"It comes to all of us, in the end," the voice said. It wasn't Azul: this was someone younger and healthier, cocky instead of vicious. She knew instantly that it was an enemy.

Someone had come to finish Falsi off. There wasn't enough time to load the crossbow. She drew her long knife and crept closer.

Giulia looked into the dining hall. The grand statues were almost luminous in the moonlight. Cafaro stood at the end of the table, addressing Falsi like a jester performing for a drunken king.

"I mean to say," Cafaro said, and she could hear the amusement in his voice, "if you ride a three-legged horse, you shouldn't be surprised when it drops you on your arse, right?" His voice rose, became strained and self-righteous. "'Oh, I've got to do right by these ladies. Got to show the world what a perfect knight I am.' Right, because you look fucking perfect too."

Giulia bent low and crept into the room.

"I mean, it's just pathetic. It's childish, that's what it is, fucking childish. What did you think, that you'd get them to sleep with you in return? You think you were going to get to fuck a noble lady in return for all this?"

Her eyes were level with the tabletop. She scurried forward.

Cafaro shook his head. "I expected more from you. I thought we were in this together. We were supposed to be together on this – all of us – and now you go and betray us all."

Falsi's eye looked straight at her.

"What?" Cafaro demanded. "What? You think someone's going to come for you?"

He turned. Giulia gasped and ducked under the table.

"What, you think someone's going to get you out of this shit?" Cafaro's boots took a step towards her. "I don't think so!"

Sudden movement, and plates and cutlery were swept down from the table. They broke and clattered around her. She licked her lips. Cafaro's legs were close enough to cut. She could reach out and slash his tendons, kill him when he fell.

"Because let's be clear about this: you are fucked!" Cafaro turned, stepped back towards his boss. His voice had flicked from mockery to self-righteous outrage. "You sold us out for nothing. All this shit you are in is because of that."

Giulia crawled out from under the table. She rose up behind Cafaro, looked for the place to strike.

"Well, you've only got yourself to blame. All good things come—"

Giulia grabbed him from behind. She threw her left hand over his face – that always panicked people – and pulled him back. Her right fist rammed the knife into his spine.

She was half-mad with hatred. Giulia staggered back, pulling him with her. She heard his muffled cries, felt his spit and blood against her palm. Her hip caught on the corner of the table and she fell onto her back, pulling Cafaro down onto her.

He flailed, grabbed at her shirt. She yanked his chin back and stabbed him in the neck, gritted her teeth and sawed through his throat.

Giulia shoved him off her and scrambled to her feet. Cafaro clutched his neck, but there was no stopping a wound like that. He stared up at her, his eyes full of horror.

"I'm going to kill all your people," Giulia said. She was panting. "Every last one of them." She flicked the blood off her knife and slid it back into its sheath. At her feet, Cafaro was still.

"Good," Falsi said. His face was drying; in a few places the blood was still sticky and damp. Cafaro had worked him over well: perhaps that was part of the training when you joined the Watch. "Can I go to Albion with you?"

He sounded half-delusional. "What?"

"Go to Albion. With you and your friends. On your ship."

"No," she said. "I've got business here. Besides, they've gone."

"No. They're here."

"What? Why?"

A laugh came from outside. Falsi flinched, as if from a blow. Giulia felt sick watching him. She'd flinched like that.

"Let's go," she said. "Listen, I'm going to pull you up. You've got to be quiet. Understand?"

He nodded.

Giulia took both his hands, stepped back and hauled him to his feet. Falsi cried out between gritted teeth, and the sound swelled around them, filling the room like a cloud of noise. She stepped in close and pulled his arm across her shoulder.

"It hurts—"

"Not long now. Just try to keep quiet. There's guards at the front door. We'll go out the back."

They crossed the hall slowly, Falsi struggling at her side. His body felt like a sack of sand, his legs two wobbling sticks. They reached the door and lurched to the top of the stairs.

"I'll do it," he said, and she helped him grip the

banister with both hands.

She loaded the crossbow and went down before him. Falsi dropped himself down behind her, one step at a time, his boots scuffing the stairs. When she reached the bottom she glanced back: Falsi was still near the top, his teeth bared like a beast. *Come on*, she willed him, *get a bloody move on*!

Halfway down the stairs, he said "Wait," and she cursed under her breath.

A guard called out in the road. Giulia stopped, her hands tight on the bow. Her palms were slick with sweat.

"Nearly there," Falsi said.

She caught him at the bottom, let him get hold of her and stepped away from the banisters. Her back and arm ached from carrying him. They struggled down the corridor, towards the back of the Scola.

As they entered the garden, Falsi seemed to lose his will, as if the cords that held him together had gone slack. He drooped in her grip, and she nearly stumbled. "I can't," he said.

Oh no you don't, not now. Her skin crawled with impatience. "You can. Come on!"

"It's too—"

She wanted to throw him down and beat him, to drive him to the boat with kicks and blows. How long before the others came looking for their friends?

"You *can*," she snarled, and she half-dragged him through the ruined garden. They lurched between the shattered trees like a lame animal, constantly in danger of falling down. At last she could unbolt the gate, and they struggled through.

She set him down on the waterfront and dumped her bow in the rowing boat, her shoulders light from the absence of his weight.

"Thank you," Falsi said as she helped him get on board.

"Don't mention it. Put your legs in." Giulia glanced over her shoulder. Nobody there. She climbed in, sending the boat rocking and making Falsi groan, and quickly unhitched the rope from the side.

Giulia was tired already. She looked across the canal and thought, *This will exhaust me. I'll be lucky if I don't just pass out on the oars.* She locked one oar into its rowlock and pushed against the bank with the other. The little boat slipped out into the canal.

In the bottom of the boat, Falsi moaned. His face was bloody, but the cuts were shallow. More worrying were the wounds inside him.

"Go to Printers' Row," he said. "There's a place there."

"Fine." The night suddenly felt very cold. She pulled up her hood.

"Go right."

Giulia pulled hard on the oars, and the boat slid across the water, away from the Scola. She kept close to the bank. On the far side of the canal, thousands of lanterns and candles glimmered in the night, like pinholes in a velvet cloth. Smoke rose against the sky, wisps against the risen moon.

They're at their strongest now, she thought. *That's what the books said: the beasts are strongest when the moon is full.*

Falsi's eyes were closed, his face tensed as if he was about to scream. "Look, Giulia," he said carefully, "I told them everything I knew. About you."

"That's all right. People do that."

He stared upwards, as if trying to find the right

words to describe the night sky. "Starting to think I'm not cut out for this."

Giulia said, "Nobody's cut out for it."

"You are. You and the old man. The others, too. When I let you stay in the Old Arms, I couldn't work out why. You did magic on me, didn't you?"

"Just try to rest, would you?"

"Doesn't matter now," he said, and he sighed so deeply that for a moment she thought he was breathing his last. But his chest still rose and fell.

Thank God.

Giulia hauled at the oars. Water slapped gently against the hull. "Have you got a family?" she asked.

"Wife and brats. Four of 'em."

"You need to get them out of town."

"You're right," Falsi said. His eye fastened on her. It was like something hiding inside a dead shell. "Thanks."

"It's all right. Neither of us had this coming." She looked out at the lights. Averrio was slowly sliding into the water, she'd heard. One day the lagoon would swallow it all, and the fish would pick it clean.

"I never meant to stay here," she said. "You know what Hugh and I were doing, before we came here? Having adventures. Like knights. We were supposed to be on a quest: meeting his old knight friends, having fun, doing some good deeds for once in my fucking life."

"This is a good deed," Falsi said.

The oars slapped against the water, louder this time. "Poor old bastard. His magic princess is with his best friend, and his best friend doesn't even want to be a knight any more. And then that priest turns up..." The rage swelled up inside her, pushing the sorrow aside. "It never fucking turns out right. Not once. I thought I'd got away from all this when I left Pagalia, but oh no, not a God-damned chance."

The oars dipped into the water. She pulled on them, feeling the ache in her biceps. Falsi was silent.

"You know, back in the day I'd get so fucking angry. All I'd feel was this rage, that these bastards could treat me like shit and get away with it – no, not just that – that they could *profit* from it. Like I was something they could tread on to get up higher. I don't know if anyone can die from fury, but I must've got pretty close. I'm not much, I know, but it's not right that they can do what they like and just walk away. Nobody gives a shit if you feel bad. You've got to *do* something – and I know what I'm going to fucking do."

"I've noticed."

She stopped, embarrassed. She'd almost forgotten that he was there. "I'm going to finish this, Falsi. I mean it."

"I believe you." He looked over the edge of the boat, peering at the land. "Left up here."

Lights reflected in the water, shimmering as the wake of the boat stirred the canal. Seeing the lights move, something shifted in the back of her brain. She thought as she rowed, her thoughts keeping her mind off the ache in her arms.

Let's say Azul is the same man Sethis talked about, the Inquisition man. Say he's been here years, maybe since the war, long enough to buy his way into the Glassmakers. Then he finds that he's in charge of some criminal business – smuggling, maybe. Perhaps it's his own decision, maybe someone else wants it done. It doesn't matter. Whatever it is, he has to do it in secret.

He needs men to help him, men he can trust: where would he look other than to his old soldiers? Varro was one of his wolves

– there are others, too. Azul has a warehouse to use for loading and unloading. Varro makes things for him. Maybe they work under the cover of exporting glass; maybe it's entirely secret.

What about the procurator? He's below Azul in the hierarchy. Azul pays him to keep it quiet, to deal with anyone who makes a fuss – like me. Through the procurator he controls the Watch. But not the Customs.

So he needs to get past the Customs men.

She rowed on, slow and tired. It all made sense so far. She and Hugh – and Edwin and Elayne – had stumbled upon a conspiracy, there was no doubt of that. They had not understood what they were seeing, but the little that they had seen was enough to mean that they had to be removed.

Her arms were numb from cold and strain. "Are we nearly there yet?"

"Not long. It's a big place, painted pink. Ask for Frannie."

Giulia wasn't sure if brothel-keeping was illegal in Averrio: if it was, Frannie wasn't doing a good job of hiding it. Her house backed straight onto the canal, painted lurid pink, draped with vines and lit up by half a dozen lanterns. Music seeped across the water as Giulia brought the boat in to shore. Her arms felt as if they were coming off: stopping rowing was even worse than carrying on. She left Falsi in the boat and struggled onto dry land.

The thin woman guarding the doorway was long past her prime, if she had ever had a prime at all. She looked Giulia over very slowly, clearly unsure whether she had come equipped for violence, theft or some new form of sexual depravity.

"Uh-uh," she said, folding her arms. "Whatever it

is, take it somewhere else."

"I'd like to see Frannie," Giulia said.

The woman sucked in her cheeks. A voice bawled something from the house behind her, just discernible over the sounds of bad music and drunkenness. The woman glanced over her shoulder just long enough to yell, "One moment, love!" before looking back.

"No, sister," she said. "Just the street for you. Now go before I make you."

"I've got a sick man here," Giulia said. "The sick man your boss pays to keep this place open. If he dies, so does your business. Would you mind fetching Frannie for me now?"

Frannie looked like a farmer's wife from a rough border town. Her cheeks and hands were red as though she'd just punched somebody out. *Perhaps she has*, Giulia thought.

Frannie looked into the boat and cried, "Oh, saints! Maria, help her get him inside!"

The thin woman helped Giulia to get Falsi out of the boat. They took his weight between them, but he groaned as if they were pulling him apart. People glanced at him and looked away. Giulia reckoned they assumed that he was drunk, or simply didn't care.

"In the back," Frannie said. Like most of the brothels Giulia had seen, Frannie's house served food and drink on the lower floor. They put the Watchman on a bed in a back room, and he lay there, sweating and grey-faced.

They stood beside Falsi's bed, watching him.

"You know a doctor?" Giulia said. "A crooked one would be best."

The big woman nodded. "There's an apothecary who checks the girls. I'll send my boy for him."

"Make sure Falsi gets proper treatment," Giulia said. "He's worse than he looks: cracked ribs, I think."

"Oh, I will, trust me. He's a sensible man, good for business. Someone really beat the shit out of him," Frannie said. There was pity and a sort of awe in her voice. "Where d'you know him from?"

"He arrested me," Giulia said. "It wasn't me who beat him up, if you're wondering. His friends did that."

"I've got a couple of *real* friends," Falsi croaked. "Get Seb and Rupe from the Watch-house. They're good people."

"We need to tell his family," Giulia said. "When your boy gets back, send him out to warn them."

"I know how to cover tracks," Frannie replied. "It's not the first time someone's got hurt here." She brushed her hands together. "What a mess," she added. "We'd better get some slack from your people for this," she told Falsi. She looked at Giulia. "He'll be fine. You can go."

Giulia said, "I need a room."

"You'll have to pay."

"Half-rates. I'll be on my own."

The big face scowled for a moment, and Giulia wondered if the red fists were going to rise to threaten her. "Fuck it," Frannie said, "it's a slow night anyhow."

Giulia woke up in the cold. She lay clothed on top of the narrow bed, arms folded and hands jammed into her armpits to keep them warm. She sat up, her cloak falling off her, and sat on the edge of the bed in the dark.

Her bandaged arm didn't feel too bad. There was a steady numbness, as though it was not so much healing as stunned. But at least it didn't hurt. Whatever Sethis had done to it, it had worked.

Or else it's about to drop off. Giulia sniffed the bandage: no rot, at least. She rubbed her eyes and stood up. *Here I am, hiding out in a whorehouse, looking for someone to kill.* Somehow it didn't seem terribly surprising. She picked up the crossbow. The wood felt smooth and natural against her palm.

There wouldn't be any Hugh this time, but she didn't mind. This was better done on her own, without anyone to slow her down. Giulia stretched in the darkness until she felt ready and keen. Then she crossed the room to the stripe of weak light that filtered under the door.

A young man sat in an armchair in the hall, a girl on his lap. They were both quite small, and looked as if the big chair had made them shrink. The girl was sleeping. Giulia wondered where she'd seen her before.

Giulia stopped before the chair, and the young man looked at her apprehensively. Softly, she asked, "Are you the doctor?"

"Yes," he said. "Are you a friend of the man in there, the Watchman?"

"Sort of. How's he doing?"

"He's badly hurt, but yes, given time..." The girl stirred and rubbed her face against his shoulder as if to mark it, and he reached down and stroked her hair.

"How long will it take him to get better?"

"Weeks, if not months. Anything faster and you'd need a magician."

It's a shame our magician has gone, Giulia thought, and then: *What did Falsi say? That they're still here? Why would they stay?*

The doctor sighed. "Maybe a good alchemist could speed it up, but that's not really my area. They sent a runner to his family. I don't know whether they'll let him stay here for long."

Giulia nodded. "Thanks."

The girl opened her eyes. "So the Watch did let you out," she said drowsily.

Giulia realised where she'd seen her – she'd been in the same cell when Falsi's men had first brought her in. "Yes. But I didn't suck the guard off, if you're wondering."

"You the one who beat Lieutenant Falsi up?"

"No."

The girl nodded slightly, as if Giulia had passed a test. "You staying here?"

She shook her head. "I'm going out. I've got things to do."

THIRTEEN

The bells tolled three in St Agorian's Church. Giulia hurried past, away from Printers' Row and towards the Great Canal. She felt tough and dangerous.

A skinny, nervous-looking man moved aside as she approached. Drunken, educated voices rippled out of an upstairs window as she passed one of the big townhouses. Laughter tinkled above her like breaking glass.

Shops stretched out on either side. In the daytime their fronts would be open, making the ground floors into little markets for spices and fine goods. Now they were closed up, padlocked and chained.

Five minutes more and she saw Varro's yard. She pulled her hood down low and continued.

The warehouse she wanted was a hundred yards further on, behind a brick wall almost twice her height. That was where Falsi's book had said the two hulls had been delivered. She stopped and listened. Nothing.

Giulia followed the wall to a small iron gate, scabby with rust. It took fifteen cold minutes to crack the lock.

She pushed the gate open until she could slip through. She waited there in the dark as her eyes took in the buildings and the cover she could use.

Junk lay around the edges of the big yard, as though a great broom had swept it out of the way. The warehouse stood alone. It was a huge brick cube, four storeys high and almost without windows, butting straight onto the canal. It looked like a fortress from here. Behind it, she could see clockwork cranes and the masts of harboured ships.

She began to sneak towards the warehouse, using the junk to cover her approach.

At the back of the warehouse, a pair of doors opened into the yard. Three men stood outside the doors, each holding a crossbow. They talked quietly, but their eyes stayed on the yard. *Damn*, she thought. *What the hell are they doing?*

People in Averrio didn't put three armed fighters outside a building for no reason. Azul had to have brought them in after he captured Falsi. Maybe he had found Cafaro's body, and it got him worried. Or the crossbowmen were guarding something especially valuable. *Something big must be happening tonight.*

Perhaps she could create a distraction. Giulia doubted it. They looked competent and smart, too shrewd to go charging off after a noise in the undergrowth. Best check the last side of the warehouse.

Giulia crept past the doors, behind an upturned rowing boat riddled with holes, and slipped into the wood-strewn area on the far side of the yard.

Suddenly she was in the landscape of a nightmare. Like tree-stumps given life, women sprouted from blocks of wood, white faces staring towards the moon as if pleading for the power to change their shape. Giulia froze.

Figureheads, that's all. Silly, getting scared by things like that.

It was then that she realised how afraid she was.

She wouldn't turn back. She'd see this business through tonight. Giulia kept low and jogged between the figureheads, weaving through the forest of bodies.

One of the guards cried, "Look at this!" and she dropped down, crouching beside a half-carved nymph, a white-painted breast at the level of her head. She heard the other guards laugh, and she moved on.

There were no windows in the first three storeys of the warehouse. For a moment she wondered about finding a grapple and a rope – not difficult in a dock, surely – and then rejected the idea. It would be far too easy to spot. By the time she was halfway up she'd have three crossbow bolts sticking out of her back. She retreated, looking for a plan.

Along the canal, rows of ships were tied up for repairs. They began just past the warehouse doors. She could see cranes and offices beyond the yard, and for a crazy moment she imagined swinging out one of the cranes, to make its boom connect with the warehouse roof. The canalside was deserted now, and the boats looked like abandoned hulks.

Coils of rope lay on the ground like snares. Tools were propped against the walls. Ropes ran from each ship to the dock, holding them in place while they were repaired.

But the warehouse was unassailable. "Shit," she hissed. Apart from the windows in the top floor, the only opening was a square hole in the roof, from which a thin trail of smoke trickled into the sky. She peered at the side of the warehouse, looking for something to hold on to, to climb. There was nothing: only the brick wall, too smooth to grab.

Giulia gritted her teeth and clenched her cold hands into fists until the knuckles were little white bumps of bone. No going back, not now. She'd hack handholds into the walls if she had to, heap timber outside the doors and burn the whoresons out.

There *was* a way. She turned to the nearest ship and looked up the mast and across the yardarm. It stuck out towards the warehouse like an accusing finger. Giulia licked her lips, barely believing herself. There was a gap between the tip of the yardarm and the roof. It could not be more than eight feet. *You lunatic*, she told herself as the plan formed inside her head. *You absolute lunatic. You must be crazy to even think of it...*

Grinning, she jogged towards the ship.

Giulia ran up the gangplank and onto the deck. She stopped in front of the rigging.

This is insane. She looked at the ropes, glistening with the first touch of frost. *Who cares if it is? Do you want to get this bastard or not?*

The ropes were cold and rough on her palms. She climbed up the rigging, hand over hand. *Look straight ahead. It's just like a ladder.*

The creaking of the ropes seemed painfully loud. Her weight dislodged bits of ice like dust, stirring up little clouds where her hands and feet had been. *Just keep looking forward. Enjoy the view*, she thought, and she felt a crazy urge to laugh.

The rigging narrowed as she approached the top. She didn't need to look down now to be afraid: she was at the height of a siege tower, the cold wind shaking her, slicing at her cheeks. Her hands trembled. *Gloves*, she thought. *Why didn't I get some gloves?*

This ship was too small to have a crow's nest, but there was a flat point at the top where the rigging joined the mast. She reached it, scrambled on and wrapped her arms around the mast.

Something caught her eye below. She didn't want to look down, but her vision moved there anyway, drawn towards a light on the dock. No, not the dock itself: it was a lantern on the next ship down. People had stepped onto the deck.

There were two of them: a hulking fellow with a beard and a broad, tallish man. They were leaning over the rail, their backs to her, and the bearded man was showing the other something on the waterline.

Giulia waited for them to go.

The bearded man stood up and turned, gesturing across the deck. His face caught the light. It was the man from the cellar, the one Hugh had impaled, the one who had helped to torture her: Cortaag.

The sight of him flooded her with rage. Giulia hugged the mast and stared down at him, wishing that the force of her gaze could punch through his head like a musket-ball.

I'll kill you, you bastard, you and your fucking master.

The other man turned around. It was Edwin.

She nearly lost her grip. Her hand slipped; she grabbed hold of the mast and clung to it like an ape to a tree.

What in God's name is he doing?

Edwin said something to Cortaag, and the torturer nodded. They looked like the best of friends.

No, surely not. They can't know each other. That makes no sense.

Cortaag smiled and gestured at the city, as if to say that it was all his. He put out his hand.

Don't take it. Don't do that—

Edwin shook Cortaag's hand. Cortaag stepped back and walked down the gangplank. The cabin door opened and a woman emerged. Her hair was light, almost blonde.

"Goodnight!" Elayne called.

Cortaag turned and waved, then carried on walking, off towards the warehouse. He passed the ship on which Giulia hid, his stride long and businesslike. Someone called to him from the warehouse and he grunted back. He reached the warehouse and was lost to view.

Giulia looked down. Edwin was showing Elayne the thing on the waterline, the thing that Cortaag had been pointing out. They straightened up and Elayne kissed his cheek. Then they both crossed the deck, steadying each another against the ice, and disappeared inside.

The deck was empty. It might never have happened. *I could have dreamed it*, she thought, and wished that she had.

They've been bought. They're in league with Azul. They must be. Why else would Cortaag be there, otherwise? Were they working for him all along? They set us up, they fucking set us up!

Her head was full of a shoal of thoughts. Her mind swam with shock, outrage, disbelief. Giulia wanted to turn it over, to work it out and feel either anger or relief, but there were other things to do. Whatever Edwin and Elayne had done – and whatever they deserved to get – had to wait.

"God damn it!" she muttered, and she discovered that her hands had gone numb. She flexed her fingers and blew across her knuckles to make them warm.

I must be mad.

She looked down the length of the yardarm, at the tapering end of the wood. It reminded her of aiming a crossbow, looking towards the tip of the bolt.

Except this time it's me being fired. She took a deep breath and thought, *Saint Senobina, blessed patron of thieves, watch over me.* She had a sudden image of the bald-headed saint, looking down from Heaven as she watched Giulia clinging to the mast, and she thought, *Fuck it, woman, do you want this or not? Then what are you waiting for?*

She turned, ran, tore down the length of the yardarm, feeling ropes and wood under her boots, faster and faster towards the tip of the beam and the empty space beyond – and leaped, legs bent, crossbow clutched to her chest like a child. *Cold*, she thought as the air rushed past her face, then *I've made it!* and her boots hit the roof and she rolled on her right shoulder, came up into a crouch and was still.

Something hissed beside her. Her hand shot out and grabbed a tile as it began to slide. She laid it carefully on the roof beside her boot.

The guards were talking below her.

"Probably bloody crows," one of them said, sniffing loudly. "Dammit, it's freezing out here! Soon as I get paid, I'm getting a decent coat."

Oh, yes! Here I fucking am!

Wisps of smoke curled up from the hole in the roof. Giulia crept to the edge of the hole and looked down. She saw a hearth below, with a fire that was not quite out. Coals glared at her like evil eyes.

Giulia climbed onto the edge and dropped down. She landed, kicked the fire-screen over and scuttled into the room.

It was windowless and hardly furnished, apart from a tatty armchair and a desk piled with paper. Giulia stepped to the door and put her ear to the wood. She heard nothing. She slid back the bolt and tried the handle. It was locked.

She stood in the dark, watching the door as she loaded her bow.

Voices from below. Men called to one another in the warehouse. Clumsy, heavy noises accompanied the shouts. They were moving things about, dragging metal on stone, banging boxes together.

She had an image of iron-bound treasure chests, fat with gold and dripping coins as the smugglers hauled them back and forth. Perhaps they were emptying their boats, taking out the goods they'd somehow sneaked past the city Customs, preparing to load them onto wagon trains and other ships.

Like Edwin and Elayne's.

Giulia pulled out her picks, bent down and got to work on the lock. It took five minutes before she felt the last tumbler give, twist slightly and spring back. She stood up and listened at the door again. Nobody outside, just the thumps and voices of men working below.

She opened the door gently and slipped through, shutting it behind her. She was in a corridor, the walls raw brick. The only light came from the narrow staircase at the far end. There was a door on the opposite side of the passage.

She stepped across and checked the door – unlocked. No sounds from within. Giulia opened it and peered inside. A little light seeped through a small window. There were several large boxes on the floor, locked with chains. A mattress and a few sheets showed where someone had been sleeping. A guard, presumably. Best of all, there were several coils of thin rope in a heap in the corner.

The window-frame looked just wide enough for her to fit through. Quickly, she tied one of the coils to the catch and looped the rope around one of the strong-boxes, just in case. She returned to the corridor.

Giulia crouched down to hide her outline. She crept to the top of the stairs, towards the noise, and squatted in the shadows with the crossbow ready to fire.

The staircase led down into a high, open hall, lit by lanterns. Massive doors stood at the far end of the hall, facing onto the canal. They were closed. A channel full of water ran down the centre, broad enough to allow a large boat to be rowed inside for repair. Eight or ten men waited around the channel, talking in little groups and passing round a bottle of wine. One of the men was Cortaag. Giulia lifted the bow and lined it up with his head. It would be a pleasure to kill that bastard, but he was not the man she wanted most of all.

Chests and boxes stood against the walls, but they were open and empty. Giulia peered down, feeling anticipation stirring within her gut. Something was going to happen, and soon.

Cortaag nodded to two men at the far end of the hall, and they hauled on chains hanging beside the door. With a slow, metallic rattle, the pulleys in the rafters spun and a dripping portcullis rose behind the doors.

Cortaag stood up straight as if jabbed in the back. "Officer!" he barked, and the other men put down the bottle, hurried into lines and stood upright along the water's edge.

People entered from the landside door. First came a tall woman in a practical dress and a heavy cape. Giulia caught a glimpse of her eyes. They were wide and staring, as if her madness was only just reined in. It was the woman from the cellar, the one who had struck her and whom she had used to escape.

After her came Azul. He wore a grey coat and heavy boots. His dark clothes and lined face made Giulia think of a widow.

She shuddered at the sight of him – not from fear, but repulsion. For a moment she wanted to spit and retch, as if she had reached for someone's hand and taken hold of slugs. Giulia swallowed, lifted the bow and lined the bolt up with Azul's ear.

"Are we all set?" the inquisitor rasped.

"We're ready," Cortaag replied. "We've got the signal from downriver."

Straight through the brain, stone dead. Then run like hell.

Azul bent down. Giulia tilted the bow to keep him in her sights. *Stay still, you little shit!*

She put a little pressure on the trigger, then a little more. Azul crouched at the edge of the channel, looking into the water. He chuckled.

Something popped up from the water.

Giulia flicked up the bow, yanked her hand away and the bolt fell out of the groove. She groped for the bolt by her side, eyes fixed on the thing sticking out of the channel.

It looked like a bent pipe. Very slowly, the pipe turned, and she saw that there was a lens on the end. It turned to face Azul, and his shoulders shook. It took Giulia a moment to realise that he was laughing.

What the hell was that? A breathing tube for a man walking on the bottom of the canal? The neck of some animal?

Then the pipe shot upwards, and a great black shadow rose under it, and it was all she could do to keep herself from crying out.

The shadow broke the surface like a whale. With a hiss of parting water the bulk of a huge machine rose into view, slopping water over the floor, rattling and creaking as it appeared. Wood and brasswork filled the channel; wet lenses and rivets winked in the lantern-light.

Giulia crouched wide-eyed at the top of the stairs.

It looked like a massive barrel on its side, tapered towards the front, held together with metal bands and shiny, folded leather. A stubby chimney stuck out of the back of the thing, where a fish would have had its dorsal fin. There was a lid on the chimney. As she watched, fascinated, the lid began to turn.

Black magic. The dryads said he knew magic. Two hulls. It was in the books. Azul bought two hulls. Varro did the work.

She could see big paddle wheels at the sides. There was some kind of rudder at the back, with a metal thing like a stretched-out apple peeling behind it.

The lid squealed as it turned, as if it pained the machine.

There's someone inside it. A person? A monster from the sea? Giulia's stomach was tight. She reloaded her crossbow.

The lid stopped turning. The room was silent apart from the slap of water on the stone floor. Giulia breathed slowly and carefully. Fear was tightening in her, winding itself up in her guts and limbs, readying her to strike and run.

The lid flopped back against the chimney with a loud clang. From her position at the top of the stairs, Giulia could see things moving inside the fish-machine, the shine of light on leather. Alicia began to cough. Azul wrinkled his nose and took a small step back.

A demon leaped whooping out of the hatch. Giulia saw a flash of metal, a hideous gold face and black limbs beneath; she flinched, and her finger jogged the trigger. The crossbow fired. The bolt slammed into the metal face, and the thing grunted and fell back.

The demon's body lolled in the open hatch, and in the frozen second before chaos broke out she realised what he really was: a dead man in a leather suit, a golden mask over his face. Coins spilled from his hands, twinkling on the fish-machine, dropping into the water.

Azul howled and flailed at the falling coins. "Get that money!" he cried. Cortaag rushed forward and Azul straightened up, pointed into the shadows and yelled, "Look!"

Giulia was up and running in half a second. She tore down the corridor and turned left as their boots clattered on the stairs.

"Get him! He's up there!"

She raced into the room, slammed the door, shot the bolts, and a hand battered on the wood. "It's locked, get a hammer!"

Giulia ran to the window and kicked out the glass. She bashed the remaining pieces out with the butt of the crossbow, snatched up the rope and tossed it out the window.

She scrambled onto the windowsill. She leaned out, grabbed the rope, wrapped her legs round it and slid down.

A figure ran round the side of the warehouse, sword in hand. Giulia dropped the last ten feet, hit the ground hard and took off towards the wall of the boatyard. Dirt slid and crunched under her boots. The guard was puffing behind her, but he was fast like a charging bull. She didn't have long – not long enough to climb the wall before he dragged her down.

Giulia dodged left, between the figureheads. She stopped, turned, and as the guard ran into view she smashed the butt of the crossbow into his eye. The man staggered and fell onto his arse, and she ran again. She left him rolling in the wet dirt, shouting promises of vengeance and calling to his friends.

Where to now? Not Edwin's ship: no, too risky. Giulia ran past one figurehead, then another, turned and saw Azul's men lumbering behind. She sped up again, pulling the bow over her shoulder as she ran. She saw a door in the wall and darted through it. Her heart pounded as if to shake free from her chest. Someone, Cortaag perhaps, was calling the men back, telling them to stop.

The Arsenal loomed ahead, its clockwork turrets slowly turning as they surveyed the bay. Giulia headed inland, slowing a little. She ran past one block, took a right into a tiny alleyway and stumbled out into a little courtyard. There was a bench in the middle. A man sat on the bench and a woman stood astride him, pulling up her skirts as if trying to find where her legs began. Giulia ran straight past, leaving them gawping after her.

She jogged down another alley, took a right and dropped into the doorway of a tenement block. She flopped against the wall, giddy with sudden exhaustion, her head spinning as if struck. Her palms stung from the rope, and the backs of her legs ached. But she had escaped. She wanted to shake her fist at them all, at the fat criminals who couldn't keep pace, to climb onto the rooftops and shout "Screw you!" at Azul and all his men. Magic, smugglers, men in gold masks, a bloody underwater ship – she wanted to shout her defiance to them all.

All you did was get away. And they'll come sniffing after you. There's nothing to celebrate. Keep sharp.

This time she was not furious for missing him. Azul had escaped again – the swine led a charmed life, perhaps literally – but she'd be back. She knew his game now, smuggling gold in from somewhere in that fish-boat thing.

God, it was cold. The ice had tightened around the city like a torture device. She pulled her crossbow across her body and hid it under her cloak. Then she stood up and began to walk. She strode through the back-alleyways with her hood up, the breath pumping out ahead of her. Thirty yards on, she remembered what else she'd seen.

Edwin's a traitor. Edwin and Elayne are on Azul's side. Fuck, how long have they been working for him?

Above, a bird screeched. Giulia thought, *Was it them who killed the priest? Were they plotting against us from the start?*

She checked herself. *Maybe they're innocent. Perhaps they don't know all of it. Perhaps they've been forced to cooperate.* A dog saw her, gave her a long, guilty look and sloped into the shadows.

Then she thought, *What will I tell Hugh?*

The sun was rising at the edge of the lagoon. Giulia watched it tinting the horizon, too tired to much care, and she turned and wandered back into the town. The fierce joy of victory was gone. Nobody bothered her as she walked to the edge of the canal. A few people milled about; none came close.

She took as roundabout a route as she could manage. Giulia kept under the eaves, out of the way of the fading moon. At one point, she felt sure that something moved above her, and she darted into the shadows and waited there, half-expecting a griffon to sweep lazily through the sky. She counted to a hundred, saw nothing more, and went on her way.

Some of the boatmen slept in their boats. It was easy to wake one and catch a ride back to Printers' Row. She sat at the bows and watched the Great Canal come to life, the first boats welcomed by the shriek of gulls.

Light fell on the water and the rooftops, on the striped mooring-poles, the pale stone bridges and the brightly-painted mansions on the waterfront. Now that she was too weary to hate Averrio, she could see how someone could come to love it.

The brothel on Printers' Row was closed. Giulia needed to get out of view. Roaming the streets dressed like a man was suspicious enough: carrying a crossbow was inviting trouble. She hammered on the door until the shutters flew open over her head. The lean-faced woman who had guarded the door last night glared down at her.

"I'm back."

The woman said, "Stay there, would you?" She disappeared inside. Giulia tapped her foot and wondered how hard it would be to climb up the facade and through the window.

The door opened and Frannie looked out. "He's gone," she said. "Went last night."

"What happened? Is he all right?"

"Two friends of his came. Said they were taking him to his wife. Sep and Rupe, they were called," she added, as Giulia moved to speak. "He seemed to know 'em well enough."

"I see. Can I wait here?"

"No. Go to the beer shop over the bridge. There's a

man waiting for you."

"Who?"

Frannie shrugged. "Rich fellow, smart looking. I don't go asking for names where they're not given."

"Right." Giulia turned and walked over to the little beer-house. Her legs ached as she climbed over the bridge. She ducked inside, into the smell of dust, hops and varnished wood, and sat down in the darkest part of the room. She pushed her crossbow under the table, then called for a drink. The proprietor set half a bottle of wine before her, and Giulia watched his hands pour the wine into a grimy cup. She let him wander away before she relaxed.

Every part of her was exhausted. Her limbs were stretched and aching, her eyes sore, her mind reluctant to dwell on anything except how weak she was. She thought about the warehouse and felt neither triumph nor disgust. Slowly, Giulia lifted the cup and took a sip.

As she drank she thought about Edwin and Elayne. *So you were playing us, eh?* she reflected, too worn out to feel much spite. *I always thought there was something strange about them. Too bad I've got to tell Hugh*, and then she felt something close to dread. She reached up and tentatively pressed her bandaged arm. It hurt a little, but the pain was dull and tolerable. She wondered where the rich man that Frannie had mentioned was.

It might be a trap. Fuck it: I've beaten one trap, I can take on a few more. She almost smiled at the idea. *Giulia Degarno, Our Lady of Battle, the hardest woman to take up arms since the angels appeared to Saint Cordelia. Right now, Our Lady of Battle needs a soft bed and a week asleep.*

Hugh came back into her mind. *How will I tell him? Finding out your beloved works for a bunch of ex-Inquisition smugglers. Sorry, Hugh, your fair damsel's actually a murderer. What a shitty thing to learn.*

So, this is it, eh? See the world, hunt the wyverns, have adventures and get rich. She looked at the bottle, now nearly empty, and reflected that she could see why Hugh had spent several years choosing beer over human company. Friends betrayed you, lovers treated you like shit and moved on to a newer and better version once you were all used up, but wine didn't care whose company it kept. Princes got drunk, kings and queens as well, all the way down the scale to women with cut-up faces who'd always be alone, and broken-down knights who'd be funny if they weren't anyone she knew.

Damn it, woman, you need a rest.

The Melancholia rose up in her. Giulia rubbed her brow, gritted her teeth and screwed her face up. It was the same old sense, the mounting desperation, the feeling of being trapped and furious. *I have to get out*, she thought, and then: *I can't get out. I want to be somewhere else, in the sunshine with someone I love and who loves me back, and I never will. I'll be stuck here forever, getting betrayed, tortured, never getting out—*

Shut up. The way out is through. You're like an arrowhead: you've gone in part of the way, and now you have to tear straight through if you want to see the light again. You have to keep going.

"Excuse me?"

She glanced up. A short, curly-haired man stood before her. He looked friendly and strong.

"Are you Giulia?"

For a moment she felt embarrassed, as she wondered what her expression must have looked like when he walked in. Then she became wary. "Who wants to know?"

"I'm from Iacono."

She peered at him, not quite alert, and he added, "Battista Iacono, the mapmaker? He instructed me to come and find you."

"Him? What does he want?"

The curly-haired man looked around. He was middle-aged, Giulia realised: his friendliness gave the impression that he was a decade younger than he actually was. "It's about the Scola," he said. "He's waiting at home," the servant added. "He doesn't really like coming into places like this."

"Too much fun for him?"

"You've met him already, then?" the man said, and he smiled.

***

"Shit," Cortaag said. "First Varro and now this. They're on to us."

"They've always been 'on to us'," Azul replied. "They've wanted us dead for years, you know that. Now they see a chance, that's all."

He watched four men lift the dead body from the underwater-ship. They lowered the man down and laid him along the side of the channel, still in his gold mask.

The men crowded around the corpse. One knelt down and carefully removed the mask. The bolt had worked its way free, and there was a red mark on the blue-grey face, as if someone had smudged a blob of spice onto the smuggler's forehead.

Azul touched Cortaag's arm. "Let's go," he said.

Alicia waited in the yard. She had no skill with people, and could be relied on to say something crass, so Azul had sent her outside while the men retrieved their dead comrade. She strolled out from among the figureheads, tall and proud.

"Let's go to the waterside," Azul said.

They walked down to the canal, the inquisitor and his two adjutants. Once they were at the water's edge, Cortaag glared at the tall buildings on the far side. "What a fucking night," he said.

"So," Azul said, "it seems that Giulia Degarno has decided to return."

"That little bitch came here to murder us," Alicia added. "Let me go after her. I'll rip her guts out."

Azul shook his head. "I think you'll find that she came here to murder *me*."

"Shit!" Cortaag spun on his heel, took three steps away, and then walked back. "It's that Watchman, isn't it? I told them to finish him!"

"Falsi isn't important. Orvo doesn't matter either. We don't need their help anymore. It doesn't matter if Lieutenant Falsi got away. What is he without his rather lowly post? His word is worth nothing now. He won't be back, anyway: he's in no shape to give us trouble. As for our friend Giulia, however..."

"So it's not the Watch coming after us," Cortaag said. "Who are these people, then? Don't tell me they're from the fucking Scola."

Azul shook his head. "Not them. The Scola are no doubt angry we closed them down, but they lack the guts to fight us properly. Artists, natural philosophers and similar degenerates: there's not a proper soldier among them."

Cortaag snorted with contempt.

"It's the woman and the knight," Azul said. "They're

freelancers of some kind. Perhaps the Scola is employing them – I'm sure they're linked somehow – but they're the ones to blame for this. To their minds we've wronged them, and they want revenge."

"They're not the only ones that want it," Cortaag growled. "That old bastard..." He rubbed his midriff, where Hugh's sword had run him through. "When I get the chance, I'll smash his fucking skull."

"And the woman," Alicia said. "She needs to go back in the chair. I know her sort."

I'm sure you do, Azul thought. Alicia had started off as a country girl assigned to his unit as a laundress. There had never been any female inquisitors, but the soldiers had disliked guarding the women of the Berendanti, seeing it as beneath them, and Alicia had volunteered. Her cheerful brutality had made her perfect for the role. As their research into the Berendanti had drawn to a bloody close, it had seemed only fair to reward her with the ability to shapechange. He remembered suggesting her to Leth, their apothecary, as a test subject. *Ah yes, the charming Brother Leth*, he thought, and the prospect of seeing the alchemist again made him feel uneasy.

A large boat swung into view. It moved slowly up the canal, a single lantern at the prow lighting its way.

"Brother Praxis will be here tomorrow morning," Azul said. "The others will follow. We'll need everything ready."

Cortaag leaned in. "It already is, sir. I can check again, if you'd like—"

"No. I need you for something else." He paused, watching the lone boat pass by. "The important thing is that our meeting passes uneventfully. We have to persuade our visitors that our operation is not just lucrative, but safe. Can you get half a dozen men together tomorrow afternoon, armed with bows and guns?"

"Certainly, sir."

"Good. I want your people armed and with their ears covered up, so they can't hear. They need to go in deafened, understand?"

Cortaag nodded. He seemed to be beginning to understand what he would have to do.

"Young Giulia told us some interesting things, while she was in the chair," Azul observed. "I think it's time we made use of them." He turned to look at the ships moored along the edge of the canal. "Send Elayne Brown an invitation."

***

Iacono lived in a large house several roads away from the palace of the Decimus. It was painted bright white in a row of yellowing homes, like the only good tooth in an old man's mouth.

"It's not right," he said, ushering her inside. "I mean, it won't bloody do. Shutting down the Scola like this – they're treating us like criminals. It's ridiculous. Ridiculous."

Dimly, Giulia realised that he somehow held her responsible. She didn't care.

"I suppose you need some food," he said.

"I need a bed," she replied.

"A bed – right, yes. Has Carla seen to that, Roberto, or is she not being gracious enough to bother these days?"

"She's done it," the curly-haired servant said. "Silly old woman," he added, and Giulia wondered who exactly he was talking about.

She nearly passed out when she saw the bed. It was a broad, high-sided thing with a canopy, the sheets fresh and smelling faintly of lavender. It took an effort to wedge a chair under the door handle, and to lay her crossbow beside the bed with a bolt ready to load. She was just able to toss her knives, bag and belt onto the floor before she flopped back and closed her eyes. Her last thought as she fell asleep was that she was sinking through the mattress, like a cushion of warm dough.

Giulia awoke in a panic, from a nightmare that was forgotten the moment she opened her eyes. The sheets were wound tightly around her fist. She sat up and slowly took off her boots and britches before she lay down again, under the covers this time. Bad dreams, that was all. Back to bed.

She still dreamed. Now she was scrambling up a huge pile of logs, knowing that an enemy was on the other side of the pile, doing exactly the same.

She could not tell who he was, but she knew that she had to beat him to the top. That was all that mattered: that it be Giulia who reached the summit first. She climbed, the logs shifting under her boots, and he sped up to match her. Her strides became scrabbling; she tore at the logs with hands and feet, clambering up the wooden mountain like an ape. And all the time her arch rival was on the other side, and although she dreaded meeting him she had to beat him to the peak.

Someone stood on the summit, at the very top. Someone in a green dress that wafted in the breeze, tied to a stake like a witch. So this was a pyre, she realised. They were going to burn the woman at the top.

Logs skidded out of the pyre, pushed out by her boots, rolling down. She could hear her rival on the other side of the heap, breathing hard. With a groan, Giulia made the final effort, and stood beside Elayne at the top.

Hands appeared at the other side of the pyre, and they hauled a man up onto his hands and knees. It was Hugh.

"Keep back," Giulia called. "I've come for Elayne."

"Me too," he called. "Let her go."

"No," she replied. "She's mine." Giulia looked down, and there was a lit torch in her hand. Hugh pulled himself up, his mouth opening in a shout – and Giulia drove the torch into the logs at Elayne's feet.

FOURTEEN

Giulia awoke in an unfamiliar room. It took her a moment to remember Iacono and the night before. She rubbed her eyes and stared blearily at the wall.

The things I do, she thought, and despite herself, she smiled.

Then she remembered Edwin and Elayne. Someone knocked hard on the door, and Iacono's servant called, "Breakfast time!"

Giulia dressed and went downstairs. The mapmaker had spread his papers over the dinner table, and she had to eat standing up.

"Sleep well?" Iacono asked.

"Fine, thank you. Look, I need to know what's happened to my friend—"

"I know. Sethis sent a messenger last night, while you were sleeping."

"What did he say? Is Hugh safe?"

Iacono said, "As far as I know, yes. He and Sethis got out with the others. Most of them have fled town. Sethis and his people are meeting outside the city, in a farmhouse about a mile up from the North Span. You know what that is?"

"It's an old bridge, isn't it?"

"That's one way of putting it. He said to meet him up there. You can borrow this." He picked up a leather tube and held it out to her. "It's the city and the islands. I've marked it on there. Not one of my most decorative maps, but it's accurate."

"Thanks," Giulia said, putting it under her arm.

"Don't crease it," he replied. "Some people have no idea how to look after things. I hope you're different."

"I'm different, all right," she said. "Don't you worry about that."

Iacono grunted and went back to work. He was clearly waiting for her to wander off, as though he'd slept with her the night before and was now ashamed. She watched him measure distances on his map, enjoying his discomfort at her being there. Then she prepared to go.

Giulia found a tough rucksack in Iacono's hall. Perhaps he used it when he went out taking measurements for his maps; she put her bag and crossbow inside. At the door she ran through the directions again, and then she said goodbye to the servants and turned to leave. It would have been unprofessional to steal the ornaments on the way out.

A thought struck her as she was about to leave. "Hey, Iacono."

"Mmn?"

"You must know this city pretty well, right?"

He looked up. "Nobody knows it better."

"Where would I find a griffon?"

"A griffon? Far out of the city. They live beyond the Island of Quarantine, out on the rocks in the bay. The Decimus keeps a few, because the griffon rampant is the emblem of Averrio, but from what I've heard, they're pretty runty things. There was word that they wanted to train them to fight, the way they used to train wyverns in the Alten mountains – but it didn't go anywhere. Like a lot of things in this city," he added, and he gave her a wry smile.

"Thanks," she said. "That's interesting. Look, you should get out for a while, you know. Out of town."

Iacono looked at her. "Out of town? But I live here."

"The Watch will be looking—"

"The Watch are idiots," he replied. "I'm going to put in a formal complaint to the Council of a Hundred about their activities. I expect that should do the trick. It's a miracle people weren't killed."

"People *were* killed. At least stay with someone else for a few days. There are some very bad people behind all this. I don't mean to be rude, but I don't think the people who raided the Scola are going to give a damn about your formal complaint."

He nodded, very slowly. "Point made," he said, and he waited for her to leave.

The street was warm in the sunlight, chilly in the shade. Giulia headed north. There were still plenty of scores to settle, but the thought of leaving Averrio, if only briefly, filled her with relief. *Dry land*, she thought. *Thank God for dry land.*

***

The North Span crossed four hundred yards of brackish water and tiny islands too sodden for any use. Centuries ago, men and dwarrows had sunk massive pillars into the water and had thrown arches over them in the style of a

Quaestan aqueduct: first in wood, then in stone. Finally, marks of permanency had been etched into its sides by the greatest fey smiths, cementing a friendship between the races that had been broken only in the War of Faith.

The bridge could fit four wagons abreast. Crews of engineers constantly checked its stability, lowering themselves down on gurneys or climbing up from barges piled high with scaffolding. A special company of Customs men patrolled the length of the bridge, and the bodies of traitors and murderers dangled from gallows fixed to its sides, where the crows would peck at them until they dropped into the muck eighty feet below.

That could be me, Giulia thought as she trudged along. *After all, I've got murder planned.* As if to answer her, one of the bodies swung round with a creak of rope and showed her its empty face, made genderless by weather and age. *You look even worse than me*, she thought. *I wonder what you did to end up there.*

A big wagon rumbled past, heaped with crates. Giulia took three quick strides and swung herself up onto the back. She sat on the rear of the wagon, watching Averrio shrink with every yard.

I'll be coming back soon, she promised the city, *back to finish this.* Azul, Cortaag, Alicia – she'd finish all of them.

But that was a long way away. The cold air pinched Giulia's nose and cheeks, made her scars feel pink and new. The cart rumbled past a little group of pilgrims who chatted and laughed as they walked, sharing a skin of wine. One of them waved at her, perhaps mistaking her dark clothes for religious garb, and she waved back. She reclined against a chest and wondered if this wagon belonged to Azul's conspiracy, taking his smuggled gold away.

At the far end of the North Span, the guards were stopping people as they came into Averrio, collecting a toll for the upkeep of the bridge. They ignored the traffic leaving the city, but they would certainly bother the driver on the way back.

She nodded to the Customs man at the end. He smiled back, realising that she was not part of the cargo, amused by her temerity.

The wagon lurched off the bridge and onto the main road. Giulia leaned back and enjoyed the sunshine, content to wait for now.

The road wound to the left, behind a little hill, and the city disappeared from view. The wagon slowed down as the gradient rose, and Giulia slipped down from the back, tugging Iacono's rucksack after her.

She opened the rucksack by the roadside. Now that she was outside Averrio, she didn't have to hide her crossbow. Carrying it made her look like a bandit, but it made her feel like an expert, too. Besides, it was best to go armed in the countryside. She had grown up in cities – Pagalia, Astrago and then back to Pagalia – and the country both awed and unsettled her.

She walked past a gang of bored labourers, spades and picks on their shoulders. They were probably part of a maintenance crew, tasked with cutting the trees back to stop robbers hiding by the side of the road. At this time of year it was pointless: most of the trees were skeletal.

Around the next corner, a tall man sat on the raised earth ridge at the edge of the road. He wore a cuirass and tough old clothes, his expression dignified but vague. As she approached, he licked his fingertips and smoothed down his moustache.

"Hugh!" she called. "Hey, Hugh!"

Hugh got up and said, "Hullo, Giulia!" He stood up, jumped down onto the road and strode over to meet her. She embraced the knight, surprising him. For a moment Giulia held him tight, then she kissed his cheek and stepped back. "God, it's good to see you."

"Good to see you too, Giulia. A few more hours and I'd have come to find you. Sethis wanted me to stay put, but you can't leave a comrade behind."

"Are you all right? What happened at the Scola?"

His expression became serious, as if he had forgotten that they were in danger until now. "Yes, fine, thanks. It wasn't much of a fight, to be honest. There were a few rough types – mercenaries, that sort of thing – but I was able to hold them off until most of the others got away. It wasn't good – but it could have been much worse."

"I'm glad you're all right."

"When the trouble started, we all went out into the garden and into the little wood with Sethis, where you and I went before. We got into Faery but we couldn't get back to the Scola."

"That's because they burned the wood while you were in there. I went back to the Scola last night. They knew that wrecking the wood would keep you out, maybe even trap you in Faery for good. They smashed the place up. I saw at least two dead bodies there."

"Yes," he said. "It was a nasty business, to be honest. Arashina knew a way out that got us into a forest a few miles north of here. Then I headed down to find you."

"Well, I'm back now." She took a deep breath. "I've found some things out. We need to talk about this, somewhere private."

He frowned. "You know, I didn't see that Watch

lieutenant at the Scola. The one who was after us, back at the Old Arms – Falsi, that's him."

Giulia nodded. "He was there, all right. You didn't see him because his men were busy pounding the crap out of him upstairs. He had a change of heart and helped me get some information. Some of the Watch found out and turned on him. They'd beaten him up in the Scola and left him in the dining hall. I managed to get him out, though. It wasn't easy. I had to kill his second-in-command. No great loss there, to be honest."

"I see." Hugh glanced further up the road. "Let's go, shall we?"

They started up the road together. The labourers were a fair way ahead, reliably out of earshot. Hugh walked with his left hand resting lightly on the hilt of his sword. "I can't say I ever liked Falsi – he always seemed a spineless sort of fellow – but that's no good at all. So, where's he now?"

"There was a rowing boat at the waterfront. I stole the boat and took him out the way. He got me to take him to a brothel."

"What? After all that?"

She laughed. "No, to recover. He knew the madam there."

"There's a surprise."

"I think he'll be all right. Two of his men took him away – ones he trusted." She glanced over her shoulder, just in case. "Falsi gave me some information. The little old man – the one in charge – he's called Ramon Azul. His men are smuggling gold into the city, at a warehouse on the docks. I went there last night. I missed Azul but I shot one of his people instead."

"You did one of them in?"

"Yes. And I found out a load of other stuff as well. Look, I really need to talk to you, Hugh. Just you and me." *And then what?* Giulia thought. *What will you do then, when I tell you that your beloved damsel and your best friend are in league with the enemy?*

"There'll be a chance for that soon," said the knight. "We're meeting the others further up. We regrouped, you see, while you were away."

"Regrouped?"

"Yes. The dryads have called a meeting. It seems they want the same thing as us, you see."

"Is that so? Well then, let's see what they've got to say."

Hugh nodded up the road, away from the city. A woman sat on a mule by the side of the track, a heavy green cloak covering almost all of her body. Her face was invisible under the hood.

"It's Anna," said Hugh, "the dryad girl you spoke to. They sent her down with me."

Giulia waved at Anna: she waved back. They walked on. "You know," Giulia said, "I was pretty worried about you."

"Likewise. I didn't like leaving the Scola without you, but I didn't have much choice."

They reached Anna's mule. Giulia looked up and saw the huge eyes under the hood of her cloak, like an owl looking out from the back of a cave.

"How are you?" Anna asked.

"I've been worse," Giulia replied. "It's good to be out of the city for a while. And you?"

"Happy," the dryad replied. "I will be going back to Faery soon. But I wanted to see you, to thank you."

"Let's say we're equal. You helped me, after all."

Anna smiled. "We are equal, then. Good." She turned the mule, and they followed her up the road.

"This is the place," Anna said. She nodded towards the west, and Giulia, squinting into the forest, made out a large, barn-shaped building twenty yards from the road. There was a thin path leading to it, hardly good enough for a man to use, let alone a horse.

"Hmm," said Hugh. "I'm sure it's better close up."

"It looks deserted." Giulia didn't want to say that it looked exactly like the sort of place where she would have laid a trap.

"The farmer who owns it is a friend of ours," Anna said. She dismounted and tied the mule's reins beside the path. Her boots sank into the damp, soft ground.

Giulia had half-expected the forest to turn to summer as they approached, the way it had done in the garden of the Scola, but as they drew near, the tree trunks became denser and even less of the winter sun broke through.

She saw a sliver of golden light in the nearest window, seeping between the shutters. To the side, horses stood waiting in a long stable. She glanced over her shoulder and saw no tracks in the mud leading back to the road. Brambles spilled onto the path, shielding it from view. They hadn't been there earlier. *Fey magic,* she thought, and she shivered, aware how far from the city she had really come.

A shape moved beside a tree, and a man stood up. He was a thin, bearded fellow, with a foolish, lopsided smile that belied the sharpness of his eyes. A bow and quiver lay next to where he had been sitting. He looked like a poacher, perhaps a tracker for hire. "Well, then," he said. "I'm guessing you must be Giulia. Go on in."

Anna opened the front door. They followed her into a dark wooden hall, strong-smelling and fusty-aired. Giulia glanced at Hugh, but his face registered nothing, as if he had been here many times before.

Thick moss grew in the corners of the room, and a vine had pushed its way through the floorboards at the far end of the hall. It had crawled up the wall and was starting to creep across the ceiling. Giulia wondered if the presence of the fey folk had made the vine appear.

Anna closed the front door, leaving the forester outside. The dryad girl said, "Here," and opened a door in the shadows. She held it open, waiting for them to go through.

They looked into a long dining hall. A fire threw light and heat across the room. A table stretched down the middle of the hall, big enough to fit a dozen people. Sitting at the far end were Sethis, Arashina, and a handsome man in late middle age, bearded and grey-haired. They had clearly just finished a meal: plates were stacked at one end of the table. The rest of the table was almost hidden by books, parchments, a pair of pistols and the powder and bullets to load them, several knives, half a loaf of bread and a rough, brown heap of tobacco in a patterned bowl.

The idea of food made Giulia's stomach turn with anticipation: the others had been eating chicken, from the smell of it.

"Giulia!" Sethis stood up, his eyes gleaming behind his spectacles. "Join us, please; we've saved you seats."

The table was wide enough to sit two across at its narrow end, and the two chairs at the far end were empty. *Like a king and queen*, Giulia thought. Sethis pulled the chair out for her. She shrugged off her rucksack and took a seat.

Two plates sat on the ledge above the fireplace, and Sethis fetched them and set them down in front of Giulia and Hugh.

"I thought you might be hungry after the ride," he said. There was a pile of grilled chicken, polenta and cheese on each plate.

"Thanks," said Hugh. "Good of you." He pulled a knife from his belt and began to saw into the chicken.

"If you need cutlery..." Sethis added.

"Mmn, fine," Hugh replied. He hacked out a lump of chicken and jabbed it into the polenta. "I'm rather hungry," he added. Anna poured out wine for Giulia and Hugh and sat down.

"Arashina you know," Sethis said, gesturing to her. Giulia nodded to the dryad, who gave her a lazy wave. Judging by the detritus on Arashina's plate, she'd eaten rather well. Giulia hadn't expected such a flimsy creature to have much of an appetite.

"And this is Lord Portharion," Sethis said, indicating the man.

The wizard? Shit, this must be serious for him to be here.

Portharion stood up and bowed. "I'm pleased to meet you both." His voice was smooth and deep. He sat down.

"You too," Giulia said, feeling the first stirrings of unease.

"Arashina called me here," he replied. "We have mutual enemies."

Arashina blinked slowly and pushed her thick hair away from her face.

Something brushed against Giulia's leg, and she

glanced down. A badger stood beside her chair. Alarmed, she pulled back, and Sethis whistled softly.

"Sorry," he said. "He's mine. Come on, boy."

Portharion shook his head, as though this happened a lot. He was quite attractive, Giulia thought, if a little smug. He would drive a certain type of woman berserk: she felt reassured that she was not quite that sort.

Sethis gestured to Hugh with a long-fingered hand. "Thanks to Sir Hugh here, we were able to escape the Scola with considerably less casualties than would have occurred otherwise. I'd like to take this opportunity to thank him for his help. Everyone?"

There was a rumble of agreement amongst them. Sethis said, "Sir Hugh, everyone," and they raised their cups.

Hugh looked up, slowly chewing a wad of food. "Very kind," he said.

The room was quiet. "Now," Arashina said, "to business. Our enemy has moved against us. The Scola has been broken up, and more importantly, the gate to Faery is closed. Giulia, you've come from the city. What's happening there?"

"Yes," Giulia said, tearing off a piece of bread. Her mind picked up speed as she tried to work out which bits of her story to leave out. "I was there last night. Where do you want me to start?"

"So that's the end of it," Giulia said, hoping that she sounded believable. "I went back to the whorehouse to see Falsi, and they directed me to Iacono. He let me stay in his house overnight, and this morning he gave me directions to come up here. So I headed out of the city and came to find you."

Sethis nodded. "It makes sense – in a crazy way. But then, this whole business is mad."

Arashina said, "The Inquisition scum are all insane. And most humans are like stupid sheep. They'd run off a cliff if they thought there was some gold at the bottom."

Giulia felt the insult, but said nothing.

Portharion leaned back in his chair. "A boat that travels underwater," he mused. "Cosimo Lannato has spoken about making a machine like that. Provided it could be sealed, and powered, it's possible."

Arashina looked at Giulia; a long, slow, alien stare. Meeting the dryad's gaze was like looking into a lantern. "It's quite a story you've told us. Shapechangers, smuggling, boats that sail like fish: if I didn't have it on good authority that you could be trusted, I'd think you were having visions."

"And you live in a magic forest," Giulia said. "Strange things happen."

"True," Sethis said, before Arashina could reply. "Personally, I don't actually live in a forest. But you do have a point."

Arashina muttered something in her own language and reached for the fruit.

Giulia swallowed and said, "So is there anything else you want to know?" She had not mentioned Edwin and Elayne. That was Hugh's business, and her own.

Something moved at her side. She looked down and saw that the badger was nudging her rucksack. Giulia tugged the rucksack away, and, disappointed, the badger turned and stomped off, snuffling the floor in search of dropped food.

"No, thank you," Portharion said. "You've been very helpful."

"I've got questions for you," Giulia said.

"Oh yes?"

She took a sip of wine. "It's only one question, to be honest. I want to know what all of this is *really* about."

The wizard peered at her. "Really?"

She nodded. "This isn't just about getting revenge on Azul, is it?" She looked across their faces, human and not, and saw the same suspicious blankness. "I mean, you barely knew who he was when we last spoke. It's about more than just him, isn't it?"

She stopped, and the room was silent. Like a lizard, Arashina closed her eyes and opened them again. She looked alluring and thoroughly alien. Giulia glanced to her left: to her surprise, Hugh was nodding in agreement. She had expected him to be shocked that she might make demands of these worthy allies. She picked an orange out of the fruit bowl. "Well?"

"Fair enough," Sethis said. "It's only right that you should know what's going on. You've been honest with us; now I suppose it's our turn."

"Go on."

"Putting what you've told us together with what we already know, it seems that Azul has been bringing in gold and diamonds, probably collected off a ship moored out to sea—"

"From the New World," Giulia said. Her thumbs skinned the orange in strips.

"Right. To get the money past the Customs, and to avoid the problems entailed with putting money from a foreign country through Averrio in the usual way, he uses this underwater boat to deliver the gold and gemstones straight to his own people. He takes a cut and then, presumably, he splits up the goods and sends them out."

"Varro's books said Azul was in the Glassmakers' Guild," Giulia said. "Maybe he uses the guild to distribute the money."

"We think so," Portharion replied. "But there's another step. To make the money look legitimate, Azul puts it through the Fiorenti Bank."

Giulia swallowed a piece of orange. "I know all this," she put in. "You thought the bank was hiding something, right? But what about the rest of it? You say Azul's sending the money out. Where's it going to?"

"We don't know for sure," Sethis replied, "but we've got a pretty good idea. First, to the rest of his crew: whoever helps move the gold and provides protection to him. Bribes, expenses, that sort of thing. But more importantly, he's sending money to the Hidden Hand. They, in turn—"

"Wait," Giulia said. "Who's the Hidden Hand?"

"I've heard of them," Hugh said. "Criminal gang. Recruits old Inquisition men. Didn't know it was real, though. They must be getting the money."

"More than that," Arashina said. "They don't just want to get rich. They want to restart the War of Faith."

Giulia said, "What? How?"

"Various ways. Hiring mercenaries. Spreading rumours. Bribing officials, and killing those who won't be bribed. A lie here, a murder there. Little actions, but they add up. A thousand little pushes towards war."

Giulia looked into Arashina's eyes. "So that's what this is all about, then. He's bringing in money to fund these people – to help them start a war."

"Exactly."

Sethis adjusted his spectacles and took a deep breath. "There is a man in the Hidden Hand who regrets his former actions. This man lives a long way from here. He remains within their ranks, but passes information on to us. Several of the Old Crusaders, as the members of the Hidden Hand like to refer to themselves, have received letters in the last few months telling them to await the call to arms. They are planning something big."

Arashina leaned forward, and her dark eyes stared at Giulia, as fierce and keen as a beast's. "The letter mentioned a meeting place," she said. "This city. Azul is gathering his old comrades. They may well already be here."

"Where, exactly?"

"We don't know. We've got ideas—"

"Show me," Giulia said. She leaned down and took out Iacono's map-case. "Here."

Hugh helped her clear a space on the table. They gathered around the map like generals drawing up a battle line.

"This is Varro's boatyard, and this is the warehouse where they've been unloading the gold," Giulia said. "But after last night, they'd be mad to meet there again."

Hugh rubbed his chin. "If these friends of Azul used to be inquisitors, they'll be rich, and old. They'll want somewhere comfortable."

"Well, Azul's in the guild of glassmakers.... Sethis, where do the Glassmakers have their guildhouse?"

Sethis leaned across and tapped the map twice with a long finger. "The Glass Islands," he replied. "They do all their work on Miriano and Buriano, to the north-east."

"Could they be hiding out there?"

Arashina said, "It's possible. But both islands are busy places. People would notice it if he brought in a legion of conspirators. Some of Azul's comrades are wanted men. They'd be afraid of being recognised..."

"Sirinara." Portharion stood a little way back, arms folded. "If it was me, that's where I'd go."

Giulia said, "What's that?"

Portharion drew an arc across the sea with his hand, parallel to the bay. "Here are the defence towers, yes? And here's the Golden Griffon. The island of Sirinara is beyond that, almost past the Isle of Quarantine.

"It's just a little place, really, a rock. But years ago the Glassmakers built a tower there from enchanted glass, a sort of fortress. They used it to show off their skill."

Giulia peered at the map, at the tiny hand-drawn waves, past a sea-monster rearing up like the thing in the glass that Elayne had showed her back in the Old Arms. Sirinara was a tiny circle, no more than half a mile across. "Does anyone still use it?"

"It fell into disrepair," Portharion replied. "During the War of Faith, it was too far outside the city to be worth having a garrison. It wasn't of any military use, and it's not a safe place to be, especially in a ship: there's a lot of rocks, and wild griffons nest out there."

Giulia said, "Sounds perfect."

"Doesn't it?" Arashina replied.

"So, what's the plan?" Giulia asked. "We can't just show up there and ransack the place. If we go in quietly, we risk being heavily outnumbered. We need allies – but I've no idea who would help us now."

"I'm going to return to the city tonight," Portharion replied. "We can't risk taking this to the City Watch, but I know people close to General Attelani, people with links to the Customs. That way we can bypass the Watchmen."

"What if they don't want to help?"

"I'll make them an offer. If they assist, I'll call up a

trade-wind that'll get the port busy. If they don't, they'll find a lot of ships suddenly get becalmed." The wizard smiled. "That's bad for business."

"Right," Giulia said. "So, if we get them to help – and we can trust them – all we need to know for sure is whether Azul and his men will be meeting on Sirinara."

"That's right. Tomorrow morning, I'll send word back here on the situation in the city," Portharion said. "You may have to return in disguise."

Giulia said, "We can do that."

The wizard pushed his chair back. "Then I'd suggest you all rest while you can. We're going to have a busy time ahead of us."

***

Giulia and Hugh stood outside, drinking wine. It was warmer than she had expected, and she could not see her breath when she exhaled. Dusk glowed between the trees.

"Funny bunch, the fey," Hugh said. "Good people, for pagans, but... odd."

"Yes, I suppose so." She stared between the trees and thought, *This is going to be difficult.*

A horse trotted out of the stable. Portharion sat on it, bolt upright. His expression, at once wise and stern, made him look like a Quaestan emperor. He gave them both a quick wave, then headed off down the path. Giulia was mildly surprised to see him ride. She had expected the sorcerer to vanish into thin air. On the other hand, it seemed that he would be riding through the dark. Even with a full moon, that wasn't easy or safe. Unless you were a wizard.

Funny how the mind latched on to irrelevancies

at times like this, as though it grabbed at any chance to wander off the path it had to take.

I really don't think I can do this.

"Hugh," Giulia said, "there's something we need to talk about."

The front door opened and Sethis stepped out, holding a bottle. "Do either of you want another drink?" He walked down between them. His friendliness made him look naive.

Giulia held out her cup.

"How's your arm?" Sethis asked.

"Sometimes it aches a bit. Otherwise, not too bad. But I try not to think about it too much."

"That's probably a good idea." He poured Giulia a drink, then Hugh. "I'd suggest getting an early night. There are beds upstairs; they're quite comfortable. We'll reconvene tomorrow morning."

Hugh said, "Look, Sethis: all this business of getting the Customs men involved in this – are you sure we can trust any of these people? Can't you just get some of your fellows together and raid these buggers instead? Summon up one of those, what's it, wickermen you have. That'd give these fellows a bit of a surprise, eh?"

"Too risky," the dryad replied. "The fey exist on sufferance here, the same as in most of your cities. To bring something like that into the city, especially without permission – our enemies would use it as an excuse to turn on us. Besides, wickermen are more Arashina's side of things than mine."

"I suppose so." Hugh looked him over. "You know, I could almost mistake you for one of us," he added.

"I'll take that as a compliment," Sethis replied. "That's the worst of living in the city: too human for my own people and not human enough for yours." He smiled wearily. "Well, I'd best be getting back. Sleep well."

He turned and walked inside. Giulia watched him go. The door closed behind Sethis, and she looked back to Hugh.

"You wanted to talk," he said.

Fear and guilt moved within her stomach, twisting together like mating snakes.

Of course I don't "want" to. I'm sorry, Hugh, but Edwin and Elayne are traitors. Bad luck, old fellow, your best friend and your damsel have sold out to the enemy. Sorry, but there you go.

"Let's go down the path a bit," she said.

Hugh lowered his voice. "Private stuff, is it? Right then, let's go."

They walked down together, towards the road. They were still out of view to anyone on the road. Giulia blew across her hands and rubbed them together.

So much for chivalry. You rescue me from Azul and I give you this in return.

"Edwin and Elayne are still in the city," she said.

Hugh stopped. "Sorry?"

"When I went after Azul last night, while I was breaking into his warehouse, I saw their ship moored up on the dockyards on the Great Canal. It was just down from the warehouse. It looked as if it was being repaired."

"Are you sure it was theirs?"

"I'm certain. I saw them both. They were on the deck."

"I thought they'd gone."

"So did I," she said. "Look, I'm certain it was them. I recognised the ship, too, the *Margaret of Cheswick*. I'm absolutely sure."

His voice flat, Hugh said, "Did you talk to them?"

"No. I was trying to get into the warehouse. I figured there might be a way to get inside via the ships, so I sneaked onto the ship next to theirs. Anyway, I saw two men on the deck of Edwin's ship, so I hid and waited for them to go away. One was Cortaag, the man you ran through. Big, tall, with a beard."

He stared. "What, the man from the cellar? I thought he was dead. He bloody well should be."

She licked her lips. "He must've healed up, like Varro did. The other man was Edwin. They were talking."

Hugh said, "What about? Was he threatening him?"

"Nobody was threatening anyone. They were just talking. Like you and I are now. Like friends."

"How strange," Hugh said. She wondered if he was really listening, if a portcullis had dropped in his mind to protect his friends. "I wonder why?"

"Cortaag is Azul's man," Giulia replied. "We know that."

"Yes, that's right. He must be up to something."

She took a sip of her wine. "That's not all of it, though. Elayne came out on deck. She talked to Cortaag as well, and they shook hands. He went away then. They're friends, all of them."

There was a pause. Hugh said, "And you're sure it was them?"

"Hugh, I *know* I'm sure. I'd know all three of them from a mile away. And this wasn't even fifty yards." Suddenly, she wondered if she really had seen them. Could it have been a trick of the light, some sort of delusion, a memory she had somehow made up? Maybe the horrors of the last few days had driven her hysterical, like some woman in a play. *No. I know what I saw.*

"Perhaps it was a trick. Maybe he was trying to bribe them," Hugh said. "You know, it wouldn't surprise me. Back in the war, we had a lot of that. Treacherous peace offers, you see, enemies trying to take advantage of our chivalrous nature... Yes, I'll bet it was that. We should warn them, you know."

"It wasn't that. Nobody was tricking anyone."

He turned to look at her. His old eyes were calm and stern, as though he was about to lecture a foolish child. "Did you hear them properly?"

"No, but— they shook hands, Hugh. They were all smiling. Listen, just hear me out. Once you think about it, it all makes sense." She felt her voice speed up a little, as though desperation was creeping in. "I mean, it was them who didn't want to run away from here when the Watch had us cooped up, wasn't it? It was them who wanted to reason it out with the Watchmen, even when they were gearing up to murder us. Shit, it was them who brought us to the Old Arms in the first place—"

"Now look here, Giulia. I hope you're not suggesting—"

"And it was them who said we should go to the docks when you killed Varro. That's where we were attacked. And it was Elayne who struck that deal with Falsi to keep us out of jail. She made him agree to it – she said so herself. Who knows what else she put in his head?"

"Giulia! Damn it, woman, listen to yourself. This is nonsense!"

But the dam was unblocked. The words tumbled out now, fast and reckless. "No, Hugh, you listen to me.. What if Edwin and Elayne were playing us all along? What if they went to the Old Arms to meet Father Coraldo? He said he was looking for Anglians. What if he came there because they told him to?" Another memory, something from what seemed like years ago: a sea monster raising its head above the water, in a piece of polished glass. "My God... Elayne showed me a piece of magic glass, the night I first met her. Azul's in the guild of glassmakers: Edwin and Elayne had a cargo of magic glass ready to go. Elayne knows who he is – she's in fucking business with him—"

"Shut up!" Hugh whirled around, and his hand was raised. "Shut up about her!"

Giulia darted back, four yards between them, heart pounding at her chest. Her left hand was up to block. Her right hand hovered at her belt, an inch away from her fighting-knife.

Giulia had seen Hugh fight many times, but he had never frightened her before. "Put your hand down." Her voice sounded shaky and low. "No man strikes me, Hugh. No-one, you hear?"

He lowered his arm as if slowly waking from a dream. "Yes, of course." The rage was gone, and the bemused old man was back. "Yes, certainly. You know I'd never hit a woman, Giulia. You do know that, don't you?"

She relaxed a little and stood up straight. She kept her legs bent, just a little, enough to leap aside. *I spoke ill of his lady*, she thought. *That's a duelling offence in the stories. It must hurt to hear that she lied to him.* And then a nastier thought crept in: *Or maybe he just doesn't like being reminded that she's not his.*

"I don't know what came over me. I'm terribly sorry. It's just – well, sometimes I forget you're not a man, if you know what I mean."

"You're not the first." Relief made her bitter.

"I always think of you as an equal, a gentleman. I am sorry. Friends?" He put out his hand.

"Friends and partners," Giulia said, and she shook his hand. Now the threat had passed, she felt the prickle of sweat at her hairline.

"Terribly sorry," he said again.

"It's all right. I know you wouldn't hit a woman."

They were quiet for a moment.

"But I've known Elayne for twenty years," Hugh said. "Edwin too. They'd never do anything like that. I know it as sure as I know anything. I'm sure there's a perfectly reasonable explanation for all of this."

And the moment was gone. *I played this wrong. The only thing I've convinced him of is that I'm an idiot.*

"Then we'll just have to find it," she said. "Together."

"Yes, that's it. Both of us together, eh? Two knights errant, bound by one quest."

"Right."

Hugh frowned. "Elayne may be in danger, though, Edwin too. We should go quietly— what's that?"

"What?" she asked, but her voice was already a whisper. They both crouched, instinctively moving aside from the path.

"Man ahead," Hugh whispered. "One man, coming our way."

Giulia drew her long knife. "You approach him. Give the word and I'll take him from the side."

Hugh strolled down the path, thumbs hooked over his belt. Giulia crept into the trees, the damp leaves brushing against her shoulders and side. She kept out of sight, watching. Hugh let out a loud yawn to announce his presence, followed by a cough. "Oh – hello there."

She could see the man between the trees, a head shorter than Hugh and a good deal younger. "Hello again," he said. "Going for a walk?"

Giulia recognised the voice. It was the forester who had been sitting outside when they'd arrived. She could have taken him easily. She walked out, treading loudly so she wouldn't catch him by surprise.

"Something like that," Hugh replied.

"Been inside? Seen the fey ladies?"

Giulia heard the relish in his tone. Some men had a taste for dryad women. She walked into view. "I've got a message for you two," the forester said. "The guards on the bridge said a man came up and left it for them. Here it is."

Hugh took the letter, turned it over in his hands.

Giulia said, "Did the guards say anything about the man who left it?"

"Nothing much at all," said the forester. "They said he was well-spoken, but dressed for travel, like a rich man's servant."

"Thanks."

"I'll be going, then. You take care."

The forester walked back down the path, between the trees. He was lost to view long before the sound of his boots faded away.

Giulia said, "What does it say?"

"It's addressed to me. We'll have a look at it inside," Hugh said.

"Wait a moment. Let's look at it out here, just in case." *In case of what? In case we can't trust the fey folk after all?*

"It's got a seal on," Hugh said. "Doesn't look like anyone's opened it."

"There's ways," Giulia replied, half to herself. "Read it out."

Hugh broke the seal and unfolded the letter. "It's

to me. Here we are: *Dear sir knight, the time for hints and requests has been and gone. Last night, your assassin whore took a dear friend from us: now we have done the same...*" Hugh held the letter up close to his face, straining to read it by the moonlight. He lowered it and looked at her, his eyes wide with horror. "Oh my God, Giulia. They've got Elayne."

"What? Let me see."

"They've captured her," Hugh said. His face was empty, haggard. "Look."

She plucked the letter from his hand and squinted at the words. The handwriting was elegant and smooth.

Dear sir knight, the time for hints and requests has been and gone. Last night, your assassin whore took a dear friend from us: now we have done the same to you. If you do not surrender at once we will treat the sorceress Elayne Brown to the slow arts that you know are available to us. Either you will come to the East dock tomorrow night and give yourself over, or you will bring a substitute to exchange for the witch, namely the murderess Giulia De Garno. Think quickly on this, for she shall not remain untouched for long.

Your friends.

For a moment Giulia hoped it was a joke, or a mistake, but there could be no doubt. Surprise stole the right words from her. "Oh, fuck."

Hugh looked staggered, bereaved. "We have to help her," he said. "We've got to get her back. If those bastards—"

"Wait a moment. Let me think."

"We need to work fast," said Hugh. He stared into the trees, as if looking for an ambush. "We have to rescue her."

"Easy," Giulia said. "Easy. We need to be sure it isn't fake."

"Fake? What do you mean, fake? That they've not captured her?"

"It's a trap," Giulia said. As soon as she'd said it, she was certain that she was right. "They want to make us go back into the city. They can't get at you out here. This way, they're bound to catch either one of us – maybe both."

"But what if it's *true*?" Hugh said, his voice wound a notch tighter. "Can't you see what they've written?"

"Come on, Hugh," Giulia replied. "This letter is bullshit. It's lies."

"But why would they lie?" he demanded. "How can you be sure?"

Giulia didn't say anything.

"You think Elayne had a hand in this?"

"I don't know. Honestly, I don't."

"*I know*, Giulia. I know she wouldn't do this. And she's in terrible danger – her and Edwin – and I have to rescue her – them. I know it." He turned towards the house. "Come on. We need to get our things."

"I don't like it, Hugh. I'm telling you, I don't like it. Listen, what if I'm right? What if they *are* with Azul? What happens if you walk in there and they're all waiting for you?"

"Giulia, I've known these people for years. They fought with me. Why would they turn on us just like that?"

"I don't know. Maybe it was the money."

"Oh, come on! They fought alongside me, against the Inquisition! Don't you know what that means? We fought to save the world from those bastards, and you're suggesting that they'd just— just turn their backs on it? Fight for the other side?"

Giulia wanted to raise her voice. She wanted to tell him that he was a fool, that this was Azul's plan to bring him down, to strike at the place where Hugh was weak. She fought down the urge. "Listen, I know it seems bad. But you've got to look at it like this. That letter was written for you to read. It's addressed to you. But I know what I saw. Edwin and Elayne know Cortaag. He's been on their ship. They're working with him."

"That can't be," he said again, but his voice was weaker. It was hope that fuelled him now, not evidence.

"It is," Giulia said. She softened her voice and put her hand on his arm. "I'm sorry, Hugh, but this is a trap."

He stepped away. "I'll be the judge of that."

She stared at him, then looked away, unsure what else she could do. Hugh took a step towards the house, and she walked beside him.

"What if *you're* wrong?" he demanded. "What if you've got it wrong, what then? What're we going to do when we find out that she's dead because we did nothing?"

"Hugh, I'm pretty sure—"

"But not *certain*, are you, eh?"

There was a pause. Giulia looked around them, as if looking for someone to back her up. "I know what I saw," she said. It sounded hollow.

"I need to think," said the knight. "Just leave me for a while, would you?"

"Of course. Go ahead." She felt furious: with him for being so stupid, with herself for not convincing him, with everything. "I'm going to bed: I need an early night. We'll talk about this in the morning."

He looked at her for a long moment, and she

wondered what he was thinking. Then he nodded. "You're right. Tomorrow morning it is." Hugh opened the door and they stepped into the hall. "Goodnight, Giulia."

"Goodnight, Hugh."

She walked up the stairs, feeling that everything had failed.

Her room was at the top of the stairs. It was small and pleasant, with a large window and a neat, clean bed. She pulled off her boots and britches, left her weapons on the floor and climbed into bed.

There was a pain behind her eyes. She sat up in bed and pinched her brow, knowing what was going to come.

Giulia didn't bother trying to stop the Melancholia. There was no point. It swelled behind her eyes and in her chest, and spread through her like poison.

Should've got out, she thought, *should've run from here while I had the chance. I should never have come here in the first place. Never should have met Hugh, never should have done anything except stay in the fucking gutter. If I put my head up, God himself would reach through the clouds and push me back down.*

That was the Melancholia talking: it had always been worst at night, creeping in like an evil lover when there was no sunshine or conversation to keep it at bay. *I ought to have stayed on my own.*

The letter was a clever move. The Inquisition had worked like that in the old days, during the war: the inquisitors would threaten a man's family, until he betrayed everyone he knew to save the few closest to him. They understood that friends and lovers were weaknesses: the strong were strongest alone.

She sat there in the darkness, waiting for sleep to catch up with her.

I don't know how I can win this. I really don't.

Giulia awoke in what seemed like the small hours. She felt worn out, used up, as if she had been drinking heavily and had narrowly avoided a hangover. There was some food left downstairs; that would help. She waited for her eyes to get used to the light, got up and dressed. She crossed the room, the boards creaking softly under her bare feet.

Moonlight streaked across the landing. It had been dark when she had gone to bed, and she turned to see how the light was getting in.

Hugh's door was open. He stood in front of the window, a black outline against the dark blue world outside. Above his head, the moon shone in like a great lidless eye, idiotic and malign. A high, strained noise came from him.

She crept closer. Hugh stood bolt upright, his back to her. His right hand was raised to his chin, not covering his mouth but partially in it.

He made the noise again. It was a thin, strangled sound, the sort of sound a distressed child might make. Giulia watched him bite his knuckles, eyes clenched shut.

She knew what that meant. She'd done it herself, when she'd been coming to terms with the scars on her face. It was either that or scream.

She made her feet scuff the floor as she approached. He lowered his hand, but he did not look around.

"Hugh? Are you all right?"

"Yes, thank you." His voice was a tiny bit tighter than usual, a little more controlled. He stared out the window. "I'm fine. Are you having trouble sleeping?"

"Yes," she said.

"Giulia, do I seem like a fool to you?"

"No," she said. "Why would you?"

"This letter... maybe it's a lie. I suppose I must look stupid, taking it as it reads, but... what if it's true? What if we do nothing, and it turns out they had Elayne?"

I told you already, she thought. *What more do you want me to say?* "We won't do nothing. In the morning we'll go after her. I'll do everything I can, Hugh. I promise."

"I know you will."

She hesitated. She felt guilty for resenting him. "I'm sorry this happened. I wish we'd never run into them. We wouldn't be in this shit, and you wouldn't be... you know. You'd be happier otherwise."

He turned from the window. She expected him to disagree, perhaps to be angry. "I probably would," he said. "But I've got no choice in it. I'm a knight. It's what I do."

"Doesn't mean you have to suffer. You could be a happy knight."

He smiled, very slightly.

She said, "We'll get Elayne back. But you don't owe her the way you think you do. Edwin does. You don't. She's not yours to owe."

He looked down at his hand and flexed the fingers, as if he wasn't sure how it worked. "I see what you're saying."

"I'll, um, go back to bed now. See if I can give it another try."

"Good idea," he replied. "You should do that."

"Yes," she said, and as she turned to go she saw him lift his hand back to his mouth.

"Goodnight," he said. "Sleep well."

"You too."

Giulia tried to imagine what Hugh must have been

like when he first met Elayne. He would have been in his late thirties, probably stronger and fitter than someone half his age, brash among men and awkward with ladies, happier spilling blood than making polite conversation. She suspected she would not have liked him quite as much then.

Getting back into bed reminded her body of how worn out she was. Giulia was too tired to think clearly, too tired even for the Melancholia. As she fell asleep, a jumble of images flickered through her mind: lords and ladies, dragons and tournaments, things she'd only seen in books.

***

Averrio twinkled in the rain, its thousand fires staring out of the night like the eyes of small animals: sometimes friendly, often wicked, never trustworthy. They were reflected on the water, as though there was a second city under the lagoon.

You could almost think that it was a good place, Hugh thought. He nudged his horse on, wanting to go faster but wary of laming the damned thing before he got there.

He had never liked cities. Only bad things could happen when you took a man out of the countryside and dumped him with a thousand other men, all squabbling over the same few coins. It was no place for a knight.

Elayne, he thought. One of those tiny lights stood for her. He saw her not in a cell, but as she had been, years ago: backlit by the summer sun, the field around her a blur of green, her hair ruffled by the breeze. He would kill anyone who put a hand on her. He would choke them with their own guts, fix them so they would never trouble a woman again.

There was a little stone guardhouse at the end of the road. Lanterns hung along the length of the bridge, marking out the way.

A man stepped out of the guardhouse, a blanket over his shoulders and a truncheon in his hand. "Halt! What's your business?"

Hugh looked down at him. "I need to get across. I'm going to see a merchant," Hugh replied.

The guard sniffed. "Why now? Can't you do that in daytime?"

"Could we do this quickly, please?" Hugh said. "I don't have much time."

A second, larger guard stepped out of the gatehouse, a piece of paper in his hand. "Sorry, no," he replied. "No crossing at night. That's an order of the Customs-house of Averrio."

The first guard sneezed.

"You've got to turn back," the second man said. "Council of a Hundred says so."

Hugh looked from one man to the other. They didn't look like fighters – barely like village yeomen, for that matter.

"You want to wait for tomorrow morning," the first guard said. "Of course, tomorrow morning, there's a toll—"

Hugh spurred his horse. It cried out and lurched forward, bouncing along under him, faster than it had gone for a very long time. "Wait!" cried the guards behind him, and Hugh smiled, remembering the horses that he and Edwin had stolen when they had escaped from the Chateau Dolour. He felt the night air against his face and drove his steed onwards, as if charging into battle.

***

"Wake up, dammit," the forester said. He sounded disgusted. "Wake up."

Giulia groaned and sat up, glad that she'd fallen asleep in her shirt. It was still dark outside. Sethis sat on the end of her bed, his pale face almost luminous in the moonlight. Arashina stood behind him, arms folded. The dryads' huge eyes and pointed chins made their faces seem like masks. She remembered stories she'd heard, of children stolen away and changelings left behind.

"What is it?"

The forester said, "The knight's gone."

"Gone?" Giulia rubbed her eyes with the heels of her hands. "What? How do you mean, gone?"

"Gone as in fucked off," the man said. "Run away."

"How'd he get away?" Giulia said.

"He climbed out of the window," Sethis replied. "Took his sword and a horse. I looked just now. We all slept through it," he added. "It makes us look rather foolish, really."

"That's about the sum of it," the forester said, and the tone of his voice suggested that he held Giulia responsible. "Gone to shop us to them in the city, no doubt," he added bitterly.

"No." Giulia shook her head. "He wouldn't do that. He's wrong about something, that's all. He thinks they have someone close to him."

"And do they?" Sethis asked.

"Not how he thinks." She looked at her equipment, still on the floor. "I'm going after him. He's in a lot of danger."

"Do you know where he'll be?" the forester demanded.

"I've got a good idea."

Arashina said, "Supposing he escapes you? What then?"

"He won't." She ran a hand through her hair. *Yes, the docks*, she thought. That was where Hugh would go, where the *Margaret of Cheswick* was moored. "How long's he had?"

The forester shrugged. "At best, I reckon he's had three, four hours' start."

"Four hours?" Giulia turned to him. "Shit. I have to go," she said. "I've got to catch him up. He's walking into a trap." Giulia looked at Sethis. "Would you good people get out and let me get dressed, please?"

"Of course," he said gently, and he stood up.

The forester stepped back nervously, as though worried she might strike him. "I just don't know how he got past me. I don't know how he did it—"

"Because he's bloody good," Giulia said.

He glared at her. "If he's so good, why do you need to go after him, then?"

"He's not good enough," she said.

"Huh. If someone pissed off and abandoned *me*—"

"He's my friend, and he's in danger. Now give me five minutes, would you?"

Sethis led the man out. "I should check your bandages," he said at the door.

"Do it later," Giulia replied, and the door closed.

She dressed and armed herself, then stepped into the passage. Sethis waited outside her room. Behind him, Hugh's door was open, and she caught a glimpse of the window by which he had escaped, where the moon had lit the corridor last night.

"You ought not to do this," Sethis said. His big eyes looked hurt. "It's too dangerous. You yourself said that he was riding into a trap."

"I'm not staying here, Sethis."

"You should be recuperating. With what happened yesterday, and your arm, you ought to be in bed." He stepped back to let her pass. "They'll be worried about this, you know, Portharion and the others."

"So? Why should I give a damn what they think?" She walked down three steps, stopped and turned. "And you can tell them I said that, too."

Sethis followed her down the stairs. Arashina stood in front of the door, arms folded.

"Don't try to stop me," Giulia said.

"I'm not. Do you intend to go after Hugh on your own?"

"That's the plan," Giulia said. "Where's Anna?"

"Back in Faery, where she should be. I sent her to warn our friends. She will find – what's the word – reinforcements for us."

"I can't wait that long. I need to leave now."

"Then go. I hope you catch Hugh up before Azul does. I'll fetch the others," Arashina said. "We'll meet on the west docks at daybreak. The enemy have made their move. Now we make one back." She held out a leather tube. "Here's your map."

Giulia took it. "Thanks," she said.

Arashina said, "Good luck, Sethis. Giulia knows the way."

"What?" Giulia said. "What do you mean?"

But the meaning was obvious. Sethis picked up a sword from the side table, a smart-looking weapon that a merchant in a bad neighbourhood might use. He slid it through his belt. As he turned, Giulia saw that there was a long knife strapped to his right thigh.

"You're not going alone," he said. "I'll help you."

She thought about it for a moment. "Can you fight?"

"You'd be surprised," he replied.

Arashina said, "Trust me, he can."

"You'll have to do what I say," Giulia said. "I'll need you to stay back when I tell you to."

"I can do that." Sethis picked up his cloak and put his spectacles on. His cloak was dark green, like that of a gentleman hunter. "I'm ready," he said.

"You'd better be," Giulia replied. "This isn't going to be easy."

The High Tower

FIFTEEN

"Edwin?" Hugh bashed the cabin door with his fist. He looked over his shoulder at the warehouse and the deserted yard. There was no trace of any of Azul's men, let alone the underwatership that Giulia had spoken about. "Edwin! Open up, it's Hugh!"

He heard someone moving across creaky boards, a dull thump and a muttered sound that had to be a curse. Bolts slid back and Edwin opened the cabin door. He looked tired and worried, almost sick.

"Hugh? I thought you'd left town. What's happened? Are you ill?"

"No, I'm fine. Where's Elayne?"

Edwin stood in the doorway, absolutely still, looking as if he might shatter into pieces. "You'd better come in."

The two men barely fitted into the cramped cabin. A lantern glowed in one corner. Edwin took a bottle from a little table and poured out two cups. He gulped his wine down instantly. For once, Hugh didn't want to drink.

"Look at this," Hugh said. He passed the letter to Edwin and stood by the cabin wall as Edwin's eyes moved slowly over the handwriting. "A man left it with the guard where I've been staying. The guard had instructions to give it to me."

Edwin sat down on the bed. His face fell as if it was starting to melt. Hugh thought that he was going to howl.

"They want me to give myself up to them, or give them Giulia. To hell with that," Hugh said. "I'm going after them. I'm going to rescue Elayne and put every one of these bastards to the sword, I swear it."

"No," Edwin said. "This can't be right. She's safe. This is wrong."

Hugh looked down at him, surprised. He seemed small, all of a sudden. "Whyever not? A woman is in trouble, Edwin. Not just any woman, either. It's time to get moving, time to take the fight to these whoresons! To teach them a bloody good lesson!" The thought of beating the daylight out of Azul's men made him feel much better. He felt full of righteousness.

"Hugh, I sent her away. There was some trouble on the docks last night. Someone broke into a warehouse, killed a workman there. Elayne's up at an inn in the city, out of the way."

"They must have found her there." Hugh glanced around, his mind spinning. "Which inn did you send her to?"

Edwin shook his head. "They can't get her. There's half a dozen men guarding her."

"Really? These men of yours: are they any good in a fight?"

"They're not my men. They work for the man who runs the boatyard. They're good people."

Hugh froze, and slowly looked down at him. "The boatyard?"

"Yes, the man who's doing the repairs on the

ship. He has a warehouse over there. He's a northerner: Cortaag's his name."

The name was like a match to oil in Hugh's mind. "Cortaag? He's Azul's man! He works for Ramon Azul!"

"Who? Hugh, you're not making sense. Who the hell is Ramon Azul?"

"He's the man who's behind all of this. He used to be in the Inquisition. He's got magical powers. Cortaag works for him."

"Magical—"

"They killed that priest. They're smugglers, bringing in gold from the New World. Varro was one of them, too."

"That's nonsense. They can't be. I mean to say, I've been dealing with Cortaag for years."

He fell silent. He looked up at Hugh. They both realised what Edwin had said, how it sounded.

"How do you mean, 'dealing with him'?" Hugh said. "Do you mean to say that you trade with him?"

"Among others, yes. Hugh, if this man is what you say he is, I had no idea—"

"Then the glass you bring back... that's his glass. You've been helping them get rich."

Edwin was sterner now. "Hugh, Cortaag's just another merchant. He carries stuff overland. If you think I'd willingly help some bunch of criminals, then you're very mistaken."

"You've been helping them. How long have you been doing this for?"

"I've not been 'helping' them. It's called business, Hugh. That's how it works. If, and I mean *if*, this man Cortaag is linked to this, I had no way of knowing."

"You're helping the enemy!"

"How the hell was I supposed to know!" Edwin was

on his feet, shouting. "He's a merchant. I don't ask whose company he keeps. Fine, maybe he looks a little bit rough. Maybe I don't want to break bread with the man. What's wrong with that?"

"Because he's got Elayne." For a moment, neither spoke. Then Hugh said, "I'm going to get her back. You know where they took her?"

"She's gone to an inn, north of here. It's called the Althanor. We've stayed there before. But there's a load of men there, Hugh. Cortaag suggested it. Said that she'd be safe with all of them."

"And you let them take her?" It came out of Hugh like a sob. He swallowed. "Come on. Let's get her back." He glanced around the room, looking for something that he couldn't name. He felt desperate to get out: not just to find Elayne, but to leave this room, to escape from the man he suspected that Edwin had become. "Well, aren't you coming? Don't you want to rescue her?"

"Of course I want to rescue her! Of course I do! But there's loads of them!"

"Don't worry about that. Trust me, we'll go through these scum like a knife through butter." He moved to go.

Edwin stood up. "No, Hugh. It's too dangerous."

"Dangerous? This is Elayne we're talking about. We have a duty. You know, I hate to say it, but sometimes you don't sound like a knight at all."

"Haven't you been listening to me, Hugh? I'm not a knight. I'm a *merchant*." Edwin's voice rose, hardened, but then it became quiet again, defeated. "I can't risk it. I just want her back safely."

"Very well. I'll do it. You stay here if you want. I'm going to do what's right." Hugh turned to the door. Edwin moved. "No, Hugh. We have to tell the authorities. Wait,

I won't let you—"

It all happened instinctively. A hand took hold of Hugh's shoulder, a hand to keep him away from rescuing Elayne. He grabbed it, turned it, locked it and twisted, all in the same movement. Edwin yelped, stumbled into the wall and sank onto one knee.

And there was Hugh's old friend, clutching his left elbow with his right hand, and it was Hugh who'd done it to him.

"Oh, shit," he said. "Edwin, are you all right?"

"You've broken my fucking arm!"

"It's not broken. It's just the muscle—"

"You lunatic!"

"I'm really sorry—"

"Are you? Really?" Pain filled Edwin's face with reckless fury. "You can have her all to yourself now, can't you? That's what you want, just like in the stories. Go on, hit me again, perfect knight. Do it. Make yourself feel clever." He took a deep, shuddering breath. Hugh braced himself for shouting, perhaps for tears, but Edwin's voice was low and controlled. "Hugh, for God and the angels' sake, don't go after her. If that letter's right, they'll kill her. *Please.*"

Hugh felt sorry for his friend. "Edwin, they'll kill her anyway," he said. "If I don't bring them Giulia, they'll kill Elayne." He paused. He felt strangely clear-headed, devoid of the fury he had expected to feel. "Even if I brought Giulia to them, they'd never give Elayne back. They want Giulia, me, you too, eventually. They'll kill us all, given the chance. It's neater for them – probably more fun, too."

"You don't know for sure—"

"They caught Giulia before, you see. It was when we

were trying to get to the ship, and those animals attacked us. She wasn't fast enough. Cortaag took her to their lair and Azul tortured her. They were going to murder her, too, in cold blood and everything, but they didn't get the chance, thank God. I managed to get her out first. Trust me, Edwin, there's no reasoning with these people. They don't care who they murder: women, children, anyone. You can't deal with people like that. All you can do is send them to Hell."

Edwin started to get up. Hugh held out his hand: after a moment, Edwin took it and heaved himself onto the bed. He sat there, cradling his injured arm. "So what do we do now?" he said.

"Never despair," Hugh replied. He felt much better now. Things were back on course. "We will rescue Elayne. How do I get to this inn?"

"It's to the north. You go towards the big tower, turn at the first canal you see and follow it north."

Hugh raised a hand. "Stay here. Your arm's hurt. Giulia will be here soon. She'll need your help."

"They'll be waiting for you."

"I suppose so. But I'm ready for them." He thought about Elayne, the way she'd smiled from across the Old Arms at him. He remembered going into that house to rescue Giulia, realising what they were doing to her. "I'm going to finish this, once and for all," he said, and he opened the cabin door.

"Wait."

Hugh paused. "What is it?"

"What if they come back?" Edwin asked.

"Do what I'd do," Hugh replied. "Slay them."

***

The docks lay up ahead: a long, quiet expanse of piers, quays and warehouses. Masts jutted into the sky like dead pine trees. A cold wind stirred the canal. It was early afternoon, but the air felt like the dead of night.

"This is it," Giulia said. She rubbed her hands together to warm them. "You see that wall, with the door in it? That leads into the boatyard, where Azul's men were bringing the gold in. See that big building behind it? That's the warehouse. There's a channel under it that lets the underwater-boat come in. Edwin's ship is just down from there."

"I see," Sethis replied. She had been pleasantly surprised so far: he was light on his feet, nimble and quick. "It looks deserted."

Giulia peered at the warehouse. It made her thtink of an abandoned fortress. "They've probably cleared out. It's what the gangs would do back in Pagalia: run and hide when the Watch comes looking."

"Except the Watch is on their side, here."

"I know. I tell you, there may be no law here, but there'll be some fucking justice before I'm done."

Sethis leaned close. He smelled slightly herbal, a little like cut grass. "Let's try the ship, then."

"All right. Listen, I don't know how you'd usually do this, but we're going in quietly, right? I don't want trouble if I can avoid it. Whatever happens, don't kill anyone unless they go for us, and if you have to, put them down quick and make sure they stay down. Are you any good with that sword?"

"I'm hardly King Alba, but yes, I'm reasonably skilled," the dryad replied. "To be honest, this isn't my usual line of work."

"It's not mine either. Let's go."

She jogged down towards the quay. The ships were as big as churches. Giulia slipped into the deep shadow cast by the hulls, the dryad running silently by her side.

On the deck of a merchantman, two lookouts stamped their feet and shared hot wine. Steam rose from their cups. A guard strolled round the lattice of jetties and pontoons, a lantern bobbing over his head like a gravelight. Giulia stopped and crouched down.

"There's Edwin's ship," she whispered. "Up there, with the white figurehead."

She pointed. Sethis nodded. "I see it."

The guard turned and walked away from them. Now was the time to move.

Giulia and Sethis were as small as birds in a herd of cattle. She did not like the ships: they were great beasts that whispered to one another in soft creaks, ready to swing together and crush the trespassers against their sides.

Stay calm, she told herself. *There's work to do.*

"We need to get on board," she said. The side of the *Margaret of Cheswick* loomed up like a cliff, far higher and steeper than Giulia remembered. Two clockwork cranes held it tight to the waterside. The big floats lying alongside looked like bodies risen from the deep. The gangplank was raised.

Sethis pointed. "What about the ropes? Or the cranes?"

Giulia did not much fancy climbing up the mooring-lines. "There," she said. A single rope hung down from the railing, trailing over the float and into the water. "I'll climb up. Wait until I give you the sign."

"Right. I'll stay here."

Giulia blew on her palms and wiggled her fingers. *Here we go*, she thought, looking at the side of the ship. There was always something mysterious – almost magical – in taking the first step over the threshold and into someone else's home. Into enemy territory.

She stood at the waterside, bent her legs and jumped. She hit the float and bounced, dropping to all fours to keep her balance. It was like crouching on a huge wineskin. Giulia waited for the wobbling to subside. The float stopped shaking and she reached out and grabbed the rope.

Giulia braced her feet against the hull and hauled herself up hand over hand until the railing was in reach. She grabbed the rail with her left hand and then the right, released the rope and heaved herself on board. She crouched down beside the railing, catching her breath as she surveyed the deck.

It was clear and nearly empty, the ropes tied off with an almost fussy degree of care. Her eyes moved to the door to the captain's quarters at the rear of the ship. There were lights on in there, and as she peered at it she saw that a panel in the window was cracked.

Giulia hurried back across the deck. She reached the railing and beckoned at Sethis. The dryad stepped out of the shadows and simply ran up the mooring line, scuttling along it like a spider on a thread. Giulia stepped back, and Sethis dropped down beside her.

She pointed at the light. "We're going in there."

They crossed the deck, keeping out of view of the cabin. Giulia readied her crossbow and loaded a bolt.

They stopped on either side of the door. "On three," she said. "Remember, if anyone tries anything—"

Sethis gripped his sword but didn't draw it. "I

know."

She reached out and took hold of the door handle. The metal was freezing against her palm. *One*, she counted, moving her lips. *Two.*

Three – she threw the door open, strode inside with the crossbow raised and shouted "Stay still! Raise hands, everyone!"

Edwin sat at a table, his right arm lifted in surrender. The left was in a sling. Papers lay randomly on the table, and on top of the papers there was a roll of bandage. A sailor stood next to Edwin's chair, a pair of scissors in his hands.

"Edwin," Giulia said.

He looked at her with empty eyes. "Giulia. Hugh said you'd come here."

"Where is he?"

"Gone. He went to find Elayne. I tried to stop him, but—" He looked down at his arm. "This happened."

Sethis looked at Giulia, eyes wide.

"Where's Elayne?" Giulia asked.

"At an inn called the Althanor. Cortaag came here last night. He said that he knew people in the Council of a Hundred who could help us." He saw her face and added, "I believed him. I thought he was a friend. So did Elayne. I thought she'd be safe with him. But Hugh said that he was in league with the men who killed that priest. He said that Cortaag kidnapped you."

"He did. Edwin, what exactly is happening here? I thought you were meant to have left the city."

"We sprung a leak. We had to stop to get the ship repaired."

"Right here, next to their warehouse? That's convenient."

He sounded exhausted. "For them, yes. Giulia, Hugh's half crazy. He's gone to the Althanor, to find her. I'd have gone with him, but—" He moved his injured arm and grimaced.

"Did Hugh do that to you?"

"No," he said, but she knew that, somehow, Hugh had been the cause of it.

She said, "I came here the night before last. I broke into their warehouse, saw them unloading the gold they've stolen. I saw you and Cortaag on the deck, talking."

"I know," Edwin said. "But—"

"Cortaag works for Azul," Giulia said. "If you didn't know that already."

"Honest to God, Giulia, I've met Cortaag before, but I had no idea... not about this."

Giulia looked at Edwin, and wondered if he might somehow be innocent. Could it have been a mistake? Could Varro have sabotaged the *Margaret of Cheswick* while it had been stuck in port, to stop Edwin and Elayne getting away? Perhaps Cortaag had been instructed to befriend the two Anglians, to dupe them into joining the conspiracy. Maybe Azul had tired of the pretence.

She didn't have the time to find out. "I have to find Hugh. How do I get to the Althanor?"

"It's ten minutes from here," Edwin said. "I can show you the way."

Giulia hesitated. Whatever he had or hadn't done, she wanted him out of the way. But Elayne was his wife, after all. "All right. Just be careful."

"I will," Edwin said. "Rollo, look after the boat. Nobody comes on board until we come back."

The man put down the scissors and nodded, as if this was, on balance, something he could just about do.

"Yes, sir," he said. "It's bad luck to have a fey on board, anyway. Or a woman."

A bitter smile flicked across Edwin's face. "You think our luck was good before they came in?"

Whatever Edwin might have done, Giulia thought, his distress was real.

Sethis opened the cabin door and they stepped onto the deck.

***

Giulia and Edwin walked out of the Althanor tavern and stopped beside the canal. The door swung shut behind them, and the rumble of voices became a murmur again.

Sethis was waiting outside. He looked at her and saw the bad news in her expression.

"They never even went there," she said. "Not Cortaag, not Elayne. The landlady never saw them enter."

Edwin looked how Giulia felt: desperate, lost. "Maybe she was wrong—"

"She says she hasn't left the place for two days solid. Nor have her family."

Sethis said, "Did the landlady see Hugh?"

"Oh yes," Giulia replied. "He came in and threatened the lot of them. They showed him that nobody was hiding there and told him what they've just told us."

Edwin raised his hand and touched his fingertips to his forehead. "Oh God." He looked as if he was about to vomit. "What're we going to do? What the hell are we going to do?"

"Sirinara," Giulia said.

Sethis nodded.

Edwin lowered his hand. "What?"

"It's an island, out beyond the bay. Portharion thinks that Azul might be staying there."

"Portharion? The sorcerer?"

"Yes. Look, Edwin, Portharion said he'd talk to the Customs people. We might be able to sail over to Sirinara."

He shook his head. "Not in this weather. The wind's either blowing into the bay or not blowing at all. Portharion could call up a wind to get us out there, though."

"So we have to wait for him to get here? There must be a quicker way. Can't we row across?"

"Giulia?" Sethis raised his hand. "There's a little boathouse to the east, owned by one of the Scola's members. We could use his boat. He's, ah, something of an eccentric, but the boat's fast. I could give you a lift to the island, then come back for the others."

"How long would it take you to get hold of the boat?"

"Half an hour at most. It depends on whether the springs are wound up."

"Springs? Never mind. Can you meet me here in half an hour?"

Edwin said, "I'm coming with you."

Giulia turned to him. "No," she said. "I'm sorry. You're already injured and we need you here. Go back to the ship, get your men armed and ready, and send out people to the Customs offices. Tell them to look for Portharion and Arashina, all right? They're on our side. Can you do that?"

"Of course I can do that. But Elayne needs—"

"Elayne needs you to get ready. Once I'm on the island, Sethis will come back for you in the boat. I'll try to find Hugh and we'll meet you on Sirinara, wherever the boats unload. Understand?" He didn't reply. "Edwin, do you understand?"

"Yes," he said. "I understand."

***

The two oarsmen worked hard as they watched Hugh preparing his weapons. They'd told him that they had been rowing people over to the islands for years, some of them very bad men, but Hugh had the feeling that they'd not seen anyone like him before.

They could think what they liked. Hugh sat at the bows and stared out, as if the force of his glare could punch through the gathering fog. The boat turned, headed north-east.

A cloud of thick mist lay outside the city, waiting for its chance to close in on Averrio. As they left the bay, the mist surrounded the boat, and it was as though Hugh was looking at the world through a piece of thin, grey cloth.

A green light appeared in the air ahead. It was a soft and sickly glow, too weak to shine through the fog, but strong enough to unnerve. To Hugh, it seemed to come from some monster risen from the depths of the lagoon.

That must be it. The place where they took Elayne.

The glow spread and swelled as they drew closer to Sirinara.

"That's it," the older of the rowers called. "The Tower of Glass."

The island lay low to the water. From the centre rose the single glowing spire. The upper two-thirds of the tower trapped the light so that it shone out of the fog.

The tower grew. It seemed as if the rowers were motionless and the island was coming straight at them:

a rock leviathan that would mow them down and smash their boat into planks.

The boat creaked with every pull of the oars. Hugh looked up and found that one of the men was staring at him.

"Problem, is there?" he said.

"No, friend," the man replied. Hugh suspected that one of the rowers was the other's son. With their coats fastened and collars pulled up, they looked like a pair of murderers in a play. "No problem at all."

The details of the island were taking shape: the wide dock and the cranes looming over it like a row of gallows. *Stop being soft*, Hugh thought. *You've stormed bigger citadels than this before.*

But not with my damsel inside.

Anger stirred in him and he squinted across the water, eager to begin. A wide, high jetty stuck out towards them, a lantern at its end and a single figure in the lantern-light. The jetty had been made for unloading big ships: the boat could pass straight under it. Behind it, closer to the island, half a dozen smaller boats lay in a row.

Those must belong to Azul's men, he thought. *They're here.*

"Aim there," Hugh said, "between the posts. As soon as I'm gone, go straight back and never tell anyone about all this. Do you understand?"

"Yes, milord," said the older boatman.

"Good fellow. Close the lantern and bring us in quietly."

The men gave the oars one last pull and the boat slid in to the dock. It slipped between the posts and under the jetty. The air smelt of damp timber and the lagoon. Hugh heard boots banging on the wood above his head. The footsteps reached the end of the jetty, turned and headed back towards the land.

Hugh grabbed one of the posts that supported the jetty and pulled the boat in close, quickly wrapped up his things and threw his bag across his back. The posts were linked by crosspieces, slimy with accumulated muck. Hugh climbed onto the nearest crosspiece, locking his arms around the upright post. He nodded to the boatmen, and they pushed off as quickly as they could. Hugh crouched there in the cold, underneath the jetty, listening. A minute passed before he heard the guard return.

The man walked past again, humming. Hugh listened to the boots stamping by overhead, felt the planks vibrate with the guard's heavy tread. The footsteps reached the end of the dock and stopped.

Hugh wondered what he was looking at, and hoped to God that it was not the boat.

The man huffed and turned. Hugh caught a glimpse of his head. The guard's face was young, too young to have been an Inquisition soldier back in the old days, but he looked crafty and alert. He began to walk away.

Silent as a spider, Hugh climbed up after him. It wasn't easy: his left knee didn't like it much, but Hugh was not to be halted by such minor things. *For God and the Land*, he thought, and the old warcry made him feel strong.

Hugh laid his bag down very carefully. The weapons were scabbarded inside, and the hilts clinked no louder than a couple of coins. Smoothly and carefully, he drew his sword. Hugh stood up and watched the guard, studying the way the man's helmet met his neck. It wouldn't be an honourable kill, of course, but this was a special occasion. You didn't call the Inquisition out to single combat, especially when the life of a woman depended on it. Hugh lifted the sword in both hands, raised it slightly above his head. A diagonal cut would do it: sever the nerve-strings and windpipe in one blow. *Here's for you, kidnapper*, he thought, and he loomed up behind the guard and swung.

***

Giulia ran down to the docks and jogged along the waterside until she saw a gap in the wall of ships. The Great Canal was ink-black and endlessly wide. She glanced back at the *Margaret of Cheswick* and wondered what Edwin was doing inside. It was probably best not to stay here long.

She tried not to think about the next few hours. Fear was beginning to seep into her bones, trying to freeze her. She rubbed her hands together and pulled her cloak tight around her shoulders.

Something pattered on the water, a steady, fast sound like dozens of small paddles striking at once. She wondered what the Scola's boat would look like. Did dryads have boats at all?

It slid into view. It seemed to have been based on a gondola: long, thin, needle-like. But a spindly mast rose up from the centre, and two huge wheels flanked the hull, one on either side. Each wheel was made up of flattened spokes – the paddles she had heard – and the light flickered between the paddles as they spun. She had seen something like it back in Pagalia, but this was a refinement on the design.

The boat approached the dock at an awkward angle, and the prow bumped against the bank. Sethis beckoned. "Come on in!"

Giulia sprang into the bows and climbed down between the great wheels. The rear of the boat was almost entirely taken up by clockwork, all cogs and coiled springs. "Is this safe?" she demanded.

Sethis beamed at her. "Oh yes. I'm not much of a sailor, but we'll be fine." He released a lever and the wheels spun backwards, pulling them away from the dock. "It's very quick, too. Just wait until the sails come out!"

SIXTEEN

Azul turned to the mirror and tugged his collar into shape. He looked his reflection over, impressed. He wore a velvet jacket under a long cloak: not actual Inquisition robes, but close enough to be reminiscent. His spectacles made him seem wise and stern. He looked like a man who knew how to get things done: how to reward friends, how to dispose of enemies, and most of all how to become rich.

He wondered whether to wear his gloves. No: this was his event, and he'd do it by his own terms. No need to hide among friends. Besides, once they saw his snake-hand again, they'd remember that he meant business.

The mouth at the end of his thumb yawned. It was a useful killing tool, but that had been very much a secondary benefit. While dosing his men up with serums derived from wolves and bears – and other things – Azul had altered his own body to be able to hibernate. When the end had come, and his old comrades had been hunted down and killed, he'd simply bricked himself into his cellar, gone to sleep like an adder in the wintertime and waited for everything to quieten down. His enemies had assumed that he'd fled. After that, it had been easy to start work again.

On the far side of the room, a pair of blue alcedo birds hopped and bickered in their cage. No doubt a storm was on its way: alcedos could foresee the arrival of bad weather. Azul reached to the side of their cage, took out a little pot and tipped some more seed into their bowl.

Someone knocked on the door – four times, in quick succession. "Come in," he said.

Cortaag stood in the doorway. He wore a silver breastplate over a black shirt. "All the guests are inside," he said. "The lower ranks are eating in the main hall. The officers are ready to meet you."

"What about the servants?"

"They went on the last boat. The dining room's ready. The food's keeping warm downstairs. My men can send it up on the dumb-waiter whenever you need."

"Excellent," Azul said. "Then we're all set." He examined his reflection again. Some faces didn't look right until they had aged sufficiently. Twenty years ago, he had looked like an angry little man: now he had the tough, weathered dignity of a Quaestan senator.

Yes, he thought. *I am in my prime, a leader of men.*

"Let's meet the others," Azul said. "They've been waiting long enough."

They left Azul's suite and headed down the corridor. Cortaag led Azul down three flights of stairs. Their boots sank into thick carpet. Azul heard his guests as he approached the head of the grand staircase.

They stood below, talking and drinking a Lyre Valley white wine that he had chosen especially. As Azul started down the steps, they fell silent. Then they started to clap.

Some of the faces he recognised from long ago, although they had been stretched, coarsened and puffed-up by age. Others belonged to old fighters he didn't know, men recommended by others or by their own reputation. There were even a couple of professional gangsters from out of town, people with useful connections among the young. But of all the guests, there was only one that Azul actually feared: the man his superiors had sent along to check the smooth running of the project. He was a small, bland man with a chubby face – Brother Praxis, the direct link to the masters of the conspiracy.

Cortaag clapped his hands. "Gentlemen, your host! Brother Colonel of the Fifteenth Legion, Lord Commander of the Cerandis District and Guildmaster of the Glassmakers' Guild: Ramon Azul!"

Azul stood on the stairs and gave them all a bow. "Good afternoon, everybody," he said. He had to strain his voice to be heard across the hall. "I'm very glad you could make it here."

A fat man in a long tunic called out, "It's a pleasure, sir!" There were laughs and a brief patter of applause.

"Gentlemen," Azul croaked. He felt an uncomfortable scratching at the back his his mouth: his throat was going to ache tomorrow. "Welcome to my humble abode."

More laughter.

"I hope you didn't have too much trouble in getting here. We'll be eating early: there's a lot to discuss, and no doubt you're hungry after travelling here. Your guards will have their supper with my men in the main hall here, directly below us. We, however, will be eating upstairs, at the very pinnacle of the Tower of Glass. Before we go up, I would like to thank you all for taking the trouble to attend. I believe that the business proposal I have for you will more than make up for the distance of the journey –

and all the flights of stairs."

The laughter was a little quieter. Several of the old warriors winced at the mention of stairs.

"Some of you I recognise as old comrades from the Holy Legions. Others I have only known by repute until now. Still others are new friends, people who travel towards the same destination as us, even though they make the journey via different routes. You are all most welcome here. Please, follow me to the dining room."

***

The wind turned and caught the sails, and suddenly Sethis and Giulia were skimming over the water, paddles whirling. Giulia's hood fell back, and the rain and the spray pattered against her cheek. She looked down into the dark water, and tried not to think of the things that lived in there.

Something glowed behind the mist like a rising, toxic sun.

Sethis sat between the great wheels, working the rudder. With each beat of the paddles, Giulia drew closer to Azul, nearer to Hugh and nearer to her revenge.

"We'll be there soon," Sethis said, his voice straining above the wind. "Didn't I say this boat was fast?"

A big wave tossed the bows up, and as they slapped back down Giulia queasily reflected that it was indeed an unusual craft.

"Of course, the mechanism's enchanted," Sethis called out. "But we dryads built the hull. There's magic in the very trees they used. I helped organise it – a gesture of friendship between the races, you see!"

She glanced down and saw that the body of the boat

was one piece, a single bit of timber somehow shaped into a hull – or somehow induced to grow into one. To the east, something broke the surface of the waves. Giulia peered out, thinking she saw a thing like a smooth rock protruding from the water, half-expecting some monster to rise up and lunge at them – but it was gone as soon as she looked, yards behind them as the boat carried them across the bay.

The mist parted and the island spread out before her.

It was long and flat, lit by great torches at its ends, covered in warehouses and living quarters for the artisans of the guild. *Like a little village*, she thought, and more of the island revealed itself as they came closer.

In the centre stood a mansion, from which rose a great tower. The entire tower was covered in glass the colour of a young lizard's back: it shone out of the fog as if it were a gigantic emerald. As the boat turned to compensate for the waves, the weak sunlight struck the tower and rippled over its surface like lightning. For a moment it blossomed with colour, and then it faded back into the grey mist.

Something sank inside Giulia's chest. The Tower of Glass was ingenious but malign, like a device for collecting poisonous gas. She pointed to a low point in the cliffs, where sand formed a natural ramp. "There's a dock there," she called. "Drop me off there."

They came in fast and low, and as they passed the rocky edge of the island she heard the screech of a bird of prey. Giulia squinted up at the tower. There were massive arches set into the glass, near the pinnacle. A platform stuck out of the side: half-fortification, half-nest. The edge of the platform was encrusted with white dung. Pale sticks lay scattered around it: bones.

Behind one of the archways, something colossal moved.

"Griffon!" Giulia yelled. "There's a griffon in there!"

"I'll bring us in," Sethis called back. The water was choppy now, gearing itself for a storm.

"Do it, quick!"

An eagle's cruel head appeared in the arch and, behind it, high, muscled shoulders. Huge claws gripped the edge of the masonry. The griffon threw back its head and screamed a challenge that rang across the island.

It drew back into its lair. For a moment the monster was out of view, and then it bounded to the edge and sprang into the sky. It sailed out, massive wings unfolding, and suddenly the beast soared above them, riding the growing storm.

"Oh, shit," Giulia cried, "it's seen us! Get us to the land, quick!"

Her crossbow was already in her hands; she struggled to load it in the rocking boat. The griffon twisted in the air, fighting the wind to stay in place.

"I'm trying!" Sethis sprang around the boat like a goblin, pulling levers and spinning wheels. Slowly, too slowly, the boat began to change course. Above them, wings batting the air to keep it in place, the griffon shrieked into the wind.

It dropped, shooting down from above, its wings folded against its sides. "Get down!" she yelled, writhing in her seat to get away from it.

"Lean to the left!" Sethis yelled. "Left!"

The dryad's voice cut through Giulia's mounting panic. She threw herself left, and the boat turned. They swung in close to the island. She heard the griffon swoop, felt the rush of air, and suddenly there was a sound like someone smashing down a door, and the starboard paddle-wheel whirled uselessly, half of its spokes shattered, flapping like a hand on the end of a broken arm.

The griffon shot past as fast as a cannonball. It folded its wings and curved away with lazy, contemptuous grace, ready to make another pass.

The boat started to spin.

"Giulia, we'll have to jump!" Sethis called, and she realised how close they were, how fast they were coming in to the rocks.

She swung her crossbow across her back. "Right!" she yelled, and Sethis ran to the bows and crouched beside her.

He flicked his hand out, and his belt was in it. "Hold this."

She gripped it, looped it round her fist.

"Are you ready?" he called, and she nodded back. "Now!"

They leaped. Giulia hit the water just in front of the rocks, grabbed hold of an outcrop and clung on. Water poured onto her back, over her face. Cold flooded across her arms and back, down her legs and spine. A flash of terror – the memory of drowning, her face freshly slashed – and she was clambering out onto the rocks, spitting out water. Sethis scrambled up beside her. The griffon came down again, screeching, and she heard the splinter of wood as it tore their boat apart. Great wings drummed against the air.

They crouched there, pressed together. Twenty yards away, the griffon ripped the clockwork out of the boat. Broken wood lay around it, bobbing on the waves. The massive beak swung down and gutted the seats.

Giulia glanced at the dryad. He looked scared and utterly determined. "That way," he said, looking along the island.

She worked her way right. Beneath the cliffs was a jumble of rock, enough to give them handholds and keep them out of the sea. They crept across the jagged boulders, the water breaking on the rocks at their feet. Sethis pointed: Giulia followed and they struggled onto the slope leading to the dock.

Together they stumbled upward, onto the island itself. Sethis pointed to an outhouse and they ran towards it. The door was bolted on the outside. Giulia tore the bolt back and they hurried inside, into the smell of tar and old rope. Sethis sat down. Giulia stopped beside him, panting, dripping wet.

"By the Lord and Lady," Sethis said. "That was close. And I used to think I was agile," he added, and he managed to smile. "Are you hurt?"

Giulia looked out of the door, at the sky. Far away, the griffon turned lazily back to its lair, no longer interested in them. It had seen off the competition, and the island was its own again. The waves were still loud, but muffled now, as if they beat against the outhouse walls.

"I'm fine, considering. How about you?"

"A little bruised; nothing more. Unlike the boat." Sethis looked through the open door, towards the great glass tower. The dryad hissed something in his own language, a long, sibilant word that was definitely a curse. "Looks like I won't be going back, then."

"Sorry." *The only way out is through.*

"There's a storm coming," Sethis said. "Where now?"

Giulia looked across the island. She pointed to the

tower.

"I'm going up there," she said. "It's where Hugh will have gone. You should hide out in one of those buildings there. Arashina said she'd come and help."

He shook his head. Rain glinted on his face and hair. "I ought to help you." He had to raise his voice. "And Hugh, for that matter. He helped us out at the Scola. It wouldn't be right for me to leave him. Besides," he added, glancing around, "I'd rather not stay here on my own."

Giulia looked at him. If Sethis was cold, he didn't show it. His resolve impressed her. He was much tougher than he looked. Who knew what he had seen during the War of Faith, what he had done to stay alive? She held her hand out and pulled him to his feet. "Let's go."

***

The gatehouse of the Tower of Glass stuck out of the smooth exterior of the building like an afterthought, crude stone against glass and smooth white plaster. Hugh hid in the bushes twenty yards away.

The wind blew the long grass flat, threw chilly rain against Hugh's armour. He crept out of hiding, leaned around the side of the gatehouse and put his ear to the door.

"It's no good if no-one knows," someone said. It was a man, quite young. "All this pulling-strings shit: it's no good if people can't *see* us, is it?"

"They *will* know." An older man, middle-aged. "Pass the bread over, would you? Thanks. But it's all about faith, right? You've just got to have faith. Then, come the moment – bang! All the pixie-lovers and foreigners and New Church and all the rest of them. And those soft bastards in Sanctus City, too. *Then* they'll see."

Voices muttered their approval. There were three of them in total, maybe four. The gatehouse was not a large building. There would be clutter inside, and narrow walls. Hugh drew his sword and a long knife, ducked under the window and rapped on the door with the pommel of his dagger.

Boots scuffed on the ground. *Have to work quick*, Hugh thought, *can't let anyone get away*. His heart felt high and fast in his chest.

The door opened a crack and Hugh shoved it open and barged straight in. A guard stumbled back, cried "Fuck!" and reached to the pistol at his side. Hugh shouldered him off-balance and stabbed him in the neck. The man dropped and the other two guards scrambled to their feet. Hugh brought up his sword and blocked a thrust from a meat-knife, then jabbed the second guard in the thigh with his dagger. The man doubled over. Hugh pulled the blade free and drove the point into the side of his neck. The third guard scrambled towards a rope in the corner of the room. Hugh hurled the dagger; it missed, and he stepped in and knocked the man's hand down from the rope as he reached for it. The guard howled and folded over, clutching his broken hand. Hugh struck him across the skull with the pommel of his sword. The guard grunted and fell.

Hugh looked down at the bodies. The first man he'd killed had a brace of pistols on his belt. Normally, he disapproved of guns, but when you were rescuing a damsel, the rules could be bent. And when you fought the Inquisition, you did not expect a fair fight, and you did not give them the opportunity to cheat.

Two minutes later, Hugh left the guardhouse with

the keys in one hand and his sword in the other. He pulled the door closed behind him.

He walked up the path, towards the gates of the Tower of Glass. They were three times his height and smooth as ice. There was a large keyhole with a brass escutcheon: the longest of the keys fitted it. A small door built into the gate swung open. Hugh hadn't even noticed it before.

He stepped through the doorway and let it swing back behind him. He stood at the edge of a courtyard, the floor made of dark grey flagstones. There were no plants or decorations.

On the far side of the courtyard hung the Inquisition flag: a simple banner quartered in black and white. Smaller white banners flanked the main one, each bearing an inverted sword.

Hugh remembered passages from the Holy Codex and *The Death of Alba*: *Though I am delivered into the furnace, my faith shall be like armour unto me... And the king beat on his door and called for the false knights to come forth and do battle with him...* "Sons of whores," he said.

He took a deep breath and checked the weapons strapped to his arms, back, thighs and belt, and jogged across the courtyard towards the tower. They meant to hurt Elayne. There was no time to waste.

***

Giulia and Sethis crept towards the Tower of Glass. A clump of tough, weather-worn trees stood between the outhouses and the tower itself, and they used them for cover and shelter from the rain. Water dripped from the branches. Giulia felt the cold weight of her sodden clothes. At least they were out of the wind – and hopefully out of view of the griffon.

Giulia looked over the smooth flank of the tower. "I don't know how we get in," she said. "There don't seem to be any windows. Or else the whole place is one big window... What do you think?"

Sethis frowned. Shielding his eyes with his hand, he peered up at the fortress, searching for a weakness in its armour. "There!" he exclaimed.

"That's just the gatehouse," she replied, unimpressed. Was this how the fey fought battles, by knocking at the front door? Then she saw what he meant. The light caught on something like a crack in the flat glass of the wall, a vertical line of shadow. She realised what it was: a small door, very slightly ajar. "You're right. Let's try it. But go carefully. There'll be men in the gatehouse."

Sethis took the lead this time. The rain muffled his footsteps, and he slipped between the trees as easily as a dog on a scent. Giulia ran behind him, the crossbow in her hands. Sethis bent almost double as he ran the last dozen yards. He reached the gatehouse. Giulia stopped a little way back, covering him with her bow.

Sethis turned the handle and pushed the gatehouse door. It swung open a little way and stopped. He leaned around and looked through the aperture. For a moment, he was still. Then he beckoned to Giulia.

She ran up and looked into the gap. The door wouldn't open fully, because there was a corpse behind it. Three men lay dead in the gatehouse. Their deaths had been bloody and quick.

"Hugh did this, I assume," Sethis said.

"Yes. They weren't expecting him."

"Odd that he left the gate open," Sethis said.

Giulia shook her head. Droplets fell from the edge of her hood. "He's in a hurry. Ready?"

"Ready."

They ran up to the main gates. Giulia pushed the glass door. It opened silently, revealing the wet expanse of the courtyard. "Keep to the edge," she said, and she entered.

A hiss from behind, and she turned to see. Sethis was looking across the yard, his small mouth closed and hard, big eyes vicious and sharp. She saw the three banners, symbols of the Inquisition, and a jolt of fear and awe ran through her like a spark. Then she pushed it away, angry that they could intimidate her. *We've got the right place, then*, she thought. Sethis muttered something under his breath, either a prayer or a curse.

They followed the edge of the courtyard. Rain pattered down on the stone and glass. Giulia watched the rooftops, remembering the beasts swarming over the skyline outside the House of Exchange. The memory made her seethe with fear and rage. At the far side, they stopped.

"It looks deserted," Sethis said.

The rain made it pointless to whisper. "Be careful: they might be hiding. We'll take the side door."

"Servants' entrance," Sethis said, and he smiled humourlessly.

The door was plain wood banded with iron, with a solid, simple lock. Giulia crouched down and slid the picks from the bracer on her right arm. Sethis held the crossbow while she worked the lock. She probed the mechanism, felt the tumblers tense, then tremble, then give against the picks. Giulia took hold of the doorhandle and Sethis raised her bow to cover her.

This is it. Here I come, into your castle. Hide from me, you little bastard, but I'll dig you out no matter what. The higher you climb, the further you can fall when I kick you off your own fucking roof. Now you can have a turn at being afraid.

She opened the door.

The door creaked as it swung ajar. She looked into a long corridor, streaked with moonlight. Doors branched off to either side. She could smell bread and beef.

They crept inside. Giulia pointed down the hallway. Sethis nodded and passed her the bow. He looked grim.

She started down the corridor, legs bent, bow held ready to shoot. She could hear something: not the rain, she realised, but something from above. It sounded like chanting. Giulia stopped to listen.

Sethis halted beside her. His eyes were on the ceiling and, as they listened, noise filtered down from above: dozens of voices, raised in song.

***

Captain Alberto Tucca was heating a flask of ale on the hearth when the nightly report came in. Fifty feet below the little stone chamber he used as an office, the sea battered at the harbour walls. The bell beside the door jangled, and a voice called, "Clockworker here to report, sir!"

"Come in."

The man outside the door wore standard Customs gear. Tucca knew his insignia but not his face: the red circle on the fellow's sleeve showed him to be one of the Customs engineers.

"Let's hear it," Tucca said. "And shut the door, for Heaven's sake. There's a storm gearing up out there."

There were some in the Customs who looked down on the engineers: they were neither sailors nor marines, and almost never left the land. But it was their work that kept the gears wound and the defence towers moving, by processes Tucca didn't quite comprehend.

The man closed the door behind him. "All organ guns and mortars are cleaned and loaded, sir. Cannon-turrets one to seven are fine. The leather winding-belt on turret eight has developed cracks, sir. We've taken eight off the main camshaft and have brought a team of oxen down to wind the mechanism by hand. We think we'll be able to replace the belt by noon tomorrow, sir."

"Good work," Tucca replied. "Make sure eight's harnessed back in as soon as you can."

The engineer bowed. "Yes, sir. One more thing, sir."

"Yes?"

"The boys on the main gate asked me to let you know. There's a man to see you, sir, asking for the captain of the guard. He says it's urgent."

Tucca frowned. It was strange, but probably unimportant. "What's his name?"

The clockworker frowned. "That's the thing, sir. He says he's Portharion, the wizard."

Suddenly, Tucca was alert. "Portharion? Is it him?"

"I don't know, sir. I mean, I've seen him and he looks like a wizard..."

Tucca wondered what the hell a wizard was meant to look like. "What does he want?"

"He says there's smuggling going on, sir, out in the bay. He says he's found a whole bunch of smugglers. He wants a patrol sent out right away."

Tucca frowned. "What, right now? Where is he?"

"He's at the front gate, sir."

"And the smugglers?"

The engineer looked downright embarrassed. "That's the thing, sir. He says they're on Sirinara, hiding out in the Tower of Glass."

Tucca glanced wistfully at his ale. Chances were, this fellow was a lunatic, or trying to pull some kind of trick. But if he wasn't – if the real Portharion had come here, and they'd turned him away, there'd be hell to pay... "Take me to him," Tucca said, and he braced himself for the rain.

***

The ground floor of the tower was deserted. Hugh crossed the hall and climbed a grand set of stairs. As he reached the landing, music started to pulse through the walls: the muffled sound of men singing. He felt as if he was creeping through the innards of the House of Glass, and that the voices were its pumping breath.

There were two big Inquis men at the end of the corridor, guarding a pair of double doors. Each wore a long, red cloak, hood up, and a steel cuirass polished to a silvery shine. They held long-handled maces across their chests.

Hugh ducked back out of sight and very carefully drew his sword. He knew the sort: an honour guard, no doubt. They had that familiar expression, dead-eyed and cynical, capable of any crime except disobedience. *Veterans*, he thought. *Proper enemies.*

Behind them, through the double doors, a man's voice broke into a new tune. Others picked it up, and soon it was a banging, stamping rhythm accompanied by a pack of shouting voices, all belting out the same war-song.

Hugh flexed his fingers around the sword and listened to the singing getting louder. A lesser man would have found it intimidating: Hugh of Kenton, favoured by God and the knightly code, was ready to fight.

There were whoops among the singing now. One voice rose up crazily and twisted into a drawn-out howl. Hugh drew his sword and stepped into sight.

***

As the guards stacked the last of the plates in the dumb-waiter in the hall, the delegates leaned back in their chairs and relaxed. Azul sent around a dish of tobacco and a tray of chocolate and sugared oranges. It had been an excellent meal, he reflected: woodcocks in a mustard glaze, followed by water-wyrm steaks, caught out in the bay. The guards refilled the glasses and discreetly retired from the room.

Halfway down the table, Alicia was smiling at something one of the guests had said. The door opened and Cortaag slipped into the chamber. He stepped close and leaned over.

"All well?" Azul said.

"Very well, sir," Cortaag replied. "The men are enjoying themselves downstairs. Looks like a storm's coming, though."

Azul looked at the wall. He could see the lights of the city very dimly through the green glass, as if someone had set out candles behind it. There was no sign of the storm up here. "Thank you, Cortaag."

"Pleasure, sir." Cortaag stepped outside, closing the doors behind him.

"That was splendid," one of the guests said from

down the table. He was a huge man, fat and wide-mouthed like an inflated toad. Azul knew that he was now something important in the Montalian school of gunnery, but once he had been a captain of cannon for the Inquisition. His tunic was taut across his stomach, like a sail in a high wind. "You keep a fine table, Azul."

"Thank you." Azul had not eaten much: these days, large meals left him bloated and drowsy. "I've always been of the view that life is too short to be eating bad food. Now, then." He rapped his knuckles on the tabletop. "Gentlemen, your attention, please!"

They fell silent. Azul looked down the table and saw rows of faces turned to him like a jury waiting to be persuaded.

He stood up and smiled.

"This has been a very pleasant meal. It's good to break bread with so many old friends – and to have the opportunity to make some new ones. However, I have called this meeting for more than the pleasure of your company. I have a business proposition for you." Azul's mouth was dry; he took a sip of wine. "Although there is no denying the extensiveness and valour of our efforts, we were never able to cure Alexendom of the disease of heresy." He licked his lips. "These days, the disease has become an epidemic. The Old Church becomes soft and weak, and the so-called New Church grows in strength. Gloria of Anglia calls herself the 'queen of the fey' and makes trading deals with the painted savages of Maidenland. I learn that the king of Bergania has signed a pact between Bergania and the dwarrows, while in the Teutic League any sort of dissent is tolerated so long as the coppers flow. Gentlemen, the world is in a bad state. I don't think there can be any question about that."

"Damn right!" someone called from down the table.

Another voice said, "What about Pagalia, up the coast? You should see who's ruling there!"

"Or Astrago!"

"Nobody in his right mind could be happy about the state of the world today. Which brings me onto the real question." Azul had to raise his voice: several glasses of strong wine had made the guests a little too talkative. "The real question is *this*: what are we going to do about it?"

Azul gave them a moment to consider it. They looked down the table at him, quiet now that he had got their attention. Only Brother Praxis looked anything other than intrigued. He was as blank as a doll.

"Well? Suggestions, anyone?"

Nobody said anything. They waited.

"I don't know the exact details of your current employment," Azul lied, "but I'll wager that everyone here lives comfortably. Some of us were able to leave our previous employment with our own private funds. Others found work elsewhere, or were fortunate enough to have estates they could use. A few were lucky enough to be helped along by the Hidden Hand, which has very kindly provided our old friends with jobs and loans – and has been, I should add, one of the main conduits through which most of you received your invitations to join me today."

Towards the far end of the table, a mousy little man nodded. He was the Hand's contact man, and his intervention had kept several of the other guests alive during the difficult times after the War of Faith.

"Our lives are pleasant and comfortable," Azul said. "One way or another, we live well – far better, our enemies maintain, than we have any right to."

There was a little laughter.

"But for me, it isn't enough." He looked from face to face, meeting one pair of eyes after another. "It's not enough to live in my mansion, surrounded by a high wall to keep the world out of sight. It's not enough to be able to afford to keep the land outside at bay: not while the world grows more rotten and polluted with every day that passes. I don't want to fade away comfortably; to die of old age in some great chamber with a painted ceiling. I, for one, am sick of dreaming of past glories. I want new ones. And I know many of you feel the same."

He gave them the count of three to think it over, to taste what he was offering.

"Is there anyone in this room who doesn't smile when they remember the old times, and wish they could come again? Anyone here whose heart doesn't stir when he hears the old songs – and whose soul doesn't flinch at the thought of pagans, heretics and fey having the ear of the lords of our land? Anyone who doesn't want to see us back where we belong?"

Azul paused again. *Let that soak in*, he thought.

A thin-faced old man leaned forward, raising a fleshless hand. "With respect, sir, that's all very well." His voice was loud and crisp. "I don't deny there's many who feel that way, myself included. But one has to be realistic, and that means accepting those days have gone. Unless you, Lord Commander, have a plan to make it all come back...?"

Azul smiled. He took his glasses off, blew across the lenses, and put them back on. "Actually," he said, "I do."

***

Hugh stood over the dead guards, breathing hard. Had fighting been this tiring the last time he had been on a quest? He wished he'd had the time to be properly shriven. Before the Battle of the Bone Cliffs, he had received a blessing from preachers of both the Old and New Churches, and from a dryad priestess to be sure. Right now, his good intentions would have to do.

He reached out and put his hand on the brass door handle. He could smell their food – roast beef – and it made his stomach turn. The singing had reached a climax now, the voices and stamping feet backed by snarls and barks. The door pulsed against his palm with the force of the sound, as if the song was trying to push its way out. It was "Brother Alonzo", the battle-hymn of the Inquis Impugnans.

"Brother Alonzo is long gone
But his spirit marches on!"

He had intended to stride right in, but there were too many of them. No, this required cunning. Knees aching a little, he bent down and looked through the keyhole.

The feast was a festival in Hell. Men were sitting around two tables, shouting and singing and drinking and cramming their faces with meat. They had women with them – most were just as drunk as the males, and a couple were half-undressed. Faces glistened with grease, sweat and beer. A man lowered a cup from his mouth – no, not a mouth, a snout. A woman laughed crazily as one of the soldiers dropped off his chair and began to change shape on the floor.

Kill them, Hugh thought, *every last stinking one. Burn*

their evil off the earth in the name of God and the Land.

But how? There had to be twenty people in there, at least. Hugh had his sword, two knives and a pair of pistols that he'd taken from the guards at the gatehouse. A frontal attack, even from a knight of Albion, would be suicide. And suicide meant they would kill Elayne.

The thought made him quick and vicious. He stood up, strode to the fireplace and yanked down the banner hanging there to get himself in the mood. Hugh paused, the cloth rolled up in his hands ready to throw into the fire.

A delicate vase stood on the mantelpiece. It was one of those weird moving things: eagles soared above a pastoral scene. Hugh lifted it down. The birds flapped their wings; the trees shivered in the breeze. Holding it made him feel queasy. He stuck one hand in and found that it was empty and dry.

One of the men at the gatehouse had carried a powder-horn. Hugh reloaded his pistols, opened the flask and poured the rest of the powder into the vase. Then he pulled a small, glowing log from the fireplace and wedged it into the neck of the vase.

He turned the door handle and kicked the door open with his heel.

For half a second Hugh saw them start to move, faces frozen like a painting of men in mid-battle. Hands raised, mouths open in the torchlight. He hurled the vase into the middle of the room.

Hugh slammed the door shut, heard the explosion, threw the door open again and marched straight in.

Shouts and screaming, things breaking, the yelps of something that was no longer a man. Hugh's sword hissed from the scabbard as he strode to the first table. A man with fangs was scrambling to his feet. Hugh split his shaven head open. Blood sprayed and a woman shrieked like a whistle.

Fast and accurate, Hugh told himself. *Put one down and on to the next.*

"Oh, God!" someone yelled from the centre of the room. "Get him! Get him!"

It began in earnest. The injured scuttled out the back door, and the healthy grabbed weapons and charged. Hugh saw hands pull down the crossed maces above the fireplace – then an axe sliced the air beside him and he blocked just in time, sidestepped and hacked into the soldier's neck, sending him crashing into the wall.

He cut down two more monsters as they tried to flee. Their yelping sang in his ears. Rage burned through his body. *Yes*, he thought, *this is it!*

"Heretic!" a voice yelled from the right, and Hugh looked into a face twisted into nothing but fangs and hating eyes. He blocked the soldier's sword with his own, drew one of his pistols and shoved it under the man's chin and blew a cloud of brain and bone into the air.

Two more charged, one half-transformed: Hugh carved the first monster across the belly, ducked low and took out the second across the knees. He rolled as it fell, came up behind it and put a boot on its back and the sword-tip through its neck. Something struck his thigh, and he felt it sink deep. A soldier bounded in from the right. Hugh sidestepped, feinted and drove his sword under the man's arm and between his ribs, found he couldn't pull it free, so he let go and scooped a mace from the ground.

He looked down, saw a dagger sticking out of his thigh and yanked it out before he could think about it. He lurched into the middle of the room. "Where's Elayne?" he shouted.

A gun banged and he flicked around. A man stared at him, horrified, holding a smoking pistol. "Misfire!" Hugh cried joyfully and struck him down.

A length of chain whacked him across the back and he stumbled, the noise from the rest of the room suddenly as distant as the sea. He saw the boards below him and thought: *No, not the floor, stay up*, and he turned, lurched into the soldier with the chain, knocked him off balance and cracked his skull with the mace.

"Scum!" Hugh picked up an axe from a pile of firewood beside the grate. "Where's Elayne? Where's my fucking damsel?"

More rushed him. He carved bodies and limbs, sent men and half-beasts to the ground. A thing that was nearly a wolf thrashed beneath the table, clawing at its back.

"Any more?" Hugh cried, giddy with fury and triumph. "Who wants to break a lance with me?"

Something struck him in the shoulder, knocking him sprawling. His boot slipped – his leg folded and he crashed onto a floor slick with blood and ale. A crossbow bolt jutted from his left shoulder. He tried to rise, but suddenly the room was full of shiny boots. A whole mob of them ran at him: he hacked two men across the shins as he struggled to get up, and a knee hit him in the eye. He fell over, twisted to avoid landing on the crossbow bolt, and reached for his second pistol.

Hands grabbed him, tried to pull him this way and that. A face came into view, a snarling, pimply youth. The boy lifted one of his boots. It filled Hugh's vision as it swung into his head, and then the lights went out.

***

"So you're talking about bringing the old days back, then?" one of the delegates asked. His name was Torvald, an ex-mercenary who had made a name for himself by being willing to do anything for his employers. *A dirty-worker*, Azul thought. *An able one at that, but nothing more.* "I could live with that."

"Damn right!" the old man beside him wheezed. *Dravaignac – he was half-senile twenty years ago. God knows how old he is now.* "It was *good* back then! We had the best food, the best wine, women from all over – hell, we had fey women too—" He broke off into a wheezy laugh as the others muttered their agreement.

The old days, Azul thought, *always the damned old days.* He felt a sudden jolt of contempt for his comrades. So what if they'd once lived like kings? Years of being hunted had turned them into neurotics and voluptuaries. He stood there and listened to them joke about the revolting dryad women, and wondered what had happened to the legion of fierce young gods with whom he had once had the privilege to march.

"Gentlemen!" he barked. "Gentlemen!"

They turned to him, surprised to hear him shout. He looked down the table and thought: *At least one of us can still give an order properly.*

"We shouldn't dwell on the old days to the detriment of today. Twenty years ago, the New World was just a dream – a novelty, if you will. Nations boasted of having put a man on New World soil; sailors considered themselves lucky to reach there alive. As I say, times change. In the last few years, Albion has established a colony on the north island of the New World, which they call Maidenland. They've struck trade deals with Paratan, the witch-king of the north. Meanwhile, various explorers have set up a line of garrison towns on the south island. Brave men have already made expeditions into the jungle and returned with considerable rewards.

"However, nobody has fully exploited the opportunity that the New World presents. In order to properly investigate the region, and to make the greatest profit, a large-scale privateer expedition is needed, using mercenary soldiers and experienced captains. I am part of a consortium that has sponsored such an expedition for the last three years. We have been very successful, but now it's time to enlarge our operation."

He met Brother Praxis' eyes for a moment. The little man looked mildly interested, as if this was diverting but would never be of any relevance to him.

"The inhabitants of the area where my consortium operates are primitive savages, ignorant of both horses and gunpowder. The only thing worth noting about these people is that they honour their pagan gods with gold. Their jewellery is golden. So is their armour, their dinner-plates, even their temple walls. Captain Arrighetti, our chief operative in the New World, informs me that their entire cities are made of the stuff. It's that gold which I intend to bring back here.

"My men have made significant inroads so far, but we are far from realising the potential of the area. And that's where you'd come in. With increased funding, we can hire more ships and more mercenaries. With that kind of military force, we will be able to take a thorough and methodical approach to the native population. In short, there will be almost no limit to the amount of treasure we can take from these savages."

He gave them three seconds to take it in, then resumed before they could start chattering.

"You'll want proof, of course. Our expeditions so far have been fairly small-scale, but they have yielded impressive results. Let me show you some samples."

Azul turned to a little trolley at the rear of the room. On it sat a polished wooden strong-box, banded with iron. He hauled the trolley forward, opened the box with a key on his belt, and lifted the lid. Around the room he heard a noise as gratifying as any lover's voice: the sound of the delegates drawing in breath.

"The merest taste of what we expect to achieve," Azul said. He held up a necklace: six fat rubies hanging from a golden chain. Azul lifted it to his neck, smiling, then tossed it onto Torvald's lap.

"Keep it. There'll be plenty more. Consider it a Lexmas present for your wife." Azul reached into the box, scooped out a handful of coins and dumped them on the tabletop. "These are solid gold."

A hand rose. It was the fat man, the ex-captain of cannon. Azul said, "Question?"

"This consortium of yours. How do I buy in?"

Someone knocked on the door, four quick, loud bangs.

Cortaag. What's this?

The joviality dropped off Azul's face. "Excuse me one moment, gentlemen. Do talk amongst yourselves. I'm sure there's plenty to discuss." He nodded to Alicia, and she stood up.

"Perhaps I can show you some more of the treasure," she began. "Look, everyone: here are earrings, made of emeralds set in gold..."

Azul stepped up to the door and opened it. Cortaag

stood outside with an Inquis man, one of the younger ones. The man was panting, his eyes wide.

"Sir," Cortaag said, "could we have a brief word, perhaps?"

As Azul closed the door the youth cried, "We're under attack, sir! We've been raided!"

"Idiot!" Azul rasped. "Keep your voice down!" He scowled. "How many?"

"Loads," said the man. "Must be a whole squad of them—"

"How many did you see?"

"Well, one, sir. But the men at the gatehouse are all dead. He broke in downstairs while we were having dinner. Sir, we managed to knock him out. They're taking him to the cellars right now." The man shook his head. "He was crazy, sir, berserk. He must have killed a dozen people—"

"What? One? You let one man frighten you? Pathetic!" Azul's mouth set itself. His eyes glittered behind his spectacles. "You are a soldier of the Inquisition. Do you even understand what that means?"

The young man nodded. "Yes, sir."

Azul leaned forward and said quietly, "It is your purpose and your privilege to fight and die for your betters. If you don't go down there and do that, if I hear any bad reports about you or any other of you gutless young bastards, I'll have Cortaag here rip off your ears. And you can tell that to your friends as well. Got that?"

"Yes, sir!"

"Now get back downstairs and kill the prisoner and anyone else who got in with him. Go!"

The man turned and ran back down the hall. Azul turned to Cortaag, who had been waiting silently with his mace in his hands.

"Send all the guards downstairs and close off the lower floors," Azul said. "Lock the doors. Have the men on the shore get to their positions. Keep the back staircase open, just in case. Understand?"

"Absolutely," Cortaag said.

"If the old man's here, so is the woman with the scars. Listen to me, Felsten – she'll be out for blood, so watch yourself. Now get going."

Cortaag gave him the blessing-salute. Azul opened the doors and returned to the delegates. They had been muttering, he realised, finding new things to worry about. He made himself smile as Alicia stepped aside. "Now, gentlemen, I do apologise for that interruption. If I might continue..."

***

A sudden bang from above, and Giulia stopped and looked up. Beside her, Sethis watched the ceiling as if it was about to collapse.

They stood in a warren of service passages, a maze of narrow, dirty corridors designed to keep the servants out of sight of their masters. They'd encountered nobody so far.

Two seconds of quiet passed, then someone screamed. Voices called out, beasts yelped and barked, the shouts of men twisted into the snarling of animals and back again.

Giulia looked at Sethis. She had never seen someone look so afraid and yet so resolute. He swallowed hard, as if it hurt. "Hugh," he said.

"Follow me," Giulia replied, and she started to

run. The dryad kept close behind her, his sword drawn. Screams and yells rang through the narrow corridors like fire through a slum. Giulia turned left and they scurried into a passage tight enough to force them into single file. At the end of the passage was a door.

The noise stopped. Someone groaned. A man called out, "Oh, fuck, I'm bleeding!" and Giulia could see him in her mind, the sense of horror as he realised how badly hurt he was. She couldn't hear Hugh.

Sethis looked plaster-white. His mouth was a tight scar above his pointed chin. "Wait," he said. "I'll go first."

"No, I'll do it. Open the door on three."

"Right." Sethis stepped to the narrow door and wrapped his long fingers around the handle. He whispered, "One."

Giulia tightened her grip on the crossbow.

"Two."

She stared at the wooden door, as if to see straight through it.

"Three!" and he pulled the door open. Giulia saw a dining hall strewn with bodies. She stepped in, checked left and right, and advanced. The room was in chaos: a dozen corpses lay surrounded by smashed plates and broken furniture. A soldier in a red cloak held another down on the table, trying to bandage him.

"Raise your hands and turn around," she said. "Try anything and I'll kill you."

The man in the red cloak turned and raised his hands. He did not look afraid. He hardly seemed surprised that she was there.

"Where's Hugh?" Giulia demanded.

"The old man is with us," the soldier replied. He spoke slowly, cautiously, but there was a kind of confidence in his voice, as if he relished the words. "He'll be dead soon."

The man on the table cried out. His hand reached out blindly, caught his friend's cloak and clenched in it.

"I hope you're proud of him," the soldier said. "Your friend's a murderer."

"I've met worse," Sethis replied, "Inquisitor." He stooped and rooted about on the floor: he was taking something off the belt of one of the dead men.

The soldier ignored Sethis. "You want to watch him," he told Giulia. He teased his cloak out of the injured man's grip, and held the bloody hand instead. "Some of these pixies get a taste for our women. I've seen it happen. He'll be on you before you know."

A bang, and a spike of blood burst from the side of the soldier's head. He fell as Giulia flinched – a second bang, and the injured man jolted and was still. Sethis held two pistols, smoke rising from the barrels.

"He was buying time for his friends," Sethis said. "We ought to get going." He pushed the guns into his belt. "These should come in handy."

Giulia nodded, shocked. "I thought you people preferred bows," she said. She'd meant to sound nonchalant: she sounded numb.

"Well," he replied, "I'm unusual."

***

The world became clear, then faded away. Trying to think straight was like reading words written on a swinging pendulum. And then, all at once, Hugh was back. He was alive once more, being dragged down a corridor by his feet. There were three of them around him, maybe more, young voices.

"What a stupid bastard, coming in alone like that. Shouldn't try it if you can't pull it off."

"He won't be alone. There'll be more."

"That's fucking crazy. Don't they know who they're messing with?"

"What? Have you been asleep or something? The mess-hall's full of corpses, son. Same goes for those poor bastards in the gatehouse. This old piece of shit good as butchered them."

I shall hit them like lightning, Hugh thought.

"Hey, he's awake!" the soldier said. "Wakey, wakey, old fart!" Hugh was suddenly aware of a face close to him. The man was bending down. Hugh felt water drop onto his face. No, too thick for water: spit. "Not long now, you old prick."

Hugh's left boot jolted out of the soldier's hand and swung downwards heel-first. The spur punched into the soldier's knee. He screamed.

Men reached for weapons, frantic and clumsy. Hugh scrambled upright and drew a knife.

His leg was bleeding, but he didn't need to run. They were already close enough for what he had in mind.

***

For every staircase designed for visitors, there was a smaller one for staff. The staff passages were poky and damp-smelling, the walls the colour of parchment beginning to rot. A row of wicker bins stood along the wall, stuffed with leaves and peelings.

"We must be near the kitchens," Giulia whispered. She pointed to a little staircase, lit by a lantern surrounded by a fan of grubby mirrors. "Up there."

She led the way. Knees bent, they crept up the narrow stairs. She halted at the top. To the left there was a doorway, and from inside it came voices and candlelight.

Giulia crouched down, leaned out and peered around the doorframe.

Half a dozen men sat at a small table, eating and talking. The low ceiling made them look like ogres. She drew back and turned to Sethis. "Six of them, having dinner," Giulia whispered.

"Servants?"

"Soldiers. There's a bell-rope at the corner. If they see us they'll ring it."

"Can you get past?"

"I think so. Look, if you want to go back—"

The dryad shook his head. His curly hair bobbed. "No. I've run from these people before – hid from them, too. I didn't know much about fighting then. I do now."

She thought of him dispatching the two men downstairs, as sharp and cold as a knife. Yes, he knew his stuff, when pushed to it. "All right."

Giulia drove off and rolled past the door in a quick whirl of cloth. She came up on the other side and pressed herself against the wall. Sethis dropped into a crouch and drove off like a jumping frog. He landed on his shoulder, rolled silently and stood up. The soldiers kept on eating.

They crept down the corridor. Alcoves on either side led into little storerooms. A row of white aprons hung from pegs in the wall, like ghosts on parade.

Further up, the corridor widened into a kitchen. There was no meat here, but vegetables lay on long racks, beside pots of spice. Knives lay on a chopping block; a bucket on the floor held dozens of apple cores. The tables and implements looked evil in the moonlight.

Sethis whispered, "Can we stop a moment? I need to load my guns."

Giulia stopped. "Be quick about it." She laid her bow down and rubbed her eyes, listening to Sethis work. *Come on, come on*, she thought. Two loaded pistols would be useful, but she had to get to Hugh – and then Azul, and Elayne.

A bell rang – a harsh, sudden jangle. Giulia's skin tightened with fear. Sethis froze, the little ramrod still in his hand.

Boots and voices sounded from behind them. Giulia glanced at the entrance. "Close the doors!"

Men ran into the far end of the corridor. Giulia caught a glimpse of three people, the first still wearing a handkerchief as a bib, and she ran to the kitchen doors.

Sethis grabbed one door, Giulia the other. "There they are!" the first guard yelled. "Get 'em!"

Sethis knocked away the doorstops and they hauled the doors closed. A gun banged. Then the doors slammed against each other, and Giulia slid the bolts. Someone barged against the other side, then pounded uselessly on the wood with his fists. Giulia stepped away, watching the doors shake as they were struck, knowing that the bolts would hold for now.

"They're just too damn slow," she said, unable to avoid smiling. She turned. "Eh, Sethis?"

He collapsed against the wall.

"Shit!" She ran to him. The dryad slid onto the floor, his hand pressed to his side. He lifted his hand away, and his palm was red and slick with fresh blood.

"Oh, fuck," Giulia said.

Sethis raised his head. His eyes were gentle. "Sorry."

Something heavy shook the doors. The impact was sharp and close.

"Come on," Giulia said. "They'll break in."

"I can't."

"Yes you can. Come on. Get up."

"Bullet wound," the dryad said. He looked down almost thoughtfully, as if it were someone else's body he was studying. "You'd best go on."

The doors crashed and shook again. The guards were swinging something between them as a battering ram. They said nothing, but she could hear them grunting as it swung.

"Up," Giulia said. "I'm not letting them have you. Hand!"

He smiled weakly and raised his hand. She grabbed and hauled in one motion, and Sethis cried out as he lurched upright. He stood there, holding his side, a little taller than her but terribly fragile.

His weakness made her angry. *This is all I fucking need.*

Giulia picked up his sword and put it in his hand. It was an elegant, wicked-looking thing, slightly curved like a cavalryman's blade. He gripped it tightly.

"Can you walk?" she asked.

Sethis nodded. He looked as if he was about to puke.

They headed deeper into the kitchen, and Giulia closed and bolted a second set of doors behind them. Light glinted on knives. The tables were long and empty as if waiting to be filled. The air smelled of spice and old vegetables.

Sethis dragged a stool out, the legs scraping on the tiles. He dropped onto it, grimacing. Giulia thought, *I should have done this on my own. I let him come along because*

I wanted someone to watch my back. I should have left him at the docks.

On the far side of the kitchen was a pair of wide doors. Giulia crossed the room and checked them: they wouldn't move. She dropped down and put her eye to the keyhole. The key was still in the other side of the lock. "They must lead upstairs," she said, standing back. "The bastards have locked them."

"They know we're here," Sethis said between his teeth. "Trapped us."

She looked at him. "How bad is it?"

"Not sure," he said. "Hurts—" He hissed and clutched himself. Giulia hurried over, not sure what to do. Was he even made like a man, inside? "Don't worry," he said. Water ran from the edges of his huge eyes. "It's all right now."

He did not sound all right. A sudden, deep admiration came over Giulia, a sense of real respect. Sethis had not just helped her, but taken the fight to the citadel of his enemies. He might not be built for combat, but there was no denying that he was fierce and brave as hell.

But bravery only went so far. He needed bandaging. She strode to the far end of the room, looking for cloth. She saw aprons on hooks. "Herbs," Sethis croaked.

Giulia nodded and pulled down a rack of little bottles from one of the shelves. She paused, listening, waiting. The soldiers had stopped trying to get in, but the room was not entirely silent. She could just hear something, a muffled, steady, repeated sound. Like footsteps.

"Someone's coming," Sethis said.

Giulia held her breath, eyes half-closed, listening. Yes, there it was. Careful but not furtive, someone was moving quietly and slowly at the far end of the room. She swung up her bow, saw a little service door there and cursed herself for missing it. Something was behind it.

There wasn't enough time to lock the service door. Giulia crouched down and worked the ratchet under her bow, drawing back the string. She took out a bolt and laid it in the groove.

The doorknob rattled. She heard a slight grunt of breath. *His head will be a small target*, she thought. *Have to shoot quickly or he'll just duck out of view.*

The door swung open. She saw hair, messy and gummed with blood and sweat. The man took another step. Giulia put a little pressure on the trigger, and the whole face came into view.

"Hugh!"

The knight stopped just inside the room.

"Giulia?"

"Hugh," Giulia said, and she lifted the bow and relaxed. "Thank God it's you!"

"Likewise."

"What the hell were you doing, running off like that? Why didn't you tell me— shit, what happened to you?"

He closed the door behind him. "I need a sit-down," he said.

Hugh needed more than that. His face, always pale, was sickly white except where it was smeared with drying blood. His moustache was solid with blood, his right eye blackened and almost shut. As he stepped forward, Giulia saw that it was even worse: half a crossbow bolt had pinned the armour to his left shoulder, and blood was oozing through a bit of cloth tied around his left thigh.

"Hello there," he said, seeing Sethis. "Bloody hell,

Giulia, this fellow's wounded—"

"I know," she said. "I'm sorting a bandage out. The griffon attacked us. We got washed up: Sethis wasn't supposed to be here. But you—"

"It's nothing too bad," Hugh explained. "Took a couple of hits back in the dining room. I got quite a few of these swine, though. I'm not letting them get away with this, you know."

Giulia wanted to hug him. "Come on," she said. "You need new bandages."

"It'll hold," he said. He looked at Sethis and frowned. "I'll give you a hand."

"It's not perfect," said Hugh, tying off the bandage, "but it'll have to do."

Sethis sat on an old chair. His shirt was open and three torn aprons were wrapped around his midriff. They were already moist with blood.

"How do I look?" he asked.

"Fine," Giulia said. His chest was lightly muscled and sleek, without much hair. Had he been human, she would have liked his shape.

"Good as new, son," Hugh said, wincing as he stood upright. "I'll do this," he said. "You check the doors."

The doors by which they had entered were now heavily barricaded. Giulia's arms still ached from dragging a butcher's block in front of them, now joined by two tables and a heap of pots and pans. She had bolted the small door Hugh had used to get in, and had wedged a chair under the handle and several kitchen-knives into the frame. They might be trapped in here, but nobody would be getting in easily.

The room was weirdly quiet. Azul's men had given

up on the outer doors, but she knew that they would be looking for a different way in.

It was getting dark outside, and the last sunlight put a queasy edge on the room. Every object seemed to have its own halo. It made Giulia feel as if she was about to hallucinate.

A few candles flickered on the table. From his seat against the wall, Sethis watched her approach. His stare made him seem like a lizard. Hugh sat bare-chested in the candlelight, holding a bloody wooden spike six inches long.

"It was an armour-piercer, luckily," he explained. "No barbs."

It occurred to Giulia that he had pulled – or cut – the thing out of his shoulder without making a sound. "Good," she said, and she took a knife to another apron, slitting it into strips.

Without his shirt, Hugh looked like an old man, his pale chest threaded with veins and scars. He was not heavily muscled: most of his ability as a fighter came from efficiency and skill, not brute force. But he was wiry, she saw, gaunt and hard. He had always been careful to avoid showing her his skin, for it embarrassed him, and she tried to be businesslike as she wrapped the cloth around his shoulder.

"You need stitching on this," she said. "It's pretty deep. Can you move your arm much?"

He flexed it. "Yes, it's not too bad."

Giulia said, "I'm fucking glad to see you, Hugh."

"Thanks. Glad to see you too."

"I thought you'd get yourself killed, taking off like that. Why didn't you wait for me?"

"Because you wouldn't have wanted to go with me."

She cut the second apron lengthways, and waited as he wrapped the strip round his arm. The wind had risen outside, and it whipped around the tower at the edge of her hearing. "Of course I'd have gone with you. Azul's here, isn't he? I owe that bastard."

"I mean about Elayne. You think she's on his side, don't you?"

"I don't know what to think."

Giulia held the knot in place as Hugh secured it.

She thought, *If Elayne makes a move against me, I'll fight her no matter what.* But what then? What would Hugh do to Giulia if she killed Elayne? She shoved the thought away, with all the other things she didn't want to think about. She had to get Azul, then find a way out for them all. That was what mattered. The rest was secondary.

Sethis raised one of the herb bottles to his lips, tipped it like a cup and chewed slowly, miserably.

Hugh finished bandaging his leg and stood up. He looked as ungainly as a newborn colt. He pulled his shirt on, then his breastplate. He said, "We ought to get going."

"Well, we've got a problem there," Giulia said. "They've bolted the door from the other side."

Hugh looked down. "We're locked in? You know another way?"

"Unless the door you came in by leads upstairs, no."

He shook his head. "It goes straight back to the servants' dining-hall, I'm afraid. We'll have to break those other doors down."

"It'd take too long. By the time we get through, they'll have their friends up here."

"We can't just stand about talking," said Hugh. "Elayne—"

"Yes, I know about Elayne. I know we have to go

fast," Giulia said. "But we can't get through. There must be something else."

"I've got powder," Sethis said. They looked round: Giulia had half-forgotten that he could talk at all. "I took some for the guns. Could blow the locks off."

"I doubt there's enough," Hugh said.

Giulia turned away, fear rising inside her once again. She wandered into the main kitchen, trying to think. Could she climb up the chimney, perhaps? No, not a hope – even if she could fit into it, it would go nowhere. She grimaced, searching the room for a way out. The window, perhaps? Could she climb the glass outside?

Three piles of dirty plates lay on the floor, stacked neatly in front of a square hatch built into the wall. Giulia opened the hatch and saw more plates. Behind them, clockwork twinkled. She reached in and found two ropes. It reminded her of a device that the scholars of the University of Pagalia had used to move heavy objects, a chamber that could travel up and down.

She stepped back, suddenly alert. "Hugh," she called, "I've just found the way up!"

SEVENTEEN

Every few seconds, the rope creaked and the dumb-waiter lurched a foot closer to the floor above. With each rattle of gears, the little box rocked and scraped the walls, and Giulia struggled to keep still.

For the love of God don't let me fall, she thought. *God and Saint Senobina, let me come out of this alive.* She had a sudden image of the rope snapping, of the box meant for a few dishes plunging into the depths of the tower. She could imagine the terror, the sensation of the world dropping away. *Stop it*, she told herself. *Why the hell did I think this was a good idea?*

The sound of her breath echoed off the walls as if she shared the box with an animal. She wanted something to hold, all of a sudden: a holy sign to clutch in her fist, prayer beads to wrap around her hand, something more than her crossbow.

The clockwork rattled, and the dumb-waiter rose another twelve inches.

A sliver of light appeared above her. *That's it*, she thought, *the way out*.

She pulled back the bow-string and loaded a bolt.

***

"So you can imagine the sort of coinage that I'm talking about," Azul concluded. He was sitting again: he felt comfortable and confident. "As to when supplies would be exhausted, I would say that it would take an extremely long time: years, if not decades. Which means, of course, a very considerable sum available both to the cause we serve, and to ourselves." He had been staring into the middle distance, rapt. Now he lowered his eyes and focussed on the hand that had gone up in front of him. "Yes? Is there a problem?"

"Your man said there was trouble downstairs," the fat man said. "He said that there'd been fighting."

Azul waved an irritated hand. "Don't worry about it, Fontaine. Some fool tried to cause trouble in the men's dining hall. There was a scuffle, a momentary lapse in discipline. That's all."

"A guard?"

"No. Some idiot from outside. A drunkard."

"From outside?" The chins swung as Fontaine drew up in his chair. "How did they get onto the island? I thought nobody knew that we were meeting here?"

"They don't know you're here. No-one does." Azul clenched his fist by his side. "One of the young men overreacted, that's all." He smiled. "Everything is fine." *You're quite safe, you bloated idiot.*

"Well, good," Fontaine said, and he settled back in his chair. "I'm glad to hear it."

"Now then, does anyone have any questions?"

"Yes," a voice rasped from the other end of the table. It was Dravaignac, white-haired and lined around the mouth. He spoke with a heavy Mittlestadt accent.

"This plan of yours. You believe it to be foolproof?"

"As good as any plan can ever be. If you want to call that foolproof, go ahead."

"Do any of our enemies know about it?"

"No."

The man glared at him, somehow unsatisfied. "You sound uncertain."

"There was a priest associated with our group. He turned out to be morally unsuited to the work, too sentimental. I disposed of him."

"Did he have associates? People allied to him?"

"None."

Dravaignac scowled. "You're sure?"

"Absolutely. He acted independently. I'm sure we all remember men who lacked the guts to follow their orders through, and we all knew how to deal with them."

"I hope so," the old man said. His voice was not used to being corrected. "Exposure of this plan would cost us way too much."

"No-one will ever know, as I have explained," Azul said patiently. "This is a private venture, using trusted people. You can rely on me to—"

"I hope so, Azul. I, for one, am disinclined to trust you to keep our enemies away from our business, when you can barely keep drunks out of your own dining room."

You stupid old prick, Azul thought. He said, "As I said, it is completely safe."

Praxis leaned over and whispered something in Dravaignac's ear. He swallowed and seemed to shrink in his chair. He looked at the tabletop.

Torvald raised a hand. "I'd like to know more about how the money is split," he said. "We fund this expedition, hire more men and ships, and the gold comes back here."

Azul nodded.

"You take the majority of the money," Torvald continued, "and we take ours. How is our share calculated?"

"Well, as I've said, our ability to bring in gold is limited only by considerations of space and weight. Provided we've got the ships, it can keep coming. I would divide up the proceeds in direct proportion to the amount you're prepared to provide to fund the venture. I think that's fair. By my reckoning, I think a ten percent investor would be looking at about twenty thousand in profit every year."

Torvald nodded, apparently satisfied. "What does your cut go towards? Does any of it go towards our cause?"

Azul said, "Yes, half goes to me, and half to the cause. I'd expect the same from everyone. I'm afraid I can't give you precise details, but a percentage is used to pay our associates in the Fiorenti Bank. Some of it will be used to help our brothers who have fallen on hard times. The majority will go towards projects of a more discreet nature. I can't go into details on those, at least not until you've joined the consortium."

"Wait a minute," someone said. "I want to know—"

"Dravaignac's right," another voice put in. "This is risky, Azul. What if your men in the New World can't deliver? What if someone else turns on us?"

"We can't take risks like that," Dravaignac barked. "Not now."

Azul looked down the table, aware of their eyes on him. "Gentlemen," he said, his voice soft and reasonable, "I have told you already. There is no risk of our men either running out of gold or of the savages preventing them from taking it. There is also no risk of our business being discovered. I have taken care of that."

"How?" Dravaignac demanded.

"I'm not at liberty to say."

"Why not? This is dangerous," Dravaignac said, before Azul had the chance to respond. "I will not be involved in a situation where we risk being exposed. I want proof that this is absolutely safe before I agree."

"Of course it's safe!" Azul tried not to shout. It was not easy.

"I don't want any part in this," Dravaignac said again. He pushed his seat back and folded his arms. He sat there sullenly, shaking his head as if ruing the foolishness of the young. "I'm sorry, but there it is."

Azul thought, *I will have you killed. It might put a bit of backbone in the rest of them.*

There was a moment's quiet. Men looked at each other across the table. Eyes met. A sort of agreement seemed to be formed among them.

Good, they've seen sense.

Torvald pushed back his chair until the headrest touched the green glass wall. "I'm out. I'll wait in the corridor if you'd prefer."

"What? What're you doing?" Azul demanded.

"I'm sorry," Torvald replied. "Before I agree to join you, I need to know more about this scheme of yours, and I need to have promises that it won't backfire on us. You seem to be unwilling to give them. Right now, it's too risky – and I don't just mean in terms of money. If this goes wrong, they'll *find* us."

All they needed was that little prod. Suddenly it seemed that all the guests were muttering, shaking their heads like a bunch of worried cows, filling the air with the sound of chair-legs scraping on the wooden floor. "Just not viable," someone grumbled. "Far too uncertain," another said.

Azul met Brother Praxis' eyes, and the little man shook his head helplessly. Azul waited for the noise to stop. He listened to his guests fretting and whining, their petulant voices filling the room like billowing smoke. He closed his eyes: it gave him only a moment's pause from the idiocy before their stupid protests pushed their way back into his mind. They had started to argue amongst themselves now, calling out across the table. He could not rid himself of them, could not make them go away, could not make these fools shut up—

"Silence!" he cried. He was on his feet, towering over them. "How dare you? You will all be silent, right now!"

They looked at him as if he was deranged. He stared back, and the words kept coming.

"You're useless! All of you – useless! Do you think we conquered Alexendom by being afraid that things weren't *safe*?

"Yes, I have enemies! So what? The weak always hate the strong. *I* remember that. *I* crush my enemies instead of hiding from them. I've been working to make us powerful again, not sitting round dreaming of the past! I—" —he jabbed himself in the chest— "I want to see our cause where it belongs. I am a loyal soldier, not some— some *weakling*, whoring and idling my life away! I give you this opportunity, and all you want to do is cut and run. You deserve nothing. You sicken me!"

He stopped, panting. They stared at him, but their expressions didn't matter. They meant nothing to him now. He had seen something much more important behind them all.

There were lights in the window behind the dining table. A cluster of lights was sliding across the water towards the island. *A ship*, he realised. *A large one.*

There were not meant to be any boats coming to the island tonight. Something was wrong.

"Wait here," he said, and he strode out of the room.

***

Half a mile from the shore, Edwin stood at the railings, feeling the vessel slipping through the water far faster than it had any right to do. To either side the storm was rising: Portharion sat at the stern, redirecting the wind into their sails. Even Elayne could not control the weather like this.

Edwin flexed the fingers of his right hand and prayed that his damaged arm wouldn't hurt too much. It was bandaged and in a sling, his cloak slung over his shoulder to shield it from the rain. He'd taken potions that had left his arm and shoulder numb. He wore his sword, ready to draw. He hoped the medicine wouldn't slow him down in a fight.

"Fine weather, isn't it?"

Arashina stood beside him, smiling out to sea. She had tied her hair back and wore two knives and a long dryad sword. Her dark clothes were soaked through, and for a moment she looked like something that had sprung from the waves.

The Tower of Glass loomed above them, glowing through the rain like a corrupted moon. He licked his lips and tasted salt.

"Are you ready to fight, friend?" Arashina called.

"Ready as I'll ever be," he replied.

***

Giulia pushed the doors open and slipped out of the dumb-waiter. She was in a corridor bathed in green light. The left wall was entirely glass, flawlessly smooth. There were niches down the other side of the corridor, and delicate vases and sculptures in each. Figures leaped and danced on the vases: she thought of the sea monster rising in the glass that Elayne had showed her.

Walking in the green glow was like being underwater. She was close: Azul had to be on this floor. She'd find him very soon.

A door opened behind her, and she darted into one of the niches and pressed herself against the wall. Shadow fell across her face. She heard a babble of voices – old men talking over one another, bickering and confused.

Very carefully, Giulia leaned out. Half a dozen men blocked the passageway. They all wore expensive-looking clothes, and one or two had a vaguely military look. It was always hard to guess the ages of the rich, but none of them could be under forty-five. The men milled around, agitated but unable to act, as though their servants had unexpectedly disappeared.

Who were all these old bastards? She caught fragments of conversation – "No safety in meeting like this" – "I told him it wasn't possible" – and wondered if Azul was holding them captive here. No, she realised. There was something about their faces, a sort of bullying confidence, that reminded her of the soldiers she'd seen taunting martyrs in religious paintings. They were dignitaries, she realised, Azul's friends, the Old Crusaders that Arashina had spoken about.

So, that was it. He'd been having a party. She felt

the urge to shoot one of them, just to spoil their fun. She stopped herself. Whoever these arseholes really were, they weren't her target. Giulia crouched down and slipped out of the alcove. Bent over, keeping close to the wall, she ran back to the far end of the passage.

There was a door here: she pulled the bolts back and opened it. A set of narrow stairs led down. They would get her back to the kitchen, and let Hugh and Sethis out. And then it would be Azul who was trapped.

***

The delegates gathered around the entrance of the dining room, eager to get away. Azul watched them from his seat at the head of the table.

They were not his soldiers anymore. Their strength was gone: they were nothing more than fat merchants and decrepit crooks, men with no ambitions beyond rotting quietly in their comfortable homes. He caught Cortaag's eye. "Get these cowards out down the back way. Ring the alarm bell for the men to guard the dock."

The big man shook his head. "They won't hear it, not in this weather."

"God damn it! Just ring the bell!" Azul raised his hands, as if about to call down curses from Heaven. He hissed and checked himself, and a hand touched his arm.

It was Brother Praxis. "Forget it, Ramon. These old boys are useless to us."

"This was beyond my control," Azul began.

"I know. I'll contact you." He dipped his head, a kind of small bow, and stepped back. "Time to take my leave."

"It was out of my hands," Azul croaked.

Praxis smiled. "Of course," he said, and he joined the mob at the door.

For a moment, everything seemed lost. Azul's comrades were weaklings, his standing within the Hidden Hand was ruined. He felt like finding somewhere safe and warm, and using the snake part of him to sleep through the winter and wake once the chaos had settled down.

No. There was still a plan to be followed through, money to be made. He'd do it himself: put the gold he'd made back into the operation, hire more mercenaries, bring in more booty from the New World. And he wouldn't have to split it with anyone else.

Azul turned to his assistant. "Cortaag, listen. I need you to get the bird ready to go. Once you're done, take the little strongbox with the jewels in it and get yourself and Alicia down to the diving-boat. Meet me at the warehouse an hour after dawn."

"Yes, sir. What of the sorceress, sir?"

"Take her up to the bird too. We're getting out."

***

Giulia hurried down the last few stairs, down to the kitchen door.

There were no guards. She yanked the bolts back and tore the door open.

Hugh stood on the other side, sword raised. He sighed and lowered it as he saw her face. "Giulia."

"Let's go," she said. "Where's Sethis?"

"He's not coming."

"What?" She lowered her voice. "He can't stay here. They'll get in and murder him."

"He says he's staying," Hugh replied. "I don't think

he's going anywhere."

She ran past him, into the kitchen. Sethis was still perched on his stool, china-pale in the candlelight. He looked up very slowly, and she saw that his chest was dark with blood.

"Oh, no. Sethis, no."

"I'm staying here," he said.

"You can't," she replied. "They'll break in. There's guards below—"

"I'm not in much of a state for running," he replied. He raised his hands; there was a pistol in each. "I've got these."

She thought, *He's going to kill himself.*

Hugh said, "Let's get going."

"Go on," Sethis said, looking at the barricade.

Giulia strode over to him, leaned down and kissed his cheek. He smelt strange, alchemical. "Thank you," she said. "Good luck."

***

On the grand staircase there were threats and recriminations. "Damn stupid business," Fontaine said, feeling for the next step with the toe of his boot.

"A total waste of time," Dravaignac replied. "Slow up: my hip hurts. What happened to all the God-damned lights?"

"Maybe it's not a complete disaster." Torvald still sounded thoughtful, despite the circumstances. "There's sense to his plan. In the hands of someone better – someone with the appropriate ability, perhaps – it might be made to work. If Azul could be replaced..."

Complaining, they moved down. Their boots

scuffed on the staircase.

"And who will take his place?" Fontaine demanded. "Azul's a high-ranking man; people respect him. It's not like changing sentries at a guardpost, you know. Who else is going to have the clout to pull off a thing like that?"

"Shush," Torvald said. "I heard something."

They stopped and listened. "Nothing," Fontaine said.

"No, I heard it." Torvald peered into the darkness with small, hard eyes. One of his comrades pushed past, sniffing and muttering.

A dryad woman stepped out of the dark two feet in front of Torvald and drove a knife into his chest.

The ones at the back heard him gasp and sputter, and suddenly a pale face and a blade were coming at them. Others followed up the staircase: a human with a sword, a second dryad. Some of Azul's guests drew their daggers, but they were unused to combat and dressed for show.

Fontaine went down squealing. Dravaignac slipped, fell, screeched as he hit the stairs and rolled over and over. Long knives flashed into paunches and wrinkled necks. Their descent became a panic, then a stampede.

***

Green light washed over Giulia's face as she stepped into the corridor. It was empty.

"There were all these old men here," she whispered. "I think they were Azul's guests—"

"Be careful," Hugh replied.

They walked down the passage together. Giulia moved in a crouch, bow raised. Hugh's boots scuffed on the floor with each limping step.

There was a doorway on the left. Giulia raised a hand and Hugh froze. She took a deep breath, put a little pressure on the trigger. She sidestepped and pulled the crossbow tight into her shoulder, ready to fire.

She looked into a dining room. It was abandoned: seats had been pushed back from the table, glasses of wine left on the tabletop. This was where the old men had been making their plans. The rear wall of the hall was pure green glass. The light made her think of witchcraft.

"Nothing," Hugh said.

They closed the hall doors and kept going. Hugh lurched along beside her like a broken machine. She could sense his urgency: she knew that he could think only of Elayne. Giulia thought about Azul and how much she wanted to see him die. Hatred swamped her thoughts for a second, and then she snapped her attention back to the corridor.

At the end they turned left.

"God almighty," Hugh whispered.

They stood at the end of a broad hall, lit by candelabra. Lenses and mirrors threw clear light around the room. Down the centre ran sheets of glass, as big as partitions, and on each sheet a different scene was replaying itself. To the left, a life-sized athlete hurled a spear, which reappeared in his hand ready for the next throw. On the right, a galleon loosed its cannons and flame blossomed on a coastal fort, then faded ready for the ship's next salvo. The rows of glass panels made alleyways down the hall. The room was for display, Giulia realised, a glittering, shifting maze built out of enchanted glass.

Something caught her eye, and she glanced left and saw a blur behind the glass at the end of the room. A second blur moved up beside it.

Giulia raised her hand, held up two fingers. She glanced at Hugh. The knight nodded, understanding. When she looked back down the hall, the blurs were gone.

Very quietly, they advanced down the centre of the hall. Fear made Giulia's limbs ache. Her palms were damp. On either side figures leaped and danced silently, as though she walked through someone's memories.

Glass exploded behind her. She ducked and whipped around and saw a black shape slam into Hugh and knock him through the next panel in a storm of glinting fragments. Hugh slid across the floor on his back, the monster crouched on his chest. Giulia leaped after them. Hugh groaned.

The werewolf lay twitching on top of him. Hugh's knife was in its mouth, the tip protruding from the back of its neck.

Giulia ducked down. The beast was warm and sweaty. It smelt of fresh meat.

She grimaced and pushed it with her boot, and Hugh slid out from underneath.

His thigh was covered in blood. The beast had pulled the wound open, and the bandages he'd applied were fast becoming sodden. Giulia stood over him as he retied the dressing. Shards of glass crunched under her boots. She looked down and saw two rows of teats on the werewolf's chest. *Alicia*, she realised. *Got you.*

There was another one. She looked left, then right. *Can they smell blood?* It had to be waiting, watching them perhaps – *There!*

He was ten yards off. He stood behind a castle like the Devil looming over a city of sinners. Giulia did not move her head. She whispered, "Stay here."

Hugh gave her a tiny nod.

The figure moved: not directly towards them, but down the length of the hall. *He's trying to get round the back. He doesn't know I can see him. All I need to do is get a good shot...*

She would only have one chance. If he didn't die, he would be on her before she could reload. She needed to get closer.

In the glass on her left, a harlequin was dancing in a pantomime. Hands raised, he skipped across the glass and away again, while a crowd of onlookers applauded silently from the background. The harlequin danced towards her—

And she danced back. Giulia sidestepped as the harlequin skipped, using him as cover, and the shadow was right before her. She lifted the bow.

"Hey!"

The shadow spun around.

The bolt punched straight through the glass and into Cortaag's eye. From six feet away it skewered his brain, and he stumbled, flailed, crashed into the wall and slid onto the floor.

Giulia loaded a fresh bolt and walked over to the body. Cortaag lay in a heap, apparently dead. She drew her long knife and made absolutely sure. When she returned, Hugh was upright.

For a moment, she thought about going without him. It would be easier to face Elayne that way. But Hugh had rescued Giulia, and she still owed him for that.

"Elayne," he said between his teeth.

"They're on the roof," Giulia replied. "Nowhere else to go."

***

A distant crash told Sethis that the outer doors had gone. He heard a jumble of voices, too muffled to make out, as they got to work on the inner door.

His side hurt, but not too much. Sethis knew some of the dryad techniques for easing pain, and the herbs he'd mixed up had taken the sharpness away. The pain had settled down into a hard, throbbing ache, pounding like a muffled hammer in his side.

He took out the little wrapped canisters from his belt. Each held enough powder and lead for a single shot. Once the inquisitors had broken in, he would be able to fire twice before he was overwhelmed. His fingers broke the canisters open, one by one, and soon gunpowder slid down the front of him like black sand, pooling in his lap.

You won't get me, he thought. Sethis drew a pistol and laid it across his lap. He reached over with his left hand and pulled the candle close.

Suddenly he felt very sad. It would have been good to die in Faery. Perhaps his soul would go back to the woodland, and his spirit would be forgiven for spending so much time in the world of men. At least he would be taking some of the enemy with him. The Lord and Lady would appreciate that.

The doors burst. He snatched the candle, raised it high, and for a moment he stared into the gap, confused. Then he tossed the candle aside, seeing the flame go out as it struck the ground, and the pain in his side swelled as he lowered his hand.

Portharion stood in the doorway, and just behind him, a man with his arm in a sling.

***

Stairs led to a trapdoor in the roof. Giulia ran ahead and unbolted the trapdoor while Hugh limped up to join her. His sword hung down, and his free hand was clamped to his side.

"Are you sure that you want to do this?" she said.

"I have to."

"Then let's get the bastard." She let the trapdoor fall open, swinging on its hinges. A square of black, rainy sky was above them. Together they climbed into the cold night wind.

Azul stood next to Elayne on the far side of the roof, the griffon at his side. It was bigger than a carthorse, muscled like a bull, and the sight of it sent a rush of terror down Giulia's spine. Elayne's hands were bound behind her, her mouth gagged. They all looked out of scale: the tall woman, the little man and the massive beast beside them, as if the perspective was awry.

The wind whipped around the tower. "Welcome!" Azul called. "You've missed dinner, I'm afraid!"

"Unhand the lady," Hugh said.

The fake jollity disappeared. "No. She's worth too much to me. And to you. Giulia told me all about that. She told me about a lot of things, didn't you?"

Giulia pulled the bow up and fired. Azul ducked; Elayne twisted free and Hugh lurched towards her. The griffon darted forward, quick as water, and its great clawed hand batted Hugh to the floor. His sword clattered on the stone. He lay there, pinned under its massive foot, its talons digging into his breastplate. Slowly, idiotically, his hand reached out towards his sword.

Elayne ran to Giulia's side. She shook her bound hands at Giulia and made a muffled, desperate sound.

"All this for nothing," Azul said. He was shouting against the storm: his voice was twisted with rage and contempt. "So weak, all of you. You, Giulia, so willing to betray your friends for a little respite from the pain. This broken old knight, chasing dreams. The great sorceress, as trusting as a child."

"People are coming," Giulia said. "You're finished."

"*No.* By the time they get here, I will be long gone. As will you!"

The griffon's jagged beak opened, and a pink snake of a tongue squirmed within.

"You," Azul shouted, his voice almost cracking. "You think you can have whatever you want. You think you can steal from me. All of this is mine, you evil bitch!" he screamed, jabbing his finger at the ground. "I worked for this. I made it. You don't get to take this away from me!" He stopped, shaking, almost in tears. "Watch, knight," Azul said. He looked at the griffon. "Kill the women."

Giulia drew her knife.

The next two seconds seemed minutes long. She lifted the knife, pushed the blade between Elayne's hands and sliced them free.

The griffon advanced, light and sleek as a panther. Hugh crawled towards his sword.

Elayne tore a wad of rolled cloth out of her mouth. "Stop!" she cried.

The griffon stopped. It looked round, a little confused, as if unsure whom it could trust. Giulia looked at Elayne.

Elayne raised her arm and pointed. A trickle of blood ran from her nose. "Kill."

The griffon turned, smooth as water, and looked down at Hugh.

"Yes," Azul said.

"*Kill*," Elayne repeated. Her teeth were clenched, her body shaking as if to break apart. Her nose bled freely now: blood ran over her chin.

The griffon looked up, at its master.

"No," Azul said. He took a step backwards. "Stop. I order you to stop!"

The griffon pounced on him, smashed him into the wet stone. Azul howled in pain. The massive beak dipped and closed around his head and he shrieked.

The griffon lifted him in its jaws. For a second, Azul's eyes met Giulia's. He stared at her like a damned soul staring out of Hell, desperate and terrified, and then the griffon closed its beak. Azul's face screamed, bled, and was gone.

The griffon raised its head, Azul dangling from its beak like an afterthought, and leaped into the air. The huge wings beat at the sky, rain glistening on feathers as it bore its prize away.

Elayne fell against Giulia's side. Giulia caught her, took her weight. She saw how sick the wizard looked, how fevered her eyes were.

"I can stand," Elayne gasped. "Oh God, look at Hugh!"

The knight rolled over onto his side. Giulia ran to him. She knelt down, but Hugh was not looking at her.

"Oh, Hugh," Elayne said. She bent down and took his hand. Giulia wondered if she could heal him. Surely not, not now.

Giulia looked out across the sea, at the distant lights of Averrio. A wave of nausea washed over her, made her shudder, and then it was gone. She took Hugh's left hand and, with Elayne's help, got him to sit up.

"You rescued me," Elayne said.

Hugh nodded. "Yes, I did," he replied, and he smiled weakly. "Probably shouldn't make a habit of it, though. I'm going to need help getting down. Giulia, do you mind if I lean on you?"

EIGHTEEN

Rain sluiced across the city in sheets. At the edge of the canal, an old man in a fur-trimmed cloak watched a family making their way towards the waterside. Their son ran ahead, golden hair bobbing like a candle-flame.

"Madam?"

Giulia looked away from the window. On the other side of the table, the clerk had finished scratching into his papers. "Sorry," she said. "I got distracted."

"We'd reached the point where you had come down from the rooftop," the clerk said, his quill raised to write. "I wondered if you had anything more to add."

"Oh, right. No," she said, "I think that's about it."

"Hmm," the clerk replied. He put the pen down. Behind him, a large portrait of the Decimus smiled across the room. The Decimus wore a white robe embroidered with gold thread, and a matching hat. He looked wise and gentle: not friendly, exactly, but a friend. The clerk seemed drab in comparison. "It's quite a story," the clerk said, managing to look completely unimpressed. "Fish-boats, griffons, men turning into beasts... quite a story." He blew across the paper in a showy way, then rolled it up. "I think that just about covers it. Thank you for being so forthcoming."

I didn't have much choice.

"Now, then." The clerk folded his hands. A signet ring caught the light. "We have an offer to make to you and your friends, in recognition of your services to the city. You will be given a generous sum of money as a reward, and access once again to your account at the Fiorenti Bank. In return, you and the knight Sir Hugh of Kenton will undertake to leave Averrio in a week's time and not to return for a year and a day. You'll be escorted to whichever exit you care to use, and then you'll be free to do as you please. As far as the money is concerned, we were thinking of five hundred saviours between the two of you."

"That suits me fine," she said. "To be honest, I'm pretty much finished here."

"Excellent," the clerk said, and he stood up and held out his hand.

"Before I go," Giulia said, "I want to check a few things."

The clerk looked at his hand as if it disappointed him. He sat down. "Very well, then."

"The Scola san Cornelio – will it be opened again?"

"Of course. In fact, the members are to be awarded a special plaque recognising their loyalty to the city in this, ah, difficult time."

"I'm sure they'll love it. And the fey folk?"

The clerk looked bothered. "Yes, they'll be recognised. The Scola will of course be permitted to continue its relationship with the fey. I'm told that the issue of recruiting a new procurator will be put to the Council of a Hundred at their next meeting."

"Good. You ought to talk to your bosses about the New World, too. Whatever's been happening out there, it's nasty. You don't want to end up connected to that."

"I will." The clerk opened his hands, as if to show that none of this was his fault. "Did you have any further questions?"

Giulia said, "No. We'll be gone in a few days." She stood up, looked at the door and paused. "Wait a minute. There *is* one more thing—"

***

Children rushed around the table-legs. It was not a large room, and Rinalta Falsi struggled to get the pot to the table without being tripped. The dog looked up, as if he already sensed the possibility of spilt food. "Sit down, all of you!" she cried. "Just sit down, dammit!"

On the other side of the table, her husband was reading a letter. He rested his forehead in his left hand, while the fingers of his right hand followed the writing down the page. His little finger was splinted.

"Rinalta, will you shut them up?" He spoke out of the corner of his mouth. Although healing, the left side of his face was still badly bruised. One of his legs rested on a stool: the apothecary had said he'd fractured a bone in his lower leg, and for now he walked with a crutch. It was getting better, but slowly, and nobody needed a Watchman who couldn't run.

"I'm trying," Rinalta said, opening the pot. "It's having you stuck at home that does it. They've got you here and they think it's a bloody holiday." She shook her head and casually pushed Felicia, their second youngest, out of the way.

"God almighty," Falsi said.

She watched him read. "What is it now? If they want their armour back, tell 'em that you pawned it."

He looked up and shook his head. "It's not that. They're making me a captain. They've given me Orvo's job."

***

The rain didn't stop all week. Hugh spent most of it in bed, in an expensive inn paid for by the authorities. He slept for days on end.

Giulia visited him every day. She found a couple of books about knights in the Scola's library and took them to him to help pass the time. On the second day she visited an armoury in the town. She had money to spend.

Giulia struggled up the steps with a metal cuirass under one arm. It was of the modern type, with plates attached to the waist to hang down and cover the thighs. Two apprentices had shined it at the armourers, and she was careful not to get handprints on the steel.

She nudged Hugh's door open and carried the armour in. Hugh was asleep. Elayne sat beside the bed. The winter sun shone through the window, catching her hair and making the sheets and her dress look fresh and clean like the colours of a painting. It occurred to Giulia that Elayne must have been quite a beauty in her day. Giulia wondered what she would look like if she ever reached Elayne's age.

The wizard was holding Hugh's hand. "He's doing well," she said.

Giulia set the armour down beside the bed. "Tell him it's from me."

"I will," Elayne said, and she smiled up at Giulia.

As Giulia walked downstairs, it occurred to her that there was a good reason why normal people didn't step off the beaten track. Human beings were meant to grow up, learn a trade, get married and have children: anything else was swimming against the tide. Maybe it was a noble thing to want something else, or maybe it was just selfish and unwise, but no normal person would do it.

Mattia the boatman was sitting in his boat, waiting for business. "I wondered where you'd got to, milady," he said. "And then I thought it might be best not to know."

She climbed into the boat and settled down on the cushions. "Is that so?"

He smiled. "Some women are trouble, they say. Where to?"

"The Scola san Cornelio, please. Actually, do you remember that floating chapel you took me to? Could we go there on the way?"

"Gladly." He pushed them off, and began to row.

Giulia leaned back and put her hands behind her head. The sensation of moving over the water was pleasant, as if she were floating. She felt light, as though a weight had been taken from her. Then she realised that the weight she was missing was fear. "You know," she said, stretching, "you're right. Some women *are* trouble. And I'm the worst of them. Or maybe the best. I'm the meanest, smartest, most deadly woman that God ever made. Lady Macgraw, Sycorath the witch-queen? They've got nothing on me."

They swung out into the Great Canal. Giulia looked across the expanse of water, at the hundred different boats going about their work, and felt a kind of tranquil sadness that she had only ever known Averrio as a place of danger.

She shielded her eyes and saw the floating shrine, with its high sides and painted sail.

They came in alongside the ship, and the monks helped Giulia climb on board. In the quiet of the little chapel, she bowed her head to Saint Senobina.

Thank you for delivering me from my enemies. Thank you for keeping me hidden, and for giving me the chance to take revenge on those who wronged me and others. But this was too close. I'm asking you never to let anything like this happen to me again. Just easy work from now on. Amen.

She opened her eyes and took a little bag off her belt. There was a tradition among thieves that offerings to Senobina had to have been stolen first.

It's a good haul this time. It was stolen even before I took it.

She put it into the offerings tray. Giulia had lied to the city clerk when she'd said that she had gone straight down from the roof. She'd slipped into the dining room, and found a little strong-box full of gold. Much of it would be going to Saint Senobina, as alms for the poor.

Mattia was waiting in the boat. "To the Scola, then?"

"Please."

Giulia watched the grand houses on the waterside go by. She knew that they were beautiful, that it was turning out to be a fine, crisp winter day, but she felt nothing much. Instinctively, she reached across and felt her bandaged arm. It was a little sore, no more than that.

They reached the Scola, and Giulia tied the boat to the little pier. Strange to think that she'd knocked a man unconscious here a few days ago.

"I'm going to be here a while," she said. "Then I'm leaving the city. Before I go, I want you to have this." She took another small bag from her belt and passed it over.

He opened it and saw the gold coins. For a moment, his eyes widened. Then he composed himself. "I don't need alms, lady. I told you that before."

"It's not alms – it's a gift. I just want to see someone rewarded who isn't a total shit."

"I can't take all this."

"Give some to the beggars, then. Just make sure someone deserving gets it. And keep a little for yourself, eh? Buy yourself some new oars or something."

"To Hell with new oars," he replied, looking back into the bag. "I'll pay someone to row *me* around the city!"

She waved as he rowed away. She knocked on the little door, and the guard let her in.

The Scola san Cornelio hardly looked as if it had ever closed. The burned trees in the garden could have been the results of an experiment in natural philosophy gone wrong. Giulia told the guard that she had come to return some books, but in truth it was Sethis that she wanted to see.

He found her at the library door. "Hello there."

"Hello."

Sethis wore a loose shirt, and she guessed he was bandaged underneath. "It's good to see you."

"You too," she said. "Should you be walking about?"

He smiled. He had one of the most pleasant smiles she'd ever seen: once you were used to the pointed chin and unusual eyes, there was something rather lovable about him. "I'm almost better," he said. "I spent a few days over the border, in the forest. It did me a lot of good. How's your arm?"

"Fine. I mean—" It had scarred. There would always be a scar there, little more than a white stripe across her upper arm, but a permanent reminder of the man who had put it there – and the fact that she had killed him.

Whenever she looked at it, Azul would be there, and all the things associated with him: the terror of the interrogation, the burning hunger for revenge, the Tower of Glass and Edwin and Elayne. She remembered Alicia and the underwater-boat, the fight on the tower roof and the sound of the griffon's beak closing on its former master's head. Screams, accompanied by the crack of bone. "Yes," she said. "It's healed well. Thank you, Sethis."

He took off his spectacles and began fussing with them. "Thank *you*. You know, to be honest, I think we happened to meet at the right time."

"How are the others?"

Sethis shrugged and smiled, as if discussing beloved but exasperating relatives. "Very well. Portharion's back on his island, which suits me fine, Iacono's back with his maps, and Arashina's very pleased, for now." He grinned. "We're meeting with the Fiorenti Bank next week. Funny how keen they've become to talk to us, all of a sudden." Sethis stopped smiling. "Look," he added, "you do realise this conspiracy doesn't stop here, don't you?"

Giulia shrugged. "How do you mean? Azul's dead. Most of the others are too. That's the end of it, isn't it?"

"One of the conspirators never attended. Leth, the alchemist."

"The one who made the wolves in the first place?"

Sethis nodded. "Yes. We want him. But we'll need to track him down, of course. We thought it might be your sort of work."

"I'm not an assassin," she said.

"I know. The thing is, it's difficult for us. There are places we can't go, people who won't talk to us... We'd need you to find him. That's all. We can deal with it from there."

"Will someone pay me for all of this?"

"Of course," the dryad said. "Nothing's been decided yet, but it's been suggested that something in the region of six thousand saviours would be fair. The work would be dangerous, though."

Six thousand! With a little effort, Giulia kept her voice level and said, "I'll think it over." *Where the hell does money like that come from? I thought the fey folk didn't use coins?*

"Thanks," Sethis said. "Do let me know."

"To be honest, I'll have to see what Hugh thinks. We take it in turn to come up with work. It's his turn, and he wants to go hunting for wyvern scales." She sighed. "We've got to leave soon. It's part of the deal: they want us out the city."

Sethis did not seem terribly surprised, but he did look sad. "Well, just ask around for me. The right people will put you in touch."

"I'm sure they will."

They embraced. To her surprise, he kissed her briefly on the cheek. It was the scarred side of her face. "I'll see you soon, I hope," he said, and he stepped away.

***

A boat crewed by four oarsmen made its way slowly down the Canal of the Five Steeples. The front of the boat was bright red. A crest flew from a flagpole at the stern.

Some people, Brother Praxis reflected, never got the hang of secrecy. He leaned on the stone railing of the Regino Bridge, and watched the boat slide under the bridge from the corner of his eye.

"A drink for you, good sir?"

Praxis turned. A man stood beside him in a scruffy blue coat, probably some nobleman's cast-off. The fellow wore a small keg slung across his body with a little charcoal burner underneath. He held up a grubby cup. "It's fine spiced ale, milord. Guaranteed to take the edge off the cold."

"No, thank you." Praxis passed him a couple of coppers: enough to make the man go away, but not enough for the fellow to remember him for long.

The red boat pulled in to the bank, and a slim man in a grey cloak stepped out. Praxis shielded his eyes with his hand and squinted at the man in grey. It was Antonio Benevesi.

Benevesi headed east. Praxis walked down from the peak of the bridge, pausing to pat the faded head of a gargoyle for good luck. It was always best to do as the locals did.

Two young men stepped out of a doorway. They were neat, scholarly-looking fellows, the sort you might find strolling down any wealthy street in Averrio, discussing the latest trends in philosophy or art. They followed Benevesi at a reasonable distance, chatting as they walked.

Benevesi passed through a long passage. Clothes hung between the tenements like curtains raised above a stage. Praxis followed, knowing where the banker was headed. He'd arranged the meeting himself.

The passage opened into a small plaza. On the far side, a woman swept a step clean. Otherwise, it was deserted.

Praxis watched Benevesi cross the square, followed by the two scholars. They stepped into an arched alleyway at the far side. He could see the brightness of water on the canal at the far end of the alley. All of a sudden, the three men were silhouettes.

The left silhouette slammed its fist into Benevesi's gut. The right silhouette threw a cord over his head, yanked it tight around his neck and dragged him kicking and thrashing out of view. The three men became part of the shadows.

After a little while Praxis felt someone beside him. He turned and saw a broad man, solid and ageing, with a broken, boxer's nose. The newcomer moved slowly, with a sort of gentle dignity. "So that's Benevesi dealt with."

Praxis nodded. "The whole operation closed down, just like that." He blew out and looked sadly across the square. "Do you know how long it took to set this up, Nuntio?"

The big man said, "I can imagine. Is that all the loose ends?"

"All the ones I can get at, for now. The Scola is under the Council of a Hundred's protection – it's much too dangerous to interfere with them. The actual assassins who killed Azul seem to have left the city. They can be traced, though. They're foreigners, so they should be distinctive enough."

"I can have my people look into it."

Praxis folded his arms. His fingertips were cold. "Please do. They certainly wrecked Azul's operation well enough. A freelance knight and a woman with duelling scars. From what I've heard, they sound like Teuts or Anglians."

"Scars? I know her," Nuntio said. His voice was flat and hard. "Warn Leth."

Praxis looked around, surprised by Nuntio's tone.

"He's not easy to contact."

"It doesn't matter. Warn him. I mean it."

"She's dangerous?"

"Very. They both are, her and the knight. Her name's Giulia Degarno." Nuntio scowled. "Make sure Leth has her killed right away. Tell him to execute the pair of them."

"I will."

"Let's go back. It's doing neither of us any good standing out in the cold."

They walked back across the square. Praxis rubbed his hands together. "I'll be glad when spring comes. Winter seems to be going on forever this year."

Nuntio grunted.

Praxis said, "So, Giulia Degarno, then. What's so special about her?"

"Well," said Nuntio, "how long have you got?"

***

"Bloody hell, it's freezing," Giulia said. "I'd go mad living here."

Hugh nodded. "You know, some call it the City of Lovers."

"I suppose people have got to do something to keep warm," she replied, and he laughed.

They stood on the harbour, looking out across the lagoon. It was still cold, but the sun warmed their faces when the wind was low. She looked at the waves and the nodding prows of the little boats tied to the pier, then out to the *Margaret of Cheswick*. On the deck, men were getting ready to untie the ropes.

A door opened behind them and Giulia glanced

around. Edwin and Elayne stepped onto the dock, their heavy cloaks stirring in the breeze.

Edwin walked straight over to them. His arm was still in a sling.

"Well, goodbye," he said.

"Goodbye," Giulia replied.

"Goodbye, old fellow," said Hugh. "Safe journey, eh?"

"You too. If ever you're in Anglia, come and see me."

The merchant stood there for a moment, as if uncertain whether anything more was expected of him, then stepped back and Elayne stepped forward.

She smiled, and her clever eyes met Giulia's before she leaned in and kissed her on either cheek. "Thank you for everything," she said. "For coming to rescue me. And for making our stay so... interesting. It's been lovely to meet you."

Giulia smiled. "Thanks," she said. "It's been good to meet you too. I just wish it had been in different circumstances."

"You should come to Anglia some time," she replied. "I promise you won't be arrested."

Giulia laughed, but it felt forced. *I was wrong about you*, she thought, and she felt unhappy that she had mistrusted Elayne just because she was honest and kind.

Or maybe I wasn't.

The chances were that Edwin and Elayne were good, decent people, whose only sin had been to want to live quietly and make a profit from their trade. That was the most likely thing: that they'd got caught up in all of this and been victims all along.

And then there was the suspicion that wouldn't go,

the feeling that, at some point, they'd realised something was wrong and looked the other way. Had they known about Azul and Cortaag, suspected where their money came from, but still done business with them? Of course, they'd never wanted to be detained by the Watch, or for Elayne to be kidnapped, but Giulia remembered Edwin on his ship, shaking hands with Cortaag, and wondered about the glass that Elayne had showed her back in the Old Arms, all that time ago.

She saved me from the griffon. The rest doesn't matter now.

Giulia said, "I don't mean to be rude, but will you do something for me?"

"Of course," Elayne replied, a little surprised.

Giulia reached into her bag and took out the tile that she had stolen from Orvo's office. Now she knew what the figures on it meant. The standing man was one of Azul's hirelings, and the body at his feet was one of the pagans in the New World, whom Azul's men had massacred for their gold. She wondered if Father Coraldo had stolen the tile, or whether the natives had given it to him to bring back, so that someone might know what had happened to them. Whatever it was, she knew what the New World Order was now: take the gold, and leave no witnesses.

"Both of you," she said. "Please take this back with you, show it to someone. Tell them what Azul's men were up to. Maybe that wizard you mentioned, Doctor Dorne. But take it to someone important, right? If nothing else, you can tell them it'll make their New Church look good."

"I will," Elayne said.

"Promise me you'll do that."

"I promise." Elayne reached out with one well-kept hand and took the tile. Giulia felt a strange pang on giving it up, as if someone she'd only just come to know was going away.

Elayne said, "And you too, Hugh. Goodbye, and thank you."

"Not a problem," Hugh said. "Happy to help, you know. I, ah, I'll miss you, Elayne. A lot."

"I know," she replied. For a moment she looked sad. Then she smiled and said, "Make sure you come and visit us in Albion. No more of this cavorting about abroad, all right?"

"Absolutely."

"Take care, both of you," she said. "God bless you both!"

Edwin and Elayne walked up the gangplank, and two sailors pulled it up behind them. Giulia and Hugh watched the crew cast off. A wind blew in from the east, filling the sails, and the ship pulled away from the dock. After a few minutes, a figure appeared on deck: golden-haired, her dress billowing around her, Elayne raised a hand and waved at them.

Giulia and Hugh waved back.

"So," Giulia said, "are you going to visit them in Albion?"

Hugh kept waving. "No. I'm done. I... it's not that I've stopped caring about them – about her – but they're gone now. Their world is different to mine. They're not the people I remembered them as being. Not quite." He sighed. "I've been thinking about what you said in that farmhouse, the night when they took Elayne. She's not mine to care about. Not to care about like that." Elayne waved one last time, turned and went below. Hugh blinked, as if he'd only just realised that he was speaking. "That sounds bad, doesn't it?"

"No." Giulia watched the ship become smaller, because she didn't want to look at Hugh. "You know, back in the old days, before I killed Publius Severra, I used to think about him all the time. I mean, every day I'd think about that bastard, how I was going to pay him back. He— he owned my thoughts, you know? He really did, without ever knowing it. And you know what he said, when I finally caught up with him? He said, 'Is that all you've been doing, thinking about me?' I couldn't believe it when I heard it."

Hugh looked down at her. "Is that what I've been like, with Elayne?"

"No, not really. It's not the same at all, of course, not anything like it, but—"

"The point stands."

"Maybe. I don't know. The thing is, you're free now, whether you want it or not. Elayne's gone, Azul's gone, Severra's gone. We're both free. It's what we do with that freedom that counts." She looked at him. "So, then, what's it going to be?"

"I think we should head out," Hugh replied. "Take to the road again."

"Good. I've got to say, I'll be happy to leave. Averrio's a beautiful city, but... not for me."

"True," he replied. "We'd best get ready, I suppose." He paused. Giulia waited, knowing that he wanted to say more. "Damn shame you're not a man, Giulia. You'd have made a very good squire."

"No, I'd be useless at that sort of thing. Too many rules to follow," Giulia said. "Anyway, we need to get out of this city before they throw us out. And if I remember rightly, it's your turn to choose."

"Wyverns it is, then," said the knight, and he turned back towards the land.

NINETEEN

Even in the sunshine, everything felt brittle. The winter light made the edges of rocks seem razor-sharp, made the long-bladed grass on the hillside look as if it would shatter if the wind blew hard enough.

Like glass, Giulia thought. *God, I've seen enough glass for now.*

She peered up the slope of the hill, trying to seem professional. To her left, Hugh had drawn his sword. Three mercenaries waited behind them, a little way apart.

We should have hired more men.

Giulia looked at Hugh. His cuirass shone like a mirror. "How's your Lexmas present?" she asked.

"Very good, thank you." He patted his steel stomach like a fat man after a meal. "I pity anyone who tries to fight a well-equipped fellow like me!"

"It's so shiny they'll go blind long before they reach you." She looked up the hill. "I'm not seeing anything, you know. Maybe we should go back."

"Nonsense. We've hardly been here an hour."

Giulia shrugged and pulled her new cloak tighter. It, and the long scarf heaped around her neck, were gifts from Hugh. "Well, if that's—"

"Down!" Hugh said. He looked behind him, at the men. "Down!"

Giulia wondered what he'd seen – then spotted it. High on the hillside, something was moving in loose, awkward bounds. From here it looked like a large green tent, half-collapsed and blown along the hilltop by the wind, all folded canvas and bent poles. Her body tensed.

"Get down!" Hugh hissed.

The thing on the hilltop opened up. The tent seemed to burst before them, and what had looked like folded canvas was suddenly a pair of outstretched wings. A body rose up, and a massive tail swung out behind it. The wyvern threw back its long neck and screeched.

Giulia dropped into a crouch and pulled her hood up. The beast bounded into the air. Its wings beat furiously, hauling it up into the sky, and then it stretched them out and soared over their heads. She turned and watched the wyvern fly over fields and trees, its shadow chasing it towards the horizon.

Hugh was smiling like a child. He stood up, brushed his knees down and grinned at the hired men. One of them clutched a musket like an oar in a storm. Another, an old Landsknecht mercenary, let out a slow, wheezy laugh.

"Magnificent," Hugh declared.

For a little while, nobody said anything.

"Well, then," Giulia said, "let's get started."

Side by side, they began to climb the hill.

Acknowledgements

Several people have helped me get Blood Under Water from its first draft to publication. In particular, I'd like to thank Alex Smith, Bryan Wigmore and Owen Roberts for their help with the early drafts; Ian Cundell for his advice on writing and website matters; my literary agent, John Jarrold; my editor, Sam Primeau; Claire Peacey at Autumn Sky for the cover art; and everyone at Verulam Writing Circle and the Science Fiction and Fantasy Chronicles forum for all their assistance over the years.

Thank you for reading this book. If you enjoyed it and have a moment to spare, I'd be very grateful for a short review, as this helps new readers find my books. For more information about what I write, including free stories, find me at:

> www.Toby.Frost.com
> www.SpaceCaptainSmith.com

Giulia will return in her third adventure, *Legion of Bone*, in early 2020...
☺

Printed in Great Britain
by Amazon